Can love beat a lust for revenge?

Nelson Anderson is one of the richest men in America, but his life has become a quagmire of bitterness and the need for revenge. Wynter O'Reilly is a gutsy girl determined to make her life better–and she just may be the tool Nelson needs. All she needs is a little polish.

To his surprise, a girl from the wrong side of the tracks helps heal emotional scars that all the money in the world can't fix. But just when Nelson realizes that, his own plot for revenge may cost him not only Wynter's love but her very life.

Books by Laura Browning

Winning Heart

The Barlow-Barretts: An American Dynasty
Bittersweet, Book One
Balancing Act, Book Two
Remember Me, Book Three
Broken Heart, Book Four

Published by Kensington Publishing Corporationn

Winning Heart

Laura Browning

LYRICAL PRESS
Kensington Publishing Corp.
www.kensingtonbooks.com

Lyrical Press books are published by
Kensington Publishing Corp. 119 West 40th Street New York, NY 10018

All Kensington titles, imprints, and distributed lines are available at special
quantity discounts for bulk purchases for sales promotion, premiums, fund-
raising, and educational or institutional use.

Special book excerpts or customized printings can also be created to fit
specific needs. For details, write or phone the office of the Kensington
Special Sales Manager:
Kensington Publishing Corp.
119 West 40th Street
New York, NY 10018
Attn. Special Sales Department. Phone: 1-800-221-2647.

First Electronic Edition: July 2011
eISBN-13: 978-1-61650-290-4
eISBN-10: 1-61650-290-8

First Print Edition: July 2011
ISBN-13: 978-1-61650-850-0
ISBN-10: 1-61650-850-7

Printed in the United States of America

To Jacob—who's shown me over the years that winning isn't always about blue ribbons or crossing the finish line first. Thank you, son.

Prologue

Sweat dripped down the man's lean cheeks, mingling with tears of pain as he labored through physical therapy. His dark hair was wet from the effort to propel himself along parallel bars, and his arms shook with fatigue.

One good step, and then slowly, painfully, he forced the other leg forward, arms and strong leg bearing much of the weight.

"I think that's enough today," the therapist interrupted.

"No!" he barked, his tone darkened not only with pain but simmering with anger and bitterness just below the surface.

"Mr. Anderson," she began in that voice he'd heard her use to warn other patients it was time they listen, "if you keep pushing yourself like this, you will do more harm than good."

"I will not be wheeled inside that courtroom."

"You'll arrive in a coffin if you don't quit!" she snapped back. "Don't forget, you have suffered more injuries than just your leg. You're also missing a few feet of intestines. Recovery takes a while. You can't keep pushing this hard."

Nelson sagged, and the therapist pushed the wheelchair under his shaking legs. His broad shoulders hunched, and he ran trembling fingers through wet hair.

"Don't you have other patients to harass?"

She sighed. "I do. You have a pool in that great big house of yours, don't you?"

"Yes, whatever good that does me. I can't get up and down the stairs."

She laughed, making him glare.

"For heaven's sake! You're one of the wealthiest men in the state— maybe in the country. Put in a damn elevator."

"That's like admitting I'll be like this," he waved a hand at his atrophied right leg, "for good."

The therapist went down on her haunches. "No, it's giving you access to an outstanding therapeutic tool. Water will help support your weight and add resistance to rebuild muscles in your leg. It will do more in half the time than grunting through exercises in here."

He glared at her. "Hand me my cellphone," he ordered in a voice accustomed to being obeyed.

"Yes, sir." The therapist found the cellphone in the pocket of his jacket and handed it to him with a slight smile.

Five minutes later, he snapped it shut with a satisfied smirk. "The elevator will be in by the end of the week when I return home."

"God, it must be nice to be filthy rich," the therapist sighed.

Nelson grimaced. "It is until you find out money can't buy everything."

Chapter 1

Three hundred dollars would stretch a long way, but pinching pennies wasn't anything new for Wynter. She and her mom had done it their whole lives. The problem was, she was down to her last little bit of cash, and as she stared at the help wanted ads, finding a job still seemed far away.

She was either over-qualified or under-qualified. With no address since she gave up the room she'd rented, some employers tuned her out right away. Wynter also had no references and no expectations the Southards would provide them. They were the only people for whom she'd ever worked.

Her mouth tightened. She stared out the windshield at a farm across the road. She wasn't ready to give up her dream. She would get into Duke. She would make her mother proud. But damn it, she needed a job.

Hell, she'd already squared everything with the high school so she could graduate, but if she didn't get a job soon, she would have to go home and admit defeat. Her options were running out.

Horses grazed in the pasture across the street, and she watched them wistfully. Wynter understood horses. She always had. It was what had landed her a job on Southard Farm. All she needed was another shot, and this time she wouldn't screw up.

She'd driven north of Durham that morning to get out of the city and weigh the choices. Right. Who was she kidding? She rationed out the last cigarettes a week before. Now she was on her last tank of gas, had just a couple of dollars left and still no job. She thought if she left town it would clear her head, so she could make a decision. Gamble one more time finding a job or go back.

She thought about her mother, how hurt and disappointed she would be. Wynter loved her, but she couldn't go back. Irene had struggled her whole life to give her daughter opportunities, and Wynter had repaid her by getting in trouble and losing a scholarship that might have changed both their lives.

Somehow, she must make it right. She would not call it quits. There must be something someone would hire her to do. She looked over at the horses once again.

On a whim, Wynter cranked the ignition and the old truck rumbled and coughed. After checking both ways along the narrow state highway, she drove across the road and down a long, neatly-manicured drive toward the barns in the distance. Bradford pears lined the smooth asphalt, mulch in neat mounds around the base and the grass mowed and trimmed. The whole farm was a showplace that screamed money.

So what are you doin' on it, trailer trash?

Stomach rumbling, she pulled into a parking area in front of what looked like a business office. Nerves or hunger? Did it matter anymore?

She stepped from the truck and slammed its door. After a quick check to make sure her hair was still in a neat braid, Wynter smoothed her palms over her jeans. They were worn, but at least this pair didn't have any tears. It was still cool, so she pulled on the sweater Mama had knitted. It was the best thing she owned.

Her knock was hesitant. Nervousness tingled and tickled the pit of her stomach. Hunger, not nerves, was making her belly as jumpy as a hoppy toad.

"Door's unlocked. Come on in."

The words were tinged with an accent she couldn't quite identify. Wynter turned the knob and pushed open the door. It was much darker inside and took a moment before her eyes adjusted. Two men sat in the room, but she directed her attention to the one sitting at the desk right in front. He was older. Besides, the other man worked on a computer toward the back and didn't even glance up when she came through the door. All she saw of him was gray-streaked hair and broad shoulders. Probably some techno-geek working on the system.

"What can I do for you, miss?" the older man asked. Wynter shifted her gaze. Her lips trembled and curved into a smile as she identified the accent as Scots. His face was round, with light blue eyes and receding gray hair. On the desk, a tweed driving cap lay as though it had just been tossed there.

"I was wondering if you might have any jobs available."

The Scotsman assessed her from the tips of her sneakers to her slender arms and legs. "Have you worked around horses, lass?"

"Yes, sir," Wynter confirmed. "I worked for a family, grooming and exercising their field hunters. I took care of the barn too, feeding and mucking out stalls."

"We don't need any grooms or riders right now," the Scotsman remarked. The last hope drained away, but she fought to keep it from showing. He hadn't said no yet.

"I do need a stall mucker." He eyed her again. "You seem a might skinny. It's a lot of heavy work. We're a training-and-show facility with twenty-five horses in active work."

"I can do it," Wynter assured him, hope rekindling.

The Scotsman's eyes twinkled. "We could try it and see. Do you have a letter of reference?"

Hope crashed back to earth with a dull thud of despair.

"No, sir, I don't."

"How about a phone number, and I'll give them a call."

She shook her head and bit her lip. At this point, Wynter felt more than saw the other man stop what he was doing while he watched too. As always, when she drew attention, heat seeped into her cheeks.

"Do you not know the number?" the Scotsman asked. "That's all right. Just give me your employer's name, and I'll ring them up."

She looked back up at the older man and cleared her throat. "The Southards fired me, sir. They won't give me a reference." He shook his head, so she continued on, "Thanks anyway for your time."

Wynter turned on her heel and hurried out the door. She'd almost made it back to the truck when she heard a younger, deeper voice.

"Wait!"

The other man stood on the porch. Her eyes widened when she saw him lean on a cane. His face was pale, as if it had taken him a great deal of effort to get outside. In the bright light outdoors, she saw brown hair streaked with gray and deep blue eyes shadowed with pain and something else she couldn't quite pinpoint, but it was the eyes that stopped her. So dark, so deep, she felt she was almost drowning in them.

"Please come back up here on the porch. I hate yelling at people." His voice held a quiet command impossible to ignore.

He moved aside, so she could sit in one of the rocking chairs out front. When she moved past him, Wynter caught a faint scent of horses, leather and some spice she couldn't quite pinpoint. For a moment, it reminded her of her friend, Wythe, but was different. His scent was familiar, comfortable. This man's scent made her stomach flutter. She shook the thought away. The man remained standing, although he supported his weight against the porch railing behind him.

"I'm Nelson Anderson. You are?"

"Wynter O'Reilly," she supplied with a challenging tilt of the chin, not sure why they were having this conversation but feeling compelled to answer him.

"I own Pheasant Run," he supplied as though that would clear things up. So, not a techno-geek. Wynter watched him warily. He also seemed a little uncertain. "What did you say the family's name was who fired you?"

Her eyes narrowed. Hypnotic blue eyes be damned! Wynter's experience with blue-blooded horsey families was they stuck together in their own clique, and it was small enough most of them knew each other. For all she knew, Payton Southard might have decided to press charges against her.

"Southard," she mumbled.

Nelson Anderson's beautiful eyes narrowed, any trace of warmth vanished. "Where did they live?"

"Southside Virginia."

There was a long pause. Anderson's gaze moved from her face to work-roughened hands. She gripped her knees, shifting with nerves, but refused to hide her hands.

"If—if there's nothing else, Mr. Anderson, I should leave." Right, because she had so many appointments in her day planner. No, it was his eyes she needed to get away from. They saw far too much.

"Wait here, Wynter." It wasn't a request. Despite the quiet demeanor, it was obvious Nelson Anderson was a man accustomed to being in charge. Leaning on the cane, he limped back inside the office. The right leg was the one he favored. Wynter stared after him with a touch of resentment. Why should she wait if they weren't hiring her? She still needed a job, and standing around waiting wasn't getting her any closer to employment.

She was about to leave when the door opened again, but it wasn't Anderson who came back through it. It was the Scotsman.

"Come with me, Miss O'Reilly. We'll try you a week and see how things go."

She jolted with surprise. "You will?" She jumped up and grabbed his hand and shook it. "You won't be sorry. I'm a hard worker and a lot stronger than I look."

He eyed her with one bushy brow raised. "I hope so. My name is Thomas Sinclair. You can call me Thomas like everyone else does. I don't stand much on ceremony, but I do expect an honest day's work for an honest day's wage."

As he spoke he headed down the steps. For a short man, he walked briskly, and Wynter found herself hustling to keep up. When they entered the barn, he glanced at the sneakers she wore. "Do you have any other shoes?"

"Just my paddock boots."

Thomas shook his head and rolled his eyes. "Manure'll ruin your boots. Look in the wash stall there to your left. See if there's a pair of Wellies to fit you."

He waited while she checked a couple of pairs before finding a fit. When she'd slipped them on, he was off down the barn, talking over his shoulder while he explained the daily routine and what her duties would be. As they reached the end of the aisle, he handed her a pitchfork, pointed to the wheel barrow and said, "You can start right now."

By day's end, Wynter was exhausted. She wanted nothing more than a hot shower and a soft bed. One out of two wasn't bad. Earlier she'd noticed a shower off the tack room at the front of the barn. She'd given up the small boarding house room in Durham, so it looked as though she would be sleeping in the truck until she got paid and found someplace to live. She scrounged up enough change to grab a couple of packs of nabs and peeked out front. There was still a light in the office but no cars in sight. Wynter grabbed the small bag containing shampoo and other toiletries, snatched up clean underwear and a t-shirt and sprinted back to the barn.

She paused as she entered, savoring the noises of horses settling in for the night. The rhythmic chewing of hay and the rustle here and there when a horse moved around its stall were as soothing as any lullaby. It was good to be back among animals she understood. All they asked was for someone to look after them and treat them well. They had no ulterior motives.

The shower room wasn't much, but it did offer a stack of clean towels on a shelf in the dressing area. In addition to the shower, the large tack room contained a washer, dryer and a toilet. Wynter grinned. She could almost live here, she thought as she stripped and turned on the shower. When the hot water washed over her, she sighed in relief. She would be sore tomorrow. Although cleaning stalls was nothing new, she'd never cleaned so many. But it felt good. She'd found a job. Things would be fine again.

* * * *

By Thursday afternoon, she wasn't so sure. She didn't get paid until the next day. Her whole body ached, and she hadn't eaten. Wynter drank water to squelch the hunger pangs, but after a while, even that didn't work. Her muscles ached even more than usual, and she couldn't wait until the end of the day. She wanted a hot shower, and then she planned to wash and dry her clothes in the tack room.

She lingered over sweeping the aisle and hanging the hoses, waiting for everyone else to leave. It was a warm spring night, and some of the amateur owners still hung out, laughing and gossiping. There was a show coming up at the Hunt Horse Complex the next week, and everyone scrambled to get ready. She looked forward to it for another reason. She might be able to pick up extra cash at the show braiding manes and tails. At last everyone cleared out, and she walked to the front entrance of the barn.

As usual, the light in the office was on. She figured they had left it that way because she never saw anyone. She grabbed her duffel bag and the sheaf of financial aid papers she'd picked up from Duke. Her grades and test scores were good enough that they were going out of their way to find the money she needed to start classes. But unless they covered almost everything, she'd have to lower her sights.

Wynter didn't linger in the shower. She wanted to get the laundry done and leave before anyone became suspicious. When she had given up the room in Durham, she had used some of her precious store of cash to buy an old sleeping bag at the Goodwill. She secured it under a tarp in the back of the truck. Although a little cold at night, it had been dry, so she'd found an old farm road in the woods just down the road where she parked the truck and slept in the back of it. Wynter wanted to wash the sleeping bag too, and it might take a few minutes longer to dry. She didn't bother separating any of the clothes. Everything she owned fit in the large capacity washer with room to spare. It was used to wash horse blankets, so it had to be big.

As the washer spun, she looked around the tack room. She was so hungry. Against the wall was the refrigerator where Thomas kept horse medications. She checked for something edible, but her stomach rumbled in protest when all she saw were vials of vaccine and boxes of horse wormer. Out of the corner of her eye, she spotted a crumpled potato chip bag sitting on top of the trash can. Wynter hesitated a fraction of a second to get herself past the gross-out factor before grabbing it and shaking it. Hallelujah! It had something in it. She almost cried with joy when she discovered someone tossed out half a bag of chips. Wynter slipped two fingers in and grabbed one, savoring the salty, starchy taste.

The washing machine beeped when it finished. Setting the bag of chips next to the papers from Duke, Wynter slipped into the laundry area and shifted the clothes and the sleeping bag from the washer into the dryer. The machine hummed as it started. Wynter settled back in a comfortably shabby overstuffed chair with the garbage can chips and the Duke paperwork. The chips were gone in pretty short order. It blunted the edge off her hunger.

She checked the dryer, took out the t-shirts, underwear and her oldest pair of jeans and restarted it. The rest of the jeans and the sleeping bag were still damp. While she waited for them to dry, Wynter tried to concentrate on the paperwork, but she was just too tired. In no time, she found herself drifting off.

* * * *

"Are you worried about the lass too, sir?" Thomas had asked Nelson that afternoon when he'd once again caught him staring after their newest stable hand, Wynter O'Reilly.

Nelson glanced behind him. "She looks thinner."

"I'm afraid the job's too much, sir, though she's giving it her best. I won't be responsible for her hurting herself or one of the horses."

Nelson had watched the girl struggle to guide the wheelbarrow down the aisle and out to the manure pile. She was tall and slender, now bordering on thin. When she had returned and passed the two men, she had smiled tiredly at them. Nelson's eyes had followed, resting on the dark auburn braid hanging from underneath the beat up baseball cap perched on her head. It swayed when she walked in the same easy side-to-side rhythm as her slender hips.

Nelson frowned. "Do what you think's best. I trust your judgment."

He had more things to worry about than the fate of one stable girl. But when he got ready to leave the office late that night to return to the house, he noticed her truck was still there. Wynter O'Reilly would not be dismissed, no matter what he might say. But now the question nagging at him was what she was doing in his barn so late? Still turning that over in his brain, he limped to the tack room in the barn. As soon as he had eased open the door, he spied her sleeping in a chair on the other side, one hand tucked beneath a cheek and her legs curled beneath her, as innocent-looking as a baby.

On her lap, resting beneath her other hand, was a sheaf of papers. Even from here he saw the Duke University logo. Now his curiosity sharpened.

As a general rule, stable girls were drop-outs or runaways. *Which are you, Wynter O'Reilly?* He limped over quietly and was rewarded when she continued sleeping undisturbed.

He saw financial aid papers, a summer school application sticking out from them. Nelson looked at the dark circles under the half-moons of her sooty eyelashes. Was this why she worked so hard? Trying to get into Duke? He glanced at the full name on the application, and noted she had put Pheasant Run's address under place of residence. He frowned again, sharp eyes taking in the still damp hair and the sound of the dryer from the laundry room.

There was a lot more to Wynter O'Reilly than had first appeared. While he whispered her name and shook a slender shoulder, Nelson wondered if the girl might be of use. She seemed to dislike the Southards. Perhaps he should find out more about her connection to that family.

Chapter 2

"Wynter." Someone shook her shoulder. "Wynter O'Reilly."

"Wythe?" she mumbled as she struggled awake.

"Nelson Anderson."

Wynter's eyes snapped open, and she struggled to focus on the man leaning over her. His scent teased her nostrils. Leather, horses, spice. She shook her head and stared into those midnight-blue eyes. Panic surged. "I—I'm sorry. I fell asleep."

Anderson grunted and grimaced as he straightened.

"What time is it?" she asked.

"Almost midnight. Shouldn't you be home in bed?"

"Yeah. I was just drying some blankets," she lied. "I'll finish then be on my way."

Anderson seemed content to wait while she went into the adjacent laundry room. Probably didn't trust her, she thought. She grabbed the rest of the laundry and the sleeping bag. What on earth was she going to do now? She couldn't very well walk back into the tack room with the stuff, so she looked around and found an empty cabinet next to the sink. It would have to do. She would sleep inside the truck tonight. Wynter stuffed everything in the cabinet and then smiled uneasily as she returned to the main tack room. Anderson watched her with intense blue eyes.

"I'll walk you out to your truck."

"You don't need to," Wynter assured him, eyes darting to the cane.

"My doctors tell me the exercise helps, so humor me." His lean face twisted.

She swallowed and looked away, anywhere but right at him. "Yes, sir."

Wynter gathered the papers together. She noticed him studying her, but he said nothing when she stood back up, holding the papers against her chest.

"Ready?"

Laura Browning

"Yes, sir."

He stiffened for a moment but didn't say a word while he limped toward the door. Wynter followed. He held the door open, and she felt herself blush. She ducked her head as she went past him. Wynter waited for him to turn off the lights before adjusting her pace to walk beside him. The silence stretched her nerves to the screaming point. When she reached the driver's door of the small truck, she looked at him. Close up she had the feeling he wasn't as old as he seemed, maybe somewhere around her mother's age.

"I'm sorry, Mr. Anderson. I didn't mean to fall asleep."

His face relaxed. "It's all right, Wynter."

She nodded and climbed in the truck. To her horror, when she turned the key, the engine turned over again and again, but didn't catch. He watched, and Wynter bit her lip. One glance at the gas gauge and she swallowed. Empty. It was what she feared.

"Anything wrong?" Anderson asked.

"I'm out of gas." She smiled at the man looking in. "It's okay. I'll walk. It's not far."

"Nonsense," he stated. "It's too late and too dark for you to walk along the road. I'll take you home. My car's in back of the office." He started to turn away.

"No, really," she insisted. "I...I like walking, and it's not far..."

"Wynter," Nelson Anderson warned, "you're being ridiculous. I'll take you home, and that's the end of it." He turned to limp toward the back of the office building.

Wynter swallowed when she climbed out of the truck. Her shoulders hunched as she dug her hands in her jeans pockets.

"Mr. Anderson?" He stopped, one eyebrow raised. She grimaced and scuffed her sneaker in the gravel.

"What?" he prompted.

"You can't take me home."

"Excuse me?" he asked as if unaccustomed to someone telling him what he could or could not do.

Wynter stared at him with defiance. "I don't have a home."

"What do you mean?"

"I don't have a home," she repeated, chin jutting. She didn't like his tone. She was already embarrassed and humiliated.

He hobbled back. "Just where have you been living the past three days?" Those eyes again. Even in the dark his gaze shot sparks of blue fire.

She glanced at the truck.

"In your truck?" His tone was incredulous. "You've been sleeping in your truck since you started working here?"

Heat flooded her cheeks. What right did he have to take an attitude? Shoulders squared, she stared back.

"Yes. I have. Not all of us are as privileged as you or your clients." She glared at him. "I can assure you, it hasn't affected my work, so it's none of your business where I sleep."

He'd reached her side by this time. She turned to walk down the drive, but Anderson grabbed her wrist. A sudden vision of other hands grabbing, touching and bruising flashed through her head. She gasped and jerked away, but this time she wasn't the one to fall. Anderson's cane clattered when it hit the driveway. A grunt of pain followed when he struck the side of the truck. It was a moment in which time slowed to a crawl. In the glow from the security light mounted on the front of the barn, his face twisted with pain and he clutched at the side of the small truck.

"Damn it!" he swore while he struggled back up.

Wynter moved as though she had just unfrozen, scrambling to pick up the cane and rushing back to his side.

"Mr. Anderson?" she asked. She shook almost as much as he did. "I'm sorry!" She hated the frantic note of panic in her voice. She wasn't sure if she was more concerned he might be hurt or he might fire her. "I didn't mean to hurt you," she rushed on. "Are you okay? Can I help you?"

"Wynter."

"Here's your cane. I didn't mean to hurt you. I'll help you to your car. Then I'll go. I—I'll have to come back to get my truck in the morning."

"Wynter." His tone commanded. "Stop. What on earth are you talking about?"

"I'm fired, aren't I?" she demanded.

His face softened, and blue eyes searched her face. "No, I'm not firing you. I know it was an accident, although I must say your reaction seemed a little extreme." His expression questioned, and around him hung an air that said if she had something to share, he was a man who didn't repeat confidences. She stared into that searching blue gaze and swallowed.

"I'm a bit jumpy. I'm sorry. It was something that happened, before I came here."

His eyes narrowed. "Where you worked?"

"Their son, Payton." When she said it, she noticed Anderson went still. "What did he do?"

"It was following a hunt. I'd gone out to my truck to change out of my coveralls. All of a sudden he was there." She stopped and swallowed.

"Go on."

"He touched me...offered me money to...anyway, when I started to punch him, he grabbed hold of my wrist and twisted. I guess I kind of flashed back."

"Did he hurt you?" Anderson's voice was quiet.

She shook her head. "No. Not really. Wythe got there and took a hunt whip to him."

"Wythe?"

"Oh. He whips in for Southard, but he's friends with my mom and me."

Anderson nodded. "Is that why you got fired?"

"Uh, no. Mr. Southard had already fired me. I laid a drag before the hunt that ended in his son's brand new Mustang convertible. I gave them a great couple of miles before the scent ended at Payton's car. Well, there were a lot of refusals at the hedge next to the house. And that was so funny because Payton's girlfriend looked like a raccoon! And then, the top was down on the Mustang, and those hounds so trashed that car. They were all over the white leather upholstery like flies on sh..."

Wynter's eyes snapped up when she heard a cough and she caught what looked like the faintest smile flashing across Anderson's face.

"Shit," she mumbled. "I'm sorry. You don't want to hear this."

Wynter turned away, a hand to her face. Jeez, could she look like any more of a kid?

"Have you eaten anything today?" The question caught her off guard. She looked up to find his gaze focused on the empty juice bottles and nabs wrappers on the passenger side. He turned those dark intense eyes on her. "And don't lie."

She shut her mouth.

"Well?" he asked again.

"I—I ate some chips."

"You haven't left here today, so where did you get those?"

"None of your..." She saw the sudden glare and continued, "Out of the trash."

"Christ!" he exclaimed and waved his hand at the trash in the truck. "Nabs and juice, and chips you got from the damn trash? Is that all you've eaten since you started work here?"

Wynter bristled. "And if it is? What business is it of yours? You're my boss, not my father. As long as I do my work, what's the big deal?"

"I'll tell you what the big deal is," Anderson snapped. "You're as thin as a rake. You have dark circles under your eyes. Yes, you work hard. Thomas and I have seen that, but you can't keep this up, Wynter. You'll make yourself sick, get hurt, or hurt a horse or another person because you can't perform. Thomas was ready to send you packing tomorrow because he'd pretty much decided the job was too much."

"No! Look, I can do it! Please give me a chance. Once I get paid tomorrow, I'll be able to get some food an—and I've found a room not far from here."

"That's enough, Wynter." He looked so forbidding.

"No. Really." Panic made her voice shake. She couldn't go back now, not when she had everything lined up. It would all work, but she needed this job. Without it, there was no way to pay her living expenses so she could attend Duke.

"I'll work harder." Wynter hated begging. Tears blurred her vision, but she blinked them away. "I can handle the job. Please!"

He grabbed her shoulder with his free hand and shook her. "Wynter. No one's firing you. Do you hear me? You can stay."

She sucked in a deep breath and felt her cheeks burn again. Never had she experienced so much embarrassment in such a short period of time. And still he watched. She struggled to calm down. When the panic receded, exhaustion took over. It was late. She needed sleep to be back at work before dawn.

"Help me to my car, Wynter," Nelson ordered in a tone that brooked no argument. "I'm taking you to the house. You will eat something and then you can bed down on a couch tonight. We'll figure something else out tomorrow."

She was too tired to argue.

Wynter noticed the Rolls Royce came equipped with hand controls to accommodate his bad right leg. She swallowed. She'd assumed he had suffered a fall or something, not that he was crippled. She stared out the window while they made the short trip up the drive.

The house stood on a hill behind the barns. It was screened from both the road and the barns by a grove of tall pine and cedar trees, so she had yet to get a good look at it. In the dark, she still didn't, just the impression of its large outline as they rounded a bend in the driveway. Anderson pulled the car around a circular drive.

After he shifted the car into park, he said very matter-of-factly, "I need your help, Wynter."

She scrambled out of the car and hurried around to the driver's side. He leaned on her while he pulled himself up. She kept hold of his elbow while he negotiated the short ramp added to the front of the house. Tension radiated from him. Getting help must bother him a lot.

Her eyes widened when they entered the front hallway. Its vaulted ceiling opened to the second floor with a winding staircase curving up along the right side. As she stared, she felt like Little Orphan Annie with Daddy Warbucks. The steps were wide enough for three or four people to walk abreast. In the dim light from a lamp resting on a sideboard, she saw the black and white marble tiles that covered the floor. Family portraits hung around the hallway and lined the stairs. Wynter had never seen anything this ornate. Even the Southards' and the Butlers' homes were nothing compared to this house.

"Damn! It—it's so big!" Wynter exclaimed before halting with an awkward grimace. "I'm sorry. That was rude."

Her boss smiled for the very first time, and it transformed his face, making him look years younger and much, much kinder. She stared at him. "You're not old! You're young!" she accused then gasped.

This time, he didn't smile, he laughed. It was a rusty sound, as though he hadn't done so in a long, long time.

"Oh! I'm so sorry. Ma's forever telling me to keep my mouth shut."

"Don't worry about it, Wynter. We're both tired. If you'll go straight through the hallway you see in front of you, the kitchen's at the back of the house. Help yourself. Mrs. Caudle always leaves plenty of sandwiches in the fridge. I'll find a pillow. There's a big couch in my study. It will be the door at the end of the hallway on your left when you leave the kitchen."

"Thanks, Mr. Anderson." She hurried past him, almost running down the hallway. She heard his slower, stilted gait and the tap of the cane while he followed as far as the hallway leading to the study.

She stepped through the doorway and into the kitchen. It was almost as big as the whole trailer she and her mom lived in. Because the overhead light cast only a slight glow over everything, Wynter thought it must work off a dimmer switch. Nowhere in the house was anything left dark. Was that because of Anderson's limp?

She looked around. What her mama wouldn't give for a kitchen like this. Stainless steel appliances gleamed in the work area, including one of the biggest refrigerators she'd ever laid eyes on. When she approached it, she ran tapered fingers over ice-smooth black marble countertops, and her gaze roamed warm, light oak cabinets. Her growling stomach reminded her of the true reason for the visit to the kitchen.

Wynter opened the refrigerator. Just as he had promised, a tray of wrapped sandwiches sat on the middle shelf. She grabbed one then made herself slow down. Ma would kill her if she saw her do such a thing. A pitcher of milk sat on the top shelf. She took it out and set it on the counter while she found a glass. She was already on a second glass and a second sandwich when Anderson stepped into the kitchen.

Her cheeks tingled with heat when his glance moved from the half pitcher of milk to the two sandwich wrappers lying next to a plate.

"Feel better now?"

She nodded, mouth full. At least she had remembered not to speak with food in her mouth. That was another thing Ma was always getting on her about.

"I'll leave you. There's a bathroom off the mudroom by the back door. Good night."

Wynter gulped the bite of sandwich. "Thank you, sir," she mumbled. "For everything."

He nodded and limped away. What an odd man. He'd be a real hunk if he smiled more.

Chapter 3

Nelson leaned against the wall in the small elevator. It hummed while it glided up to the second floor. From there it was just a few feet to the bed. He'd lied when he said Thomas was keeping an eye on her. The truth was *he* was the one watching. Thomas would have turned her away when she couldn't give him a reference, but as far as Nelson was concerned, being fired by the Southards was perhaps the best reference she possessed.

He'd clamped his jaw shut to keep from laughing out loud when she slipped into the story about the kid's car. After he stripped off his clothes and sat on the edge of the bed to get the painkillers, he thought of her again. Wynter was like a rough-cut stone, edges and hidden facets waiting to be drawn out. A few flashes of her potential were already obvious in that gorgeous auburn hair and creamy complexion. Given the right advantages, she'd be a knockout.

There was more to her, though, than just looks. He saw how hard she worked. She was the first one there in the morning and from what he had observed, the last one to leave at night. Character. It was rough, but it was there, and it was what kept his thoughts coming back to her again and again. Nelson learned enough concerning Wynter O'Reilly to know she needed to stay. The most important thing he'd discovered was as much as Payton Southard the Third might consider her trailer trash, he desired her.

Nelson rubbed the aching muscles in his scarred right leg, thinking and considering the possibilities. Perhaps there was more he could do than ruin Southard. If he turned their duckling into a swan, it might be an even sweeter revenge. Just how much would it irk snobs like the Southards to see the stable girl they'd fired taken under the wing of Nelson Anderson? Very closely under his wing.

* * * *

It took Wynter a few minutes to realize where she was when she woke up. When it dawned on her, she sat bolt upright and looked around. Panic hit her like a punch in the gut. She was late. The rising sun was already lightening the sky outside Nelson Anderson's study window.

She jumped off the couch and snatched her jeans back up before throwing on the rest of her clothes. After jamming on sneakers, she plaited her thick hair in one long braid down her back. When she glanced at the clock on the fireplace mantel, another wave of panic shot through her. Almost six. An hour late. Shit.

Her first instinct was to dash out of the house, but then she saw the crumpled blankets and pillow from where she'd slept. Some things her mother had ingrained all too well. Her hands shook while she folded the blankets and laid them on the couch. After setting the pillow on top, she darted down the hallway. The house was still quiet when she slipped out the front door, eased it shut and ran down the drive.

The barns stood almost a half-mile away. Wynter was in full-fledged panic now. She rounded the bend that would bring her in sight of the barns when the nose of Anderson's Rolls glided around the corner at the same time from the opposite direction.

She couldn't stop. The car swerved as she tried to leap sideways, and her hip slammed into the fender before she stumbled backward to the trees. A cedar branch grazed one cheek, but otherwise, the dense foliage cushioned the worst of the fall. Even so, the impact knocked the breath out of her. She heard the car door fly open and the incessant beep from the ignition alarm.

"Wynter!"

She rolled over and struggled to a sitting position when she heard his feet hit the pavement. "Stop!" She gasped and sucked in a deep breath. "I'm fine! Don't get out."

He cursed so vividly even Wynter was taken aback. "Come here, damn it, so I can see you're okay."

Wynter pushed out from the cover of the dense cedar trees and limped over to Anderson's side.

"See?" Her irritation turned to concern when she saw how pale his face was. "Are you all right?"

"You're bleeding," he mumbled.

"It's just a scratch." She swiped it with the back of a hand. "What were you doing? I thought you were still asleep." She glanced toward the barn. "I gotta go. I'm late."

The color returned to his face, but he still seemed distracted when he said, "I went down to explain to Thomas. You're fine. No one else is there yet." His voice once again assumed its usual commanding tone. "Get in. I'll take you back down there."

"You don't…"

"Wynter," he snapped.

"Fine." She did her best to stomp around the car, but each footfall shot pain through her bruised hip. She winced when she bent to get in.

"You are hurt," Anderson accused.

"Just a bruise. I'll be fine," Wynter replied and stared out the window. This wasn't how she had planned the morning. She wanted to be cool and polite, able to thank him for how kind he'd been. She sighed in frustration. Instead, she had come off looking like a total idiot. Again. "Just take me to the barn, please. I have work to do."

They didn't speak anymore on the way. Wynter got out with a mumbled thanks and heard him backing the car to head to the house. When she walked through the barn door, Thomas was there measuring feed. He glanced up and set the feed scoop back in the barrel. Wynter jammed her hands in her jeans pockets and scuffed the toe of one sneaker.

"Sorry I'm late," she muttered, half expecting the taciturn Scotsman would give her the sharp side of his tongue. She'd heard him berate one of the grooms the other day. Thomas Sinclair possessed a very creative grasp of the English language and could dress someone down without a foul word ever uttered.

"I've already given the horses their hay. You can do the grain and the water, lass." The surprise must have shown because for a moment, the older man softened and said, "Mr. Anderson explained your situation."

Wynter nodded in embarrassment, face averted.

"You're a hard worker, Wynter O'Reilly. I'll give you that. So let's give it another week, this time with food and shelter, and see how you do."

She turned with a quick, grateful smile and nodded. "Thank you. You won't be disappointed. I promise."

Sinclair grinned. "I know I won't. You'll be living in the apartment over the barn. Mr. Anderson's orders."

Wynter shook her head. She had seen how much people charged for such apartments, even if they were small, and she needed every extra penny to help cover school costs loans and grants wouldn't cover. "I can't afford it."

"Rent's free. Mr. Anderson says that's in return for the additional security you'll provide being around the barn all the time."

She started to protest and then closed her mouth. The two of them had figured everything out so she could have no reasonable objection. Truth was, it sounded almost too good to be true. A real apartment. And free meant more school money.

"Thank you," she said at last, pushing aside pride for practicality.

Thomas smiled again as he headed for the door. "I gassed up your truck too." He stopped with his hand on the knob. "Look, lass, if you run into trouble, Mr. Anderson's a good man. He'll help."

She nodded. After he left, she stood in the feed room and blinked away hot tears. Never had she met people like this, except maybe Wythe. Based on her experience, rich people were like the Southards and the Butlers. They wanted to look down their noses at families like hers because she couldn't buy everything she wanted, and she wore thrift store clothes. Kindness wasn't something she was used to.

She measured the rest of the feed from the list on the wall and concentrated on her work. Once the horses were fed and watered, she checked the schedule posted in the tack room to see which horses would stay in to be ridden later and which were to be turned out to pasture.

Exercise riders showed up around seven, along with a couple of grooms who knocked dust and dirt off horses with their brushes. Wynter collected the blankets where they threw them on the floor. Dirty ones went into the washer. Those soiled with shavings, she took outside to brush.

* * * *

Nelson's first surprise came when he made a few phone calls to people he knew at Duke. As a member of the board of trustees, he figured he would open some doors for Wynter.

"She doesn't need any doors opened, Nelson," his friend told him over the phone. "The girl's test scores are sitting right in front of me. She's got an all-but-perfect SAT. Oh, excuse me, it appears she's ten points off perfect in English."

Nelson chuckled. "Anything else I should know?"

"The finances are shaky. It appears she won a full scholarship from something called the Southard Foundation, but it was yanked a couple of months ago. We're working with her on some loans now."

Nelson's eyes narrowed. So in addition to firing her, the bastard pulled the college money out from under her. Was there no end to how low the Southards would stoop?

"Tell her she's got a four year full ride," Nelson declared. "I'll pay."

"What do you want me to call this sudden scholarship?" Jason Hairston asked in some amusement.

Nelson's mouth twisted. "Call it the Allison Memorial Scholarship fund. Start it in the fall so she won't be too suspicious. I'll continue it for one incoming freshman student each year after this. Full ride, based on academic excellence and demonstrated financial need."

Nelson hung up the phone with a small feeling of satisfaction. *Strike one*, he thought. It might be a small hit, but it was still a hit.

His major plan of action was progressing nicely. Already he'd put out information and set up what appeared to be solid investments. Then he had tipped Southard's broker. Only Nelson knew the companies were ready to go belly up.

* * * *

Once the horses were turned out, she picked out stalls at a fast pace because she had an appointment at Duke to finish filling out paperwork. Wynter had put it off because she'd had no address to give them until now, and even better, she could also give them a tuition deposit. It wouldn't leave much for gas and food for the coming week, but she could get by since she'd be living right above the barn.

She whistled while she worked. It was one of the happiest days in a very long time. She finished the last stall just before eleven. Now the rest of the day was free until five in the afternoon when she brought horses in for the night. Wynter hurried to empty the last wheelbarrow full of manure on the pile in the back. After putting the tools back in the shed, she crossed over to the office. Thomas came out with the checks.

"Here you go, Wynter." He grinned. "Your first check."

"Thank you." Her gaze dropped to the amount printed on the paper and she swallowed. There must be a mistake. She'd never made this much at the Southards. As much as she needed the money, she didn't want to risk losing the job if this was an error.

"Thomas," Wynter whispered before he passed her on the way to the barn. "This can't be right." When he frowned she hurried on, "It's—it's too much money."

Thomas relaxed. "There's no mistake, girl. Mr. Anderson believes in paying the help. In return he expects hard work, make no mistake."

She looked at the amount on the check and grinned. "Damn. I mean thanks. Thanks a lot!"

She turned toward the truck, still smiling.

"Where are you going?" Thomas inquired.

She laughed. "School, Thomas. I'm going to school. Don't worry, I'll be back in plenty of time for afternoon feeding."

Wynter felt lighter than she had in a long time. She stopped at the convenience store across from Pheasant Run to cash the check. When the man saw it was from Nelson Anderson, he handed her the money, no questions asked. She bought an apple and a big bottle of water and aimed the rattletrap truck toward Durham.

After parking outside the financial aid office, she glanced around and couldn't keep down the sense of anticipation she felt. She was going to Duke! Spring semester classes had finished the previous week, so the campus was almost deserted, but she still felt an air of challenge. Before heading inside, Wynter washed her face and hands with the water left over in the bottle and changed her soiled t-shirt for a fresh one. The papers were in her hand, and the money was in her pocket.

It was almost an hour later before she left. She was registered. They would let her start on a part-time basis over their summer session. Plus, the financial aid people said they had discovered another scholarship for which they felt sure she qualified. It would cover tuition, come fall. Now she just had to buy books. The other things she needed she didn't even want to think of at the moment. She had managed advanced math classes and her other high school courses without either a computer or a calculator. She would make do with using the library until she saved enough money for a computer.

She knew she should head back, but she still had time, so she took a few minutes to walk around campus. Over the past year, she'd looked at so many brochures and pictures she felt she knew her way around already. It was quiet now, but next week it would reawaken with students and faculty. The fall would be even more exciting. Wynter grinned when she headed back to her truck.

She should tell her mother where she was, what was going on. The thought struck her as she turned the key in the ignition. No. Not yet. Not until she was truly settled. The sting of what happened at home was still too fresh. Wynter found that out last night when she had jerked away from Nelson Anderson and almost sent him sprawling. She wasn't ready yet to talk to her mom—or Wythe. She thought about the letter she'd left her mother.

> *Ma—I'm sorry. I got in trouble today. It was*
> *just supposed to be a prank to get even with Pay,*
> *but it got out of hand. Anyway, Mr. Southard fired*
> *me—and he's taking away my scholarship.*

I can't take it around here anymore. I'm leaving
to see if I can find a way to get into college
somewhere, even if it's not Duke. I promise I'll
take care of myself and get in touch with you
once I'm back on my feet. Please don't worry.

But she knew Irene O'Reilly would worry. Wynter tamped down her guilt with the knowledge Wythe Bradshear would be there to comfort her. Wythe was always there. And maybe with her gone, he'd do something about the way he'd always watched Mama.

Just a little longer. When I've got summer school under my belt, I'll let her know then.

She headed out along the tree-lined road bordering campus and back to the highway. Pheasant Run. What a great name. So much classier than Southard Farms.

And Nelson Anderson was different than anyone she'd ever encountered. He seemed much older than what he was. Wynter wondered what had aged him. Then there was the whole thing with the leg. Whatever happened had been bad enough to make permanent changes around his home. The hand controls on the car. The ramp to the front door of the house. Plus, she'd heard what sounded like the hum of an elevator after he'd said good night. Those weren't things a man with a temporary injury needed or even wanted. In fact, he acted like a man waiting for things to get even worse.

Chapter 4

As summer wore on, Nelson made a point to catch glimpses of Wynter whenever he could between work and business trips that drained what energy he had recouped. He looked forward to those glimpses. They were a tonic, especially when he saw her gaining weight and looking healthy and happy. He couldn't help feeling a bit like she was one of the young show horses they trained. When the time was right, she'd be ready for the show ring too.

God knew she had the lines of a Thoroughbred. One evening, he had passed her while she ran along the main road in shorts, a sports bra and beat-up sneakers. Her strides had been easy and ground-covering as though she was accustomed to running long distances. He had watched her slim, graceful form in the rearview mirror until another driver honked, and he realized he'd almost crossed the center line. Yes, her body would make men sit up and take notice, but that was just part of the package. The girl possessed a brain.

On another occasion, she'd been curled up in a rocking chair on the front porch of the office, engrossed in an advanced mathematics textbook. One hand had balanced the book and the other had twirled the braid she wore. Nelson had found himself wondering how long her hair was, and how it would feel to run his fingers through her thick tresses. Did it feel as silky as it looked? He had imagined the strands lying in contrast against her milky skin.

God! She was way too young for him. He turned away in disgust. What on earth was he thinking?

He'd found her another time, after a long day of caring for horses at a show, curled up on a horse blanket on top of the hay bales in the feed stall of a show barn. Thomas had started bringing Wynter along to groom and braid horses, although he was under strict instructions from Nelson not to overwork her. If the older man had thought anything of it, he had hid his feelings well.

As Nelson had watched her sleep, he had felt heat stir in the pit of his stomach. She had lain on her side. His gaze had traveled her long legs to the curve of a hip and the dip of her waist. Her t-shirt had ridden up to reveal the pale, creamy skin of her flat stomach. When his gaze had moved to the swell of her breasts, he'd swallowed. He had pivoted away, the move almost making him lose balance.

She was a means to an end, he reminded himself, just a means to an end. He took a guess at her size and ordered clothing the next day. It was time he started playing Pygmalion.

* * * *

Wynter saw Anderson rarely, but when she had mentioned something to Thomas, he had said the younger man was away on business. Then she'd see him at some of the shows at the Hunt Horse Complex in Raleigh. Sometimes she had caught him watching her. It made her nervous, because her whole body heated up every time. It was as if his dark blue eyes were some kind of laser that set her on fire.

"Wynter," Thomas called. "Quit daydreaming, lass. I want you ready to go with us this afternoon. You squared away with your classes?"

She set down her book, stood and stretched. "Yes. Is there anything left to pack?"

"Take your braiding gear with you. You can pick up some extra money."

Wynter blinked. "You'll let me take on customers outside our horses?"

"If it doesn't cut into what you must do for me, I have no problem with you pickin' up extra cash. Figure you must need it, what with your schoolin'."

She wanted to hug him but was afraid it would embarrass the crotchety Scotsman. Instead, she smiled. "Thanks, Thomas."

This show was bigger than the last one she'd attended. More riders from outside the state. After she recognized a couple of riders from Southside Virginia, Wynter tucked her giveaway hair up under a baseball cap and introduced herself to everyone outside of Pheasant Run as Win Riley, short for Winifred she told them with a wicked grin as she explained her mother's awful sense of humor.

After she had landed the first braiding jobs, more followed over the next three days. As fast as she'd finish one horse, someone else would head her way.

Wynter resorted to wearing leather gloves when she worked around the barn. Her fingers were raw and numb from sewing in so many tiny braids.

Every time she grimaced with the pain, though, she'd pat the growing wad of cash in her pocket. By the last day of the show, she had pocketed more than eight hundred dollars.

Though she knew he was around, she had hardly seen Nelson Anderson during the entire show. While she stood in the warm-up area near the indoor arena that last day, he rode past in a covered golf cart. A thin, blond-headed woman with more gold on her fingers than sense in her head drove the cart, gesturing and talking as she went. Nelson looked bored and distracted, as though he wasn't listening at all.

"Hey, Wyn," a Mexican teenager about two years younger than her yelled from the middle of the ring. "You got any smokes on you?"

She caught Nelson's head turning out of the corner of her eye, but then he was past and headed around to the front entrance to the arena.

"Sure, Rico. Come and get one."

The teenager jogged over and jumped the railing of the ring. She handed him a cigarette. He lit hers then his own. He was from Southern Pines, where he worked for a big Hunter/Jumper barn. He and Wynter had hit it off after he'd heard her swearing a blue streak at one of the horses she'd been braiding . He'd promised to teach her Spanish if she would teach him the swear words she knew. It had sounded like a good deal to her because, heaven only knew, she commanded a wide vocabulary of acceptable and unacceptable words.

"You leaving tonight?" he asked in heavily-accented English.

"Yeah. Thomas wants to get the horses back to their own stalls as fast as possible."

"Too bad. We have a big party on the last night."

Wynter shrugged. "I'm not much of a partier. I have classes tomorrow."

"Oh. GED?"

Wynter shook her head. "College."

It set her apart, and Rico's manner cooled. "I see you next show then."

He was off and already calling out to another girl groom. Wynter smiled. Dropped like a rock, but she didn't care. She lit another cigarette and took a deep draw on it.

Wynter O'Reilly, Duke University Freshman. Nothing would get her down, not hands that hurt like hell, not even the persistent stiffness in her neck and shoulders. She rubbed the back of her neck. She would have loved nothing more than to massage it, but her fingers were too sore.

She watched the horses in the warm-up ring. As she continued to rub her neck, some of the tension dissipated. As usual, it was chaos. Trainers barked at their students while riders made turns and called "Heads up!"

before the fence they wanted to jump. It was always amazing, she thought. There were seldom, if any, crashes.

"Smoking, Wynter?"

She dropped the cigarette and remained standing, still staring at the ring while her hand dropped to her side. She felt like a child caught doing something wrong. Why she wasn't sure. Slowly, she turned to see Nelson Anderson, this time behind the wheel of the golf cart, and no one with him. His expression was unreadable.

"Hi, Mr. Anderson." Wynter shifted from one foot to another. "How are you?"

She hadn't spoken more than a passing greeting to him since the morning he'd dropped her off at the barn. He scooted over to the passenger side on the cart's bench seat, using the cane to give him leverage.

"If you don't mind, I could use your help. I need you to give me a ride out to my car, then turn the cart back in to the show office."

"Sure." She climbed in. How hard was it to drive a golf cart? What she didn't count on was the interrogation that went along with it.

"What's with the hat?" he asked. "You have lovely hair. It's a shame to cover it."

"I—thank you," she said, flustered.

"So, why the hat?"

"I-I was just trying to keep my hair out of the way while I worked."

"You wouldn't happen to be the Wyn Riley everyone hired to braid their horses?" He paused, and she glanced sidelong to find him staring at her gloved hands and the loose grip she maintained on the steering wheel. After she stopped the cart at his car, he continued to sit. "Take off your gloves, Wynter."

"No, that's all right," she responded, "I'll keep them on."

"Take off the gloves," he ordered.

His tone put her back up, but God she needed this job. So she stripped off the gloves and let her hands drop back in her lap, hoping he wouldn't see them since her fingers dangled between her thighs. Instead, he surprised her by reaching over and lifting one hand. He turned it over, rubbing her palm while he stared at the raw skin of the thumb and first two fingers. He turned her hand back over and set it down.

"How much money did you make?"

The quiet firmness in his tone told her it would do no good to lie or even tell him it was none of his business.

"Eight-hundred and fifty dollars."

He arched one dark brow at the amount. "Was it worth ruining your hands?"

"I need the money," she retorted, and feeling stung by the criticism, added, "not that you'd know anything about that. You've always gotten everything you wanted."

Anderson's mouth twisted with bitterness and his expression closed like the shutter on a camera. "Not everything. No. Some things money can never replace. All it buys you in the end is some satisfaction, and you should hope like hell you never have to learn that lesson."

She assumed he had been referring to the leg and whatever happened to it. "I'm sorry. That was stupid of me and childish."

He sighed. "You start classes tomorrow, don't you, at Duke?"

"Yes," she replied in surprise. She had told no one about signing up, so she'd assumed he'd seen the papers the night she had fallen asleep in the tack room.

"How will you take notes in your classes, Wynter, if you keep butchering your hands trying to make money braiding at every horse show?"

"I'll figure it out," she began, an edge of anger and rebelliousness not far from the surface.

Anderson's fingers grasped her chin. "I'll pay you *not* to do it. A thousand dollars per show."

Wynter pulled back in shock and suspicion. "I-I don't understand."

His smile lifted one corner of his mouth. In a man less handsome, it might have been called a sneer. "You heard me. I'll pay you one thousand dollars above and beyond what you make if you will *not* do any braiding."

"I couldn't do that," she stammered, gut twisting even as she refused the tempting offer. "I—it's not right."

He looked off in the distance, his blue eyes remote. "It's the least I can do. I don't know much about you, and I won't pry, but you must be an outstanding student to have made it into Duke with your background. Furthermore, you must have incredible drive to pursue your education," he turned and reached for her hand again, "if you're willing to do this to your hands to help pay your own way. Accept the offer, Wynter. I won't repeat it."

With that he climbed from the golf cart and limped over to the Rolls. She watched while he started the engine and drove off. That was one of the strangest conversations she'd ever had. Someone willing to pay her *not* to do something? She shook her head. Not likely. Rich people always had some motive, something they wanted to hold over another person's head. The Southards had taught her that lesson all too well.

Chapter 5

Irene O'Reilly stared out the kitchen window of the trailer, her gaze not even absorbing the bright foliage of the trees in the woods beyond. Did all mothers go through this? Had her own mother ever wondered after she had left?

"I can hire a detective, Irene." Wythe Bradshear tried again to convince her to look for Wynter.

"She's legally an adult, Wythe." She shook her head. "I had hoped she would send me some news by now, but I won't pressure her."

"Wynter has always been hot-headed, but I never considered her thoughtless." Wythe's voice held irritation.

"Wythe…"

"Yes, thoughtless and cruel. She has no business putting you through this kind of hell."

His chair scraped, and his big hands rested on her shoulders before he turned her from the window to face him.

"Please let me hire someone to look. You don't have to make contact, but it would give you some peace of mind."

It was so tempting to let Wythe help. But she wanted to give Wynter until the end of the year. Whether she was on her feet or not, Irene knew Wynter would never let Christmas, her birthday, pass without some word. She shook her head again.

"I have to give her a chance. I have to have faith."

Wythe snorted in frustration.

"I know you like things black and white. You like to take action," she said. "They are the very qualities that make you so successful with the corporate acquisition stuff you do. But Wythe, parenting isn't like that, not single parenting. There are a lot of gray areas."

He raked a hand through his wavy, brown hair. Like always, it was just a bit too long, as though he couldn't be bothered to take time for a haircut when there were so many other things to do.

"If you'd like to stay for dinner," she offered, "I can give you a haircut."

He grinned, his face boyish with amusement. "Your hints are getting less subtle."

"If not, I can let you borrow some of the ponytail holders Wynter left behind."

This time Wythe laughed. "Ah, Irene O'Reilly, if people knew what a smart-ass you are." He shook his head. "I'm afraid I can't stay tonight."

"Hot date?" she inquired, hoping instead to hear it was some business matter as it almost always was.

"Not really."

Her heart sank. Maybe not a hot date, but a date all the same. She watched Wythe turn and grab his suit jacket from the back of the kitchen chair. "I stopped by on my way home from the office to change clothes. I'm meeting an old college friend in South Boston tonight."

She smiled, hope springing up. "He or she?"

"Nosy tonight, aren't we?" Wythe grinned back. "*She,* if you must know. Trish Staunton. Her family's from around here, and we hung out some."

"Good luck."

She watched him go out the door, her smile in place until the door shut behind him. Irene blinked and bit her lip. She would not feel sorry for herself. Even if he never became anything else, Wythe was her best friend. It would be enough. It must be.

She remembered the first day they'd seen him. Ten years ago. He was home from college for the Christmas holidays. Irene and Wynter had just arrived in Danville, where she'd tried to get hired at Dan River Mills, but she didn't have a job yet. Money was tight. Everything went to renting a cheap room not far from the mill. Wynter's birthday was Christmas Eve, and Irene had nothing to give her. Not an easy thing to tell an eight-year-old. It would have been even tougher to explain she'd had no money for dinner either.

Somehow Irene convinced Wynter they were eating out. She didn't have to know it was a church soup kitchen where they served meals to the hungry and homeless. Irene smiled when she remembered how excited Wynter had been. They never ate out. Anywhere. Not even a hot dog from the convenience store. They couldn't afford it. Wynter had thought it was a wonderful treat. As they went through the serving line, her eyes had landed on Wythe. When her daughter had smiled at him, he'd smiled back. It was the most beautiful sight Irene had ever seen.

"Guess what?" Wynter had told the young man as he served them turkey, while Irene had snuck glances at his handsome face. "My name's Wynter, and me and my ma are eating out tonight because it's my birthday!" Wythe had glanced at Irene, and she'd wanted to fall through the floor. What must he be thinking?

But without even missing a beat, he had laughed at Wynter. "Is it really your birthday?" At her vigorous nod he had asked, "How old are you? Sixteen?"

Wynter had giggled and twirled one braid around her finger. "No, silly. I'm eight years old. Ma says I'm the best Christmas present she ever got."

Wythe's eyes had darted to Irene and he had smiled again, genuine respect lighting their brown depths. "Well," he'd said, turning back to Wynter, "we'll have to see what we can do for your birthday celebration."

They had almost finished eating when Wythe had come back into the room carrying a sheet cake with eight candles stuck haphazardly in the top. Irene had noted with chagrin they looked like candles from the advent wreaths scattered around the church. He had lit the candles, and the entire kitchen staff had sung *Happy Birthday*. Wynter had laughed in delight, and Wythe had laughed right along with her.

God knows, Irene thought, whether he had ever realized he had been more of a father to Wynter than any man they had known. He had made her give him their address before they'd left. The next morning when they had awoken, there had been a package out front with a note saying, "To Winter, from Santa." It was the same teddy bear Wynter had left behind when she'd run from home in the spring.

Chapter 6

"Wynter!" Thomas Sinclair shouted down the length of the barn. "Come on out here, lass, and put on your paddock boots before you do."

Wynter wrinkled her brow while she stowed the pitchfork and wheelbarrow in the shed. She had hoped to grab a little down time before she left for campus. It was one of those bright fall days she loved. The sky was crisp and clear blue, and the trees blazed in an array of colors from palest yellow to a deep, rich red. At home, Wythe would be hunting or hacking out in the afternoons. She missed those rides with him. He was the first person to put her on a horse.

While she worked, she took off the sweater Mama had knitted. It was too warm for mucking stalls, and she didn't want to get it dirty. After grabbing her paddock boots from the back of the truck, she slipped them on, zipped them up and sprinted out to the ring while she pulled her sweater back on to hide her threadbare shirt.

Thomas stood holding the reins of one of their show jumpers, a big bay mare named Rosie, but her attitude on life was anything but. In his other hand, Thomas held a hard hat.

"I need your help. Rosie's rider just quit on me. Put on the helmet and hop up, so I can see what you can do. The mare's already entered this weekend in Raleigh."

Wynter looked at Thomas dubiously but strapped on the helmet and adjusted it to fit. "I haven't ridden in six months, Thomas," she warned when she put her foot in the stirrup and swung up. She settled in the saddle, making Thomas smile as he handed her the reins. "And I'm self-taught."

"You'll be fine. Take as long as you like getting your legs under you. Rosie likes a long warm-up."

"Okay." She started the mare like she had most of the field hunters she'd exercised, working at a walk on a long rein until she picked up on the mare's rhythm. Rosie moved big, even at the walk. Slowly, Wynter collected her, getting her to step under herself more and engage the hind end. There was a lot of power back there. She'd seen the mare jump, and she'd known Rosie was talented, but also temperamental. While Wynter rode, one of the mare's ears flicked back and forth before rotating forward again. It was as though she asked who was on board.

"Push her up to a trot," Thomas called.

Just a light squeeze of the leg, and the mare responded with a smooth transition into the higher gait, still maintaining her rounded profile, hind end engaged and front on the bit. The mare floated across the ring. Wynter tested her responsiveness with a couple of leg yields down the outside length of the arena, then at the corner asked for the canter transition. Once again, it was smooth.

"Take the oxer on the diagonal whenever you're ready," he instructed.

It was the smallest fence out there, a shade over four feet. Wynter circled and looked for the line to the fence, Rosie smooth and collected beneath her. When she turned to line up, the mare's ears flicked backward and forward, and Wynter felt her back off the fence, so she squeezed her forward. It was to reassure the nervous horse she knew what they were doing, and the mare should trust her. Rosie's stride equaled out, but Wynter felt her picking a big spot. Rather than ask the mare to insert another stride, the girl pushed her forward even more. Rosie sailed the oxer with plenty of room to spare.

"Now the outside line."

Wynter nodded at the trainer and looked around the turn. It was a triple. A two stride to a one stride, all verticals and all big. She narrowed her eyes. It was more than she was used to from her experience exercising field hunters, but Rosie could do it if Wynter could boost the mare's confidence. The horse ticked the first jump, and Wynter felt her start to waffle.

"No, you don't," she hissed near the horse's ear. "You can do this, Rosie, stay with me."

Since the mare had flattened out, Wynter rebalanced her, and when they cleared the second element, collected her even more. One stride and they were up again, the mare powering off her hindquarters. It wasn't pretty, but they cleared all three.

"Bring her over," Thomas ordered.

Wynter blew out a breath in relief and patted the mare on the neck while she brought her down to a walk on a loose rein. Only then did she turn back to where Thomas leaned against the fence. Her breath caught and heat rose to her cheeks when she saw Nelson Anderson and an older woman standing at the rail. Thomas, who smiled with a bit too much satisfaction, stood next to them.

She'd been set up.

Wynter nodded at Nelson, and he returned it, expression unreadable. She'd seen very little of him since that night at the show in Raleigh when he had offered to pay her not to take braiding jobs. She had taken him up on his offer and set the money aside. It would go for school expenses or to help her mother, nothing else. Other than the odd glimpse at some of the horse shows, he'd spent a lot of time away on business she guessed. She glanced at the older woman next to him with a nod and a slight smile. "Good morning, ma'am."

"Hop down, girl," Thomas chided, "and introduce yourself properly."

Wynter felt herself blush as she leaned over to give the mare another pat, hoping some of the color would leave her cheeks before she faced everyone. How the hell would she know how to talk to someone who was a client? She was just a shit shoveler. Wynter hopped to the ground and glanced at Thomas.

"Shouldn't I walk her first, Thomas? She's sweaty." She said it with a hint of pleading, but the trainer wasn't going to let her off the hook.

"I'll take her around while you make your introduction." He held out his hands for Rosie's reins, and Wynter handed them over to him before unstrapping the helmet and shaking her braid loose from where it had been tucked up to help make the hard hat fit.

"What glorious hair, child," the older woman next to Nelson commented. Wynter saw his glance flick over her hair then away. When the older woman stretched a hand out, Wynter placed hers in the woman's palm. The older woman held on after shaking it and turned Wynter's palm up. "No stranger to work, I see."

"No, ma'am." When she once again became aware of the dark blue eyes studying her calloused hand, Wynter wanted to curl it behind her back. She remembered once in school how Tory, Payton Southard's girlfriend, had made fun of her work-roughened hands.

The older woman dropped Wynter's palm and smiled. "Call me Miss Olivia. My real name's Olivia Rutledge, but my husband's long gone, thank God, so I prefer Miss Olivia. I'm too old now to drop the Rutledge name."

Wynter giggled. She couldn't help herself. She'd never met anyone quite like this woman.

"Stop, Olivia," Nelson said with unexpected humor. "Wynter's hard-headed enough without you adding fuel with your misandry." He turned toward Wynter, his deep blue eyes searching her face before he looked away. "Let's do this right. Olivia," he said formally, "I'd like you to meet Wynter O'Reilly." Nelson turned to Wynter again. "Wynter, this is Miss Olivia Rutledge, a neighbor as well as a client."

She smiled at the older woman, liking her kind expression. Laugh lines surrounded her eyes and mouth. "I'm very pleased to meet you, Miss Olivia."

"Nicely done, girl."

Wynter glanced at her in confusion.

"The ride, I mean," Miss Olivia added. "I never did like the last girl. She was too rough, too abrupt. Rosie didn't like her, but she likes you."

"Thank you. She's a wonderful horse."

"Then it's settled? You'll ride her this weekend in Raleigh?"

Nelson and Wynter both turned their heads at the same time to stare at Miss Olivia. "What?" they said in unison, Wynter with confusion and Nelson with fury.

"Sure she will, Miss Olivia," Thomas said, having just arrived back around the ring with a now cooled-out Rosie.

"Thomas," Nelson warned. "Don't you think we should discuss this first?"

Thomas looked at his employer. "I wouldn't enter the girl in an equitation class, Nelson, but when it comes to raw talent, she's one of the best I've seen. Gutsy too. Do you know," he continued, adding fuel to the fire, "she hasn't ridden in six months, and look what a fine job she did!"

Wynter's confusion grew when Nelson's face darkened with anger. "What on earth were you thinking?" he snapped. "The girl's not ridden in six months, you've not seen her ride, and you put her on the most complicated mount in the barn?"

Wynter recoiled in hurt confusion from his anger. She knew how to ride, damn it, and she'd done a good job with the mare. He had no right to be so angry.

"I would never have let her jump the horse if I thought she would hurt the mare!" Thomas protested.

Nelson's hand sliced through the air and slapped against the fence. "It's not the mare I'm concerned about."

Silence followed the unexpected outburst and everyone looked at him with expressions ranging from satisfaction to Wynter's stunned confusion.

"I'm fine with it," Wynter ventured. She saw Nelson was embarrassed.

He glared at them. "Then settle it among yourselves. I have work to do." He turned on his heel and limped toward the office.

Olivia chuckled, meeting Thomas's twinkling blue eyes as she pulled a crisp twenty from her wallet. "You were right, Thomas. I would never have believed it after what had happened last fall."

"Am I missing something here?" Wynter questioned, wondering what the bet was.

"Not at all, my dear," Miss Olivia smiled. "Pay no attention to us or Nelson."

"I'll take Rosie and untack," Wynter volunteered, but Miss Olivia shook her head.

"Let Thomas do it, my dear. The old coot should earn his feed every now and then. I'd like to chat with you for a few minutes before you leave. Thomas tells me you have class soon."

"Yes, ma—Miss Olivia."

Thomas and Rosie disappeared into the barn. With regret, Wynter watched the mare go. She had enjoyed riding her. Rosie had plenty of talent, she just needed confidence.

Olivia Rutledge put a hand on Wynter's arm to draw her attention away from the mare. "Rosie is my mare, Wynter. She was born on my farm...the last foal out of my old hunt mare. Even as a foal, I saw she had potential, so I brought her over here to Thomas because I've known him for years, and I trust him. But so far, Rosie hasn't lived up to our expectations. If Thomas trusts you to ride her, so do I. I want you to ride her this weekend in Raleigh."

Wynter longed to say yes, but she shook her head instead.

"If the problem is money, dear, I'll pay you to ride. There are two classes. One Friday evening and one Saturday evening."

"It's not that, Miss Olivia," Wynter stated. "I can't. I mean, I won't go against Mr. Anderson's wishes." She stared at the older woman, pleading for understanding. "He's been very kind to me, kinder than almost anyone, except maybe my Ma."

Olivia Rutledge laid a thin, veined hand on Wynter's arm. "Don't you worry about Nelson, my dear. I'll handle him. You just concentrate on riding these next few days."

Wynter smiled, allowing hope to grow. "I'll have her ready for you, even if I don't ride this weekend." She glanced at her watch. "I should go. I have midterms coming up soon. It was nice to meet you, Miss Olivia."

Olivia Rutledge laughed. "Oh, trust me, the pleasure was mine."

Wynter sprinted back along the barn, afraid she would be late. It was a tough semester, with both accounting and economics courses. She hadn't told anyone at Pheasant Run how many hours she took. If everything went according to plan, she would have her undergraduate degree in two, three years at the most.

She ran up the narrow stairs into the loft and turned to the entrance of the small apartment. It was an afterthought to the barn, but she was glad they had added it. Set up as a studio apartment, there was a small kitchenette with a table and two chairs, and a futon served as both couch and bed. No phone, no TV. It wouldn't suit many people, but it was perfect for Wynter. She could study in the evenings uninterrupted. The faint sound of the horses in the barn below drifted up. The one drawback was the bathroom was the one downstairs off the tack room. She took to showering at night, so she avoided the risk of running into anyone.

After grabbing backpack and sneakers, Wynter ran back again and sprinted for the truck. It had been acting up but started without a hitch.

While she drove to campus, she thought again of Miss Olivia's offer. Wynter wanted nothing more than to ride Rosie, but it would make a tough weekend. She had planned on asking Thomas to let her stay back at the farm to study. With two midterms Monday morning in Accounting and Political Science, she would have to find a way to get it done, if Nelson gave the okay. And just when had she started to think of him as Nelson?

Wynter fumbled for a cigarette while she drove. She'd seen the way Nelson had looked when he'd caught her smoking, but it wasn't as if he were her dad—or anything else—a small voice inside her head taunted. She tried to deny it, but Nelson fascinated her like no one else ever had. She recalled his outburst beside the ring. Why would he worry?

* * * *

Nelson stood next to the ring every morning the rest of the week, watching, but saying nothing while Wynter rode Rosie. Thomas delighted in taunting him as he set the fences higher and made the combinations tighter and the turns more technical.

They were tougher courses than she'd ever ridden, but she sensed when she'd made a mistake. If there was no time to correct and jump safely, Wynter pulled Rosie up. She refused to damage the horse's growing confidence.

It was Thursday morning, the day before they were to leave, and Nelson was once again standing watch at the side of the ring. Although he'd told Wynter it was all right to ride, she had sensed a worry deep inside him he couldn't let go.

He seldom spoke all week, and this day had started the same. He scowled while he watched them warm-up, and his expression never lightened the entire time she rode. It was distracting, but Wynter tried hard to ignore him.

"That's enough today," Thomas called from the center of the ring. "Walk her out before you dismount."

She nodded and loosened the strap on the helmet. Keeping her long braid tucked up inside it made her head hurt. She hadn't dared mention to anybody that she owned nothing to wear, and nobody had said anything, so Wynter decided she would stop by a consignment tack store that afternoon. If she was lucky, she might be able to find everything she needed without putting too much of a dent into her computer fund.

When she passed Nelson, he stopped her. "Come get me in the office when you've finished. I have something for you." He turned without another word and limped away.

Wynter stared after him. She missed the Nelson Anderson she'd first met, she realized. The man from that horse show in Raleigh. The man who had rubbed her palm with his thumb and told her not to cover her hair because it was lovely. This Nelson was abrupt and remote. Wynter gulped and turned Rosie away to continue walking around the ring.

It was almost a half hour later before she had finished untacking, grooming and settling Rosie back in her stall. She could have dumped the work off onto one of the grooms, but it didn't feel right. Wynter wanted to get as close to Rosie as possible in the time remaining before the show, but the real truth was she tried to put off the meeting with Nelson. Her feet dragged when she headed toward the office. She pulled the sweater back on, but the rest of her was getting pretty scruffy. She glanced down at her favorite jeans. There were holes in both knees, and they were so worn on the thighs, she knew she should get rid of them soon. It would have to wait now. She couldn't buy riding clothes and new jeans.

Wynter knocked on the door.

"Come in," Thomas's voice boomed from inside.

As always, Nelson was in the back corner on a computer. She wondered about that for a moment and then dismissed the thought.

"I've put Rosie back," she said before turning her attention to Nelson. "Mr. Anderson, you asked me to come get you."

He looked up from the computer screen he'd been studying. "Right. Just let me log off, and I'll be right out."

His mood seemed lighter than in quite some time. Wynter smiled and was relieved to see his face soften a bit. He never quite smiled, she thought, as she went out the door. During the months she'd worked here, Wynter had seen him smile a handful of times, but she remembered him laughing only one time—when she'd told him he wasn't old.

She cocked a hip against the porch railing. A few minutes later, the door opened and Nelson came through. Automatically, she moved to help him shut it, but he waved her away.

"I can get it, Wynter," he barked. "I'm not a complete cripple."

She retreated, feeling stung. Something of what she felt must have shown. When Nelson turned, he paused as though he wanted to say something then decided against it. Wynter followed while he led the way down the steps to the back where the Rolls was parked. He popped the trunk with a remote key as they approached. When Wynter stopped beside him, she looked inside to see several boxes.

"These are for you, Wynter." When she hesitated, Nelson urged, "Go on, open them."

Her fingers shook. She saw the labels on a couple of the boxes. There were boots, breeches, a helmet, jacket, shirt and stock tie with a diamond studded pin nestled inside. She gaped at everything, stunned someone would do this for her. She felt her throat tighten. She would not cry. She would not.

"Well?" Nelson prompted.

Wynter couldn't answer, couldn't even look at him. Without thinking, she turned and buried her head against his shoulder. He staggered before she felt his arm circle her and pull her closer. Finally, in a choked whisper Wynter managed, "Thank you. Thank you so much."

Nelson's arm tightened, surprising her when he leaned his head against hers, cheek on her hair.

"You never ask for anything," he murmured, "do you, Wynter? What were you planning to ride in?"

She rubbed a hand across her eyes but still stayed where she was in the circle of his left arm. "I found a consignment tack shop. I was going to check there after class today."

Nelson cleared his throat, and Wynter stepped back, feeling uncomfortable.

"I saved enough money in my computer fund," she rushed on, "so I figured I could spend that. I'll be happy to pay you back," she added with determination and trepidation. She'd seen the labels on everything, and they weren't the economy brands.

Nelson slammed the trunk shut and glared. "It's a gift, Wynter. Can't you leave it at that?"

"No, damn it!" she shot back. "You're all the time pushing money at me! I-I'm not used to it, and it makes me uncomfortable."

Nelson raised a brow. "Oh? Then you'll enjoy the next part for sure. I need you at the house at five. My tailor and a friend who specializes in fitting boots will be at the house to make sure this fits."

Wynter laughed. She couldn't help it, but then her anger flared. "That's not even funny! You might be my boss, but I don't have to sit here and let you make fun of me." She glanced at her watch. "I have to go. I've got class."

When she spun around to head to the truck, Nelson called, "Five o'clock, Wynter. I'm paying these guys good money to get this done."

* * * *

She thought about it all afternoon. Who was he kidding? Who on earth had a tailor and boot maker in this day and age? Wynter couldn't let go of it. It made it hard to concentrate on her lectures, which in turn made her even angrier. She had two exams Monday and three more that week, not to mention the paper she was still finishing. Her last class ended at four-thirty, which left just enough time to get back to Pheasant Run. The angry part of her wanted to go back to the barn, but she was curious.

Had he been serious?

In the end, curiosity won, and she drove past the barns and up the driveway to the house. In daylight, it was even more imposing than at night. When she made the turn around the trees, Wynter saw three cars parked in the circular drive beside Nelson's Rolls Royce. She parked the beat-up truck next to them, deciding she was either the brunt of some kind of joke, or Nelson Anderson had far more money to throw around than she had imagined. That thought made her want to turn tail and run. In her experience, having money was not a good thing.

Wynter knocked on the door. Mrs. Caudle opened it and smiled. They'd met at the barn and taken an instant liking to each other. Even as rich as he was, Nelson didn't like having a lot of household staff. In fact, as far as Wynter knew, Mrs. Caudle was it.

"Wynter! Come in. Mr. Anderson's been waiting. I've set everyone up in the sitting room off the study."

Wynter stared.

"Are there really people here to make sure the riding clothes fit?" she asked, feeling a wave of horror wash over her.

"Oh, yes," Mrs. Caudle went on, oblivious to Wynter's evident discomfort. "And a dressmaker Miss Olivia brought over."

"A what?" Wynter backed out the door when Olivia Rutledge appeared in the hallway.

"Wynter! You're here. Excellent." Olivia crossed the hallway and grasping her by the elbow, pulled and pushed her along. "We'll start with the riding clothes."

The next hour went by in a haze of both embarrassment and anger. Everyone talked as though she wasn't there while they prodded, poked and pinned. They turned her around and touched her in places no one but her mama and the doctor had.

Wynter had just stripped out of the riding clothes and handed them out the door of the small guest bath. She was ready to change and get the hell out of there when a silky dress in deep green was thrust through the door.

"Put this on, please," the dressmaker said in a no-nonsense voice.

She held the dress up. It seemed a bit short, she thought, but otherwise it wasn't too bad. The dress had long sleeves, with a high, boat neck style neckline. It was then she turned it around to unzip it and gasped. It was cut low enough in back there was no zipper. That was it. Wynter stood a moment in her bra and panties before she thrust the dress back out the door at the dressmaker.

"I will *not* put that on," she informed her. "I won't wear it. There's no back to it! I've had enough poking and prodding." She slammed the door in the woman's face.

A hushed conference was going on outside. She heard Nelson's deeper-timbered voice too, and her humiliation was complete. After a moment, the door cracked open and another dress was thrust through it.

"One more, miss, please," the dressmaker begged.

Wynter accepted it, but it seemed very similar to the other one until she held it up. Although the front was cut in a wide "V" neckline, the back matched it, making it overall a much more conservative dress. She shimmied into it, eyes widening at the hem. It ended just below mid-thigh! She wouldn't be able to move without showing more than God ever intended.

"Come on out, dear, so I can see what adjustments need to be made."

Wynter cracked the door enough to peek out. Miss Olivia and the dressmaker stood nearby. On the other side of the sitting room, Nelson stood looking out the window. Wynter wasn't sure what he looked at since it was dark outside, and they'd already turned on the lights inside.

He straightened, balancing on the cane while he turned toward the room. For a moment, she saw his deep blue eyes darken. She swallowed.

The dressmaker was already pinning. "We'll take it in some here at the waist and the hips. It seems fine over the bust."

Wynter blushed when Nelson's gaze shifted to her breasts before sliding down to rest on her long legs. A gnawing discomfort in the pit of her stomach made her squirm then yelp when the dressmaker pricked the side of her hip.

"Are you done?" Wynter whispered. "I-I need to go. I have studying to do."

"Almost, dear."

Wynter touched Olivia Rutledge's arm. "Miss Olivia, why do I need a dress? I'm just riding Rosie, right?"

"Of course, dear," Miss Olivia said. "But there's also the exhibitors' party Friday night."

"I can't go to that," Wynter gasped. "I've never been to a party. I-I wouldn't know what to do—or say."

"Of course you can," Miss Olivia assured. "Nelson will bring you."

Wynter glanced at Nelson. He once again had his back to them while he stared out the window. It was then she realized he stared at her reflection. Her outraged expression must have shown. She saw the sudden quirk of his mouth reflected in the window. Damn him. It was useless to object now. She would find some way to get out of it.

"There. Done." The dressmaker patted Wynter's hand. "Don't worry. I'll have the dress ready and waiting for you."

"Can I go now?" she asked in a somewhat shaky voice. "I have to study."

The dressmaker and Miss Olivia nodded, but it was Nelson who was her undoing, making her heart beat with a heavy thud when he turned from the window and smiled. "You look lovely, Wynter."

Chapter 7

By the next afternoon, she was a mess. Her classes passed in a haze. She rushed from campus to the Hunt Horse Complex, where she found Thomas and the Pheasant Run stalls. Nelson and Olivia Rutledge were out front, still seated in the golf cart Nelson drove in order to get around. They turned when she walked toward the stalls.

"We were beginning to worry," Thomas remarked. When she brushed a strand of hair from her face with a hand that shook, his sharp, blue eyes narrowed. "Are you all right?"

Wynter nodded, tensing her jaw so her teeth wouldn't chatter.

"Well," he continued as though he cheered on a reluctant hound in the hunt field, "go change. You've got an hour to warm up before your class is called. Chances are with your inexperience, they'll put you in early."

She nodded again. Trying hard to remember her manners, Wynter turned and smiled at Nelson and Miss Olivia before heading inside the tack room to change. She did okay until she attempted the stock tie. Her fingers shook so much she couldn't get it adjusted, never mind get a decent knot.

"Damn this thing anyway!" she swore. She mumbled more obscenities concerning the maternal heritage of whoever invented stock ties. The curtain shifted to one side and Nelson limped through the opening. Wynter glared her frustration. "What do you want?"

"To help," he responded.

His tone took the starch right out of her. She dropped her hands from the tie and stood there. "I'm sorry," Wynter apologized. "I—I do need help. I can't get it adjusted correctly."

Nelson stopped in front of her and leaned the cane against a nearby trunk. Putting most of his weight on the good left leg, he turned his attention back to her tie. "Relax, Wynter. I'll have it tied in no time."

His fingers were swift and steady. It was obvious it came from years of practice. While he worked, his unmistakable scent drifted up to her and she inhaled, eyes closed. It should have been calming, and in some ways it was. But at another level, the scent of him left her wanting something, she wasn't quite sure what.

"You must have done this a lot," she commented, an edge of nervousness still tightening her voice.

Nelson finished pinning the tie in place and looked at her without any humor. "A year ago, you would have been competing against me."

She stared at him dumbfounded as without another word, he picked up his cane and limped back out of the tack room, shoulders straight and stiff.

Nelson and the golf cart were gone, as was Miss Olivia. Thomas stood there waiting. The Scotsman beamed when she came out.

"You look grand, Wynter. Are your nerves settling down any?"

"Some."

"You missed the course walk earlier, but they're on dinner break right now, and I've gotten us permission to take a look at it anyway. Let's go."

He led the way to another golf cart and they climbed in. In a couple of minutes, he parked it outside the door near the entrance to the ring. Wynter saw one of the grooms walking Rosie around the indoor warm-up area when they passed. She looked beautiful, sleek and shining, ears and crown covered with a crochet and cloth "hat" to help deaden the noise inside the arena.

Wynter started to put her helmet on, but Thomas stopped her. "Leave it. We still need to finish your hair."

When they walked the course, she felt some of the nervousness leave. It was not as high or as tight as the courses Thomas made her train over at Pheasant Run. On one level she registered what Thomas said, the strides and the pacing sinking in even while part of her mind wandered—noting how different the complex looked now that she was in the ring instead of on the outside like a spectator. *Huge* didn't describe it.

When they walked the triple combination along the wall where most of the spectators were seated, Wynter felt an uneasy prickle along the back of her neck and glanced up. Seated in a box near the edge of the ring were Payton Southard and his wife, along with the Butlers, and both Tory and Payton the Third. She saw a moment of startled recognition on Mr. Southard's face before he masked the expression.

Her gaze found Nelson seated in a chair at the very top. No way could he negotiate those steps. Olivia Rutledge stood next to him. Her smile reassured Wynter, who nodded, but couldn't quite manage one in return.

"Wynter!" Thomas barked. "Did you hear a word I said?"

Wynter smiled at the older man. "Don't let her flatten out going into the triple, but once I'm done and have made the turn to the water jump I should let her run like hell. Would that sum it up?"

Thomas grunted. "Smart-aleck kid."

When they exited the ring to go out to the warm-up area, Miss Olivia met them at the in gate. She handed Wynter a slender box. "I thought you might enjoy these."

Wynter's eyes widened when she opened the box to find a pair of chocolate brown leather gloves. The leather was so fine and supple they felt almost like a second skin going on. She smiled at Miss Olivia and hugged her. "Thank you. What a wonderful gift!"

Her stomach rolled as she started the warm-up on Rosie as she always did with flat work. It calmed her and the mare, and helped Wynter concentrate on what she must do. She felt Rosie's nervousness ease when she asked her to move under herself and down onto the bit. Wynter smiled when the mare rounded, her hind end pushing off like a piston as she asked for alternate leg yields.

Wynter ignored the other riders in the warm-up area. She had to. She had already glimpsed a couple of faces she recognized from magazine articles. She wouldn't let it psych her out. They must be schooling younger horses. Although this was an A-rated show, it wasn't one of the better known ones.

When Wynter saw an opening, she turned Rosie down the center line to the vertical schooling jump in the middle of the arena. Her ears flicked, and Wynter felt a test coming as the mare started to back off from the fence. With strong legs and seat, Wynter pushed forward and felt Rosie relax and go. When they landed, Wynter patted her neck. They would be okay.

Thomas was right. They were among the first to go, but that suited Wynter. She hated waiting because it gave her a chance to get nervous, a chance to think about the people in there watching. She shook her head to clear it as the announcer called her number. She barely heard him continue with the horse and rider's name as she pushed Rosie into a trot, halting before the start to salute the judge. Then they were off.

Rosie felt liquid and powerful beneath her as they approached the first fence. Over the last few days, Wynter had felt the horse's confidence soar and her pace even out. It paid off now. When each fence loomed before them, the powerful mare pricked her ears forward, eager to take it on. Instead of pushing, Wynter found herself half-halting the mare to keep her from flattening out.

At last, they took the brick wall and made the turn to the triple line. When they approached the first element, a flash went off, making both Rosie and Wynter hesitate a moment. It knocked her off stride, and Wynter knew as they came in they would have to adjust. The option was take it big or ask the mare to stick in another short stride. It was almost automatic— Wynter pushed the mare forward. The line was set as a two stride to a one stride, so she would gamble on getting her collected back after this vertical. Wynter heard a gasp go up from the crowd when Rosie picked a big spot.

"Come on, girl!" she urged the horse when she powered off the ground. "You can do it!" Wynter did her best to just stay out of Rosie's way while she flew over the fence, leaving plenty of air between the top rail and her feet. As soon as the pair landed, Wynter sat down and brought Rosie back hard, collecting for the one stride, another vertical to an oxer. She seemed to bounce in place as she shortened her stride and powered over the jumps.

The horse responded instantly to Wynter's legs and the shift of her weight, executing a tight turn and galloping forward toward the water jump. One, two, three. Wynter asked for the takeoff, and the mare responded with a strong finish over the ten-foot spread. She grinned at Thomas when he met them at the gate.

"Good girls!" he praised them both. "That's what I've been waiting to see from this mare!" He patted her neck and grabbed the reins as Wynter hopped down. "Don't wander off. You're clear with no time penalties, so you'll be in the jump-off." Wynter nodded while she watched Thomas hand Rosie off to the groom. "You've got fifteen minutes!" he called when she headed outside.

It was quiet outside the door, isolated almost, even with the traffic of horses and grooms going back and forth between the warm-up ring and the arena. Wynter took off her helmet and leaned against the wall outside the door. The coolness felt good. She sucked in a deep breath, feeling the tension drain away as she released it.

"Hey, Wyn!" a familiar voice called. "Nice ride! You sit a horse even better than you swear."

Wynter laughed with sudden relief and turned sideways to lean against the wall. "Rico, that was just what I needed. Thanks!"

"Here," he said, offering a cigarette. "If you liked that, then a smoke should help."

She stripped off her gloves and shoved them in the pocket of her jacket before taking the smoke. Rico offered his cigarette to light it from. She handed it back and took a deep draw.

"No kidding," the teenager continued. "You're good. An' I thought you were jus' a groom! Where you learn to ride like that?"

Wynter shrugged. She hadn't. She just had more guts than sense and often put the Southards' field hunters at obstacles their owners would have fainted at, had they seen it. She had jumped rows of round bales and pine trees fallen across trails through the woods. There had even been a car or two and a few farm wagons in there. Wynter stamped the cigarette out under the heel of her boot.

"I taught myself until I rode Rosie then Thomas fixed me," she explained as she grinned at Rico. "And trust me, I still need a lot of fixing!"

They both laughed.

"I see you've landed on your feet."

Wynter stopped laughing. She knew that voice. Payton Southard, Junior. She felt more than saw Rico vanish into the darkness. *Great!* Just when she could have used a little moral support, he had disappeared. Squaring her shoulders, she straightened and eyed the older man.

"Yes, I have. Not that it's any of your concern." She felt a surge of confidence. This man was no longer the intimidating influence of the past few years. "I'm paying my own way through Duke, Mr. Southard. Dean's list, both summer sessions. Can you say the same of your son?"

"Why you…" he blustered, taking a threatening step forward when a cold, furious voice interrupted.

"I wouldn't finish what you're about to say or do, Southard."

She turned to find Nelson standing there, a Nelson she had never seen look so cold. His eyes glittered and his jaw was hard with a fury out of proportion to the situation. He turned to her and softened. "Wynter, Thomas needs you inside. They're resetting the course for the jump-off."

She nodded and walked by him without a word. For once in her life, she feared saying anything. With that look Nelson had become a stranger. After she shut the door, she still heard the voices from outside as they drifted around the gangway where the horses entered. She couldn't hear what was being said, but the bitter, angry edge was obvious, as was the fact the two men knew each other.

Wynter found Thomas leaning against the rail, watching while the height on the fences was adjusted. She stood next to him, gaze on the ring and asked, "Thomas, how does Mr. Anderson know Payton Southard, the man I used to work for?"

He tensed, turning with a slight frown. "Why do you ask?"

"They're outside. Mr. Southard stopped to…speak to me. Mr. Anderson came out to get me, and he seemed angry."

Thomas glanced at the door behind them. "It's not my place to tell you. That's something you'll have to take up with Nelson." He seemed anxious when he said, "Stay here, lass, I'll be right back."

Thomas hurried out the door, leaving her to stare after him in confusion. What was going on? When she started to go after him, Olivia Rutledge chose that moment to come down the steps. Wynter smiled, happy to see her, but still worried what was happening outside—and why.

"What a wonderful ride. I was so concerned when that girl in the front row took that flash picture as you headed to the triple. I hardly dared breathe, but you and Rosie cleared the fence anyway."

"Thanks, Miss Olivia." She glanced over toward where the Southards sat, Payton, Junior joining everyone else. He looked pale, but it could have been a trick of the lighting inside the arena.

The announcer gave a five-minute warning for the jump-off. It would be short. Just four other horses went clear. Wynter drew the first go. She put her gloves back on and found both Thomas and Nelson behind her. An aura of controlled anger still hung around Nelson. He barely acknowledged the greetings of other riders when they came and went.

"Warm back up," Thomas said. He had his game face on now, so Wynter nodded while she tucked stray hair under the helmet and snapped the harness. "Go for clear first, speed second—but don't dawdle. Like we practiced. Tight, tight turns. Rosie can jump these fences almost from a standstill if you make her believe."

The groom brought the mare forward, and Thomas gave Wynter a leg up. She settled into the saddle and turned Rosie on a loose rein while they trotted out to the warm-up ring to loosen things up. Wynter wouldn't take another fence before the jump-off. The announcer called the class and their names. With a tight smile at everyone gathered near the in gate, she trotted the mare through the opening to the middle of the ring, turned and saluted the judge, then nudged Rosie into a collected canter. Everything else faded as Wynter found the first fence and turned toward it. Seven jumps, laid out in a twisting pattern with two turn backs before a long gallop to the finish. She concentrated on doing just what Thomas had instructed.

Rosie wasn't as relaxed as before. Taking a chance, Wynter slowed down a notch, asking for collection. The horse's ears flicked before she responded.

"You can do it, Rosie!" she encouraged as they reached the first fence. "Come on, mare. Show them what you've got!"

She did. Collected, ears forward, she powered over the fences then made beautiful tight turns. They approached the last fence, the in gate in sight. It was a high vertical that forced Wynter to resist the temptation to let Rosie flatten out going in, but when they landed, she leaned forward and hissed at the big mare. Rosie leaped forward. They finished with one time fault.

The groom met them at the gate. Wynter vaulted off Rosie, beaming while she patted her neck. "Thank you, lady."

The first person she saw when she turned to the rail was Nelson. For the first time since she'd met him, she saw him smile with pleasure. It lit his blue eyes, banishing the shadows always lingering there. It relieved the lines in his face and made him seem the thirty-two years she now knew him to be.

"Wynter."

Impulsively, she stepped over to the rail and wrapped her arms around his neck. She squeezed him and felt strong arms encircle her, the cane still grasped in one hand while he hugged her back.

"Thank you!" Wynter released him and looked straight into his eyes, laughing. She looked around at everyone, Thomas, Miss Olivia, and back at Nelson. "Thanks to all of you for giving me a chance." The last couple of words came out in a sob. "I'm sorry," Wynter apologized, laughing and crying, and then moved back in embarrassment when she realized Nelson's arms still held her. Heat burned her cheeks. "I'm sorry," she said again, ducking her head.

Nelson startled her by chuckling.

"You are a treasure, my dear," Olivia Rutledge said matter-of-factly. "You have no idea how much."

The next horse finished with four faults after pulling the top rail on the last fence. Wynter glanced over her shoulder and said, "I need some air. I can't stand here and watch the rest of this."

She walked down the gangway, crowded with horses and grooms, and stepped around the corner for a breath of cool night air. She glanced up as the door to the spectators' area opened, and Nelson stepped through. He leaned on his cane. As much exercise as she knew he racked up, tonight was too much and it was beginning to show. She started to say so but thought better of it. He was her boss, and she had no right to say anything to him.

"Did you need me?" she asked.

He leaned against the cement wall behind him. "No. But like you, I didn't want to stand there and watch the rest of the jump-off. When you have a good round, it's like waiting to see yourself go up in flames."

Wynter smiled hesitantly. "That's what I thought."

"You did a great job tonight, Wynter, in case I didn't already tell you."

She looked over at him and asked, "What did you mean earlier when you said you would have been my competition last year?"

He started to answer when Thomas peered around the corner. "Get in here, girl!" he beamed. "You placed second! Get on your horse and take your victory lap!"

* * * *

Could a night get any better than this one? Wynter thought as she showered in the hotel room Miss Olivia had booked.

The older woman was a firm believer in comfort and spared no expense to make sure she found it. After Wynter's victory lap, she had whisked the girl into her car and told everyone they would see them in a couple of hours.

Wynter came out of the bathroom with her hair wrapped in a towel twisted on top of her head. Olivia Rutledge had already donned the proverbial little black dress. There was no telling how old it was. The style was timeless, and the quality was without question.

"Sit here, child, while I work magic on you." She waved the brush with a flourish.

Wynter laughed and took a seat. She soon realized Miss Olivia wasn't kidding. In a matter of minutes, the older woman had brushed out Wynter's long, damp hair, pinned it up in a neat French twist and applied light makeup. Wynter stared at her reflection in amazement. Still wet, her hair gleamed a sleek, dark auburn, and having it pulled back from her face highlighted delicate cheekbones. Whatever Miss Olivia had done with the makeup she'd applied, Wynter thought her eyes sparkled a deep emerald, framed by her thick lashes.

"I look so different," she said wonderingly. "I've never worn makeup before."

Miss Olivia raised her brows. "Where did your mother hide you?"

Wynter shrugged. "I never did girly things. I worked. I studied."

"You look beautiful." Olivia smiled in the mirror. "You just have no idea, do you?" She patted Wynter's shoulder. "Your dress is hanging in the closet along with a bag of lingerie and some shoes."

"They aren't high heels, are they?" Wynter asked while sudden visions of wobbling and falling flat on her face came to mind.

"No, dear," Miss Olivia answered chuckling. "Not only am I aware of how challenging heels can be to someone not used to them, but you don't need them to enhance either your legs or your height. God blessed you."

"I used to run cross country in high school."

"Instead of dating?"

Wynter laughed when she stood up. "The students at my high school wouldn't date me. I'm the trailer trash."

She disappeared around the door of the closet, reappearing a few minutes later in the altered dress. It fit like a second skin now, making her a bit self-conscious.

Olivia Rutledge clapped when Wynter walked back. "You are not trailer trash, Wynter. If you're ready, we should go."

It took only a few moments to get back to the hotel suite where the party was already in full swing. Wynter tried to hang back behind Miss Olivia when they entered, but she would have none of it, taking Wynter by the elbow and keeping her by her side. Heads turned. The whole room paused for an instant before the buzz of conversation continued.

Wynter relaxed until she realized the rider who won, the one she'd guessed was schooling a green horse, walked to her side.

"Excellent riding this evening," he remarked. "Haven't seen you on the circuit before." He glanced at Olivia. "Another of your *protégées,* Miss Olivia?"

The older woman smiled as if enjoying a secret joke. "Actually, she's Nelson's discovery, Chris. Meet Wynter O'Reilly. Wyn, this is Chris Stevenson."

The young man glanced over toward the windows, his eyebrows rising. "If she's Nelson's discovery, then I won't detain you. He's never been much of a party animal, and he seems a bit put-out tonight."

When Wynter looked in that direction she saw why. In the corner, not more than ten feet from him were the Southards. Her breath caught, and her newfound confidence plummeted. Years of teasing and taunting had taken their toll, and she felt like the trailer trash they'd always called her.

"Stop it!" Olivia whispered. "You're slouching. Put your chin up and walk on over to say hello. Nelson looks like he needs cheering up, and whether you realize it yet or not, you are the cheerleading squad."

Wynter smiled at Chris Stevenson before she walked toward Nelson.

The buzz of the party faded into the background while she studied him. He seemed tired. At that moment, he glanced in her direction, almost as if he had been checking for her arrival. His deep-blue gaze locked on hers. Wynter felt a jolt of heat, as if he had reached out and touched her.

The room was crowded, and it took some time to reach him. Various people stopped and congratulated her. She thanked them politely, but turned back each time to Nelson's intense regard. The closer she came, the tenser he looked.

When she reached him, his right hand gripped the cane until his knuckles turned white. He rotated his left hand palm up. Without thinking about it, Wynter slid hers into his. Again that jolt of heat rose from the pit of her stomach. His gaze searched her face before devouring the rest of her. Part of Wynter wanted to curl up and hide, but then she remembered what Olivia had said and smiled.

"Do I look okay?" Wynter asked with concern when he continued to look at her without saying a word.

To her surprise, he smiled lopsidedly. "You're breathtaking."

This time even her ears got hot. "I don't feel that way," she confided in a shaky voice. "In fact, I don't feel much like me at all."

"You do to me." Then Nelson did something that would have seemed out of place had he been anyone else, but it fit him. Lifting her hand, he pressed his lips against the backs of her fingers. "You are the loveliest woman in the room, Wynter O'Reilly. Never forget it."

Chapter 8

Wynter ducked her head, feeling overwhelmed and confused. She'd never seen Nelson like this before. He continued to stare through half-closed eyes. His hand circled her wrist, and his thumb rubbed her palm almost absently. While he continued, Wynter's lips parted and her breathing became shallower. What was he doing?

"Please, Mr.—"

"Nelson," he corrected. "Call me Nelson."

How could she feel panic and a desire to lean against him at the same time? His voice, eyes and gentle stroking of his thumb against her palm stirred aches in places she'd never guessed could ache. She didn't know what was happening, and it made her as nervous and skittish as an untamed foal.

"Nelson, I…"

"Ah, here you are." Olivia joined them then, breaking some of the tension. She had Thomas in tow, looking uncomfortable in a coat and tie. Wynter forced her gaze away from Nelson's, her smile shaky. Relief warred with disappointment at the interruption. Nelson released Wynter's wrist, and her heart slowed its fluttering, nervous pace.

"So what do you think, Nelson?"

He smiled at Olivia, surprising even her. "She's the loveliest woman here," he teased, "except for you, of course."

"Bah!" Miss Olivia snorted. She handed Nelson a drink, then pressed a glass into Wynter's hand. When Wynter eyed it, Olivia reassured her. "It's a small glass of wine. Try it."

Nelson leaned forward and took the glass, handing Wynter his drink instead.

"Olivia," he warned, "don't throw too many things at her at once." Blue eyes flashed as he turned to Wynter. "Try mine. It should be innocuous."

She glanced between the two of them, sensing a sudden tension. "I shouldn't stay long," Wynter offered. "It's been a long day, and I still have some studying."

"I'll run you home in a few minutes," Nelson said. His tone was the old Nelson, brooking no argument.

His gaze slid to where the Southards and the Butlers stood talking with a small group of horse owners and riders from Southside Virginia, making Wynter wonder yet again what the source of the tension was between them.

When she glanced over that same way, she caught Pay staring. His gray-eyed gaze slid down the length of her, resting a long time on her breasts before sliding along the slender length of her legs. In some ways he did no more than Nelson the night the dressmaker fitted the dress, yet Pay's regard made her skin crawl, while Nelson's made it tingle.

She moved closer to Nelson. To her surprise, he let his arm slide around the back of her waist, hand now resting possessively against a hip. Again she felt that flutter and instant heat. For a moment, she thought she had jumped from the frying pan into the fire.

"Relax," he murmured. "You're fine, and I can assure you those people will not come over here."

Wynter tilted her head to look at him. "This is nice, but I…I don't want to stay. If you don't mind, could we go—soon?"

He nodded. "In a bit."

While Nelson talked with Olivia Rutledge and Thomas, Wynter took a small, cautious sip from the glass Nelson had handed her. *Good! Just ginger ale.*

She was now shielded from view of the Southards and their group by both Olivia and Thomas, helping her to relax a bit. Despite compliments from both Olivia and Nelson, Wynter still felt uncomfortable. This was not her world. She was much happier in the barns with the Ricos of the world.

Wynter skimmed a hand over the material of her dress. She couldn't remember the last time she had worn one, but certainly not since she had been a girl, of that she was sure. Mama had always been too poor to buy a nice dress or go anywhere she might wear one.

Once they had moved out to the country, it had become hard for Mama to get to mass. When they had gone, it had been a casual service. Once Wynter had started working for the Southards that had stopped. She'd had horses to tend seven days a week.

Wynter glanced left. The hotel suite's large French doors opened out onto a balcony, and she wondered if she might slip out there for some fresh air, then chided herself. What she hoped was she would run into someone who would let her bum a cigarette. Nelson's arm dropped from around her while he talked with Thomas and Olivia.

With a mumbled, "Excuse me a minute," Wynter escaped. She knew Nelson glanced after her, but he was trapped for the moment. Nevertheless, she felt midnight blue eyes follow her.

It was cooler on the balcony where several groups of people were scattered. Wynter walked to the edge and looked up at the sky. This was not like being at Pheasant Run. There you saw every star in the sky on a clear night, but here the lights from the city made it difficult to see any of them.

"I see you've shaken off Nelson." It was Chris Stevenson, Wynter saw with relief. She knew from what she'd read in the magazines he was in his mid-twenties, one of the rising stars of the jumper circuit. She also knew he had a reputation as a party boy.

Wynter smiled, not sure how to take his flippant remark. "I think they're plotting strategy for tomorrow."

"What are you riding in?" he asked. "It's always nice to know who my competition is."

Wynter grinned. She couldn't help it. She felt a lot more like her normal self around Chris. He might be rich, but right now he spoke to her as just a rider. "I have no idea. Until Monday, the closest I had gotten to any of the horses at Pheasant Run was washing their blankets and mucking their stalls."

Chris Stevenson laughed disbelievingly. "You're joking."

"No," Wynter replied seriously. "I'm not. Rosie's rider quit, and Thomas had already entered. He put me up on a whim I think, but it worked out."

"You've obviously ridden elsewhere. Were you on the circuit out West?" Chris asked, trying to place Wynter somewhere in the show-jumping world.

She shook her head and launched into her exploits, first with Wythe's hunters and then with the Southards. She soon had Chris Stevenson laughing with genuine amusement. He wasn't half bad when he dropped the party boy attitude.

He pulled a pack of cigarettes from his pocket and offered one. After lighting hers, he lit one himself.

"Please tell me you didn't really jump the master of the hunt's Lexus with his horse!" he exclaimed, gray eyes twinkling.

She nodded. "And we didn't even leave a scratch on it!"

"So are you telling me you've never had formal training? And you're competing in 'A' shows?"

Wynter smiled bitterly. "Kids from my background don't get riding lessons, Chris. We're the ones shoveling up the shit behind the other kids—literally and figuratively."

He looked somewhat uncomfortable. She knew his background. He was one of those other kids, from a moneyed family with a dad who'd shown and evented for years. He flicked the cigarette at a nearby ashtray.

"If Nelson dumps you," he purred, moving closer, "you can ride anything you like at my barn."

"I have no intention of dumping her, Stevenson." Nelson's tight voice startled both of them.

Wynter was relieved because Chris made her feel uncomfortable. When she turned, she saw Nelson's blue-eyed gaze flick to the cigarette. Swallowing guiltily, she stubbed it out.

"Mr. Anderson," Wynter said, not feeling as if this was the same man who'd asked her to call him Nelson just a while ago. "Did you need me?"

His glance shifted from Chris Stevenson and back.

"It's time to go," he stated and turned to walk away, leaning on the cane.

She smiled an apology at Chris. "Sorry, gotta go. Boss's orders."

Chris's look was cynical. "I can see. I'll see you tomorrow, Wyn."

She found Nelson waiting by the door. He cupped an elbow while he escorted her to the elevator. The car already idled in front of the hotel lobby. Wynter stopped suddenly, almost throwing him off balance.

"I need my things!" she said in a panic when she remembered.

"It's handled. Your books are already in the trunk.

Instead of feeling grateful, Wynter felt irritated, as if her life was no longer her own. "Did you put my truck back there too?"

Silence stretched between them and their gazes clashed.

"Don't be bitchy, Wynter. It's late and I'm tired."

Knowing Nelson couldn't keep pace, she strode to the car, opening the door herself and sliding in before he could get there. He tipped the bell boy then limped around to the driver's side, putting the cane where he could reach it once he got home. Some of her anger drained, leaving her feeling small and petty. He was tired. It was more pronounced now than earlier in the evening. She started to offer to drive but saw from his hard expression he was already angry. He slammed the door without a word and put the Rolls in gear, heading north to Pheasant Run.

By the time he turned up the long drive, Wynter struggled to stay awake. She didn't notice they had rolled right past the barn and her apartment until they had climbed the hill to the house.

"You forgot to drop me off," she murmured.

"I want you to stay at the house tonight. Mrs. Caudle prepared a room."

Again Wynter felt anger flare. *What right did he have to always manipulate things?*

"Stop the car!" Angrily, she fumbled with her seatbelt.

When she reached for the buckle, Nelson's right hand shot out to stop her.

"No!"

Her eyes widened at the panic that colored his outburst, and she jerked back in sudden fright. "What's wrong?" she whispered.

Nelson stopped the car and put it in park. He pulled his hand away from hers and rubbed it across his face, leaving it over his eyes just a moment.

"I'm sorry," he apologized, a hoarse edge to his voice. He sat there a second or two before sighing. "I'm sorry," he said again. "I should have talked to you. I wanted you to get a good night's sleep without having to worry about anything. Mrs. Caudle will be there. She is most nights." He leaned against the headrest. "Damn it, Wynter. I just wanted to do something nice."

She studied his profile in the lights from the dashboard. Right now he looked older, tired, and she felt childish. He had taken the time and the thought to have someone gather her clothes and books. He'd offered moral support at her first show. He'd even showed up at just the right moment to get Payton Southard away from her. And in return, she had given him complaints. She hadn't wanted to go to the party. She hadn't liked not being consulted about what he was doing.

Wynter stretched a hand out and touched his arm. He stared.

"Do you want me to take you back to the barns?" he asked tiredly.

She squeezed his arm. "No. Keep going."

"Are you sure?"

She nodded. Nelson put the car back in gear. When they stopped near the front porch, he looked away in embarrassment. "I'm sorry to ask this," he sighed, "but I hate to bother Mrs. Caudle at this hour, so do you think you can help me get into the house?"

Wynter saw how he hated asking, how much it bothered him to need help. She nodded and his face softened in sudden relief. Years of hard work, along with being taller than the average woman, sometimes paid off. She supported him to the point of half carrying him inside the house. It wasn't easy. Nelson was not a small man. Close to six feet in height, he possessed the slender, muscled build of many of the riders she'd seen. That helped. Wynter wrapped an arm around his waist, while he wrapped his left arm around her shoulders, leaving the right hand free to use the cane.

"There's an elevator at the end of the hall, next to the kitchen."

She helped him inside and down the hall, lit only by the lamp on the sideboard and then slid open the elevator door. It was big enough for two people at most. Nelson leaned against the wall once inside, closing his eyes. When the small cubicle stopped and the door slid open silently, she once again put her arm around his waist.

"Down the hall to the left."

Double doors at the end of the hallway stood open. The soft glow of a lamp spilled onto the floor inside. While she helped Nelson down the hall to the room, she thought about the oddity of the situation. The room was large and airy, with floor to ceiling windows that lined the wall across from the bed. Mrs. Caudle had already turned back the covers. The light came from the lamp on the night table next to the bed.

"Where…" Wynter hesitated.

"Just help me over to the bed." A note of embarrassment crept back. He seemed distant, as if somehow disassociating himself from the Nelson Anderson who must ask for assistance.

When she helped him to the side of the king-sized bed, she caught a glimpse of a small silver-framed picture on the night table. It showed a dark-haired woman laughing into the camera lens, a blond-headed toddler balanced on her lap, and a Nelson she didn't know. This man smiled openly, eyes twinkling with laughter, hair brown and windblown, with scarcely a touch of gray in it. *My God! His wife? His child?* She had never heard anyone speak of them. She tore her gaze away from the picture and let her eyes swivel back to the Nelson she knew. His eyes closed as if in pain.

"Can I get anything for you?" she whispered, gaze once more on the picture.

"A glass of water. There should be some on the table to your left."

Wynter poured him a glass from the pitcher of ice water and returned to the side of the bed. Nelson popped two pills and reached for the glass.

When he had finished, she took it and returned it to the table. When she turned, Nelson was still where she had left him. She glanced at his clothes, then back up to find him watching her.

"Do you need..." she began, but Nelson cut her off.

His short laugh held a bitter edge. "Most of the time I manage to dress and undress myself. I won't put you through that, Wynter, but I need help with my shoes."

She nodded and swallowed while she knelt on the floor in front of him with no regard to the dress she wore. She picked up his left foot and untied the dress shoe. When she touched his ankle to pull it off, she once again felt that ripple of electricity from the pit of her stomach. She cradled the right foot with even more care. After taking off his shoe, she peeled off his sock, and her eyes widened when she saw the scar that began just below the ankle and disappeared under his pant leg. Still without a word, Wynter set his foot back down and removed the other sock. When she finished, she met Nelson's dark blue gaze.

"Is there anything else?"

"Just one thing," he said, and he reached out to touch her hair. "Would you let your hair down?"

She looked up in surprise. An invitation to join him in bed she might have anticipated. That would fulfill her expectations of someone rich like him, but this disarmed her. Wynter let her head drop forward to pull out the hair pins in the back. It was a simple enough request to grant. Once free, her hair fell forward over her shoulders and down her back. It waved from having been put up while it was still wet. She let her hands drop. Her gaze rested on Nelson's hands where they hung between his legs.

"I—I should go," Wynter mumbled.

"Just one more minute." Nelson's voice was uneven. It was a plea, not a command, and it startled her. Blue eyes searched her face and expression. His hand stretched toward her hair. "May I?"

She nodded. He didn't demand, he didn't take. He asked, and that she could never refuse. The fingers of his left hand slid around a thick lock of hair, the strands trickling over it and between his fingers.

"You once accused me of not understanding want or need because I have money." When she tried to speak he placed two fingers over her mouth. "I saw you looking at the picture on my night table."

Wynter nodded, glancing once again at the laughing Nelson and the woman and child with him.

"My wife, Lindy, and our daughter, Allison. They're dead. And even with all the money I have, I can't bring them back," he continued. "So you see, Wynter. There are some things money can't buy."

She dropped her gaze in embarrassment before he continued. "And I know as much as you work your heart out trying to earn it, all the money I have won't buy *you* either, will it?" It was more a statement of fact than a question.

His hand slid from her hair to her chin, tilting it up so she was forced to look at him. He was in a strange mood tonight. Wynter wasn't sure if it was from the pills he had taken, the fatigue or something else. His gaze searched hers a long moment before he smiled tiredly.

"Your room is at the other end of the hall. Good night, Wynter."

She looked back when she left. Nelson sat on the edge of the bed, a closed, remote look on his handsome face.

The guest room was beautiful, not as large as the master suite she'd left Nelson in, but still almost as large as the whole trailer in which she'd grown up. She stripped off the fancy clothes and let them fall to the floor. Bending over, she rolled down the sheer stockings Miss Olivia gave her and then straightened again and let her hair fall where it brushed against her hips. She was too tired to braid it tonight, so she slipped in between the covers.

But instead of going to sleep, thoughts tumbled through her brain of Nelson, his wife and daughter, the open hostility to Payton Southard. Nelson's leg. Suddenly it clicked. She hadn't paid much attention to the details at the time, but now some of it came back. She remembered reading a headline "Accident Kills Wife and Daughter of Electronics CEO."

Why had she never made the connection? But she knew the answer: she'd been too wrapped up in her own troubles to notice anything else, too wrapped up to pay any attention to a man who dropped into her life now and then, but when he did…

Once again, her own situation rose to haunt her. She knew without a doubt the Butlers would waste no time telling her mother they had seen her. She would have to call. The thought kept her tossing and turning all night. She had treated her mother abominably these past few months, but she couldn't let her find out from people like the Butlers how her circumstances had changed. This was something she must do, and it was past time she did so, way past time.

* * * *

Nelson Anderson sank against the pillows after Wynter had left, waiting for the medication to kick in and give him some peace. Her hair was even longer and softer than he'd imagined. He swallowed and closed his eyes, but images of Wynter ran like a movie. Her impulsive hug when she'd come out of the ring. The strain in her face when she'd faced Payton Southard. The way she'd turned every head when she'd entered the exhibitors' party. The sight of her hair falling like a silk curtain around her while she had knelt on the floor in front of him. *God!* He wanted to grab her, to thrust himself between those long legs, and the intensity of his feelings shocked him.

It had been almost a year since he'd been with a woman. Until Wynter had shown up on his doorstep a few months ago, he hadn't thought he would want another woman. Not after Lindy. Not after what had happened to them.

But Wynter was different. He smiled and his eyes drooped from the effects of the pills. Wynter was like spring. How ironic. She was fresh and new and vibrant. And he admitted he wanted her in a way that had nothing to do with revenge on the Southards but everything to do with the heat and longing and protectiveness he felt every time he was around her.

He slipped into a drug-induced sleep that dulled the constant pain, along with his thoughts and most importantly, his dreams. Because above everything else, Nelson Anderson didn't want to dream. It brought back the memories. He didn't want to remember. It was still torture, and he couldn't face it. It left him feeling even weaker.

Chapter 9

It was after eight when Irene's phone rang. Wythe had stopped by while heading to town to see if she had wanted to join him for breakfast since she had the odd day off from the Butlers. Her employers had left town for the weekend.

She looked at him, dwarfing the kitchen, and shrugged. Wythe was the only one who ever called, so Irene couldn't prevent a bit of worry when she picked up the phone. Had the Butlers changed their mind at the last moment?

"Hello."

"Ma," a quiet voice on the other end said. "It's me. Wynter."

"Wynter!" Irene gasped, knees going weak. Wythe jumped up and crossed over to her side. He helped her to the chair at the kitchen table before sitting on the other side. "Are you all right, honey?"

She heard Wynter's breath catch on the other end and knew her daughter was crying.

"I'm fine, Ma. I am. I am so sorry I left you like I did. It was childish and stupid. Can you forgive me?"

"Wynter? If you're in trouble, Wythe is here. We can come get you. Just tell us where you are."

Irene heard a soft laugh on the other end. "No, Ma. I'm not in trouble. In fact, just the opposite. I don't know why I didn't call you sooner. I just got so busy between my work and my classes and riding Rosie."

Irene ran a shaking hand over her forehead. "Slow down, Wynter. What are you saying?"

She listened in amazement while her daughter recapped the past few months. Wynter finished by asking, "Can I come see you next weekend? I miss you."

Tears streamed down Irene's face. Her own daughter asked to visit? How had they reached a point where she thought she might not be welcome?

"Of course you can, baby. We could drive there to watch you today. It's not that far."

"No!"

"Wynter?" Irene asked again with suspicion. "Is there something wrong? Are you sure you're not in trouble?"

Wynter reassured her and then said she had to go. Before Irene got her phone number or address, she'd hung up. Irene let the phone fall. Wythe shoved the chair back, came around and knelt in front.

"Irene. Is everything all right?"

She looked at him in confusion. "I think so. Wynter says so." She smiled at him, so happy she was beside herself. "Wythe, she's almost finished her freshman year at Duke, and she's been on the Dean's list."

Wythe pulled her up into a big hug, lifting her feet off the ground when he did.

"Stop, Wythe!" Irene gasped. "You big oaf! Put me down!"

As he did, his face darkened. "Things are going well and she didn't call you until now?" His thick brows drew together in a frown. "That doesn't sound right. Where did she say this show was?"

"The Hunt Horse Complex."

"Get yourself ready, Irene. We're going on a road trip."

"But Wythe," Irene protested, "She didn't sound like she wanted us there."

Wythe arched a thick eyebrow. "Do I look like I care? You haven't seen your daughter in six months. I'm taking you there."

Irene looked at him in surprise and then hugged him. "Have I ever told you, Wythe Bradshear, you are my very best friend in the whole world?"

* * * *

Wythe smiled like a choir boy, but inside he chafed. "Friends" was not what he'd envisioned. In fact, when it came to Irene O'Reilly, friendship was the very last thing on his mind, but it was all she seemed to want from him. And like the sap he was, even after ten years, he kept sniffing around, hoping she would notice he was a man instead of just a friend.

Over the last six months, he'd watched the hope Wynter would return disappear. Several times he'd stopped by and held Irene while she had cried in his arms.

So, yeah. He would take Irene to see Wynter, but he sure as hell would find out what was going on and why Wynter had waited so long to contact her mother. He already had a sneaking suspicion why she'd broken her silence. Though Wythe was no longer close to either the Southards or the Butlers, he'd heard through some other friends that the two families went to watch some of the jumpers in Raleigh.

Wynter must have run into them. Wythe's jaw tightened. He would never forget walking back around the barn to apologize for making her face Payton Southard and seeing Payton the Third assaulting her. Wythe had lost it then, using his hunt whip to slash at the teen.

If anything happened to Wynter, anything that upset Irene again, Wythe would put an end to it. He shook his head. He wanted to see Wynter settled and happy because until that happened, Irene would never agree to a relationship with him.

"Come on, Irene. Let's go find your daughter."

Chapter 10

Wynter had found a long silk robe in the bedroom closet and tied it around her waist before she'd gone in search of a phone. She'd snuck across to Nelson's room to make the call because she'd remembered seeing a phone there last night. He'd still been sound asleep and snoring lightly. Whatever pills he'd taken had knocked him out. Perfect.

It hadn't been an easy phone call. Even though Wynter wanted to see her mother, she didn't want her in a hornet's nest at the show grounds, particularly if the Southards were back again. It had hurt to tell her not to come, to tell her she would visit the next weekend instead. Wynter had hung up the phone and laid her head in her arms on the table.

God how she missed her! Ma and Nelson were almost the same age, but she was so worn with caring for a child over the years it almost made Wynter sick. She had called Wynter her best Christmas present ever, but had she been? She didn't even want to think about it. The years Irene O'Reilly should have been enjoying high school and college, she'd spent raising a baby on her own. Wynter had seen how her hands sometimes cramped with pain after hours working at the threading machines in the textile mills.

Mama was still a young woman, and she didn't even know it. Thick tears rolled out of Wynter's eyes, running across her nose and down her cheek onto the sleeve of the robe she wore. If she earned a bit more money, she would be able to send some home. She'd never said she needed it, but Wynter knew how much the money she'd made at the Southards had helped their budget. Mama had lacked that for the past six months, ever since Wynter had taken off.

"Wynter?" Her name came as a groggy question from behind. She turned to see Nelson struggle into a sitting position. She had counted on his exhaustion and the medication he'd taken to keep him asleep while she'd called. "What are you doing in here?"

She ducked her head, letting her hair fall in front of her face while she wiped wet eyes with shaky fingers. "I'm sorry," she said with a smile she was far from feeling. "I had to call my mother, and I saw the phone in here last night, so…" she trailed off. It sounded lame, even to her ears. And the question she was afraid would come, did.

"What was so important that you called your mother at eight in the morning?" His sharp gaze caught her when she dug the toes of her left foot through the carpet. "Don't lie, Wynter. I can always tell when you're getting ready to." He grimaced while he readjusted the way he sat in the big bed. She averted her gaze from his bare chest.

"Do you need anything?" she asked, trying to divert him.

"Don't change the subject, Wynter," he growled.

She turned away, her hair tumbling over her shoulders, hiding part of her face from him. "She didn't know where I was."

"What did you say?" Nelson barked.

She stared at him mutinously. "She didn't know where I was, all right? I left home after that day when…after the Southards fired me."

"And you just called this morning?" He sounded angry and looked it too. His blue eyes glittered, their sapphire depths almost black.

"I didn't want someone else telling her where I was. I wanted to do it. She works for the other couple with the Southards last night," Wynter added by way of an explanation.

"Why did you wait so long?"

"I don't know!" Wynter wailed in frustration. "I told her in the note I left I would call when I got on my feet. And then when it took so long…"

"What do you mean 'when it took so long'? How long were you gone from home before you ended up here?" he snapped.

"A month. And then I was so busy between working and studying, it wasn't easy to find a phone, and I didn't call collect because she doesn't have much money." She paused and stared at Nelson. "And I miss her so much I can't stand it." And to her horror, thick tears rolled from her eyes again.

"Come here." His eyes softened and he patted the bed next to him. When she hesitated he reassured her by saying, "I'm not going to do anything to you."

Wynter crawled on top of the covers. When she saw his left arm open, she slid up next to him and laid her head against his bare chest. He rubbed her arm, and his right hand stroked the hair from her face. Gently, he wiped the tears away with his thumb.

"You never mention your dad," Nelson prompted.

Wynter snorted. "I don't remember him. He left my mother before I was a year old." Her chin trembled again. "She always tells me I was the best Christmas present ever, but I don't believe that. She quit school because of me and married a man who left. Her family disowned her. Some Christmas present," Wynter added bitterly.

Nelson pressed her hard against him and turned up her face. "Listen. She told you the truth, and I can tell you with the certainty of someone who's been a parent." His eyes darkened, but this time with a different emotion than anger. His voice thickened. "Even to this day, I would give anything, including my own life, just to see Allison one more time. I would go anywhere, do anything to hear my little girl laugh and see her play." He cleared his throat and swallowed hard. "It's a whole different level of love, Wynter. When it happens to you, it will change your life forever."

Impulsively, she touched his cheek where one bright tear escaped the corner of his eye. Nelson looked away as though he was embarrassed confiding something so private to someone. Her heart ached. This man had suffered such incredible pain, and she now knew who'd been responsible: Payton Southard the Third. He'd been driving the car that had run the Andersons off the road and into a tree.

Wynter remembered the details now of the press coverage. His wife had unbuckled her seatbelt to attend to their daughter when the accident had happened. Now she understood his reaction last night when she'd started to unbuckle her belt. Lindy Anderson had been thrown from the car and killed on impact. Their daughter had been trapped, along with Nelson who'd been unable to reach her while he'd watched the girl bleed to death before rescuers had freed either of them.

While Wynter recalled the details of the accident, she turned and put her arms around him. "I'm so sorry, Nelson. My troubles are so trivial compared to what you've been through."

"No one's troubles seem small to them." His hands stroked her head, his left arm sliding down her back to her hips. When his hand moved, the tenor of his breathing changed along with hers. Again, Wynter felt that flutter in the pit of her stomach. His right hand tilted her head up. Her lashes fluttered when she saw him lower his head until their lips were a breath away.

"Tell me to stop," he murmured hoarsely. All Wynter managed was to shake her head and then her hand cupped the back of his neck and pulled him closer. Instinctively, her lips parted then meshed with his. The flutter in Wynter's stomach flared with a heat that made her limbs feel heavy and weak. His left hand cupped her buttocks, and he lifted her against him.

She felt his whole body tremble as he pulled his mouth away from hers and took a deep breath. "God in heaven, Wynter," he murmured, "what have you done to me?" He let it out on a shaky laugh. "Go away, Wynter." He half-growled the words but smiled. "I promised I wouldn't do anything to you, and I am a man of my word."

Relief and disappointment poured through her at the same time. Relief that he wouldn't find out how inexperienced she was, disappointment she wouldn't experience more of those mind-numbing kisses. He tasted as good as he smelled, she decided.

"If you'd like a swim before breakfast," Nelson said, "there's an indoor pool in the basement."

"A pool?" Wynter asked. "Inside your house?"

Nelson laughed again. She liked it when he laughed. He didn't seem quite so formidable. "Yes," he mocked, "inside the house. I swim every morning."

"I'll pass," Wynter smiled. "I need to study this morning." She refused to admit she had never been swimming. Other than wading in a few creeks, she'd never been around water.

"Make yourself at home, Wynter. Mrs. Caudle arrives around eight-thirty."

"I thought you said she was here last night," Wynter shot back.

Nelson smiled. "I lied."

She hurried back down the hallway and shut the door to the room she'd slept in. Her clothes were in the trunk of the Rolls. She glanced at the robe she wore. No way was she going outside in this on the remote chance someone might see her. On a whim, she returned to the walk-in closet where she'd found the robe hanging on the door. The closet was filled with clothing. Wynter touched a few pieces tentatively, afraid they might be his wife's clothes, but they smelled and felt new. Then she checked the sizes and realized they were the same as what she wore. In bemusement, Wynter opened one of the built-in drawers. Underwear, bras—all her size and all new. She hesitated, but the temptation of it was too great.

In just a few minutes, she had re-braided her hair, showered and slipped on a turtleneck and a pair of slim-fitting corduroy trousers she'd found in the closet. She checked again. Yes, there were shoes too. She felt a bit like Shirley Temple in *The Little Princess*, but she wasn't so sure she liked it. Wynter was used to doing without—or working to pay the price for what she got in life. The problem was this time she wasn't sure what price Nelson Anderson might want.

She heard the elevator, so she assumed Nelson was going swimming. Wynter left the room and flew down the stairs to the front door. It was another bright, fall day, and she sucked in the crisp air with a smile. After popping the trunk on the Rolls, she found her books and backpack and toted everything back in the house.

Nelson had told her to make herself at home, but she wasn't sure where, and the house was so damn big. So far, she'd seen just a fraction of it, so she decided on the sitting room off the study where they'd been Thursday night. At least she wouldn't get lost.

After depositing the books, Wynter returned to the kitchen where Mrs. Caudle had made coffee and was laying out a plate of croissants with fresh butter and jam. Wynter's stomach growled.

"Good morning, Wynter. I hear you did everyone proud last night."

Wynter hesitated a moment, surprised she would take an interest. "Thank you, but it was Rosie, not me. I was just along for the fun."

Mrs. Caudle laughed. "I've been around here far too long to believe that. Help yourself to some coffee and croissants. There are plates in the cupboard behind you if you want to take them with you. Mr. Nelson said you had some studying to do."

"Thanks. I do. I have midterms coming up and a paper due next week too. I'll have to wait until I get back to campus for that since I have to use the computers at the library for my research."

Mrs. Caudle looked at her quizzically and then shook her head. "Whatever, dear. Just let me know if you need anything else."

Wynter smiled and walked back down the hall to the sitting room. It was more than an hour later before she heard Nelson's uneven gait in the study, the squeak of a chair and the unmistakable sound of leather moving when he settled himself at the desk. She went back to her accounting book, fingers flying while she worked problems on the calculator she'd spent some of her wages to purchase. She enjoyed the exacting nature of accounting, but she also enjoyed the political science class she'd opted to take. It looked at the changing role of religion in world politics, in particular, the rise of Islam in future geopolitical decisions.

Wynter tucked her accounting book in the backpack and opened the political science notes and textbook. This one she knew would be an essay test. She read through the lecture notes, twisting the end of her braid around and around the fingers of her right hand. Her left tapped the pencil in sync with the swinging of her leg.

The sound of a soft chuckle made her glance at the doorway where Nelson leaned against the doorjamb. "Are you ever still?"

She wrinkled her nose at him. "This is still."

"Take a break and come outside. It's a gorgeous day. My doctors say I need to walk, and I could use some moral support. Hell, I may need some actual support," he added wryly.

She slammed the book shut and leaped off the couch. "Sold! Just let me get my sweater."

Nelson took his hand from behind his back and held up the sweater her mother had knitted. "Already got it."

"Thank you," Wynter said with surprise. She pulled the sweater over her head then flipped her long braid out. "I'm ready."

Nelson led the way out the backdoor and down a ramp past the pool, into the woods beyond. The path had been manicured to make it easier for him to negotiate, but it still mimicked walking along a trail through the woods. Benches stood at intervals along the trail. They passed two of them before Nelson motioned her over to the third one where he sat. His face was sweaty and pale, and his chest heaved. As he rested the cane next to his leg, his hand shook.

Fear coursed through Wynter. "Are—are you okay?"

He nodded but didn't speak. He reached a hand in the left pants pocket, brought out a linen handkerchief and wiped his face. He looked up and grinned. Her breath caught at the pure joy in his expression.

"I made it," he gasped. "To the third bench."

She looked back along the trail and understood. The benches were markers, measurements of progress in walking. Wynter smiled back at him and looked at the right leg stretched out in front of him. On impulse, she touched him on the thigh and heard a soft hiss.

"What happened to your leg? I mean, I remember hearing about the accident." She saw his mouth twist, but she pressed on, "But no one reported what happened to you."

Nelson looked at the leg. "I was pinned in. The whole right side of the car was crushed along with my right side. My leg got the worst of it, but I also lost part of my small intestine." His voice grew distant. "They wanted to take my leg off, but I wouldn't let them. I was moved to Duke and declared a 'no information' patient to prevent the press from doing some sort of deathwatch. Next Saturday will be one year since it happened. I've undergone three surgeries. I still have one more to go, but it has to wait."

Wynter bit her lip. She wished she could take the pain away and give him some of her strength. She wished she could ease the grief she saw when he talked of his wife and daughter. Instead of telling him, she handed him the cane.

"Come on. I'll give you a hand. You shouldn't sit too long."

She held out a hand to balance him when he pushed himself back up. They walked along the path in the sunshine of the late fall morning. To a casual observer it looked as though he rested an arm around the shoulders of an attractive young woman, and she in turn had an arm draped around his waist. Only Nelson and Wynter knew how much of his weight she supported the rest of the way back to the house.

* * * *

It was afternoon before they returned to Raleigh. Mrs. Caudle had laundered and pressed her riding clothes. Her boots were polished to a mirror-sheen. After she loaded everything in the back of the Rolls, Wynter went back to the kitchen to find the older woman and thank her. Mrs. Caudle brushed away her thanks.

"It's no more than I used to do for Mr. Nelson. I'm just glad to see him taking such an interest in the horses again. Up until this spring, I thought he would sell the whole farm."

The words stuck with Wynter on the drive to the fairgrounds. She went to check in with Thomas while Nelson limped to the office to get keys to a golf cart. She hadn't quite reached the stalls when he pulled alongside.

"Hey, little girl," he called. "Wanna drive my golf cart?"

Wynter laughed at him and jumped up on the driver's side after he slid over. His left arm rested across the back of the bench seat while his right hand grasped the silver-topped cane. They crunched to a halt in front of the row of Pheasant Run stalls. Wynter jumped out and grabbed her clothes before spinning around to take them into the tack room. From behind her, she heard a familiar voice in a heated discussion with Thomas. Wynter dropped the clothes on a chair and came back out, eyes wide.

"Mama?" she whispered when she saw her petite mother frown at Thomas like a mother bear defending her young. Wythe Bradshear was next to her, his expression guarded.

"Mama?" Wynter repeated. She dropped the brushes she'd brought out and rushed toward her mother. Irene held out her arms, and Wynter buried her face against her mother's hair, holding on, afraid to let go. Everything else faded away. Mama had come. Even though she told her not to, she still had come.

"I missed you so much," Wynter sobbed. "I missed you each and every day. But I was afraid to call, afraid to cause you even more trouble than I already have."

"Wynter," she scolded gently, voice shaky. "You're my daughter, no matter what." She smiled, took her hand and squeezed it before she stepped back to examine her daughter. "I see you're not eating again."

"Ma!" Wynter protested, casting an embarrassed glance over her shoulder. Nelson sat in the golf cart wearing a lopsided smile. "I am eating! It's just…"

"No excuses, Wynter."

She scowled when she heard Wythe chuckle. Nelson joined in, followed by Thomas.

The older man stepped forward and held out his hand. "It's a pleasure to meet you, Mrs. O'Reilly. It pleases me no end to meet someone who leaves Wynter speechless."

Wynter scowled while she bent to pick up the brushes. "I have a horse to attend."

"Aren't you going to introduce us?" Wythe needled.

"Nelson, meet Irene and Wythe. Mama and Wythe, meet Nelson and Thomas. There. Now y'all know one another, and everything's wonderful. Excuse me."

She stomped down the aisle until she came to Rosie's stall. The mare nickered when she approached. Wynter crooned while she opened the door, letting the brushes fall to the floor while she pressed her hot face against the horse's warm, silky neck. God she needed that. Her head was so mixed up right now, and smelling and feeling the warm solidness of the big mare was like coming home.

Mama had come and Wythe along with her. Wythe had come with her? Wynter peeked out the stall door to where the two of them stood talking to Thomas, Nelson and Miss Olivia too. Wynter noticed Nelson remained in the golf cart, the cane tucked out of sight somewhere. She understood his reaction, especially with someone as big and athletic as Wythe standing there.

From under Rosie's neck, Wynter watched Wythe and Mama. Although they didn't touch, he hovered. He towered over her petite mother, but otherwise they fit together—like they always had, she realized. They both had rich, brown hair. Mama's glinted with golden highlights, while Wythe's sent off highlights of a deep, fiery red. She studied her mama's face. Irene looked relaxed and much younger.

In fact, watching Wythe, Nelson and her mother, she realized they were right around the same age. Wynter frowned. She really did not want to feel shut out like she did right now. She liked neither the feeling nor the resentment that went with it. Her mother said something and Nelson laughed. Jealousy raced through her, shame following on its heels.

Wythe slipped an arm around her mother's shoulders, and Wynter felt the tight ball in her stomach loosen. Out of habit, she checked Rosie from head to tail for any bumps and scratches, her thoughts going back to Wythe. He had been around, it seemed, ever since her eighth birthday. He had been the first person who put her on a horse. He had taken her mother and her to the movies, on picnics and hikes through the mountains Irene had missed so much from her childhood there. When another round of textile layoffs hit, Wythe had helped her mother find a job with the Butlers, then had helped them move out to the country.

He had always been around. He'd attended "graduations" from elementary school and middle school. If there was a father/daughter event, Wythe had volunteered to be "Dad." Once, when she'd gotten in trouble at school for something she didn't do, Wythe had gone with her to see the principal. Wynter still remembered the principal's face when he'd asked Wythe just who he was, and Wythe had responded seriously, "I'm Miss O'Reilly's attorney, sir." They'd laughed about that one for a long time.

Wythe and Mama? She hoped so. Mama deserved someone good like Wythe.

Wynter had finished rubbing Rosie when Thomas appeared at the door.

"Course walk's in ten minutes, Wyn."

The jumps were higher than the day before. They had bumped up a level today. Thomas talked while they walked, pointing out striding and potential trouble spots. There were more lines today with fewer but sharper turns, so a lot more potential for a mare like Rosie to flatten out if Wynter wasn't paying attention.

Nelson waited for them in the golf cart when they came out the back of the arena.

"Where are Mama and Wythe?" Wynter asked. She knew he'd given them a ride up when she and Thomas had left.

"Checking out some of the booths inside. Hop in."

Wynter jumped up on the back, letting Thomas have the seat next to Nelson who cast her an odd look before setting the golf cart in gear. The ride back to the barn was bumpy but short.

While she dressed, nerves got the better of her. Wynter sat on the tack box shivering, teeth chattering. She heard the tack room curtain rustle as it was pushed aside.

"You all right?" Nelson asked when he crossed the floor. He stopped and rubbed her shoulders with one hand. "Nerves?"

Wynter nodded. Her shaking slowed down. "Would you tie my stock tie, please? I don't think I can do it."

She handed him the long white tie and made room on the trunk. While he concentrated on tying it, she studied his features. They were sharp and well-defined, his nose long and straight. The eyelashes were thick, and his mouth was wide with a firm, full lower lip. Wynter felt that ripple in her stomach again. It must have shown on her face.

Nelson finished tying the tie and let his hands slide along the top of her shoulders to her arms. Eyes dark and half-closed, he stared at her.

"Wynter?"

Her hands splayed against his chest. She felt the slow, steady beat of his heart, and remembered how he'd looked that morning with tousled, dark hair and the sheet bunched around his waist. Her lips parted on a shaky breath. Nelson lowered his head and pulled her closer to him.

This time when they kissed, it was different. There was no gentleness in it, just pure, raw heat. Nelson's tongue touched her lips, and she opened her mouth. Her insides melted. She was sure of it. Wynter moaned against him. She wanted, she wanted...

Nelson broke the kiss with a shaky laugh and set her away from him before he ran trembling fingers through his hair. "You need to finish getting ready," he remarked and smiled.

Wynter smiled back, shaken but happy as well. "Thank you, Nelson." At his arched, inquiring brow she added, "For tying my stock tie. I liked the finishing touches in particular."

Nelson laughed. It was a deep, rich sound and for a moment, she glimpsed the man he had been before the accident. She wanted that man in the worst way. Grabbing the cane, he rose and limped to the door. He started to say something, paused and then murmured, "Good luck, Wynter."

Chapter 11

Thomas waited outside with Rosie. He gave Wynter a leg up and walked beside her while they headed to the warm-up ring. She wouldn't be as close to the top of the start order tonight, he informed her. Rosie warmed up like clockwork. Each time Wynter rode the mare, she felt the horse's confidence grow. That also made her tougher to ride because Rosie became stronger and more aggressive. When they entered the arena and stopped to salute the judge, the mare danced.

"Easy…" Wynter whispered when they turned and circled toward the first jump. It was not a pretty round by any means. Rosie pulled, Wynter checked, but as they reached each fence, the mare powered off the ground until they turned down the final line, and Wynter realized their striding was wrong. Years of jumping obstacles that wouldn't fall down gave her a keen sense of getting into a fence. With a one stride in and out coming up, the spot was too long to ask the mare to jump big. The choices were clear: Wynter could pull up and take a refusal, which would knock them out of the competition, or she could ask her to add the stride and try to power their way through it. Wynter checked the mare hard. Rosie added the stride, putting them a touch close.

"Come on, girl," Wynter urged as she gathered herself and pushed off. The jump was so powerful it forced Wynter to clench her legs to stay in position so she would not interfere with the horse. Her stirrups slid off her feet. There was no help for it. She would have to ride the rest of the line without them. She was barely aware of the gasp from the crowd followed by dead silence while Rosie powered over the last two jumps. When they landed after the last fence, Wynter kicked her on across the line.

Nerves caught up with her after they exited the ring. Thomas waited at the in gate, took one look at her and said, "I've got her. Hop off."

She slid off the mare's back and sprinted around the outside corner of the arena. Blessedly, there was a trash can right outside. Wynter leaned over it, gagged and vomited. "Here." A wet handkerchief was pressed against her shaking hand. "Wipe your face."

Wythe. She looked over her shoulder.

"Anderson's with your mother, calming her down, if that's who you're looking for. He asked me to come here," Wythe tacked on.

She started to hand him back the handkerchief, but shoved it in her pocket instead.

"Jesus, Wynter," he growled. "Do you know how lucky you were? You should have pulled up."

She glared at Wythe. "I'm being paid to ride—and win. And damn it, that's what I'm going to do."

"You could have killed yourself and that horse," Wythe barked back. "As it was, I thought Irene would faint, and Nelson didn't look much better. Use some sense."

"I did!" she snapped, irritated at his attitude. "I know what this mare can do. She wanted it. There was no way I was going to pull up."

Thomas stuck his head around the corner. "They're resetting for the jump-off. It's just you and Stevenson. No one else went clear tonight. Not a surprise with this course design."

Wynter glared at Wythe. "Please tell everyone I'm okay." She pulled the gloves back on and snapped the harness. Wythe turned and stalked off as Thomas gave her a leg back up. They announced the order of the fences for the jump-off.

Chris Stevenson rode up and grinned. "Ladies first," he motioned with his crop.

"Eat my dust, rich boy," Wynter shot back before she rode back into the arena. Rosie jigged and kicked out while they circled. Her ears flicked back and forth. At some level Wynter registered the fact she and the mare shared the same mood. Just a little irritated and a bit antsy, but when they approached the first fence, Rosie's ears snapped forward and she was all business. Wynter rode aggressively, drawing a couple of gasps as well as applause. When they rode back through the gate, she smiled at Chris Stevenson.

"Beat that."

She heard him laugh when he pushed the big gelding forward and rode into the ring. Thomas was next to Wynter along with a groom who sponged the sweat off Rosie and threw a wool cooler over her hindquarters.

"Just stay up," Thomas said. "You've either won it or placed second, so you'll be doing a victory lap either way."

A moment later, Chris Stevenson came back out on the big gelding, shaking his head. "I couldn't even touch your time. Maybe I'll try schooling over my BMW, since jumping cars works so well for you."

"Yes." Wynter laughed. They won. Rosie and she won. She grinned while they took their victory gallop. When she glanced up in the stands as she passed, the Southards and the Butlers sat motionless. The older Payton glared. Resisting the impulse to stick her tongue out at him, or worse, she smiled.

Her gaze searched the back row where Wythe and Mama were seated near Nelson and Miss Olivia. Nelson talked with Wythe. Irene waved at Wynter, and she waved back. Miss Olivia hurried down the steps to meet her at the exit. After Wynter left the ring, she pulled Rosie up and jumped to the ground. The groom caught the mare's reins, loosened her girth, then threw the cooler over her and led her away.

"What a brilliant jump-off!" Olivia Rutledge said. "Now I'm seeing what I expected out of Rosie. You two make a wonderful team, though I don't mind saying you scared us to death in that first round."

"Thank you, Miss Olivia. Rosie is a talented horse, and I'm so glad you gave me this opportunity. I'll never forget it." Wynter hugged her.

"Oh, you're not done. I don't expect this to be a one-time thing." She handed Wynter a check that made her eyes widen. "We're through this season, but I want you thinking big, Wynter. This mare can take both you and her to a whole new level. Talk to Thomas because it's *you* I want on her next season." She grabbed Wynter by the elbow and pulled her along with her back through the stands. Several people stopped them along the way to compliment Rosie and their performance. A girl, no more than ten, stepped in front of Wynter.

"Can I have your autograph?"

Wynter stared and laughed. "You want *my* autograph?"

"Sure. If you beat Chris Stevenson, then you must be *really* good!" Wynter blushed when she handed her a pen and her show program. It was then she noticed the girl wore a brace on her leg. Wynter paused.

"What's your name?"

"Allison," she answered with a smile. Wynter's breath caught in her throat.

"Do you ride?" she asked the girl who nodded. So Wynter wrote, *To Allison—Let's ride together—Wynter.*

She looked at the program. "Wow! Thanks."

"Where do you ride?" Wynter asked, and Allison gave the name of the therapeutic riding center that was one of the beneficiaries of the show. "I'll see you there one day, okay?"

The girl limped back to the row of people she sat with, showing them the program. When Wynter looked at some of the other kids, it struck her how much she took for granted good health and a strong body. Her eyes searched for Nelson a few rows up. He watched with a curious intensity.

"I invited your mother and Wythe to spend the night," Nelson told her when she reached them. "But Irene says no. See what you can do."

"Mama?"

She saw her mother's glance shift several rows down to where the Butlers were seated. "I have to work tomorrow. Today is free because there's a party tomorrow evening. Tory's birthday."

Wynter frowned. She couldn't help it.

"Your life might have changed in many ways, Wynter," her mother reproached, "but mine hasn't. It's my job."

"Wythe?" Wynter appealed to him. Maybe if there was something between the two of them, he could do something.

He shook his head. "She's as stubborn as you." Then he added with a teasing grin, "Just quieter about it."

Nelson laughed, causing several heads to turn in surprise. Wynter looked down a moment and sighed. "All right. But can I still come up next weekend?"

It was Irene's turn to look at her oddly. "Of course, Wynter. You're always welcome home."

She kissed her mother and then got a big bear hug from Wythe. "Put me down, Wythe!" she protested, which made him lift her even higher off the ground while he laughed. She glanced back over her shoulder and caught Nelson staring at them, nostrils flared and lips tight. "Wythe! Put me down."

He tilted his head at her tone then set her back on her feet. "See you next weekend, princess."

She watched them go—Wythe so big he was almost overpowering, and her quiet, too serious mother. Why had it taken so long to see how well they fit together?

She sat in the seat at Nelson's side and unbuttoned the forest green show coat she wore.

"There's a grand prix and a puissance coming up. Do you want to stay or go home?" Nelson asked.

He didn't look as tired tonight. Although Wynter should study, she still had Sunday, and she did want to see a puissance.

"I'd like to stay, if you don't mind."

"Do you want to change?" he asked, looking at her dusty riding clothes. "I can run you down to the barns, and we'll grab a hot dog on the way back.

She laughed at him. "You eat hot dogs? Somehow I can't picture that."

Nelson glared. "Not only do I eat them, I like them all the way—you know, chili, slaw, onions, mustard."

"Now you're talking!"

They walked side by side out to the golf cart, Nelson's left hand rested on the small of her back. His limp was more pronounced, so she slowed to stay even with him.

It was a half hour later before they sat back down. Wynter handed Nelson his coffee, then sipped on her tea. Miss Olivia had taken Thomas out on the town in celebration. So it was just Nelson and her.

The Grand Prix was first. The fences and spreads made what she jumped look small in comparison. Chris Stevenson, she saw from the program, rode in this and the puissance—on his regular jumper, of course. While he walked the course with the other riders, he glanced up in the stands, saw Wynter and grinned. She waved and grinned back, giving him a thumbs-up before slurping the last of the tea. Since it would still be a few minutes before the Grand Prix started, she put a hand on Nelson's arm to get his attention.

"I'll be right back. There's something I need to do."

She wanted to find out more about the therapeutic riding program. The woman seemed surprised when Wynter came over and introduced herself. She smiled again at Allison who was sitting right next to her.

"I'd like to stop by," Wynter told her. "Do you still ride in cold weather?"

The program's director smiled. "Thanks to a very generous donor last year, we now have a heated indoor arena, so yes, we do."

"I have to finish this semester, but I'm off for a month around the holidays. Would it be okay if I came out to help some?"

The woman looked stunned at Wynter's offer. Allison spoke up. "Oh, yeah! That would be great. I can show you Sparky. He's the pony I ride most of the time," she added by way of explanation.

The woman handed Wynter a card with directions scribbled on the back just as the announcer called the class. Wynter excused herself and started back to where Nelson sat. A couple of men she didn't know were deep in conversation with him but stood at her approach.

"We'll talk Monday," Nelson ended the conversation when she sat. The two men nodded, smiled briefly and left.

"Who were they?"

"Just some business associates. Stevenson's on course," Nelson prompted, drawing her attention away from the two men and back to the ring. They seemed familiar, but she couldn't place them. With a shake of her head, she looked back at the arena.

Chris was having problems with the horse tonight. The stallion seemed distracted and unwilling to focus on what he was doing. After the fourth jump with a dropped rail, Chris pulled up and excused himself.

"Too bad," Nelson said. "That's a nice stallion, although he's getting some age on him now. I think that's why Stevenson's bringing along several other younger prospects."

A rider from the DC area won the Grand Prix. Nelson seemed to know the woman, but Wynter wasn't familiar with her name. The puissance was up next. The announcer let everyone know Chris had scratched the stallion but would still be competing on a mare he'd brought with him.

Wynter's excitement built while she watched the competition. With each round, another layer of bricks was added. It was already at the point where neither horse nor rider could see over it. What a test of strength and trust, she thought, asking a horse and rider to jump something when they couldn't see where they would be landing.

Wynter clutched Nelson's sleeve as they watched. He smiled at her excitement, and covered her hand, squeezing slightly. Again, the woman from northern Virginia won, but her highest jump at six and a half feet was well short of the record. Wynter tugged on his sleeve, but before she could speak, he warned, "Oh no, you don't. You are not taking any of our horses in a puissance!"

She smirked. "Whatever you say, boss."

"Wynter!" he ground out. "I'm serious."

She took one look at his face and relented. "Okay, okay." He looked tired. "Are you ready to leave? If we hurry we can beat the crowd."

She helped him as much as he would allow when they left the building. It was hard sometimes to know when to offer help and when to stay out of it. Nelson was a proud man—and a stubborn one.

While they drove home, he turned on the radio to the University of North Carolina's classical music station. Wynter closed her eyes and let her head fall back against the seat. It was a far cry from the salsa that often blasted around the barn. The soft seats, the soothing music and a bad night's sleep caught up with her and she drifted off.

"Wynter?" the quiet voice startled her. She opened her eyes to see Nelson studying her. "I was beginning to worry," he murmured. "I've called your name twice already."

She stretched in the seat and smiled. "I'm sorry. I must have fallen asleep."

He brushed away a stray strand of hair. "You've had a long day."

Wynter looked around. They were in front of the house, not the barn, but she was too tired to argue about it. Nelson probably needed some help anyway. She straightened and rubbed her eyes before unbuckling the seatbelt. "Not just me. Stay there. I'll come around to help you out."

Nelson had already swung his legs out of the driver's side door. With his right hand on the cane and the door, and the left hand grasped in Wynter's, he stood.

"Thanks." His tone seemed flustered. "You make this a whole lot easier."

They entered the house much the same way as the night before, but before Wynter could press the button to the second floor, Nelson stopped her. "Down," he murmured. "I need to get in the hot tub."

The smell of pool chemicals was the first thing that struck her when the door opened. She'd never even seen an indoor pool. The lights were dim, coming from the pool itself and the hot tub, which stood next to windows along the back that looked out on another pool in the backyard.

"Wynter?" Nelson's tone was hesitant. She spun to look at him. In the dim light, it was hard to tell, but he seemed unsure of himself.

"What?"

He mumbled something and she asked him to repeat it. He cleared his throat. "Would you help me undress?"

Her eyes flew to his, wide with surprise, and she swallowed. "I—I've never. I mean…"

"It's okay," he said stiffly. "I'll manage. You're tired. Just go on to bed."

"No," she said, trying to sound more confident. "I can handle this."

"You don't have to make it sound like Chinese water torture," he remarked.

"That's not it at all," Wynter protested. She looked him up and down. "Do you want to do it closer to the hot tub?" She closed her eyes in chagrin. That sounded so not the way she'd meant it.

Nelson chuckled. "I'd like to do it anywhere with you."

She gasped and stepped back.

He put his hand out. "I'm sorry, Wynter. That'll be fine."

She guided him around the edge of the pool to a bench next to the hot tub. Trying to keep her mind on what she was doing, she removed boots and socks, then helped him to stand. She steadied him while he pulled his sweater, then shirt over his head. When she looked at the expanse of bare chest, she swallowed hard again. For someone with physical limitations, he was in amazing shape. Her fingers touched the belt buckle, but he stopped her.

"I'll do that," he said brusquely. "Just steady me."

The quiet, humid atmosphere set her nerves jangling. Wynter kept her eyes fixed on some point over his shoulder when she heard the rustle of pants hitting the floor. He leaned on her while he stepped out of them.

"Hand me a towel," he commanded. Wynter reached behind him and grabbed one off the table, careful to keep her gaze above the waist but below eye level. "You might want to undress."

Now she met his eyes. "Huh?"

He smiled ruefully. "I'm too stiff to get in on my own. I need your help."

Heat stirred between her thighs and her breasts ached. This was becoming worse by the minute. He was almost naked, and it appeared she might have to be too. And he wanted her to get in the water. With him.

"H-how deep is it?" she asked, eyeing the bubbling water.

"Just two to three feet."

"Okay." Wynter stepped behind him and turned her back, stripping off her clothes before wrapping one of the big white towels around her and tucking it in. It covered her torso, but not much else. Her shoulders ached from the combination of Rosie and Nelson, but she would never let him know. She stepped back in front of him.

"Get in," he instructed. "Just guide my right leg and I'll worry about the rest of me."

When she stepped over the edge of the hot tub and put her legs in, she gasped in surprise. It was warm, and the water bubbling against her legs soothed her sore muscles. Darting a glance at Nelson, she smiled. His blue gaze was unreadable in the dim light. After sitting on the edge, he pivoted, catching hold of the right leg to lift it over the edge. When he was ready, she did as he'd asked, guiding his right leg out as he levered into the water with his strong arms and left leg.

He had barely settled when she heard the sound of a wet towel being slung over the edge of the tub. Her eyes widened. He had nothing on.

Laura Browning

Nearly-naked nothing. In the buff was more like it. The bubbles in the hot tub made it impossible to see anything, but Wynter's heart still beat faster. She started to climb out, but Nelson's hand on her wrist stopped her.

"Stay," he whispered. "Sit next to me. The water will help soothe your muscles. You must be sore after the ride that mare gave you."

Wynter nodded and sat, back straight while she acclimated to the water.

"Relax," Nelson ordered, "and slide down some so you can soak your shoulders. If you're worried about getting your hair wet, grab a towel and wrap it."

She shook her head and let herself slide down until her neck and head were all that protruded from the water.

"I'll take your towel," Nelson offered.

"No," she gasped. "That's okay. I'll keep it on."

Nelson chuckled and slid down, leaning back and closing his eyes on a loud sigh. She regarded him with a wary gaze a moment before enjoying the feel of the water as it bubbled against her legs and arms. It was like sitting in a glass of soda water the way it fizzed. She twisted the towel a bit, trying to let some of the water jets soothe her back then undid it and tossed it onto the pool deck. Nelson chuckled again when he heard it hit.

"Now, isn't that better?" His voice was a deep whisper of sound that echoed around the dim pool room.

"Yes," she agreed.

She wasn't sure how much later it was she felt Nelson's hand trail along her cheek. She opened her eyes, startled to find the water still, and nothing underneath it left to the imagination.

"Oh!" She sat up and turned her back, crossing her arms over her breasts.

Chapter 12

"We need to get out." Nelson said gently, trying not to frighten her. "Fifteen minutes is it. If I promise not to look, will you find us some dry towels? There are terry cloth robes in the closet behind you."

Wynter scrambled out and wrapped a towel around herself before handing him one.

"Thanks. Get the robes," he prompted. "I've loosened up enough I can manage."

He took a deep breath when he heard her pad away on bare feet. He'd forgotten the automatic timer. When the jets stopped, he'd devoured the sight of her slender, creamy-skinned body. His cock had stiffened until he now sat with an erection so hard it slapped straight up against his stomach.

He levered himself out of the tub, and seeing she was still rummaging for the robes and additional towels, he limped over to the bench and dragged a damp towel across his lap, wadding it to hide his hard-on. She'd spent enough time around horse people, he doubted she was still a virgin, but sometimes she acted so innocently he couldn't be sure.

Better not shock her. When she returned, he sat with the towel draped across his hips. She had already wrapped herself in one of the robes. Her face was still flushed from the heat of the tub, and her emerald eyes glowed. When she handed him the robe, he thought she looked like a kitten ready to curl up and go to sleep.

He shrugged into the robe and asked, "Are you hungry?"

"A little," she admitted.

Thank God. He knew it was crazy, but he wanted to prolong their evening. It was one of the reasons he'd stayed at the horse show, because he'd figured that was the only way to keep her with him.

He belted the robe, arranging it to disguise his still throbbing cock.

"Let's go upstairs. Mrs. Caudle often leaves me something in the fridge in my study. We can eat in the sitting room and turn on the gas logs. Your hair's damp."

He was prepared for her refusal. Instead, she smiled at him. "You have no idea how wonderful that sounds."

A short while later, she curled up on the couch, her hands wrapped around a mug of cocoa. Nelson sat at the other end, right leg stretched out along the length of the sofa. A wineglass dangled from his fingers while he watched her through narrowed eyes.

She seemed unaware of how gorgeous she was. It was that unselfconscious side of her that made him believe she was still inexperienced when it came to men. He knew it should stop him, but he couldn't banish visions of her. He wanted her with him. He wanted to slide himself into her.

God, what was he thinking? He hadn't made love to a woman since the accident. But he wanted her, and he knew he was capable. He'd at least tested that out like any self-respecting male. But there was a big difference between using a hand and making love.

Nelson swallowed a sip of wine. On the coffee table in front of the couch were the remains of a tray of cheese and fruit. When he looked at Wynter again, she stared at the flames from the gas logs, smiling.

"You look like a contented cat," he murmured, "curled up, ready to fall asleep in front of the fire."

She tilted her head and grinned at him. "This is nice, Nelson. These past few days have seemed like a dream. I keep wondering if I'll wake up in the morning to find it's disappeared."

She'd given him an opening, and he grasped hold of it.

"It can be like this as long as you like," he remarked, trying to keep his tone casual.

She glanced at him questioningly.

"I'd like you to stay here, in the house," he clarified.

She narrowed her eyes. "And what strings are attached?"

"None." He wouldn't force her into anything. He wasn't going to buy any woman. But this was shaky ground. Poor as her background was, he feared anything he gave her might smack of him trying to bribe her. As he watched her, it was obvious her thoughts were already headed that way.

"The room I slept in last night. The closet that happened to be stocked with clothing, in my size. You planned this," Wynter stated. "You set me up."

She straightened, her expression showing both outrage and hurt.

"Wait," Nelson commanded. "Hear me out, please." She looked at him suspiciously. "There are no strings, Wynter," he said as he ran fingers through his hair. "I've seen how hard you've worked over the past few months. How you struggle to get your work and your studying done. Your mother's right. You are too thin. You don't take enough time for yourself.

"I can help. I've been blessed with more material goods than I can ever use. I live by myself in a huge home. Stay here, Wynter. Let yourself be taken care of for a change instead of always struggling to make ends meet. Let me do that while you bring some laughter to my life."

She stared at him. There was so much longing in her expression, yet the distrust was more than evident. And damn them, he knew from where that came. The Southard family—father and son—had done a real head job on her.

"There are no strings," he repeated coaxingly. "Only those you create."

* * * *

She set her mug down. It was a way to delay, a way to give herself a moment. He'd revealed more to her with words and expression than he'd probably intended. Oh, there were strings, emotional ones so powerful she was afraid to even name them. She had felt it almost from the first moment she had seen him standing on the porch outside the barn office.

At some point, she must step out of her comfort zone. She was more than willing to take risks when she rode Rosie, so why not here, why not now with Nelson? Her stomach fluttered.

What did she know about him? What did he know about her? She thought of his kindness, the way he'd faced off with Payton Southard. The way he'd kissed her. Wynter looked back at him, staring into his midnight-blue eyes.

"I'll stay."

And then he did something she seldom saw him do. A gentle, beautiful smile curved his mouth, and tears welled in her eyes.

"Let me unbraid your hair," he murmured. She slid closer on the couch and turned her back. His fingers were swift and gentle when he undid her long braid, fluffed her still damp hair and eased his fingers through the length of it, stroking without saying a word.

She sensed the way the repetitive movements helped him unwind and realized they did the same for her. She relaxed, staying that way even when he pulled her back against him. His breath was warm on her ear as he rubbed his cheek against her head.

"You have the most beautiful hair I've ever seen," he rumbled. "It burns with such a deep, rich fire, yet it feels cool like silk. I touch it and think about my hands on you—how you will feel that same way—sleek, cool and on fire at the same time."

Wynter's breath caught in her throat as his hand brushed against her breast when he caressed a lock of hair curled over her shoulder. She turned her head and found his mouth very near her own.

"Nelson?" Her voice was a whisper. Need filled her from her breasts up to her cheeks. He tilted her chin up and kissed her. Wynter twisted and slid her hand up around his neck. This time there was no tentativeness as his tongue tangled with hers. The kiss was a drug that sapped the strength from her limbs and set pulses throbbing in other areas.

She leaned against him, sucking on his lower lip. His hand slid under the edge of the robe and caressed her aching breasts. Her breathing was ragged and uneven. She had never been touched like this before, and it made her feel so heavy and slow she couldn't think straight. Control slipped from her grasp, and panic made her tremble.

"It's okay," Nelson soothed, as if he sensed her fear. "I won't do anything you don't want."

"That's just it," she admitted. "I don't know what I want."

She felt him hesitate. Just an instant, a momentary stillness of his hand while it caressed her.

"What do you mean?"

He lifted his head and she saw the sudden wariness there. Wynter shook her head. Now was not the time to mention her complete lack of actual experience.

"Nothing. It's all right."

She pressed her mouth against his and slipped her fingers inside the robe to touch the muscles of his chest. He felt as tight and firm as he looked. He groaned when her fingers brushed a small, masculine nipple.

His long, elegant fingers slid to the belt of her robe, loosening the tie so the terry cloth parted and fell away. His hand shook when he brushed it along the length of her torso, from breast to hip. Wynter felt him tremble and realized it only increased her own need.

"God in heaven, Wynter, you're so beautiful." His voice shook with repressed passion. "I told you no ties, and I mean that. I won't take this any further if you tell me you don't want it. We'll stop now if that's what you want."

"I want you." She leaned forward and nibbled at his full lower lip. Deciding she should be more aggressive, she let her hand slide over the muscled planes of abdomen until her fingers circled the silky skin of his erection.

He groaned deep in his throat. While her hand moved in a slow motion, he closed his eyes and let his head fall back. Wynter's gaze flicked between what her hand was doing to him and the expression on his face. It was so powerful to see how much she affected him.

"I want to feel you against me," he murmured a few minutes later.

Wynter stood and let the robe fall around her ankles. Nelson watched her with eyes dark with passion. That look alone was enough. She didn't care if he assumed she possessed experience she didn't have. She saw need and knew it echoed her own. Whatever they did together would be beautiful because it was him.

Nelson reached out, running one hand behind her to cup her bottom while the other hand slid upward between her thighs. At the intimate touch, she nearly collapsed against him. Her legs shook. He turned, still seated on the couch, one leg on either side of hers. Wynter's eyes drifted downward. His cock glistened, swollen and ready. Imagining what he would do with it increased her nervousness.

"Wynter?" he inquired. "Is anything wrong?"

She shook her head and then leaned forward to put a knee on either side of him so she straddled his lap. They would do this, together.

"You'll have to be on top," he murmured. She heard the tightness in his voice. This man so used to control now yielded it. She nodded, afraid to say anything as he guided himself between her thighs. He pressed upward and into her, and she knew the moment he realized what he encountered. His eyes widened.

"Wynter?"

He frowned, but before he could do more, she grasped his shoulders with her hands and forced her hips downward. She gasped from the momentary sting and the feeling of fullness inside her. He felt even bigger than he looked. Her hands clenched against his shoulders, and her head tipped forward.

"Lord, Wynter!" he ground out. "Be still. You should have told me you'd never been with a man. Easy, darling."

He caressed her with hands and lips until she relaxed.

"Let me guide you."

With hands still on her hips, he eased her along his thick shaft, in and out, gaze never leaving hers. After her body adjusted to the feel of him inside her, heat built until she felt almost faint.

"Nelson?" Wave after wave of heat rolled over her, taking her breath away and tightening her muscles.

"It's all right, baby. Go with it. Come for me."

A startled whimper left her and then she threw her head back with a long moan, barely aware of Nelson lifting her clear of him when he groaned and released in powerful spurts against them both.

She collapsed against him shakily. His hands stroked her hair and back, and he buried his face against the side of her head.

"Oh, Wynter," his voice broke as he held her. "What a beautiful gift."

* * * *

Nelson stroked her silky hair while she nestled against him until her breathing changed rhythm and she dozed. One hand rested against his chest trustingly. He swallowed at the sudden emotion that spiraled up from his gut and lodged in his throat. Christ, he was near to bawling. Not the epitome of manliness.

But what an incredible gift. Her first. That had never happened, even with Lindy. Nelson had suspected from Wynter's kisses she hadn't had much experience with men, but it never occurred to him he might be her first.

Casual relationships, heterosexual and otherwise, were not unusual on the horse show circuits. He'd lived around that world long enough to become cynical when it came to sex.

Yet Wynter had avoided that somehow. She'd had little experience, just a natural sexiness and comfort with herself that had made their lovemaking an easy, enjoyable experience. A gift. Nelson stroked her cheek with the backs of his fingers. She had given him the gift of herself.

He swallowed again. How could he have ever envisioned using her for revenge against the Southards? Not now. Never. Yet she had become another reason to seek revenge as far as he was concerned. Both the older and younger Southards had done their best to destroy her life, like they'd destroyed Lindy's and Allison's lives.

He would stop it.

He had already been providing protection for Wynter, even if she didn't know it. Bodyguards were a way of life for him. Nelson paid them to be as unobtrusive as possible but there nonetheless.

He'd also paid them well to keep their mouths shut. He never asked what they saw or heard. He'd never intruded on Lindy's privacy, although perhaps he should have, and he did not ask any questions of Wynter. He had added the guards after she'd started classes at Duke, in part because of what she'd revealed about Payton Southard the Third.

Chapter 13

Irene glanced at Wythe while they drove home from Raleigh. It was almost impossible to read his expression in the dim light from the dash, but he'd been quiet ever since they'd left.

"Wythe," she said, breaking the silence. "Is something wrong?"

He hesitated a moment before he admitted, "I'm concerned about Wynter."

"Why?" Irene asked, feeling a surge of alarm. "Everyone seemed so nice."

"Do you know who Nelson Anderson is?"

Irene shook her head. Although the name sounded familiar, she wasn't able to place it.

"Anderson Electronics?" Wythe prompted again.

She gasped. "Isn't that the man whose family died in the wreck Pay Southard caused?"

"One and the same," Wythe responded.

"So why should that be a concern? He seems like a very nice man."

Wythe sighed. "I'm afraid Wynter might be in way over her head. Anderson is not a simple man, Irene. He is to computer hardware what Bill Gates is to software. I sat in on the last phase of Pay's trial. Anderson won't be content to let him off easy like the courts did. I already have some suspicions he's set wheels in motion to that effect." His tone hardened. "But it will be a cold day in hell before I tell Payton Southard."

Now Irene was worried. She remembered the news articles about the accident last fall. She also knew a lot of what had happened never made the papers. It was amazing in this day and age how money and influence still kept plenty of things hush-hush.

It had been late on a Friday night. Pay had attended a football game where he'd spent the whole game in the stands drinking from a flask of whisky he'd smuggled in with him. Then he had gotten behind the wheel of the big Range Rover his parents had given him when he'd turned sixteen. He'd driven home the wrong way down a four lane highway. He'd swerved out of the path of one car into Nelson Anderson's, clipping it and sending it out of control down an embankment. It had flipped over and wedged against a stand of trees.

Irene closed her eyes.

He had watched his own child bleed to death.

She knew how deep her hatred would go if she stood in his shoes. But she was still confused by Wythe's concern. "Why should hatred of the Southards affect how he looks at Wynter?"

Wythe sighed. "I'm worried he might somehow involve her in his efforts to get revenge."

"But Wythe," Irene pointed out, "you don't know for sure he's even bent on revenge."

"Let's keep our eyes open, okay? That's all I'm asking." He reached across the seat of the jeep and squeezed her hand. The contact caught her by surprise, especially when he continued to hold her hand.

When they stopped in the driveway, he faced her. "So do you feel better having seen your daughter?" His tone was light and playful.

"Yes. Thank you for taking me, Wythe. It was kind of you."

He ran a hand through his hair and smiled teasingly. "There was no kindness involved. I got you to myself for an entire day."

Irene laughed. "You are too funny, Wythe Bradshear." She opened the door and jumped out of the jeep. "I should go. It's going to be a long day tomorrow at the Butlers. Will you be there?"

"No. I'm not high on their list since I beat their daughter's boyfriend with a hunt whip."

She waved after she unlocked the door, and he flashed the lights at her before starting the jeep's engine. As she watched him back out of the drive, she had the feeling he hadn't been honest regarding what bothered him when it came to Wynter and Nelson Anderson.

After Irene stretched out in bed, she kept thinking of Wythe and the way he'd held her hand. And what was with the comment about him getting her to himself all day? At last telling herself she imagined things she wished were real, she rolled over and went to sleep.

Chapter 14

Wynter rolled onto her side the following morning and studied Nelson's sleeping form. He seemed more relaxed, his face softer. Over his shoulder, she glanced at the picture on the night table. It was different. Now there was just a picture of Allison, laughing at the camera while she hugged a doll against her cheek. Wynter's eyes wandered back to Nelson.

He had been so tender after that first time on the couch, stroking her face and her back until their breathing had eased. Then he'd wrapped her in the robe she wore and held her close the whole way upstairs in the elevator. They'd showered together, his hands gentle while he washed away the evidence of her first time with a man. When she'd tried to caress him, he'd held her wrist.

"No, not now. Give yourself a chance to recover, just sleep with me."

But they'd both awakened again during the night. He'd pulled her on top of him, spreading her legs and slipping his silky shaft inside her. They had come together languorously. His hands had bracketed her hips in place while he'd pumped in and out of her.

The room was lit with a dim nightlight, so it had been impossible to see his expression, but Wynter had heard his ragged breathing and known what they'd done together had affected him as it had her. Once again, he had withdrawn from her at the point of climax, spilling his seed over his belly.

She looked at that flat stomach now with its sprinkling of dark hair. The covers twisted so his right leg stuck out from under them. In the light of day, Wynter saw the scar that started at the ankle and extended the entire length of his leg. Portions of it seemed newer than other areas. Older scars crossed his abdomen and circled his hip. She traced her finger along the one on the leg.

He woke up and smiled at her. Wynter smiled back.

"I have to go to campus," she murmured.

He ran fingers through his bed head and blinked. "Duke?"

She nodded. "I have a paper to type, so I need to use the computers at the library."

"I have computers here." Nelson frowned in confusion. "Just use the PC in my study."

She shrugged. "All right. It saves me a trip."

"Does that mean we have time for…"

"Nelson!" She laughed at him, but her laughter soon stopped when he stroked between her thighs.

"Do you know how much I love being inside you?" he whispered. "You feel so hot and wet on my fingers."

While she watched, he brought them to his mouth and licked the wetness glistening on them. Wynter's sex throbbed, and she melted against him, a now-familiar weakness stealing over her whole body.

In the end, it was afternoon before she started on her paper. Nelson showed her what she needed to know to operate the desktop in the office before announcing he was going swimming. Wynter smiled at him, her mind already formulating her ideas for a loose outline, shaping them into the beginning of her paper. Writing was not her favorite activity. She much preferred manipulating facts and figures. She even enjoyed theorizing in economics, but for once she admitted this particular political science class grabbed her attention. She never noticed the time passing until she hit a snag. She was missing some information that would have been easy enough to find at the library, but she wasn't there.

"Nelson?" she called, having heard the elevator hum several minutes earlier.

"I'm in the kitchen," he said, his voice drifting down the hall.

She saved what she was working on and padded in her sock feet into the kitchen. Nelson was munching on a piece of chocolate cake he'd found in the fridge. His thick hair fell across his brow when he glanced up.

"What did you need?" he asked before taking another bite.

"Your help," she muttered with embarrassment. "I'm not very computer literate. We never owned one, and I didn't get much of a chance to use the ones at school. Can you show me how to look for things on the Internet? I need some information for my paper, and I don't have it here."

Nelson finished the milk. "Sure."

He moved more easily after swimming. Wynter followed him down the hallway and listened while he showed her how to use a search engine and locate the information she needed on the Internet. Wynter grabbed his hand and kissed the palm.

"Thank you," she whispered. His eyes darkened and then he smiled when he pulled his hand away from her.

"I wouldn't do that if you need to get this paper done. I would so like to take you back to the couch in that sitting room for a repeat of last night." He waggled his brows.

Wynter laughed. "Maybe in a few minutes. Just let me get these ideas in my paper and reference them, and I'll take you up on that."

Nelson smiled. "I'll be waiting—very impatiently."

She laughed and waved him away. She copied the information he'd helped her locate, along with the source, and then reopened the Word program. When she searched the list of documents for hers, the name Southard jumped out at her. Wynter paused and stared at it a long time.

It read "Southard Plan." It would be so easy. Her finger hovered over the mouse. The pointer sat on "open" in the dialog box. One click, that's all it would take. One click to violate the trust of the man who'd opened his home and shared his body with her.

She took a deep breath and moved the mouse to double click on her paper. Forcing herself to concentrate, Wynter added the information, put in her footnote and saved the file to the flash drive Nelson had given her. That way, he'd explained, she could insert the drive at the library and reopen her paper if she wanted to work on it there.

She closed her notebook and packed her backpack. She felt pretty comfortable about her midterms, but decided she would go to campus early to get in some last minute review. Nelson and Thomas had made it plain she was not cleaning any more stalls. She would ride, that was it, but not in the coming week since they knew she had tests to get through.

Wynter found Nelson with his briefcase open, reviewing a thick sheaf of papers. He looked up when she entered, smiled and tucked the papers back inside. After closing and locking it, he set it on the table in front of the couch and leaned back, his gaze drifting over her. He pointed to the bottle of wine on the table.

"Would you like a glass?"

Wynter laughed. "And you were riding Miss Olivia about giving me one."

"Ah, but that's different," Nelson said. "Now I'm hoping to get you drunk, so I can take advantage of you." He poured a small glass and handed it to her.

She sipped it. Sweeter than she expected, it went down very smoothly. She swallowed the rest of it and held her glass out for more. Nelson arched one brow at her and laughed.

"Sip, Wynter. You're supposed to *sip* it."

She shrugged. "I didn't know. Besides, I was thirsty."

"Come here," he growled.

She curled up next to him on the couch, leaning her head against his shoulder. Her fingers twirled the end of her braid. Nelson's hand stroked her head and came to rest on her shoulder.

"Let your hair down," he whispered against her ear. "I want to touch it, touch you. Your hair is such a turn-on. Damn."

He pulled back, staring at her with hungry eyes.

Something wild burst forth in her. He did nothing to hide his naked, unadorned need, and it was intoxicating. Seeing it gave her a confidence and daring around him she never would have suspected she possessed.

Wynter stood, turned her back and undid the long braid, fluffing her hair out until it covered her back all the way to her bottom. Nelson had some soft jazz playing on the stereo, so she closed her eyes and allowed her body to sway with the beat. When she moved her hips, she heard him suck in breath and shift position on the couch.

"Christ, Wynter. You make me ache."

Slowly, with her back still to him, she unbuttoned her shirt and let it slip off her shoulders. Her front-snap bra followed and then her fingers dropped to the drawstring on the silky pajama style pants she wore. She untied the bow, and they slid down over her hips, hanging a moment before a soft sway to the music in the background sent them pooling at her feet. The only thing that remained was the lacy hip hugger briefs she wore. Raising her arms, she slid her hands under the curtain of her hair, lifting it enough to give Nelson a good view of her derriere. She let her hair drift down again before hooking her thumbs in the band of her briefs and turning around. She licked her lips when she stared at his heavy, sensual expression, his lids half-closed and his lips parted. Wynter slipped the briefs lower, stopping at the swell of her pubic bone while she continued swaying to the music.

Nelson's breathing was heavy, his gaze following her movements as if hypnotized. He made no attempt to disguise the way his erection tented his slacks while he watched her. When their eyes met, he cupped himself with one hand to shift his cock.

Heat pooled between her legs and she smiled. Wynter slid her hands back up her body and down over the swell of her breasts, her fingers brushing over her taut nipples. She tossed her hair back and heard Nelson groan. His hands grasped her hips and pulled her toward him. Cool, controlled Nelson buried his face against her stomach, breath hot against her skin. His hands moved to her briefs and tugged them over her thighs before they dropped on their own at her feet.

She ran her fingers through his thick hair, stroking it back away from his forehead. His hands cupped her butt, bringing her sex hard against his lips. She gasped when he caressed her. His tongue probed the moist lips of her core. When he found the bud of her clitoris, Wynter felt as though the sun exploded around her with heat and light.

Her legs shook and when they started to give way, he leaned back, pulling her across his lap. With unsteady fingers, he reached for his belt, but Wynter brushed his hands aside. She wasted no time opening his clothing and helping him strip. She was desperate to touch him. Her hand circled his shaft, caressing its silken length.

He growled and slipped his fingers along the slick folds of her sex. "Do you have any idea how wonderful you smell, how sweet you taste?" Eyes heavy-lidded with passion locked with hers. "I can't wait much longer, Wynter. Your teasing, your touch, have me so close to coming right now, right in your hand."

She whimpered. The picture he created made her even wetter for him. Soon, soon he would lift her up, so she could slide down onto him, taking his length deep inside her. To her surprise, he rolled her underneath him and stretched out on top of her.

"Nelson?" she questioned.

He groaned against her lips. "I want to try it like this. I have to try." He shuddered. "I want to bury myself in you Wynter, so deep, as deep as I can get."

Putting the brunt of his weight on his good left leg, he parted her thighs and thrust inside her strongly. They moved together in unison, bodies colliding and parting and colliding again. As he shook with a powerful orgasm, he pulled free and fell back against the couch, pulling her with him while he touched and caressed her. His clever fingers worked on her and in her, until she whimpered and shook. When her own climax crashed through her, she swore he came again, hot and warm between them.

* * * *

She started to go to her own room that night, knowing Mrs. Caudle would arrive early the next morning, but Nelson halted her with a hand on her wrist.

"Sleep with me, Wynter." It was a request, but she saw an odd vulnerability in his expression when he made it.

She nodded and they walked to the bedroom, arms around each other's waists. Nelson held her close, hands tangled in her long hair, which lay in silky, curling strands across his belly. Their legs tangled together, and she slid her arms up over his shoulders. Her lids felt heavy. While she drifted in that gray area between sleep and wakefulness, she thought she heard him whisper, "Wynter, my spring, my love."

She woke to the sound of the kitchen door shutting. When it dawned on her that meant only one thing, her eyes snapped open and she sat up, one eye on the clock. Seven. Wynter scrambled off the end of the bed and snatched up her clothes. *Oh God*, she thought, *please don't let Mrs. Caudle come upstairs to wake anybody up.*

"What are you doing?" Nelson sounded groggy and seemed half-asleep. "Come back to bed, Wynter. Come for me again."

He looked so little-boy innocent, but Wynter was more concerned at the moment with someone catching her naked in his room.

"No," she objected. "Mrs. Caudle's here!"

"Shall I call and ask her to bring us some coffee?"

"Nelson!" When he started to pick up the phone, she slammed her hand on top. "This isn't funny!" Her lower lip trembled. "Stop it!"

The laughter drained from his face. "Wynter?" he pressed. "Are you ashamed of what we did?"

"No! I just don't want her to think badly of me!" She held her clothes in front of her like a shield.

"I don't think that." He frowned. "Why would she?"

"Because that's what happens to people from *my* world," she retorted. Before Nelson could say anything else, Wynter fled down the hall, staying close to the wall while she crossed the open landing between his end of the house and the one where her room was situated.

She felt like an idiot. No doubt the other women who'd been in his life would have handled everything with poise and unflappable cool, not gone into full panic mode. But she wasn't from his world, and she didn't know a fucking thing about men.

An hour later, she stood out front beside her truck, swearing like a sailor. She kicked the tire on the driver's side in frustration and tears of pain sprang to her eyes. *Great! Just freaking great. As if this morning could get any worse.*

Just then, the door opened and Nelson came out. She had never seen him in a suit and tie before. His hair was brushed away from his face, and he looked remote and forbidding. This wasn't *her* Nelson, the man who'd spent the past two nights bringing her to multiple orgasms. This was someone she didn't know, and if she was honest, someone she also found more than a little intimidating.

"Is there a problem?" he asked stiffly, his gaze taking in her panicked expression.

"My truck won't start!" she wailed. "I have an exam in two hours, and I need to review the material again!"

He eyed her beat-up truck with distaste. "Grab your things and get in the car. I'm headed that way, anyway."

She sagged with relief. "Thank you, Nelson!"

He smiled briefly. "At least we aren't back to Mr. Anderson."

He didn't speak while they drove to Durham. She got the feeling a lot of other things occupied his mind. She told him where to drop her. Several heads turned when he pulled the Rolls up to the curb. As Wynter started to hop out, he stopped her with a touch. "I'll pick you up here at four. Good luck, Wynter."

"Thanks, Nelson." She flashed him a small smile and shut the door of the Rolls. It purred when he put it in gear and accelerated back into traffic.

Behind her, she heard one of her accounting classmates whistle. She looked at him. She'd seen him in class several times watching her. He was what a lot of the kids in her high school would have called a computer freak. Very smart. Very strange.

"You keep mighty interesting company."

"Nelson?" she asked.

"Nelson? You call the head of Anderson Electronics 'Nelson?'"

"Yesss," she said, drawing the word out.

"Holy shit!" he exclaimed. "The guy is like the Bill Gates of computer hardware, didn't you know?"

She stared at him, but her knees felt shaky, and her hands felt cold and clammy. Even computer idiot that she was, she knew the name Bill Gates.

"No," she said, "I didn't know."

The guy looked at her as though she had crawled out from under a rock. "Man," he said, "you are some strange chick."

His comments kept reverberating through her head. *He's like the Bill Gates of computer hardware.* After her last exam, she went to the library and sat at the computers. She had no idea how she'd done on her exams, but she knew one thing. She needed to find out who Nelson Anderson was. She disliked being caught off-guard.

As he'd shown her, she searched the Internet, but this time, *he* was the subject of her research. She had a lot to learn concerning the man she'd made love to for the past two days. She found articles in *Money*, *Forbes*, *The New York Times* and *The Washington Post*. She even located an article in *Cosmopolitan,* listing the world's sexiest CEOs. In that one, he ranked a whole lot higher than Bill Gates. As Wynter read, disquiet replaced curiosity. With it came the cynical voice that always reminded her where she came from.

What on earth could someone like Nelson Anderson want from her? Wynter O'Reilly, trailer trash nobody, whose only experience with a father was bearing his name?

She grabbed her backpack and trudged back to where Nelson was supposed to pick her up. She was early, so she sat beneath a nearby tree and lit a cigarette. Her hands shook. She was in way over her head. Maybe she shouldn't feel that way, but realizing how well-known he was scared her. She fought back the urge to cry. While the cigarette dangled from the fingers of one hand, she picked at the frayed threads around the hole in the knee of her jeans with her other. She'd put them on this morning because they were her favorite pair, worn to the point they were butter soft. Wynter dropped her hand to pick at blades of grass next to her feet and rested her chin on her knees.

She had tossed her second cigarette in a row when she heard a horn honk. She looked up to see the Rolls pull up to the curb. After throwing her backpack in the backseat, she slid in and shut the door. She didn't look at Nelson while she buckled her seatbelt. Before pulling back into traffic, Nelson pulled at her belt to make sure it was buckled.

"I'm not a child, Nelson. I can buckle my own seatbelt," she snapped with her face turned toward the passenger side window.

There was a long pause before she heard him ask, "How did your exams go?"

"I don't know."

"Were you able to get more work done on your paper?"

"No."

Another long silence. "Are we going to keep having conversations that consist of you making monosyllabic responses?"

"No. We could just *not* talk. That would be fine."

She gasped when Nelson jerked the car over to the side of the road, and she stared at him.

Midnight-blue eyes blazed back at her, and his generous mouth thinned. "What exactly is your problem, Wynter? Did you decide you had enough fun fucking this weekend, and now it's time to move on?"

The words shocked her. In the months she'd known Nelson, she'd seldom heard him swear and never like that. Oh, she'd heard the words—in fact, she'd used them a lot over the years, but she'd never heard him use them. Before she could say anything, he continued.

"Am I too old or too crippled for you to be seen with? Is that it?" Beneath the anger, she saw a faint touch of pain and uncertainty he couldn't quite mask.

"You're too rich," she whispered as she stared out the passenger window once again. God, she sounded like such an idiot, but she felt even worse. She had nothing to give a man like him. She was a poor kid who knew so little of life. She'd never even been in a hotel until the night of that exhibitors' party.

He exhaled in frustration. "My being rich is not something I can change," he stated as he put the car back in gear.

And that was at the heart of their problem. He lived in a mansion, and she was accustomed to a single-wide with a bedroom no bigger than the closet in the room she now occupied.

Chapter 15

The rest of the ride back to Pheasant Run was silent. Wynter turned alternatives over in her mind. She could return to the barn apartment. After all, she'd never really moved out. She might live with Miss Olivia, or she could stay where she was. When they reached the house, Wynter grabbed her book bag.

"Wynter." Nelson touched her arm. "We need to talk."

She closed her eyes for an instant and sighed. "We do. But not right now. I…I need some time to think. Can you understand that?"

His mouth tightened, but he nodded his head.

She raced up the stairs without another word. She found her sneakers in the closet. Mrs. Caudle had washed them, not that it had helped much. Digging through the things in the walk-in closet, she found a pair of leggings and a sweatshirt.

What she needed was a long run. It had helped her put some of her anger and disappointments in perspective when she was still living with Mama, so maybe it would help now. Something had to help, because her insecurities were eating a hole right through the middle of her chest.

It was close to sunset when she slipped out the front door. She noticed her truck was missing. Wynter couldn't think about that now. It had probably been towed somewhere. She rounded the side of the house and found the path Nelson had used. He'd told her there were trails through the woods, miles of them. That was just what she needed. She stretched and set off at an easy ground-covering pace. She had run cross-country for four years in high school, competing in the state meet until her senior year, when she had made the choice between running or earning money.

As her legs worked, she let her mind wander. She had to be practical, she kept telling herself. She needed her job riding. She needed to earn money for college. She had asked Nelson what strings were attached.

He'd said only the ones she tied. Why couldn't she accept what he had offered?

Because you don't deserve it, her inner voice taunted. She was the gawky stable girl, not the type of woman a man like Nelson Anderson wanted. No, *needed*, she corrected herself. She recalled the photograph of his wife. Lindy had been beautiful, like supermodel stunning.

Wynter laughed. She had nothing to offer him, and if she took all he'd offered, what did that make her? She didn't want to feel bought because if he bought her, discarding her would be just as easy. She wouldn't let herself be vulnerable and hurt the way her mother had been.

Why would he even want her? He was older, sophisticated and rich. He could have anyone he wanted. Why her?

A glance at her watch showed she had been out over an hour. It was dark, and she hadn't come up with any answers. After running onto Nelson's path again, she slowed down to give her breathing a chance to return to normal.

In the dark, the house looked huge from the back where it was three stories tall with wings that came off the main structure. There were a lot of lights on, inside and out. *Was it always that way?* Wynter walked along the edge of the woods until she reached the driveway. When she stepped onto the pavement and into the path of the floodlights, a crisp no-nonsense voice challenged her.

"Who are you, and what are you doing?"

"Huh?" She stopped in startled surprise.

One of the men she'd seen at the show in Raleigh Saturday night stepped out of the shadows. His hostile posture relaxed when he saw her, although he still frowned.

"You'd better come with me, Miss O'Reilly," he stated, grasping her elbow.

"Get your hands off me!" She yanked her arm out of his strong grasp and jumped back from him, hands fisted at her side. "Who the hell are you?"

"Security, miss," he said in a voice meant to calm her. "We've been looking for you."

"Why?" Then on a sudden note of worry, she continued, "Has something happened to Mr. Anderson?"

"He called us when he couldn't find you in the house. You'd better come in and talk with him."

When he started to escort her, she stopped and stared at him with hostility and exasperation. "I think I can find my own way in, thank you."

She wiped some of the sweat from her face with the hem of her sweatshirt. She had slipped at one point running because her sneakers weren't suited for it and didn't have enough tread. Dirt stained her knee and the palms of her hands, so she rubbed them on her leggings, trying to get the worst of it off before she went inside. Of course that made her look filthier.

As soon as she walked through the door, she saw Nelson. He balanced on his cane, talking to the other man she'd seen at the show. She heard him say, "Okay, then. You guys can leave. Thanks for the quick response."

"That's why you pay us, sir."

The man nodded his head when he passed her and let himself out the door. When Wynter looked at Nelson, she swallowed. His skin was pale and expression taut. The anger burning in his eyes was tinged with something else, but she couldn't place it. He looked her up and down coldly.

"Where the hell have you been, Wynter?"

Her glance slid away from the intense stare then back again. She had nothing to be ashamed of. "I told you I needed to think. I went for a run."

"And didn't tell anyone?" His tone made it sound as if it were the stupidest thing anyone could have done.

Her eyes narrowed. "I didn't realize a weekend of "fucking,' as you put it earlier, made me answerable to you for every move I make."

Nelson dismissed that with a wave of his hand. "It's common courtesy, Wynter. But more than that, a man in my position has to take some precautions. It's easy to become a target. Those two men have followed you since you started classes at Duke. When you just disappeared—"

"You've had me followed?" Wynter took a step back, feeling as though he'd hit her. "People have been *spying* on me?"

She was horrified and embarrassed. He didn't trust her. Wynter blinked back the furious tears that sprang to her eyes.

"Were you afraid I would steal the silver or something?" she murmured and then brushed past him and shook off his arm. "I think I have the answers I needed."

She ran up the stairs, ignoring him when he called her name. Wynter ran down the hall to the room Nelson had prepared for her and slammed the door. Frantically, she gathered up her book bag then searched the closet for her own clothes. She kicked off her sneakers and stripped off the clothes Nelson's money had bought, not wanting them touching her skin. Wynter wiped her eyes after she pulled her jeans back on, found a t-shirt and the sweater her mother had knit and then slid her bare feet back into her sneakers. No tears. She'd walked into this with her eyes wide-open. What remained, she would get later. She had just swung her book bag onto her shoulder when Nelson burst through the door.

"What are you doing?" he demanded, his breathing ragged.

"I'm leaving." She glared at him, angrier than she ever remembered being. When she started past him, he reached out an arm, but she knocked it away. "Don't touch me!" she spat at him between gritted teeth.

"Wynter! It's not what you think."

She spun on him. "You don't know what the hell I think! At least my price has gone up. Payton Southard offered me fifty bucks and expected me to fall right for it. I guess you figured you would up the ante. Well, it worked." Her lip trembled as she continued. "But even trailer trash has some pride, Mr. Anderson Electronics, and I won't be followed around by some goons waiting for me to step out of line. I can pay my own way. I don't need you. I don't want you or your money, and I wish I never, ever met you!" The last came out on a sob of pain and fury. "You're no different than the rest of them. Y'all think you can buy anything and anyone. Well, not me!" She shook her head while she backed away. "Not me."

Wynter turned on her heel and ran down the stairs, jumping the last few, almost falling on the polished black and white marble floor. She heard Nelson shout her name as she ran out the door, but she ignored him. She refused to look back. She had no truck. God knew where it was, but at that moment, Wynter didn't care. She secured her backpack and ran. She could hitchhike once she reached the highway.

She wanted to go home, but above everything, she was focused on school. She had enough money in her pocket to get her through the rest of the semester. She would rent a room somewhere near campus. If she was careful, she might make it the next month without needing a job. Then she'd go home. She'd go to school somewhere near Mama. Community college was better than nothing. She kept running, and sweat poured off her face and down her back while she struggled downhill with the load of textbooks on her back. She almost made it to the bottom when she stepped wrong. She teetered a moment before her book bag shifted and her ankle gave way. She crashed and rolled several feet into the underbrush of the pine trees.

"Damn!" Growling in frustration, she struggled to get up, but pain shot up her leg as she put weight on it. She reached down in the dark to feel it. It was already starting to swell.

The fury that had propelled her thus far drained away, leaving her feeling tired and more dejected than she ever remembered. She lay back on the ground and flung one arm over her face. Hot, burning sobs wracked her body. She cried like her heart would break. It felt as though it was breaking. After the weekend she'd shared with Nelson, the way in which she'd shared herself, she felt as if he'd flung it back in her face.

Wynter didn't know how long she lay there, half-dazed with pain, before she heard Nelson's car on the drive. The purr of the huge engine was unmistakable. He almost passed her. She wasn't sure what caught his attention, but at the last moment, the car stopped with a jerk. The door opened and she heard the tap of Nelson's cane as he got out of the car.

"Wynter?" He sounded strange, subdued, but she was too tired at that point to put more of a read on his mood. "Are you all right?"

She laughed bitterly. "No. It appears I can't even run away without fucking that up too."

"Come back to the house. We should talk."

Laughter turned back to tears. "I can't. I've hurt my ankle."

Nelson slammed the door. In the glare of the headlights, she watched him limp around the front of the car. "Hand me your book bag."

She wiggled out of the straps, wincing when she shifted her ankle, and handed it over to him. He turned and set it on the hood of the car.

"Can you get up now?" His voice held a harsh edge.

Wynter rolled over onto her hands and knees, the pain in her ankle making her feel light-headed.

"Give me your hand."

She looked up from under several strands of dangling hair and saw his left hand stretched out toward her. She put her hand in his and got her good foot under her before powering up. Nelson pulled her to her feet, but she scrambled to keep from falling against him. Wynter stood unsteadily, wincing again when she once more tried to put weight on her ankle. Nelson guided her to the side of the car, still half-supporting her while he opened the passenger door.

After putting her inside, he flipped open his cellphone, spoke briefly and then shoved it back in his pocket. He picked up her book bag, carried it around the car with him and tossed it on the backseat.

Wynter leaned back and closed her eyes. *Why was everything so complicated?* When she'd left home, she'd wanted to find a job and go to school. Why had she let herself fall in love with a man like Nelson Anderson? She'd finally admitted it while she'd lain on that hill, her ankle throbbing with pain. She hadn't run away because he'd had people follow her. Certainly not because she'd hated him. She'd run because she'd fallen in love with a man so far out of her realm she wasn't even sure they inhabited the same planet.

He couldn't love someone like her. She wasn't rich or sophisticated. She was a naïve teenager who'd never seen the inside of a hotel, let alone been out of Virginia or North Carolina in her entire life. The tycoon and the trailer trash. It was like one of those sappy old movies her mom liked to watch.

* * * *

Nelson glanced at Wynter's averted face. In the light from the dash, he saw a smudge of dirt and streaks from her tears.

Damn it. If he hadn't fucking overreacted when he couldn't find her, this would never have happened. But when he'd discovered Wynter was nowhere around the house, he'd worried. Stupid, he now realized, but he lost logic and clarity when it came to his decisions concerning Wynter. He hadn't' turned Anderson Electronics into the corporation it was by running on emotions, and now those unaccustomed feelings made him do and say things out of his norm.

If he wasn't such a damn cripple, he'd have caught up much faster, but he'd staggered on the drive, saving himself on the fender of the car before he fell. He growled in frustration at the injury that had turned him overnight from a grand prix level rider and athlete into a near invalid.

He glanced at her tensed form as she huddled in the leather passenger seat. Who was he kidding? Why would he even think someone like Wynter would be interested in him? She was young and vibrant with everything ahead of her, and he was in limbo, existing rather than living life.

The only thing that had kept him going all these months was the need for justice. When it seemed he wouldn't get that through the courts, he'd looked for other means to avenge what Payton Southard had done to his family.

At least that was the way he'd felt until Wynter had arrived at Pheasant Run. She'd brought hope. He'd seen it the first day she'd walked in. Hope and determination. She was a drug, but like an addict, he was tearing them both up with the craving.

He turned out of the drive onto the highway. Instead of driving to the hospital in Durham, he drove the opposite direction. No way were they headed to the hospital. Too much potential for publicity. Nelson Anderson showing up at the emergency room with a young woman in tow would be too much fuel for the gossips. John would know what to do.

He glanced at her again, wanting to touch her cheek, to tuck the straggling hair back into her braid, but most of all wanting to take away her pain.

He'd almost missed her coming down the drive, almost passed by, but at the last moment, the lights of the Rolls bounced off some reflective material—her book bag, her shoes? He wasn't sure, but it caught his eye and he'd jammed the brakes. And then? Oh yeah, that feeling useless part. She was hurt and in pain, and he'd done next to nothing to help. Every instinct told him she'd needed to be carried, but lame as he was, he could do little more than take her book bag. What a man.

While he maneuvered the twisting road to the doctor's house, Nelson cast worried glances at her. Wynter hadn't said a word. Her eyes were closed. He felt that ache again in the back of his throat.

Would she laugh if she knew how he craved her?

Somehow he'd never imagined the reaction she might have to the bodyguards. How could she even assume they were spying on her? That he would think so little of her?

How could she believe anything else? Her experience with people of money was far from favorable. She was a teenager from an impoverished background who just happened to be brilliant. She hardly knew him other than the fact he was her boss—some crippled, older guy she pitied. Enough she'd let him bed her? Nelson shied away from that thought, but it couldn't be ignored. Her reactions had screamed how insecure she'd felt against his age and position, but he'd chosen to ignore those signs until now, intent on possessing her.

Things would change, he decided. He would back off. It would be the best thing for her. She was just a kid, and she needed a chance to experience life, not become someone's mistress.

Oh, but he wanted so much more. He closed his mind to that line of thinking. That was behind him. He wouldn't take that risk again, the gamble of having and losing a family. He'd learned that lesson. Marriage. A family. *No.*

Chapter 16

The opening of the passenger door startled her from an uneasy doze. Strong, efficient hands reached in and picked her up, but they were not Nelson's hands. She looked around in confusion. They were outside someone's home, but not Nelson's. Confusion turned to panic.

"Nelson?"

"It's okay, Wynter." His voice came from behind her while she was carried inside. "We're at a friend's house. He's a doctor."

After a glimpse of a strong jaw and gray hair, she closed her eyes in pain and embarrassment. The doctor carried her to the living room and set her on the couch. With quick, sure movements, he stripped off her shoe, rolled up her pant leg and ran his hands over her foot and ankle. He manipulated the joint, asking what hurt and where, tested the feeling in her toes, then propped her foot up on a pillow.

"Right off the bat, young lady, I'd say you've done a mighty fine job of twisting your ankle. I don't believe you've broken anything. That's the good news."

He stood up and looked at Nelson. "I know you're avoiding a visit to the emergency room, but she needs an x-ray." He looked at Wynter's ankle. "I'll wrap it tonight, but I want you to bring her by in the morning, so I can take pictures and make sure there's no hairline fracture or anything torn. In the meantime, ice it to help cut the swelling, so we can get a better picture of it tomorrow."

Nelson nodded. "Thanks, John. I'll bring her by first thing."

The older man looked at Wynter curiously, his sharp gray gaze moving over the scratches on her hands and face. He wrapped her ankle with the same no-nonsense approach he'd used in examining it. He left the room and returned a moment later with a pair of crutches.

"This will get you through the next few days."

Nelson was quiet while they drove back to the house. He carried her book bag in and helped her to get settled in the living room. It was a larger, more formal room than the sitting room in the back. Wynter supposed he'd put her in there because it wasn't as far away. It also didn't have any memories attached to it that the two of them had shared. She'd never been in this room, but then there were a lot of rooms she'd never been in. The walls were covered in pictures. One color photograph in particular caught her eye. It was Nelson on a huge chestnut, caught at the moment when the two had crested a jump. The picture was cropped so you saw the horse's head and Nelson's. They both wore keen, intense expressions.

"I've brought you a bag of ice and a couple of pain pills John said I might give you." His tone was almost impersonal. Wynter swallowed the pills and handed the glass back. He set it on the table and then walked over to a sideboard, which held a decanter and glasses. He poured himself a shot of whisky then came and sat in a chair across from her. "We need to talk."

He'd said that earlier. She didn't want to, but she knew it couldn't be put off, so she nodded. Her consolation was Nelson looked as uncomfortable as she did

"I told you the truth, Wynter, when I said you might stay here, no strings attached. What I told you then is still true. I won't go back on my word."

She stared at her hands and nodded.

"Things got out of hand this weekend," he continued, still in that impersonal tone. "I promise you, it won't happen again."

He didn't want her. Wynter clenched her teeth together against the hard knot of pain. What had happened had been a mistake. He'd just said so. It hurt so much more than she'd expected.

"You're welcome to stay here. I want you to." Nelson paused before he said brusquely, "I may need your help. If that's a problem, tell me now. I'll hire someone."

She heard the strain in his voice. She knew how much it would hurt his pride to hire a nurse. Just like it hurt her pride to stay when he didn't want her—at least not the way she now craved him. But it was a way to be near him.

"No," she said in a small voice. "I don't mind."

"Look at me, Wynter." His voice was quiet but firm. She turned her head. "I'm sorry you didn't know who I was. I guess I was arrogant enough to think everyone did, but I will not apologize for my wealth. My family worked hard, and so have I to make Anderson Electronics what it is.

"You have a real chip on your shoulder when it comes to money." When she started to protest he continued, "No, it's my turn. You had yours earlier. All I've tried to do since you came here was ease the way for you, and you've fought me at every step. If I overwhelmed you, I'm sorry. I don't know much of your background."

He swirled the contents of the glass. "I haven't given you any more than what are daily necessities from my viewpoint. Obviously it's been more than that from yours."

She nodded, once again staring at her hands. She twisted her fingers, but she couldn't stop.

"I will not stop providing you with the things I think you need. Period. Get used to it. There is no ulterior motive, so quit looking for one."

This was Nelson Anderson the CEO speaking. She heard such finality in his voice. It was a clear statement that there would be no discussion, no argument.

At any other time, she would have taken offense, but Wynter was drained, physically and emotionally. Had it been just twenty-four hours ago he'd caressed her so intimately? It seemed like a lifetime. But she wanted something, even if it was just a touch, something to let her know he still wanted her. Wynter's eyes drooped from the pain medication.

"Do you want to go upstairs?"

"No." She wanted to stay in this room with the pictures of Nelson, the man she'd glimpsed this weekend, the man she now craved as much as any addict craved a fix. "I'll stay here tonight, if that's all right?"

He nodded. After covering her in a thick afghan that hung on the back of the couch, he dimmed the lights and left the room. Silent tears leaked out of the corners of her eyes and wet the thickness of her hair. She felt lost and more alone than ever. What had she done? If she'd just chilled and not gone ballistic over the security guys...

It was a long time before she slept.

* * * *

Mrs. Caudle helped her in the morning. While she cleaned up, the housekeeper laid out clothes for her, then helped her dress. Wynter felt the heat of embarrassment in her cheeks and couldn't quite meet her eyes. The older woman placed her hands on either side of Wynter's face and looked her in the eye.

"You have nothing for which you should feel ashamed. Things will work out. They always do."

Wynter nodded and smiled faintly.

"Here're your crutches. Mr. Nelson is waiting for you out front, and he's already put your books in the car, in case you feel like attending class after the doctor."

Wynter's smile faded somewhat when she got into the Rolls. Nelson glanced at her, but she noticed he didn't check her seatbelt like before. She knew she had caused that.

"Ready?" His question was light and impersonal, and Wynter's chest tightened.

The ride to town was quiet. Wynter recognized the glitzy medical practice where they parked. The doctors were among the Fellows in Family Practice at Duke's medical school. There were some awkward moments while Nelson dealt with insurance issues. Wynter filled out a medical history and handed it back. As always, under questions regarding her father's health history she marked "Unknown."

The nurse opened the door. "Dr. Holt will see you now." As Nelson started to rise too, the nurse smiled at him. "She'll be out in just a moment, Mr. Anderson."

Wynter wanted to protest, wanted to beg him to come in with her, but he was already seated again. The briefcase was open, and he withdrew files without glancing up at her. She chewed her lower lip and followed the nurse.

John Holt unwrapped her ankle, took another look at it, and then sent her upstairs for an x-ray. When the technician finished, she stuck her head out from the cubicle. "You can return to the exam room. It will just take a few minutes. Do you need help?"

Wynter shook her head. "No. Thanks. I can find it." She hobbled to the elevator and back to the room. She thought about telling Nelson she could pay her own bills, but the look on his face when they'd arrived had made her discard that idea. She was afraid to disrupt the uneasy truce between them. She heard the sound of the doorknob turning, and the doctor returned with the film envelope in his hand.

"You were lucky, Wynter," he said. "You do have some stretching of the ligament on the outside of your ankle, but there isn't any tearing. This will take some time to heal, though. I'd like you to stay on the crutches at least a week, and we'll go from there. Now," he continued matter-of-factly, "let me see the scratches on your face and hands." He examined each of the red marks. "Nothing major. Use some antibiotic cream on them to keep them from getting infected. Is there anything else we should discuss?" he inquired.

"I don't think so," she replied. *What else could there be?*

He tapped the pen on the desk as if trying to come to a decision. "Are you on any kind of birth control?" he asked bluntly.

Wynter's eyes opened wide. God. She'd never thought of that. "No."

"Don't take offense. It's my job to ask. Nelson's never brought anyone in here before. Are you two intimate?"

Wynter nodded. "Yes."

"Then you should be on something." After further questioning about her medical history, he filled out two pieces of paper. "Two prescriptions. One for Motrin and another for the Pill. I believe in being realistic, Wynter." He rose and shook her hand. "Take care. I've known Nelson a long time. He means well."

With that, John Holt was gone, leaving Wynter feeling as though she had been visited by a polite tornado.

She picked up her crutches and hobbled to the waiting room. Nelson held the door for her. After helping her into the car, he stowed Wynter's crutches in the backseat.

"Where to?" he asked.

"The drug store. I need to fill two prescriptions."

"I can take care of those for you," he offered moving to take the prescriptions out of her hand.

"No," she said in sudden alarm and pulled the papers away from him. "I-I can do it. It's all right. In fact, just drop me off on campus, and I'll take care of it."

Nelson arched a brow but did as she asked. After helping her out of the car he asked, "Four?"

She nodded. "Yes. Thanks." At his raised eyebrow, she clarified, "for taking me to the doctor."

His mouth quirked, then he nodded and turned, making his way back to the driver's side.

The wind had picked up by the time of Wynter's last class, and the weather took a frigid turn. She hurried as quickly as she could on the crutches, not stopping to get the jacket she'd stuffed in her backpack earlier. Nelson already awaited her.

This time, he didn't get out of the car, which surprised her. She glanced at him when she tossed her crutches and backpack onto the rear seat then collapsed in the front. Nelson had yet to say anything. When she looked at him, lines of pain and fatigue etched his face.

"Are you okay?" Wynter asked hesitantly.

"Just tired. I had several appointments."

She sat on her hands to warm them up some. "I could always hitch a ride into town, you know. You don't need to drive me."

Nelson glanced at her with a startled expression when he pulled away from the curb. He opened his mouth then just smiled. "Thanks, Wynter, but I'm making the trip anyway, so it's no trouble."

Mrs. Caudle had prepared dinner and placed it on the dining room table, rather than in the kitchen, when they returned. One look at the silverware she'd set out, and Wynter felt the nerves in her stomach tighten. She'd never seen so many utensils and had no idea which ones to use.

"I'm not that hungry," she lied, but her stomach growled and gave her away.

Nelson rolled his eyes. "Knowing you, the last thing you ate was breakfast. Am I right?"

She thought a minute. It had taken a lot longer to get between classes on crutches, and she hadn't stopped because she'd feared she would be late.

"I ate some—"

"Nabs," Nelson finished with disgust.

"You try getting around on these damn things…" Wynter trailed off when her gaze landed on Nelson's cane. *Oh God!* She looked away, chewing on her lower lip and wanting to sink through the floor in embarrassment. She blinked to get the sudden tears out of her eyes.

"We'll eat in the dining room," Nelson said, filling the awkward silence and ignoring her remark. "Mrs. Caudle set a formal table for a reason," he added as he helped her to her seat. "We're having dinner guests tomorrow night. People interested in placing their jumper string with Thomas."

"That's great!" Wynter enthused.

"They also want to talk with you about riding."

"Riding?"

Nelson smiled slightly. "Word gets around fast. At any rate," he continued after he sat adjacent to her, "dinner tomorrow night will be with the Daltons, their two children, Thomas, Miss Olivia and you."

Wynter swallowed when she looked at the silverware and glasses in front of her.

"I don't think I can do this, Nelson," she admitted, a hitch in her breathing.

"Of course you can," he reassured. "I'll help you through everything tonight and make sure you're seated next to me tomorrow night. Miss Olivia can be hostess."

Two hours later, she felt as though her head was spinning. "I can't do this!" she cried in frustration. "I'll never remember all this shit!"

Nelson lifted the napkin to his lips. "Please don't say 'shit' at the dinner table."

She threw her napkin at him and fumbled for her crutches. It was a big joke to him, but she had never seen so many dishes and glasses and forks and spoons. "It's not funny! Please don't make me do this," she begged. "Please. I'll meet them in the barn and talk to them there. Please."

Nelson covered one of her hands. "Wynter, I promise I will not let you make a fool of yourself. You'll do fine. Let's go upstairs and take a look in your closet."

She refused to speak the whole way. Nelson ignored her. With his left hand he flicked through several dresses until he landed on a silky midnight blue one with a high neck in front and a deeper "v" in the back. "This," he pronounced with satisfaction. "You can wear this."

After they walked back out of the closet, his hand touched her long braid. Wynter felt a tingle shoot down her spine. His tone was gruff when he said, "Miss Olivia will come over ahead of time to help you with your hair."

When he turned to go, Wynter asked, "Can I use your phone? I want to call my mother and tell her I can't come up this weekend."

Nelson looked irritated. "Wynter, don't ask. Make yourself at home."

She raised her chin as she stared at him. "I just figured I needed permission to make sure it didn't interfere with any plans you might have already made for me."

"That's unfair."

"Is it?" she asked. "You should stand on my side a while, Nelson. See how it looks to you."

His eyes narrowed, but his control was imperturbable. "I'm going back to my study to do some work, so you're welcome to use the phone in my room if you'd like."

"Thanks." She ducked her head and swung past him on the crutches.

It wasn't an easy conversation with Mama. Wynter knew she was disappointed and worried. After she finished the phone call, she was exhausted, and her ankle hurt. Too tired to go back downstairs, she limped down the hallway to her room. She needed to study, but her concentration was shot. She also couldn't sleep. Most of the night she tossed and turned, worried about her ma, about the dinner party and aching to make things between Nelson and her right.

* * * *

When she came downstairs the next morning, he took one look at her and shook his head. "Do you have any exams today?"

"No. Not until Friday."

"Then skip class. You look like you haven't slept. Let Mrs. Caudle fuss over you and just take a day for yourself. Hell, go and play in the pool or sit in the hot tub."

It was tempting. She thought of the hot tub.

"I'm leaving, Wynter." He spoke in a tight voice. "So you can quit worrying I'll breathe down your neck."

As Nelson's white Rolls disappeared down the drive, she stared after him. This wasn't how it was supposed to be when you fell in love, was it? She smacked her hand against the doorjamb and turned back into the house.

Mrs. Caudle fussed through the morning, fixing Wynter a pot of hot chocolate and settling her on the couch in the sitting room where she took a long nap.

At lunchtime, Wynter went to the kitchen. She stood in the doorway, her fingers clenched around the hand rests on her crutches. "Mrs. Caudle?"

"What dear? Is your ankle bothering you, or are you just hungry?"

"Neither, really. I…would you let me help set the table for tonight? I thought you might explain again about the silverware, the napkins and glasses—that kind of thing."

The older woman smiled in understanding. "Of course I can, Miss Wynter. It can be a bit overwhelming, can't it?"

Wynter nodded. "I don't want to fu…make a mistake tonight."

While they worked, with Wynter hopping from chair to chair placing silverware and napkins, Mrs. Caudle explained what everything was once again. When she was through, she felt better. It boosted her confidence and eased her nervousness.

A few hours later, she sat in the hot tub, her hair swirling around her as she leaned back and closed her eyes. She let the bubbles swirl around her. She had unwrapped her ankle and left her clothes folded on a nearby bench.

She remembered what had happened the last time she'd been here. It had been the precursor to making love with Nelson the first time. He'd said there were no strings, but there were. Her heart had formed them, and right now those strings were an aching knot right in the middle of it. She wiped a shaky hand across her eyes. She didn't like where they stood in their relationship, but she also wasn't sure how to change it.

"You shouldn't stay in too long," Nelson stated from behind her.

Wynter sat up, bumping her ankle against the side of the tub then yelping in pain. "You scared me!"

"I can see that," Nelson observed, appearing out of the corner of her eye. He had a towel wrapped around lean hips. "Mind if I join you?"

Wynter shook her head and closed her eyes again to avoid looking at him while he slipped into the tub on the opposite side.

"How's your ankle feeling?"

"Better now." she replied, opening her eyes. "Nelson, I need to get out. Would you mind looking the other way?"

He leaned back and closed his eyes, a small smile hovering around his mouth. "I'm not looking. You have a couple of hours before our guests arrive."

All she wanted was to crawl back in the tub and kiss him, but she didn't know how to bridge the distance between them.

* * * *

Wynter was dressed and seated in the living room before Nelson arrived downstairs. Olivia Rutledge had fixed her hair in a loose knot that left a few tendrils curling on the back of her neck. Wynter liked this style better than the sleek French twist. While they waited for Nelson, Olivia took pity on Wynter's nervousness and handed her a small glass of sherry.

"Here, drink this, dear," she soothed. "It will help your nerves."

When Wynter started to toss it back unceremoniously, the older woman prompted, "Sip it. We don't want you sliding under the dinner table."

She laughed and did as Olivia had instructed. Wynter set the glass down when Nelson came in. After greeting Olivia with a brief kiss on the cheek, he stopped in front of Wynter and slipped a small leather box from his pocket. "I have something for you."

He handed her the box with a tight smile. Wynter glanced up and took it, her hands trembling as she opened it. Two teardrop shaped pearl earrings lay inside along with a larger pearl pendant on a fine gold chain. She sucked in a quick breath and looked up at Nelson. "I—I can't..."

"You can accept it, Wynter," he affirmed. "Would you like some help?"

Without waiting for an answer, he sat next to her on the couch and turned her toward him. First he took the earrings out and fitted them in her ears, dropping the plain gold studs she had worn into his jacket pocket. When his hands reached around the back of her neck and fastened the necklace, she looked up at his face. Whatever he saw there made him pause. His own eyes darkened before he masked the expression. Wynter looked down, her fingers touching the pendant reverently. It nestled against the material of her dress, just above the swell of her breasts.

"Ah, Nelson," Olivia Rutledge said. "That is the perfect touch and not too overpowering for someone of her age."

Nelson's lips tightened at Olivia's words. Snapping the box shut with a decided click, he stood and limped to the sideboard to pour himself a whisky. He was as remote as when she'd first met him. Thomas was the next arrival, followed by Mrs. Caudle announcing their guests.

Wynter concentrated to make sure she smiled at the right times when introductions were made. Everyone chatted a few minutes before Mrs. Caudle's announcement that dinner was served.

The housekeeper winked at Wynter when she swung past on her crutches. Wynter smiled back, feeling at once more at ease than she had all evening. As Nelson had promised, she was seated to his left. She sensed his surprise as course followed course and Wynter chose the right utensil and glass.

She conversed with the Daltons who were seated across from her. Their son, a lanky thirteen-year-old, was on her left. Wynter felt him staring at her through much of the meal, but she refused to let it bother her. If the worst she dealt with was an annoying teenager, then she would count the evening a success. She made polite conversation, dabbed her mouth with her napkin as she'd been instructed and followed Miss Olivia's lead when leaving the table.

The real discussion about riding began in the living room while everyone but the two Dalton children drank coffee and after-dinner drinks. The family seemed surprised by Wynter's lack of formal riding instruction but was still interested in having her campaign their horses. They were even more surprised when Nelson explained she studied at Duke and any show scheduling would need to accommodate that. At last the evening was over and everyone left, including Olivia and Thomas.

Nelson smiled at Wynter when the door closed behind Olivia. "You were wonderful. I told you everything would be all right."

Wynter smiled wanly at him, but the knot in her stomach all evening now unraveled in a most unpleasant way.

"Excuse me," she whispered and without waiting for an answer, she swung down the hallway to the guest bathroom.

* * * *

That was where Nelson found her a few moments later, doubled up over the toilet and dry heaving between thick sobs. *Jesus!* Guilt twisted inside of him. He'd pressured her into the evening, knowing how new she was to anything other than work and studying.

He slipped an arm around her waist while his right hand smoothed the hair back from her face. When she finished, he handed her a linen handkerchief which he'd dampened under the faucet. Wynter pressed it against her face and neck, and then held it over her eyes.

"Why didn't you tell me you weren't feeling well?" he demanded.

"It's just nerves," she dismissed. "Thank you for your handkerchief. I'm going to bed, Nelson. Good night."

So formal. So cool. He missed the fiery girl with her long braid and her pugnacious attitude. She brushed past him, and he drank in her sweet scent. He wanted to touch her, feel her long body stretched next to his. He wanted to hold her and tell her everything was all right. But he didn't reach out to stop her as she stuck her chin in the air and left.

Chapter 17

Thursday evening Irene O'Reilly's phone rang. Wythe was out of town wrapping up a complicated estate case, so it wouldn't be him calling. Perhaps Wynter? Irene had been uneasy ever since her daughter's call about her sprained ankle. It was more than the injury. She felt in her gut something was going on between her daughter and Nelson Anderson. When she'd shared her concern with Wythe, half-expecting him to tell her she was over-reacting, he'd also voiced concern.

So when she picked up the phone and heard Nelson Anderson identify himself, she was surprised—and cool.

"Mrs. O'Reilly, how are you?"

"I'd be a whole lot better if I heard from you how my daughter is doing. She's never sounded as down in the dumps as she did when she called Tuesday."

"That's the reason I'm calling. I'd like to invite you here since Wynter can't visit you. It would be a pleasant surprise for her."

By the end of the conversation, she had agreed. Wythe, though he didn't know it yet, would bring her down Saturday afternoon and they would spend the night. She hung up the phone feeling much better regarding Wynter—and Nelson Anderson. A man who meant her harm wouldn't go to these lengths to please her.

* * * *

Wythe returned the following afternoon. When Irene heard the jeep in the driveway, she jumped up to meet him outside. Fall's bright blanket of color was fading, leaving some of the trees behind the house bare. When Wythe rounded the corner of the trailer, he beamed at her. Those eyes always made her melt.

She knew he still saw Trish Staunton on occasion. Irene wasn't sure how serious it was, but she didn't want to know. If she discovered he was serious about Trish, it would be the blow that crushed any hope Irene held. She might be foolish for wanting him, but it didn't stop how she felt—how she'd felt for a long time.

She smiled back, leaning against him to give him a hug before he started up the steps.

"Wythe," Irene greeted him as she dragged him inside the house, "you'll never guess who called yesterday."

He tilted his head. "The President? The Pope? That's it," he decided, "the Pope is nominating you for sainthood for working at the Butlers."

Irene laughed while she poured him a cup of coffee. "You're so bad, Wythe Bradshear! And you're the one who helped get me the job."

His face sobered. "Don't remind me."

"Anyway," Irene continued, not wanting to talk about the Butlers, "Nelson Anderson called. He's invited me to visit Pheasant Run this weekend. He's also invited you, that is, if you don't already have plans?"

She almost sagged with relief when he answered, "None I can't cancel. You know I'd be happy to take you down there, Irene."

She smiled. "You do so much. I feel like we take and take from you."

He surprised her then. Stretching out an arm, he caught her around the waist and pulled her onto his lap. When she started to bounce back up, he held her. His warm, sherry-colored eyes looked into hers a long time. His tone, when he spoke, was serious.

"Never think that. You've given me so much over the years. Your friendship is something I value above anything else. And besides," he said, once again the playful Wythe she knew and loved, "where else could I have the two most beautiful women in the county on my arm, even if one of them is stubborn and hard-headed?"

"Wythe! You shouldn't talk about Wynter that way."

"Who said I was talking about Wynter?" he asked innocently.

She pushed off his lap and smoothed her hands over her jeans, flustered by the heat in his eyes.

"I have to work tomorrow morning, so it will be the afternoon before we can go. I'm nervous, Wythe. Mr. Anderson said it would be a casual weekend, but I just don't know. I mean, it's not as though we have anything in common. What if he's like the Butlers and the Southards?"

Wythe surprised her again. "Screw the Butlers and the Southards. You can hold your head up among any of them. Call the Butlers and tell them you're not feeling well. We'll leave earlier, and I'll take you to lunch on the way. It's off the beaten path, but I know a great little restaurant in Hillsborough."

His brown eyes were somber when he stood. "I'm dead serious, Irene. Call them and tell them you won't be in tomorrow. You deserve some time for yourself."

* * * *

Wythe was back just before eleven the next morning. It was a warm day for early November. Irene felt him watching her while he helped stow her bag in the back of the jeep.

"Did you do something different with your hair?"

She was surprised he'd noticed. "I just put some layers in it. It was getting too heavy."

"I like it," he remarked, "but then I like your hair no matter what you do."

She looked at him and burst out laughing. "You're silly, Wythe! Let's get going!"

They took their time. He drove along the back roads through the North Carolina countryside. There were miles and miles of woods and farmlands lining the two lane highway that led them to the town of Hillsborough.

Historical markers dotted the small community every few feet, most going back to the Revolutionary War. Wythe pulled the jeep over along the main street through town. The restaurant was just a block or so up from the courthouse, tucked in among antique shops and clothing stores. Irene found herself perplexed when she looked up at Wythe. Why was he doing this? He seemed so different, and it threw her off-guard.

It was late afternoon when they turned up the long tree-lined drive at Pheasant Run. Irene's heart beat faster when she looked at the well-groomed pastures with immaculate dark-brown wood fencing. Horses grazed here and there, turned out in lightweight sheets since it was a warm day. She couldn't see the house through the trees, but Mr. Anderson had said it was up the hill beyond the barns. When they rounded the stand of evergreen trees, the house came into view.

"Wythe." Irene's breathing hitched when she saw a home that made even the Southards' house look small. "Maybe we should just stay a couple of hours then head back home."

He reached over and grabbed her hand. "You'll be fine, Irene. Calm down and chin up."

Anderson waited for them at the front door. Wythe had used his cellphone to let him know when he and Irene would arrive. Irene studied him while he limped toward them, the cane in his right hand. His dark, gray-streaked hair lifted in the gentle, late afternoon breeze. Although he wore baggy cotton twill pants and an open-collared shirt, they were tucked in and belted. Even casual, there was an air of formality and reserve surrounding him. It was hard to imagine him with someone as wide-open as Wynter.

His expression was tinged with a bone deep seriousness, which nothing appeared to shake loose. He'd been that way at the horse show. Even when he smiled, like he did now, that somberness never quite disappeared.

Irene guessed that might be the effect of losing a wife and child. It dawned on her as they got out of the car it was a year ago, almost exactly, when it had happened. Maybe that's why he'd invited them, to distract him.

"Irene, thanks for coming." He squeezed her hand before turning to Wythe. "Wythe. Good to see you again." He extended a hand and Wythe took it, exchanging firm handshakes.

When they walked inside the large front hall, Anderson lowered his voice. "Drop your bags here for now, and we'll get you settled in upstairs later. Wynter's in the back sitting room, reading for one of her classes. Just follow me. I know she'll be thrilled to see you."

Nelson led the way down the hall and through the study. It was obvious he'd been working when Wythe had called. Several neat stacks of papers lay on the desk, along with a coffee cup and the open laptop.

Nelson hung back at the doorway. "Go in."

When they rounded the doorway into the bright room, Irene saw Wynter sitting on the couch, one leg stretched out, the bare foot and ankle wrapped in an Ace bandage. Her crutches were propped nearby. She seemed very at home in Nelson's house. It gave Irene momentary pause, but later she could find out more about why her daughter appeared to be living in this mansion.

"Wynter?" she murmured, knowing how lost her daughter always got when she read.

Wynter looked up, her fingers stilling where they flipped the end of her braid back and forth. Her dark green eyes widened in surprise before she broke into a huge smile.

"Mama?" She dropped her book and jumped up, then winced when she put weight on her ankle. "Oh damnation."

As she overbalanced, Wythe jumped forward and grabbed her shoulders to steady her before handing her the crutches by her side. Wynter smiled her thanks and gave him a quick hug before maneuvering around the coffee table and over to her mother.

Wynter's smile trembled when she looked at Irene. "Oh, Ma! I'm so glad to see you again. You have no idea how hard it was to tell you I

Laura Browning

couldn't come up this weekend. It's been such a bad week. I had midterms and a paper due and then this happened Monday and—how did you find the house?"

"Slow down, Wynter!" Irene laughed. Looking up at her daughter, she touched her cheek. Wynter did look a bit pale and there were circles under her eyes as though she had not slept well this week. "Mr. Anderson called and invited us after you'd called saying you couldn't make it."

Wynter's gaze slid over Irene's shoulder to where Nelson stood behind her. What Irene saw in her daughter's expression before Wynter masked it made her catch her breath.

"Thank you, Nelson," Wynter murmured sincerely. "Thank you so much."

She hugged her mother tightly, and Irene squeezed her back, wishing she might ease the longing she saw in Wynter's eyes. Irene looked over her shoulder at Nelson Anderson, surprised to see the same look on his face. Oh, yes, there was something going on between the two of them, but neither one of them appeared happy.

Nelson cleared his throat. "Mrs. Caudle left us a cold buffet supper in the kitchen. We can eat whenever you like or have a drink and relax."

Wythe spoke up. "Drinks sound nice. We stopped for a late lunch, so drinks would give Irene and Wynter a chance to catch up."

Nelson looked at Wythe. "If you'll give me a hand, I'll show you where you can put your bags. We'll get the drinks on the way back."

Wythe grinned and winked at Irene. Nelson had maneuvered things to leave mother and daughter alone together. "Not a problem," Wythe responded.

The two men disappeared back through the study. Irene turned back to Wynter, who set her crutches aside before she twisted around and sat on the couch. She patted the space beside her, still smiling at her mother.

"Ma. I thought I would die when I had to tell you I couldn't come. Even if I hadn't busted up my ankle, my truck's in the shop. Nelson says it's on its last leg, and we should just get something else."

Irene's eyes drifted from the lightweight cashmere pullover Wynter wore to the tailored cotton trousers. They were a far cry from Wal-Mart and Goodwill where it seemed they'd always shopped over the years. How could Wynter afford them?

"I can't buy you anything else," Irene said quietly. "Helping you with the truck was the best I could do."

Wynter looked at her mother startled, and Irene realized her daughter hadn't' meant *her* when she'd talked about a new car. At least Wynter had the grace to blush as the implication became clear she'd meant her and Nelson. Just what the hell was going on? Wynter had told her she lived in the apartment over the barn, but her daughter seemed very at home in Nelson Anderson's house.

"I have some money saved up," Wynter admitted. "I could get something of my own."

"You said 'we', Wynter," Irene prompted, noticing Wynter avoided meeting her eyes. "Is there something you need to tell me? And before you start making something up, young lady, let me remind you I'm not an idiot. I can see how comfortable you are here. I can see the clothes you have on."

"I live here," Wynter admitted, then added, her eyes pleading for understanding, "but it's not what you think, Mama. I have my own room. I'm not," she paused and this time turned a bright pink, "you know."

Irene frowned at her daughter. "That's what everyone will think. Heavens, Wynter, what was going through your head? What kind of man would just hand you the world on a platter and ask nothing in return?"

A quiet voice behind her said, "I would."

Nelson Anderson moved quickly, despite the limp, standing behind Wynter, left hand resting on her shoulder. Dark blue eyes flashed, but he kept his voice impersonal.

"I don't need to tell you what a hard worker your daughter is. I admire that. She's accomplished more in just a short time with guts and intelligence than a lot of people manage in a lifetime. Why shouldn't she reap some benefits?"

He gestured at the room around them with an elegant hand. "I have more material wealth than anyone could need. Why shouldn't I share? Your daughter has been on the dean's list two semesters at Duke. When she finishes this semester, she will already be starting her sophomore year. I admire her dedication and her grit in getting admitted to school on her own." He paused and looked at Irene with absolute seriousness. "I will do whatever I can to help her, and there are no strings attached."

Irene held her chin up and looked him in the eye. "I'll take your word for that, but you should understand—it's my daughter I'm entrusting to you."

He met her eyes just as squarely. "And I understand just how important she is."

Irene's gaze flicked to Wythe who stood watching through narrowed eyes. She knew she would get an analysis of things later. Right now, though, he stepped in to change the subject, setting the tray he carried with him on the table in front of the couch and pouring drinks for everyone. While Irene sipped her wine, she watched and listened to the conversation around her.

Wythe asked Wynter what she was studying this semester, which in turn launched a discussion of international politics and the role religion played. It was beyond her, Irene thought.

She'd always been more interested in human behavior than world issues. And right now, she found the behavior of at least two people in the house odd. Despite the words and the assurances there was nothing going on, Irene knew. She saw the change in Wynter, an awareness of herself as a woman, and very definitely an awareness of Nelson Anderson as a man.

So Irene studied him while they sat deep in conversation. She knew he wasn't much younger than her, and that made him just a few years younger than Wynter's father. Given the fact Irene had been no more than a child when she had gotten pregnant, though, the age difference was not something to make anyone raise a brow. Plus, Wynter had always been mature in ways far beyond her years. It was her inexperience with the personal side of male-female relationships that worried Irene, however.

It was well after dark when Wythe said, "I don't know about the rest of you, but I could go for some food now."

Nelson set the whisky glass down. "Sorry, Wythe. It's in the kitchen. All we have to do is eat."

He led the way. When Irene looked around with the practiced eye of a professional, she envied Mrs. Caudle. This was a step up from the renovated antebellum kitchen in which she worked at the Butlers. The table was already set, condiments left on ice in the middle so they wouldn't spoil. Irene made note of some of the things Nelson Anderson's housekeeper had done, figuring she could use some of her tricks at the Butlers. It might get her out of there earlier some evenings. Irene moved automatically, fixing people's plates, but Wynter's hand on her arm stopped her.

"You're our guest, Mama," she said quietly. "Sit down."

While Nelson poured sweet tea for everyone, Wynter uncovered the trays of cold cuts and crudités.

"So how do you like school so far?" Irene asked when Wynter set a plate with sliced bread on the table.

"I love it. Duke's campus is beautiful."

Wythe shook his head and placed a hand over his chest. "It hurts my heart to see it, both the undergrad Virginia half and the Carolina Law School half."

Nelson arched a brow. "A Tarheel fan?"

Wythe laughed. "Should I leave? I'm a bit overwhelmed by the Duke Blue around here."

It was a boisterous meal once Nelson and Wythe got on the subject of basketball. The two men went back and forth about which school's team was having a better season. Wynter didn't have any particular allegiance. But if Irene knew Wynter, she had her head so into her classes most of the time she might not know basketball season had even started.

Wynter excused herself from the table when everyone had finished, disappearing around the corner. She came back on one crutch, a small birthday cake in her other hand with a lighted candle on it.

She set it in front of Nelson with a shy smile and then turned to Wythe and her mother. "Now I know why Mrs. Caudle kept insisting on baking a bigger cake than I suggested. She was in on this surprise." She looked at Nelson. "Happy birthday," she said. "Make a wish and blow out the candle."

Nelson blinked a couple of times, a small smile touching the corners of his mouth. For just a moment, he hesitated before he blew out the small flame.

"What a nice surprise." He looked up at Wynter, who still hovered, and squeezed her hand. "Thank you."

She sat back down while cake was passed around. Irene noticed Wynter didn't eat much of hers. She seemed on edge about something, her glance darting to Nelson. When Wynter saw he'd finished the piece of cake, she reached under the table and came back up with a small gift bag.

"I have something for you," she said to Nelson. "I hope you like it." Irene heard the uncertainty in her voice and wondered.

Nelson smiled at her. "You didn't need to do this, Wynter."

He reached inside the bag and withdrew a flat, rectangular object wrapped in tissue paper. Wynter studied him while he unwrapped it. A moment later, Nelson's smile faded. The hard planes of his face softened, making him look at once younger and more vulnerable. He blinked several times in rapid succession. Irene saw cradled in his hands a framed miniature of a little golden-haired toddler staring back at him with the same dark blue eyes he possessed. On her face was a beautiful smile showing off deep dimples on either side of her mouth. It looked like a small oil painting.

Nelson's brows drew together as if in pain, and he bit his lower lip before he set the painting down.

"Damn!" he swore. His jaw clenched and unclenched. "Excuse me." Grabbing the cane he walked out of the kitchen in the direction of the study. Wynter looked as though she was about to cry.

"Mama?" she asked uncertainly. "Did I make a mistake?"

Wythe was the one who reached out and grabbed her hand in his large one. "No, Wynter. No mistake. Just give him a few minutes. I think you caught him off-guard. You know it's also the one year anniversary of the accident."

Wynter's eyes widened. "I didn't think of that."

"Here," Irene said briskly, "let's get everything cleaned up. Wythe and I can do it. Just tell us where everything goes. Why don't you gather up that miniature and take it in to Nelson."

Chapter 18

Wynter looked at the small picture resting against the tissue paper. Even though Wythe said she hadn't made a mistake, her stomach turned. Nelson had looked so upset.

Way to go. She picked up the picture with half a mind to just sneak it up to her room. When Wynter left the kitchen she almost passed the hall leading to the back part of the house, but as if her body had a mind of its own, she found herself headed to Nelson.

She saw him before she heard him. He stood facing the desk, hands braced on its polished top, his broad shoulders shaking. Wynter's heart clenched. Just then she heard him sniff and reach for the linen handkerchief she knew he always carried in his back pocket.

She hurried forward, but then halted in the door.

"I'm sorry," she blurted. "I thought because the picture sat next to your bed…shit! I'm such an idiot."

He turned to her, eyes red and cheeks damp. *Oh God!* He was crying. Her hand clenched around the miniature.

"I'll get rid of it," she whispered. "I'm sorry…"

"Don't you dare." Nelson's voice was thick and hoarse when he opened his arms. "Come here."

He took the miniature from her like it was a precious jewel and set it on the edge of the desk. "Thank you, Wynter," he murmured. "It's the most beautiful present you could have given me. I love it. I…" he paused and swallowed, then continued, "thank you."

She touched his cheek just below his eyes, feeling the dampness. "You're sure?"

He pulled her into his arms and buried his face against her neck while he tangled one of his hands in the hair at the back of her head. He trembled and she leaned against him, wrapping her arms around his waist and hugging him. Her throat tightened too.

"Please don't push me away," Wynter whispered.

He squeezed her then turned his head to kiss her. It was a pledge, a promise, but neither of them could put words to it at that moment.

* * * *

The hallway to the study was dim, and Irene stopped in the shadows at the scene in front of her at the end of the hall. If Irene had any worries about how Nelson would treat her daughter, they disappeared the moment she saw them wrapped in each other's arms. His expression when he looked at Wynter burned with such intense love it almost hurt to watch.

She backed a few steps down the hallway and said in as normal a tone as she could muster, "Wynter? Nelson? We have coffee ready."

She walked forward and found Nelson still leaning against the desk, the miniature now cradled in his hand. Wynter stood nearby twirling the end of her braid once more. Irene smiled at both of them. "Where shall I have Wythe take the tray?"

Nelson set the miniature down and smiled. Irene noticed the thick eyelashes seemed a bit spiky as if he'd wiped his eyes. She smiled back at him with more warmth than she'd had prior to witnessing Wynter and him together.

"Just bring it to the sitting room," he said. "I believe there's a Carolina game on, if Wythe wants to watch it."

From just behind Irene they heard, "You got that right."

The rest of the evening passed pleasantly. Nelson and Wythe immersed themselves in the ball game, and Wynter took her mother on a tour of the house. She used just the one crutch and put some weight on her ankle.

"Are you supposed to be doing that?" Irene asked when they returned from the pool area to the first floor.

Wynter's grin was a guilty one. "No. But there's nothing torn, Ma, and I can't keep hobbling everywhere. You can't imagine how hard it is to get around campus. Nelson's been dropping me off and picking me up, but I still walk between classes."

Irene nodded. Wynter would do what Wynter would do. "Just don't overdo it, honey. Did you twist it running?"

She hesitated a beat before she said, "Yes. Let me show you the living room. It's one of my favorite rooms in the house."

Hmm. She'd lied, but Irene let it go.

She understood why the living room was one of Wynter's favorites as soon as she entered. It was filled with horse-related artwork, along with quite a few photographs of Nelson jumping. "I didn't realize he was a rider too."

Wynter shook her head. "He's not. Not anymore. From what I can see, that's a real shame too." She grabbed her mother's hand and took her over to the far side of the room. "There's something else I want to show you."

In an alcove near a bay window stood a wall of photographs of a variety of subjects. They were composed with creativity and lit with available light. Among them was the picture of the little girl in the miniature. There was a second picture that showed the same girl, this time laughing while she patted the cheeks of a dark-haired young woman.

"Nelson took these pictures, Mama. Can you believe it? They look good enough to be on exhibit."

Irene nodded before pointing to the picture of the woman and child. "Is that his wife and daughter?"

"Yes." Wynter's tone was somber. "Lindy and Allison."

Irene touched her daughter's hand and smiled at her. "Now I understand. What a wonderful, thoughtful gift you gave him, Wynter."

Irene was proud of her daughter. Wynter had left their house in Virginia an intelligent but often rough and callous girl. Now she had become a young woman with both inner and outer beauty.

* * * *

She surprised her again the following morning. When Irene came downstairs, Wynter was in the kitchen frying bacon and flipping pancakes. Oh, Wynter could cook. In fact, she cooked rather well, but her arm had to be twisted. Irene supposed it was another sign of maturity.

Wythe and Nelson arrived at the same time, both of them with wet hair. "Swimming," Wythe explained when he sat next to Irene. Nelson stood just inside the door watching Wynter.

"Are you cooking?" he inquired in a note of stunned disbelief.

"Yes," she responded, flipping a pancake up in the air and catching it on her spatula. She grinned at him.

Nelson looked aghast and turned to her mother. "Can she cook?"

"Yes," Irene replied, not sure where this conversation was going. "She's quite good. It's just not always easy getting her to do it."

He looked back at Wynter, his tone accusing, "If you can cook, can you explain why you believe Nabs constitute a legitimate meal?"

Wythe almost spit out a sip of coffee when he laughed. Irene rolled her eyes and covered her mouth to hide her smile.

Wynter glared at them as she set a plate of perfect, golden pancakes and crisp bacon on the table.

"Very funny. I just happen to have more important things occupying my mind."

"Yeah," Wythe responded, "like plotting complicated drag hunts that end in someone's car?"

Irene was relieved to see Nelson laughing.

"How did you become friends?" he asked Wythe.

Irene began an abbreviated version of the Christmas Eve dinner, but Wythe stopped her by placing his hand on hers. "Let me."

"I was home from college and helping out at the local church soup kitchen. It was Christmas Eve, and I volunteered as a way out of my parents' annual holiday bash. I was working on the serving line when I saw this pretty young woman come in with what I figured must be her sister." Irene stared at Wythe in surprise, but he ignored her. "The girl," he continued, "had the brightest, most beautiful red hair I'd ever seen."

Wynter shifted with embarrassment.

"When they came through the line, the girl stared at me with great big green eyes that sparkled brighter than the lights on the Christmas tree. Then she smiled, and I knew I was a dead man."

Nelson chuckled.

"I smiled back of course," Wythe said, like everyone knew there was nothing else to be done. "That opened the flood gates. In the space of probably, oh, ten seconds, I knew her name, the fact it was her birthday and that her mother was taking her out to dinner."

Wythe paused and looked over at Irene. She had never seen such an intent, serious expression on his face. "I looked again at the woman with her. I'd thought they were sisters. She looked embarrassed, and I didn't want her to feel that way. Everyone falls on hard times at some point. For some of us it's financial. For some it's emotional.

"When I asked Wynter if it was her birthday, she informed me her mother told her she was the best Christmas present ever. And I got choked up. It was pretty obvious they owned almost nothing, and this young mother was doing the best she could for her daughter."

"Wythe," Irene whispered uncomfortably, "Nelson doesn't need to know this."

"Oh, but it's a great story," Nelson protested.

"Then let me tell the rest of it." Wynter smiled. "When we were done with dinner, Wythe brought out a birthday cake, complete with candles!"

"I swiped them from the Advent wreaths," Wythe explained.

Nelson laughed aloud this time.

"I'm telling this," Wynter scolded. "It was the most beautiful birthday cake in the world, and everyone sang. When I got up the next morning, there was a package on our porch. A teddy bear from Santa. Wythe admitted last year he'd given it to me."

Wythe looked embarrassed, and Irene was still floored by the telling of the story.

"I decided right then and there," he continued, "that I would never let two such beautiful females get away from me, so I've been tagging along ever since."

"Wythe!" Irene scolded him again

Wynter laughed and helped ease the sudden tension between Wythe and her mother. "He's been *annoying* me ever since is more like it!" But there was real affection in her tone when she said it.

Wythe glanced at his watch. There was a faint flush on his tanned cheeks. "I hate to rush things along here, but I have some work to do in the office today before my first appointment tomorrow morning."

Nelson raised an eyebrow. "An attorney who works?" His light tone took the offense out of the question. "What type of law do you specialize in?"

Wythe grinned. "I'm not a litigator. My specialties are estates and some corporate law—a lot less messy most of the time."

Before they left, Wythe picked Wynter up and gave her a big bear hug. "Take care of yourself, spitfire," he said gruffly.

Irene caught an odd look, almost one of envy, on Nelson's face when he watched Wythe swing Wynter off her feet. Yes, there were undercurrents there, but she wondered about some of the undercurrents in her own life.

When they headed back to Virginia, Wythe was silent once more. He didn't dally on the back roads this time, instead taking the four lane highway north into Virginia. When they pulled up to Irene's trailer, Wythe hopped out and pulled her bag from the back. He carried it inside for her, refused an offer of coffee and headed for the door.

Then he almost made Irene fall through the floor. With eyes still on the door, he asked, "Would you have dinner with me tomorrow night?"

Oh Lord, Irene thought, *don't let me screw this up.*

"I would,Wythe."

He turned and smiled, looking relieved.

"I'd like that a lot," she finished, feeling shy.

"Great! I'll pick you up at six."

After he left, she stared at the door a very long time.

Chapter 19

"Is everything ready?" Wynter asked Mrs. Caudle for what felt like the hundredth time and then she shook her head. "I'm sorry. I know I'm bugging you."

Mrs. Caudle laughed. "No, dear. You're fine. I know you're anxious. It's been over a month since Mr. Nelson left on his business trip."

Oh, how well Wynter knew. He'd left the week following Mama and Wythe's visit. They'd shared a few days when Wynter felt they'd grown closer, but then he'd packed to go. He had kissed her and caressed her but had avoided taking her to his bed again, and Wynter had been too inexperienced to know what to do.

So he'd left on a trip that had taken him to places she'd only ever imagined. The worldwide trip had been designed to market Anderson Electronics' hardware and the wireless components they'd developed. He had sent postcards from most of Europe and Russia, and had emailed a few times a week. He'd called from Japan. That had been two weeks ago at Thanksgiving, and he'd sounded tired. Since then, she knew he'd traveled to Australia, New Zealand, Hong Kong and India.

Thomas drove to the airport to pick him up since Wynter had a final exam that conflicted with getting there. It didn't take her as long to complete as she had feared, so she could have picked him up, but she drove the farm truck back and forth between campus, and she doubted Nelson wanted to ride in that. He had wanted to buy her a car before he'd left, but she had protested until he had let it drop.

At last Wynter heard the car in the driveway. She had grand plans of showing Nelson how mature and sophisticated she now was. Wynter hoped it would change the almost avuncular way in which he had treated her since her mother's visit. In the end, she flew out the front door and jumped down the length of the ramp before she pulled open Nelson's door.

"Welcome home!" She gushed and grinned at him.

He smiled tiredly. Wynter realized just how exhausted he was when he made no protest about her helping him out of the car. Thomas carried his bags in the house, so Wynter wrapped an arm around Nelson's waist.

"Lean on me. You're tired."

"Your ankle…" Even his voice was hoarse with exhaustion.

"Is all better," she finished with a grin, "so lean on me." While they made their way up the ramp, she asked, "Do you want to go straight to the hot tub?"

He shook his head. "No. I want to say hello. I want to sit on my own furniture."

His eyes opened in surprise when he walked into the front hall and saw the big banner hung across the second floor balcony that said in Duke Blue "Welcome Home!" Tired as he was, Nelson still chuckled.

"You have way too much time on your hands, Wynter. Maybe I should have Thomas put you back to cleaning stalls."

She grinned at him again, feeling happy. Her head was still close, making it even easier to see the lines of weariness etched in his face. It would seem that even using a private jet with more room to move around couldn't erase the effects of more than a month of travel around the world.

Wynter didn't understand the sense of urgency in getting the trip completed before the beginning of the year, but Nelson said it must be done. Looking at him now, she wondered if the urgency was due to his health. That frightened the hell out of her.

"Let's go to the living room," she suggested. "It's closest. And Mrs. Caudle can just bring our supper in there."

The older woman fussed over him before saying she would see them in the morning. Thomas had long since returned to the barn office to finish up for the evening. As Wynter straightened up the tray Mrs. Caudle brought in, Nelson leaned forward and touched her hair.

She smiled at him, wondering what he wanted. He patted the stool in front of the chair. "Sit, Wynter and let me look at you." She sat, but felt heat spread over her cheeks as his gaze continued to take in everything about her. He reached out again, this time picking up her long braid and unraveling the thick locks. Wynter turned around and slid closer, so he didn't have to stretch so far. His fingers combed through her hair.

"I've missed this," he murmured while he continued to stroke.

"I missed you," Wynter admitted.

He might never be able to love her, she thought, but she would no longer fight what she felt. She had missed him so much while he had been gone, she'd ached. Mrs. Caudle never said anything, but Wynter knew the housekeeper was aware Wynter had crawled into Nelson's empty bed on many nights where the scent of him had still lingered, because it had soothed her to sleep when nothing else would.

Wynter felt his hand still just an instant before he resumed the gentle stroking. They stayed like that a long time, until she felt his hand still again. She turned her head, saw he had dozed off and studied his face as he slept. Faint circles rimmed his eyes, and he looked pale. She ached when she looked at him, wishing she could give him some of her own energy. Wynter wanted to let him sleep, but she was afraid to leave him where he was. He needed the hot tub and he needed his own bed.

"Nelson." She shook him when she called his name. Her hair fell in a curtain around their faces. "Nelson? Wake up."

His eyes opened and stared at hers. "Wynter? Are you real this time or just another dream?"

Her throat tightened. "I'm real," she reassured him.

"Good." Nelson seemed ready to fall back asleep, but she shook him again, gently.

"Please, Nelson, wake up. Let me help you to the hot tub."

He struggled to focus, closed his eyes again for an instant then opened them once more. Wynter smiled. Now she saw Nelson in those deep-blue depths.

"Thanks, sweetheart. I need that." He inhaled. She stood and offered her hands to him.

The hot tub looked inviting. After she twisted her hair up in a knot at the back of her head out of the way, she helped Nelson sit on the bench near the tub and undressed him. Wynter kept her mind blank while she removed his clothing. *The more impersonal, the better.* When she'd finished, she told him to wait so she could change, and she'd help him into the tub. It was a sign of just how exhausted he was when all he did was nod.

Once he was settled, Wynter started to move opposite him.

"No," Nelson murmured. "Stay here, next to me." His arm settled on the back of the tub behind where she sat. "Talk to me."

"About what?" Wynter giggled.

"Anything. I just want to hear your voice. How did your finals go?"

She was grateful for an impersonal selection, so she talked first about school then the horses. The Daltons had indeed brought their string of jumpers to the barn for Thomas and her to work. Their son and daughter each owned horses they would show in the children's jumper divisions, but there was one stallion in particular they'd wanted Wynter to campaign along with Rosie. When Wynter finished, she saw Nelson's eyelids droop again.

"Let me help you upstairs. As tired as you are, I'm afraid you'll fall asleep, and I won't be able to move you."

He shook his head as if to clear it and ran hands through his hair, fingers combing it away from his forehead. "Okay. Are my bags upstairs? I need some pain medication."

She jumped out of the hot tub, not even trying to hide herself when she dropped the wet towel and went in search of a robe. She brought one back for Nelson too. He managed to lever himself out of the tub. Wynter studied the strong muscles of his arms and back. Years of riding had given him a lot of strength, but it was obvious his upper body had grown even stronger out of necessity since the accident.

She left Nelson at the door and told him she would find his medication before stopping by her room to change. She found the medication in the study and noticed the miniature sitting there. He must have taken it with him on the trip.

When she returned, Nelson sat on the edge of the bed, clad in a pair of silky sleep pants, but his chest was bare. She handed him the pills and a glass of water.

"Do you need anything else?"

He set the glass aside and looked at her. His expression was so naked with loneliness, Wynter inhaled sharply.

"You. Will you stay with me?" he muttered. "At least until I fall asleep?"

She nodded and lay down. It was cool in the room and Nelson murmured, "Get under the covers, Wynter. I won't do anything to you."

She saw the pain pills making his eyes droop even more. She snuggled under the covers, breathed in the scent of him and sighed.

"That sounded happy," Nelson mumbled.

She smiled. She'd waited more than a month to inhale his familiar scent. "It is. I'm glad you're home. I missed you."

He put an arm around her and pulled her against him. She rested her head in the crook of his shoulder. "I missed you too, Wynter." His voice rasped against her ear. "You have no idea how much."

She tilted her head to look at him in the dim light, but his breathing had evened out. He was asleep. She touched his cheek. If he'd missed her just a fraction of how much she'd missed him each and every day that was more than enough.

"I love you, Nelson." She whispered the words, knowing he wouldn't hear them, but also knowing she must say them. She planned to stay just a few minutes longer before she returned to her room. But she never made it, falling asleep curled next to his warm, masculine body.

* * * *

At some point during the night, Nelson woke her up tossing and turning. He was restless, sweating and mumbling in sleep. She couldn't catch what he said, but whatever nightmare hell he was in ended when he flung an arm out, and a low keening moan pushed its way out of chest and throat.

"No!"

"Nelson," Wynter interrupted. "It's a nightmare. Wake up."

His eyes opened. For a moment, he was disoriented and then his tense, frightened expression relaxed with relief.

"Wynter. Oh God."

Her heart twisted when he grabbed her and crushed her to him. He whispered against her hair. "So real, so fucking real. We were driving to our house at Smith Mountain Lake. It was happening again, and I couldn't reach her. My baby." It started pouring out of him and once started, wouldn't stop.

"The car was upside down. I was pinned in my seat, and I still couldn't get to her. Allison was so scared and kept calling me, and I couldn't do a damn thing. I saw her face. She was so frightened. I talked. I told her how much I loved her, how everything would be all right, but it wasn't. It wasn't!

"It seemed like forever before anyone came. I shouted for help, but no one was there. And she bled to death. A piece of metal from the door severed her femoral artery, and she fucking bled to death! And the drunken, idiot teenager who caused the accident got off with a slap on the wrist for killing my daughter.

"It should have been me," Nelson railed. "Children aren't supposed to die before their parents, and she was just a baby."

Sobs racked his long body. It was painful to hear, painful to realize in the time since the accident he'd held the grief in check and never gotten it out. He held Wynter until she struggled to breathe. She stroked his face and chest, her own tears mingling with his. It hurt to hear him in such pain. Wynter continued whispering, soothing nonsense words, anything that came to mind to help him relax. At long last, he hugged her.

"Jesus! I'm sorry about this. It just came crashing in."

"It's okay, Nelson."

He wiped a hand across his eyes and swallowed. "Stay with me. I can't be alone, not tonight. I've already lost so much. I don't want to lose you too."

She saw the need in his face and knew he wasn't talking about her just staying with him through the night. It might never be love, but it would be enough. He might never say the words, but she would. And she would stay with him.

She gazed into his intense blue eyes. "I will never leave you, Nelson. I love you."

His eyes searched hers, and the tortured expression relaxed. Just before he grabbed her face with both hands to kiss her, he smiled. It was the most beautiful smile Wynter had ever seen. His tongue parted her lips, and he moaned against her mouth. His need was evident. His cock was hot and hard against her thigh.

When he started to undress her, Wynter smiled and pushed him back. The first streaks of dawn lightened the sky outside as she stripped the pants from him and bent over to kiss his flat, hard belly.

"Wynter, you don't…"

"I want to."

She circled his hard shaft and caressed him from his balls to the darker, swollen head. Her thumb brushed across the tip of him. He jerked in her grasp and moaned.

"I want you in my mouth," she whispered, staring at him.

"Yes. Oh, sweetheart. Whatever you want."

She brushed her tongue where her thumb had just stroked, then took him between her parted lips. Not sure if what she was doing was right, Wynter let the whispers and groans guide her.

"I'm going to come."

She lifted her face at his hoarse moan and smiled. "This is for you, Nelson."

His hot eyes met hers. "Stroke me. I want you to watch."

She moved her hand, stroking faster and concentrating on the tip until Nelson arched up toward her and cried out. His hands reached for her, pressing her against him while tremors shook the length of him. Resting her head against his chest, she listened to the rapid hammering of his heart until it slowed, and the trembling in the hand caressing her arm eased and steadied.

At last, he chuckled. "You're amazing, Wynter—a constant source of surprises. Give me a minute, and I'll be glad to return the favor."

She grinned at him. "I will so take you up on that idea."

They made love two more times before she heard the kitchen door open downstairs. When she shifted toward the edge of the bed, Nelson held her.

"Don't go, please," he pleaded. As if he thought she needed reassurance, he continued, "You have nothing to be ashamed of Wynter."

She smiled at him. "It's not that, Nelson. I promised a little girl I would come watch her ride this morning." She explained about the therapeutic riding center and meeting the girl in Raleigh.

"I'll take you," Nelson stated.

"That's okay. I know you must have loads to catch up on here. I can drive the farm truck."

"No. I'd like to go. Then we're going car shopping."

She brushed the hair back from his face and kissed him on the lips. The kiss heated up until Nelson eased her away.

"Go!" he said with a laugh. "Before we end up here all day."

She grabbed her t-shirt and shorts and sprinted out of the room, long hair flying loose around her.

* * * *

They arrived at the riding center about an hour later. It wasn't elaborate, but it was neat and tidy. The highlight of the farm was a large closed-in arena just beyond the house and barns. Nelson seemed tense when they got out. Wynter decided it must be concern over the uneven ground around the place.

The first person she saw when they walked inside the arena was Allison. She was already mounted on a chestnut pony with a long shaggy coat. The pony looked as though it had lived enough years to know more than most humans. While one person led the old gelding, another volunteer walked beside Allison, steadying her.

"Miss O'Reilly!" The girl grinned in delight. "You came! This is Sparky," she said, nodding at the pony. "Isn't he great? Come on down. They won't mind."

Wynter looked at the woman who ran the center, and she nodded with a smile. The woman's gaze turned to Nelson. It took her a second, but she seemed to recognize him, her eyes widening in surprise.

"Mr. Anderson. What a nice surprise. The arena has worked out well!"

Wynter's gaze swiveled to Nelson. She recalled the center's director saying their arena existed thanks to a generous benefactor. Nelson shrugged.

"I'll wait here," he said quietly. He nodded at the little girl. "What's your friend's name?"

Afraid of the pain the reminder of his own daughter might cause him, Wynter looked at him and said hesitantly, "Allison."

His face whitened for a moment. His sharp gaze jerked once again to the girl, and Wynter was relieved to see his color return.

They stayed for Allison's lesson, and before they left, Wynter promised to come again next week. She made her way back to the Rolls and saw Nelson stop the woman at the center. He handed her a check and picked his way back to the car. As he pulled out onto the highway, Wynter stared at his hawkish profile.

"You surprise me, Nelson. I'm used to people who want to brag about how they help the less fortunate."

"Don't make me out to be a saint, Wynter," he cautioned. "I'm anything but. Let's go find you a car." He turned and smiled at her, but there was an edge to it that didn't quite reach his eyes.

* * * *

An hour later, they stood in the showroom of a local import dealer. Nelson saw the sticker shock on Wynter's face when they first walked through the door, and he knew it would get worse.

"Black or green?" he asked while they looked at two BMW 6-series cars.

"Nelson!" Wynter protested, her green eyes glued to the sticker. "I don't need something like this."

She sure as hell needed something. Her truck was a deathtrap not worth the price of fixing. He wanted her to have something nice, not because of who he was, but because she deserved some luxuries.

"Wynter, it's just a car, and it's my money. Trust me when I say you won't bankrupt me."

Hell, he wasn't sure that was even possible.

She looked from him to the cars. Nelson knew the problem went back to her upbringing. Irene had taught her to pinch pennies until they screamed for mercy, yet he was getting ready to pull out the black AmEx. The only consolation was he doubted she knew what that meant. All the better. She would think he paid for it over time.

"Black or green?" he prompted again. The salesman stood nearby, keeping his mouth shut.

When Wynter turned her head and grinned at him over her shoulder, Nelson caught his breath. No matter how often he saw her flash that smile of hers, she took his breath away.

"Green. It's my favorite color."

He stared and then smiled at her. "Mine too."

The salesman promised to deliver the car the next day after they'd checked everything and cleaned it up. When Nelson handed the black card over, the man's eyes widened. He knew exactly what he held.

"Will you want the car in your name?"

Nelson shook his head. "It's hers. Wynter can sign the paperwork."

After they'd dotted the i's and crossed the t's, Nelson took her to lunch at a small restaurant near Duke's hospital. It was a favorite of his because it was so close to the offices where he'd spent a good deal of time and easy to get in and out of. Since the accident, he appreciated that a whole lot more than he once did.

The waiters knew him by name. It seemed everyone had cleared out from campus for the holidays, so the restaurant was half full. When they sat, Wynter looked around her with wide eyes.

"What's up?" Nelson asked. "Do you want to go someplace else?"

She shook her head. "No. This is fine. I," she hesitated. "To be honest, I've never been in a restaurant like this. Mama took me to Schoolfield Lunch once when I was a kid, but you just sat at the counter there."

"Schoolfield Lunch?" Nelson pictured a little hole in the wall.

"In Danville, right across from the mill. I mean Dan River Mill. It was a textile company. They're tearing it down now."

He thought of the places his parents had taken him as a kid. Ski trips in Colorado and Europe. Dinners at five-star restaurants in New York. He took so much for granted.

"They have a wonderful grilled salmon, Wynter, if the menu's too overwhelming."

She smiled with gratitude.

They had almost finished when John Holt came through the door with another man, Nelson's surgeon, Peter Wallace. This was not what Nelson had wanted, preferring to keep the surgeon on the back burner. Holt nodded and smiled when he saw Nelson and Wynter.

"What a pleasure to see you both again." Dr. Holt studied Wynter. "You look much better, young lady. Ankle giving you any problems?"

"No, sir."

"Have you met Nelson's surgeon?" Wynter's eyes swiveled to the other man, and she shook her head. Holt introduced them.

"I've heard a lot about you, Wynter," Peter Wallace told her with a small smile. Nelson coughed, but he saw Peter was going to be difficult. What a surprise. He'd already voiced his opinion about Nelson having delayed the final surgery. Peter arched one thick, blond brow as he turned light-green eyes to Nelson. "We're ready for you. The week after Christmas."

Nelson straightened the silverware. "Right."

The two men excused themselves and headed away from the table.

"What did he mean they're 'ready for you?'" Wynter asked. "Is anything wrong?"

Nelson shook his head reassuringly. "It's what I hope will be the last surgery on my leg and hip." He smiled and arched one eyebrow. "If it goes according to plan, it should make a lot of things a whole lot easier."

Wynter gaped for an instant then looked down at the table, making Nelson laugh. Several heads turned, including the two doctors'.

Chapter 20

Irene heard rumblings around the Butler home. It was amazing sometimes how people like the Butlers talked in front of the hired help as if they weren't even there. The Southards were just as bad if not worse. That was how Irene knew of some of the recent investments Payton Southard and Lance Butler had gambled on. All of them had gone bust.

She had been told she would get no Christmas bonus. Irene was disappointed since she had hoped to buy Wynter something nice. Instead, she was back to knitting. Wythe had helped her buy the yarn, telling her it was his way of pitching in on a gift for Wynter. It rankled—Wythe always coming to her rescue—but the years had also taught Irene to be practical and know when to keep her mouth shut and her pride stomped down. It just got old having to stomp so much.

The yarn she'd used for Wynter's gift was soft lime-green cashmere. The needles were so fine a gauge her hands ached at night, making it hard to sleep. But the finished product would be worth the pain.

She set the knitting aside when she heard Wythe's knock on the door. It was Saturday evening, and he'd volunteered to come by and bring dinner when she'd told him she was too tired to go anywhere. Dinner, either out at a restaurant or eaten as takeout, had become a regular occurrence.

So had Wythe's long looks. She had given up hope so long ago that he would look at her as anything other than a friend, she was now afraid to hope for anything else.

He pushed the door shut and smiled at her. His cheeks, which always seemed tan because of his olive skin, were rosy from the cold.

"Takeout from your favorite steak house!" He reached into the jacket pocket and produced a bottle of wine. "And wine—no screw top."

She laughed at him, feeling much better. When she started to stand to get plates, Wythe waved her away. "You've worked hard all week, I'll do it."

"Like you do nothing?"

He grinned. "Sitting in an office and staring out at Main Street in Danville is not slaving away."

She watched him, a smile on her face. Having Wythe visit was like having a large, boisterous puppy around because his outlook on life was always so sunny. Perhaps that wasn't fair, since she knew Wythe had another side. She had seen him deal with some tense situations over the years. Wythe possessed a cold temper and a razor-sharp tongue when he was angry. She was glad she had never been on the receiving end of it.

"Ready!" He held a chair out, and Irene smiled after she sat. She ate the vegetables and potato on her plate with blissful enjoyment, but left her steak knife next to her plate.

After a few minutes, Wythe asked, "Is there something wrong with your steak?"

"No." Irene picked up the knife, but she didn't have the hand strength to cut. Her fingers ached.

"Irene?" Wythe's voice was low and concerned. "Is it your hands again?"

She couldn't hide her surprise. *He knew?*

Without waiting for her response, he reached over, took the knife from her and cut the steak into bite-size pieces. Irene closed her eyes and tilted her head away. She hated depending on anyone for anything. The knife clattered on the table, Wythe's big hand turned her chin.

"There is no shame in getting help," he said.

He took both her hands in his huge palms, warming and cradling them, somehow knowing even rubbing them would cause her pain. She watched in shock when he raised her hands to his mouth and pressed his lips against her fingertips.

"You have beautiful hands."

She tried to slip them away from him, her breath coming out half on a sob. Her hands were ugly. Her fingers were rough and red, already showing effects of arthritis.

"Look at me," Wythe commanded. When she met his eyes, he continued, "I love everything about your hands. These hands worked hard for the love of someone else. You sacrificed these beautiful hands to raise a daughter. What could ever be wrong with that?"

She blinked at him several times and gave up. Tears slipped down her face while she stared at him. Wythe raised her hands once more, pressing them against his cheeks.

"I love your hands."

"Wythe?"

He jumped up and stalked to the kitchen area. When he returned, his expression was once more the jovial Wythe she knew.

"Sorry," he apologized.

She touched the sleeve of his sweater. "Don't be. I just…what's happening, Wythe?"

She couldn't stand where they were, but she didn't want them back where they had been either. What she was feeling must have shown on her face.

Wythe slid from the chair next to hers, kneeling in front of her while he braced arms on either side of her. His gaze locked with hers. "What's happening? Whatever you want to happen, Irene. I've been waiting for you since I was twenty-one years old. So you tell me. What is it you want?"

She must have misheard. He'd waited ten years for her? Irene had nursed him through a couple of college romances. He was still seeing Trish Staunton as far as she knew. So now he wanted her to believe he'd waited for her? She felt wary. This was not the Wythe she knew.

"That's not funny." Her voice thickened. "We've been friends too long for you to make fun of me."

Wythe leaned closer, brown eyes narrowed and serious. "I am not now, nor would I ever make fun of you."

"You've never…" She shook her head and tried again. "What about those girls in college? What about Trish?"

He dismissed them with a wave of a hand. "They were never you, but you never wanted me the way I wanted you. You treated me as a friend, a brother." He shook his head. "So I gave up and fell into that role."

He looked at her again, and Irene saw the depth of emotion there. "But I can't do it anymore, Irene. I don't want you just as a friend. I want you as a lover, in my bed and in my life."

She swallowed but couldn't think what to say.

"Tell me now if you don't feel that way," he ground out, "and I'll go. But if I leave, I won't be back. I can't do this anymore. I want more from you than friendship."

Life without Wythe? She couldn't even imagine it. He had kept her going during times when she had been down. He'd given her relief when raising a daughter like Wynter had overwhelmed her. He had always been there. Mustering her courage, Irene leaned forward and put her hands back to his cheeks. She pressed her lips against his, softly, tentatively and then had no idea where to go from there.

Wythe did. He pulled her closer and opened his mouth over hers. Irene responded and deepened the kiss. When her tongue touched his, he groaned and pulled his lips away from hers. Before she said anything, he swung her into his arms and carried her over to the couch. His strong hands shook when he stroked her hair and her arms.

"I've waited for this so long." His voice was hoarse with emotion.

She slid her arms up around his neck and buried her face against the firm, tanned skin there.

"Oh, Wythe." She sighed. "I think we've been at cross purposes."

"What do you mean?" he rumbled.

"I gave up hope you would ever see me as a woman."

He laughed. "I've never seen you as anything else."

She pulled back and accused, "You sure hid it well."

"*I* did?" he barked. "Every time I turned around, you put me in my place telling me what a wonderful friend I was. I got the message that was what you wanted."

She smiled at him. "Never."

"All those cold showers. All those nights of just me and my hand," he growled against her lips. "And I could have been here."

Hands more urgent this time, he pulled her hips against him. She felt the hard length of his erection push against his jeans.

"Irene?" His liquid brown eyes were warm and questioning.

At her nod, he stood with her in his arms. It frightened her how easily he picked her up. She'd never told him of her past with Wynter's father, Colin. She didn't want to remember the fear. Some of that must have shown on her face, though, for Wythe paused and stared into her eyes.

"Don't be afraid of me. I would never…will never…hurt you."

However, a few minutes later when she lay on the bed watching him, she was afraid he might break that promise. She trembled as she watched him strip. Almost eighteen years had passed since she'd been with a man, and Colin had never been concerned about her pleasure, let alone if she had been ready.

"Irene. This is me. Wythe." His quiet voice broke the silence in the room and penetrated her frightened thoughts. The bed shifted with his weight as he stretched out beside her. He cradled her in his arms, whispering her name, breathing compliments while he caressed her from head to toe, taking her clothes with him as he went. His lips and tongue traveled from her breasts to her belly and lower, parting her thighs gently.

"Wythe?" She gasped when his face hovered near her core. "I've never…"

"It's okay, sweetheart," he soothed. "Lie still. Let me taste you."

And he did. The intimate caresses drove her mad until she didn't know whether to pull him closer or push him away. She ran her fingers through his thick brown hair. *This was Wythe*, she marveled. *Wythe*. Her friend and her lover. He tasted her with lips and tongue, laving and suckling until she whimpered and arched up against him. Heat roared through her, spreading out from her swollen sex in tidal waves of pleasure she'd never before experienced.

When she thought she could stand no more, he shifted so he knelt between her thighs. His hands caressed up and down the outside of her legs.

"Irene?" he asked again. She held her arms out to pull him closer. With a groan he guided himself inside her. She sheathed him tightly, drawing another groan from him. His breathing was thick in her ear when he moved inside her. Wanting to melt beneath him, Irene wrapped her legs around him and pulled him closer still. His movements were slow at first, but then she tightened around him. Grasping her hips in his hands, Wythe thrust hard against her, picking up the pace until they gasped in release. She felt his cock jerk when he came deep inside her.

He rolled onto his back, carrying her with him.

"God, I've dreamed of that over the years," he said huskily, shakily. "And it was so much better than anything I'd imagined."

She stroked her fingers over the thick tangle of hair on his chest, imagining him touching himself while he thought of them together and felt a welling of heat yet again.

"I never knew it was like this," she murmured.

Wythe rolled onto his side and stared at her. "Marry me, Irene."

Irene's breathing stopped. She searched his face but saw nothing other than sincerity.

"You go from ten years of waiting for me to 'marry me' in one evening?" she teased.

Wythe shrugged. "I see no reason to wait. We've already waited ten years. So what do you say? '*Come with me and be my love.*'"

"Now you're being silly, Wythe." Irene laughed. "I don't remember the poet, but I do remember Wynter waltzing around the house quoting the poem."

Wythe touched her hair and traced a finger along her collarbone.

"Christopher Marlowe," he supplied. "'*And I will make thee beds of roses and a thousand fragrant posies,*'" he continued. "'*If these delights thy mind may move, then live with me and be my love.*'"

The last was said close to her lips as he once again kissed her—slow, drugging kisses that melted her from the inside out.

"Marry me," he murmured between nibbles of her lips and throat. Fingers stroked between the wet folds of her sex. "Marry me." Lips suckled her breast. "Marry me."

"Yes. Oh yes, Wythe!" She sighed when he drew her into his mouth.

He pulled her hips forward, his rampant erection pressing against her belly. "Soon, Irene. I want to hold you all night, every night. I want to pour myself inside you, feel you wrap yourself around me. I want to make babies with you. Beautiful babies with brown hair and hazel eyes."

For the second time in the space of a few minutes, her breathing halted.

"Wythe? Do you really?" Irene asked in wonder. She loved being a mother. It was the one thing she regretted—that Wynter would be her only child.

Wythe laughed. "I want as many babies as you will give me, and I don't want to wait. We've already waited too long. In fact," he said with a grin, "since we've already started, perhaps we should continue."

He rolled onto his back then lifted her and guided her down onto him. She gasped when she felt how ready he was again and then laughed when she moved her hips and heard him groan deep in his throat.

* * * *

When the phone rang the next morning, she was startled to hear Wythe's voice answer the call.

"Hello." He paused then looked over at Irene with a mischievous grin. "No, Wynter, there's nothing wrong with your mother." He ran a hand over her hip and squeezed. "In fact, I can tell you with certainty she feels just fine."

"Hand me that phone, Wythe Bradshear!" Irene ordered, feeling heat rise in her cheeks.

Wythe laughed, tossed her the phone and bounded out of the bed, naked as the day he was born. Irene had a tough time listening to Wynter as she watched him leave. His broad, muscular shoulders led down to a trim waist and narrow hips and long, long legs, muscles bulging from years of riding.

"What?" Irene said distractedly.

"Mama! You haven't heard a word I've said," Wynter accused from the other end of the phone line. "What is going on? Are you sure you're all right?"

"Yes," Irene replied. "Everything's wonderful. So what were you saying?"

"Nelson's having surgery the Tuesday morning following Christmas. He's inviting you both for the entire weekend, and I wondered if you could stay a couple of extra days just until he gets through surgery."

Irene heard the tension in her daughter's voice. Wynter hated to see anything hurt and could work herself into a state.

"Christmas is no problem, honey," Irene told her after Wythe came back in the room, still naked but now carrying two cups of coffee. "But I'll have to check with the Butlers to let you know about the rest."

Wythe grabbed the phone. "Whatever it is you're asking Wynter," he said with a laugh, "she can do it, and she doesn't need to ask the damn Butlers!"

"Wythe! You stop that swearing! No wonder my baby has a mouth like a marine sergeant!" Irene snatched the phone back, this time scowling at Wythe for real.

"Mama? What is going on?" Wynter insisted.

Irene heard that edge in her voice. She looked at Wythe who grinned, and she shook her head. She would deal with him and the whole matter of the Butlers later.

"Wynter," she soothed. "Everything is all right. In fact, it's more than all right." Irene glanced at Wythe who looked at her with so much love shining through his brown eyes it took her breath away...again. "Wythe and I are getting married."

She held the phone away from her ear when she heard a scream from the other end and then a clatter as if the phone had dropped.

"Irene?" It was Nelson speaking this time. "Is everything all right? Wynter is bouncing on the bed like it's a trampoline."

Bed? The thought swept through her. *Whose bed? Did it matter?* They were in the same room, just as she and Wythe were, she reminded herself.

"Wythe and I are getting married."

"Congratulations!" Nelson said. "When?"

"We haven't worked that part out yet," Irene said, before adding, "he just asked me last night." She talked to Nelson a few more minutes and before she hung up told him she would let them know something by the end of the day.

Wythe disappeared again. This time, though, he'd pulled jeans on over his lean hips. Irene showered and dressed and found him cooking breakfast. She raised one eyebrow at the number of dishes he'd already dirtied. She would have to keep him out of the kitchen. Even if he cooked, the mess he left behind was incredible. When they finished eating, Wythe reached across the table and took her hand.

"All kidding aside, Irene," he said soberly, "give your notice to the Butlers. You've worked long enough. Let someone take care of you."

The thought made her uneasy. Colin had wanted her at home. He'd made her dependent on him for everything—and then he'd left.

"I don't know, Wythe."

He smiled. "If someone told you, you didn't have to work anymore and could do anything you wanted, what would it be?"

The answer was easy. She'd thought about it many times. "I'd go back to school, Wythe. It's always bothered me not finishing high school and going to college."

He stroked her hand. "I can give you that opportunity. I want to. I make an excellent living at what I do, Irene. And it's not work to me because I enjoy it. Please let me give you that same chance to find what you enjoy." He paused and grinned at her rakishly. "And should you decide what you want to do is stay home and have my babies, that's fine too."

She laughed. "You might regret those words!"

* * * *

She gave her notice the next day. Lavinia Butler was aghast when Irene told her why. The look on Mrs. Butler's face said more clearly than words that it had never occurred to her Wythe Bradshear would ever look at Irene as anything more than a quick tumble in bed. Irene put her chin up.

"You'll be with us through Christmas, right?"

Irene looked her square in the eye and said, "No. I'm done, Mrs. Butler. I won't even be with you through today."

She stiffened. "I won't give you a reference."

Irene smiled and handed her the house keys. "Mrs. Butler, I don't need one. I hope you and your family have a pleasant holiday season."

As she walked to the car, Irene grinned. That had felt *so* good. After so many years of saying "Yes, sir" and "No, sir" just to keep a roof over her child's head and food on the table…that had felt wonderful. Irene told Wythe the very same thing when he bounded inside the trailer.

"Great!" He swung her around in a big hug then set her on the corner of the couch. "Stay there," he said while he fumbled in his jacket pocket. "I want to make sure I do this right."

He pulled a small box from his pocket and went down on one knee in front of her.

"Wythe, you don't…"

"Yes, I do, Irene. I've carried this ring for the last six years. It was one of the first things I bought after I got out of law school. I want to do this the right way."

He held the box open. Nestled on the dark blue velvet was a sparkling diamond set in white gold. It was simple and elegant.

"Irene O'Reilly, will you marry me?"

She nodded, speechless. Her hand shook while Wythe picked the ring up with large, lean fingers. Cradling Irene's hand, he slipped the ring over her finger. "Now," he said, grinning, "was that the right way?"

She smiled, tears of joy sliding down her cheeks. "There are romantic depths to you I would never have guessed. I will come with you and be your love."

He smiled. "Good, then you won't object if we pack your suitcases and you move in? I want you in my house and in my bed. No more nights without you."

Irene just laughed. It seemed they were making up for ten years of waiting in pretty short order.

Chapter 21

"They're going to be here," Wynter told Nelson after talking to her mother the next day.

He looked up from where he worked on the laptop. "That's super, Wynter. Have she and Wythe set the date yet?"

"No. They just keep saying soon."

Nelson turned off the laptop and closed it. "Why don't we invite them to get married here? Christmas Eve."

"Are you serious?" Wynter asked.

"Sure," Nelson replied. "They'll just need a North Carolina marriage license. I'll take care of the minister. You and your mom work everything else out—that is if they like the idea."

Wynter went around the desk to where he leaned back in his chair and gave him a hug. "That would be the best birthday present! Thank you! Thank you!"

"That's all you want?" he teased.

"It's more than enough. Why?"

Nelson shook his head and ran a lean hand over the top of the laptop. "No reason."

Wynter shook her head at him and left the room again to call her mother back. She and Wythe surprised her by jumping at the idea.

The next week and a half passed in a blur of activity. Wynter even forgot about her grades until Nelson pointed out they'd arrived in the mail. He quirked an eyebrow at her.

"Shall I?" he asked, waving the envelope in front of her.

Wynter glanced at it while she kept one eye on the florists decorating the hall with long strands of evergreen and holly. A twelve-foot tall Christmas tree already stood in the curve of the staircase.

"Sure, I don't think I'm in for any surprises."

Nelson tore open the computerized printout and glanced at its contents. He shook his head. "Wynter, Wynter!" he said in a chagrined tone. "You're slipping."

"What do you mean?" she asked, her attention now riveted on the envelope he held. She jumped up and snatched the paper out of his hands. After scanning its contents, she smacked him on the arm with it. "Nice try, Anderson! I have one 'B' in a required English Lit course!"

She glared at Nelson but found him laughing. "Finally, I get some attention. I was beginning to think nothing could get your nose out of these wedding preparations."

"Feeling neglected?" she asked with mock sympathy.

"Yes," Nelson said. "But we could work on that," he added suggestively.

Wynter glanced around at the florist and four assistants decorating the hall and the rest of the house too.

"Right now?" Nelson smiled. Wynter tugged at her earring. "Nelson, there are people everywhere!"

"I know one place they won't be." He grabbed her hand. "Come with me."

When they stepped inside the elevator, he punched the top button. The car didn't stop on the floor with the bedrooms. It continued up another level to what she assumed was the attic. The door opened onto a huge loft area that stretched almost the entire length of the mansion's main wing. Wynter looked around in wonder. Several dormer windows overlooked the outdoor pool and patio, but there were no windows on the front side of the house. A billiard table stood at one end of the room, while a huge home theater system dominated the other end.

"I haven't been up here in over a year, but I can assure you no one will disturb us."

Wynter laughed. "I guess not. I didn't even realize it was here. What is it? The man cave?"

He grinned and picked up a remote. Soft music surrounded them, coming from speakers placed around the room. Nelson returned and led her over to the large sectional couch. It was as deep as a bed. He put the cane aside and sat, pulling her halfway across his lap. His hands went to her long braid.

"I'm glad I'm the only one who sees your hair this way," he whispered when he ran fingers through the thick waves. He lifted several strands to his nose, inhaling deeply. "The scent of it, of you, is the best aphrodisiac I know of."

Wynter turned and rested her head against him. Her hands stroked his chest and circled his shoulders. She could stay like this forever, she thought, when his lips met hers. His kisses drugged her, creating a deep lassitude that made her feel weak and heavy at the same time. Nelson pushed her back into the pillows of the couch, one hand still wrapped in her hair while a free hand slid underneath the waistband of her pants and lower still until he found the nub of her clitoris. When she arched against him in need, Nelson chuckled low in his throat. He continued kissing her as his fingers stroked. When he slipped them inside her swollen passage, Wynter arched against him in sudden release.

"My, my, my," Nelson chuckled from just above her ear. "It seems I wasn't the only one wanting this."

She growled at him. He was in a playful mood today, so Wynter pushed him onto his back and helped him strip. Her clothes followed, adding to the tangle already on the floor. When he turned on his side, she pushed him back and straddled his hips.

"My turn now." She smiled and lowered herself.

* * * *

Mama and Wythe arrived the next day. When Wynter saw her mother get out of the jeep, she ran down to greet her. She had never seen her look like this. Irene's light brown hair was layered around her face, highlighting its heart shape and delicate bones. Her hazel eyes shone with warmth and joy. Wynter hugged her.

"Oh, Mama! We're so glad you're here. You look wonderful!" Wynter stepped back as Wythe joined her mother. When the two of them looked at each other it was like seeing two halves form a whole. Wythe couldn't take his eyes off Irene. It was as if after ten years of pretending they were just friends they now had to make up for lost time.

"I'm so happy for you both," Wynter told them.

Impulsively, she gave Wythe a big hug. He wrapped arms around her waist and lifted her off the ground, laughing as he swung her around.

"Just please don't start calling me Daddy." He grinned when he set her down. "At least not yet."

Nelson limped forward, smiling at Irene and Wythe. "Come inside. It's cold out here."

Wythe and Wynter picked up their bags and brought them in while Nelson took Irene's arm. He said something which made her smile and laugh. No, Wynter thought, she had never seen her mother so carefree.

"Let's get these upstairs," Wynter said when they came in the front hall. At the top of the stairs, she turned left.

She heard Wythe clear his throat behind her. "We can put them all in one room."

Wynter looked at him over her shoulder and laughed when she saw a faint tinge of pink in his olive cheeks.

"Wythe Bradshear!" she scolded in a horrified voice. "Are you living in sin with my mama?"

He coughed. Wynter laughed.

"It's okay. Mama told me she'd moved in with you and put the trailer on the market." Wynter paused as she set the bags down and gazed at Wythe. "How could I object?" she asked, gesturing around her. "I'm in no position to pass judgment. Besides," she said, smiling at him, "you've made Mama happier than I've ever seen her. Why did you wait so *damn* long?"

He barked with laughter. "Ever to the point, aren't you?"

She smiled tightly. "Not always. Maybe not as much as I should be."

She turned away, but Wythe touched her shoulder and turned her around.

"What's wrong?" he murmured. "Is it something between you and Nelson?"

"No," she said. "Don't pay any attention. I'm just being silly."

How could she tell him she envied her own mother? Irene had found a wonderful love with Wythe, one she could see was returned a hundredfold. Wynter loved Nelson, but most of the time she felt he treated her like another possession. Yes, he wanted her, he even needed her, but she wasn't sure he loved her.

Wythe hugged her. "Give him time, Wynter. Nelson Anderson still has a lot of ghosts he needs to put to rest."

Irene and Nelson were still in the hallway when Wythe and Wynter came back down the stairs. Irene was oohing and aahing over the tree and decorations. She looked up at her daughter as they came down the steps.

"Wynter, the house looks beautiful. Nelson tells me you oversaw this."

Wynter smiled, pleased at her praise. "I wanted it just right for tomorrow afternoon."

* * * *

And it was. Wynter helped her mama get ready. She wore a beautiful winter-white dress made of lightweight wool that floated to just below her knees. "Mama! This is so pretty," Wynter told her when she zipped up the back, laughing when her mother blushed.

"Wythe helped me pick it out." She looked at Wynter in the mirror. "He is the most wonderful man," she said softly. "I sometimes wonder if this is real. He quotes love poetry. Every time I turn around he's doing something for me."

Wynter smiled at her. *Wythe quoted poetry?* He always seemed like such a big, powerful take-charge type. Who would have guessed the heart of such a romantic beat inside him? But then, hadn't he waited ten years for her mother?

Wynter slipped her pearl pendant around her mother's neck and fastened the clasp. "There's your something borrowed," she told her. Irene touched the pearl studs in her ears.

"These can be the something old," she explained. "They belonged to Wythe's grandmother."

"Your dress is new." Wynter grinned at her and arched her brows. "And I've already seen your lingerie, Mama, you wicked thing. That's your something blue."

They both laughed. Irene looked Wynter up and down. She wore the dark green dress she'd worn to the Exhibitor's party. It had taken her some time, but she'd pulled her hair back in a sleek French twist. Irene smiled at her.

"You look lovely. Happy birthday, Wynter."

"Oh, Ma, this is the best birthday present you could give me." Wynter smiled through sudden tears. "Just seeing you so happy and radiant! Are you ready?"

She nodded and smiled at her daughter. Irene radiated beauty and confidence that Wynter had never seen before. She handed her mother a bouquet of camellias nestled in a bed of magnolia leaves and pine sprigs. Nelson stood waiting at the bottom of the stairs. He was dressed in a dark dinner suit, white shirt and pearl-gray silk tie.

"Allow me to do the honors," he said and extended an arm. He glanced at the pearl pendant around her neck then up at Wynter. He smiled with such gentleness she almost stumbled on the steps. She followed while he and her mother walked the few feet to Wythe.

The groom stood in front of the Christmas tree, next to the minister, a retired chaplain from Duke. Wythe's dark suit and white shirt mirrored Nelson's, but the tie he'd chosen was a green as deep as the magnolia leaves in her mother's bouquet. Wynter had often seen Wythe in formal fox hunting attire as well as business suits, and he'd appeared comfortable in both. But this afternoon, he looked ill at ease.

Nelson placed Irene's hand in Wythe's outstretched one before he stood at Wythe's right hand. She went to her mother's left and took the bouquet from her. When the minister began a simple and traditional service of marriage, she glanced at Nelson. He stared back, blue eyes veiled by half-closed lids. He was once again the remote Nelson Anderson whom she'd first met, his face betraying no emotion.

She swallowed, stared at the creamy camellias and listened while the chaplain read the familiar verses from the bible.

"Love is patient and kind, love is not jealous or boastful, it is not arrogant or rude. Love does not insist on its own way, it is not irritable or resentful, it does not rejoice at wrong but rejoices in the right. Love bears all things, believes all things, hopes all things, endures all things."

The minister asked for the rings, and Wynter slipped off her thumb the heavy gold band she'd been carrying. Irene's hand shook when she took it. Wynter glanced at Wythe, touched to see his eyes brimming with tears. Again, she felt a momentary stab of envy that her mother would know such devotion from a man. Then she reminded herself Irene had waited ten years for this.

When they exchanged the rings, Wynter watched Wythe slide one of them on her mama's finger, her eyes filling with tears. The two people she loved most in the world next to Nelson would now have a chance to bring happiness to each other after having waited so many years.

She realized Wythe and Mama were kissing. As Nelson clapped Wythe on the back and smiled at him, Mama turned to Wynter.

"Congratulations, Mama," she said. "If ever there are two people who deserve all the happiness in the world, it's you and Wythe. You both have given me so much, and now you've given me the most beautiful birthday present ever."

Wythe turned and heard the last. Clasping Wynter's face in between large hands, he bent forward and pressed lips to her forehead.

"It's me who owes you, Wynter, because without *you* we might never have met."

Nelson led the way to the study where Mama and Wythe signed the marriage license along with the minister, and then Nelson and Wynter witnessed it. The minister declined a drink, saying he still had evening services and didn't think anyone would forgive his having liquor on his breath. So Nelson escorted him to the front door while Wythe poured drinks for everyone else in the living room. Mrs. Caudle laid out a small buffet in the dining room, including a delicious-looking homemade cake to go with it.

When everyone had finished, Nelson looked at Wythe and Irene. "The small fishing cabin on the pond on the other side of the property is all ready for you," he said and smiled at them. "I thought perhaps you might enjoy some privacy. Your bags are in the back of your jeep, Wythe. You're welcome to stay there as long as you like."

Wynter smiled when Mama's cheeks turned pink, and Wythe laughed. "Don't worry about Christmas morning, Mama. We'll understand if y'all aren't here at the crack of dawn!"

Her breath hitched as she watched Wythe pick up her mama and carry her out to the jeep. Thomas or someone had written *Just Married* across the back windshield. Wynter waited, watching until she no longer saw the taillights. Even then she was reluctant to go in, reluctant to face some of the questions about her relationship with Nelson.

"Wynter," he murmured from just over her shoulder. "It's cold. You should come inside."

She nodded and brushed past him. She would have headed for the stairs, but he stopped her.

"Don't go yet." His words were quiet and firm. "Come back to the sitting room."

She waited for him, her head bowed. She had experienced too many emotions and felt drained. Watching her mama and Wythe had made her happy but also sunk in despair. They'd met as equals, both giving and receiving. All she did was take. Nelson had provided her with a job, a house, a car. She'd also discovered he was behind her scholarship. Every stitch of clothing she wore came from him. And what did she give him in return? Nothing.

She followed him to the small sitting room off the study, but she was restless. She paced the room from the windows that overlooked the woods, to the French doors that led to the back terrace and down to the pool. Nelson poured two glasses. Whisky for him, sherry for her.

He handed her a glass and then sipped his drink while he stared at her over the rim. "What's wrong, Wynter?"

She looked away, unwilling to meet his eyes. "Nothing."

"Bullshit!" he snapped.

She ran a hand over her sleek hair and rubbed her neck. "I guess it's just been an emotional day. As happy as I am for Mama and Wythe, I feel drained." She looked at Nelson. "I know that doesn't make sense."

Nelson set the glass down and pulled her against him. He bent his head and kissed her on the lips. It was more a kiss of comfort than passion.

"I have something for you," he murmured. "Turn around."

Wynter turned her back and felt something cool nestle between her breasts while Nelson's nimble fingers fastened the clasp at the back of her neck. A diamond heart on a chain as fine as gossamer. "It's beautiful," she murmured dutifully as one small, hot tear dropped onto her chest and slid down underneath the diamonds and in between her breasts. "Thank you, Nelson."

"You're beautiful. Happy birthday, Wynter."

Nelson pulled her back against him, his hands sliding over her shoulders, cupping her breasts. She swallowed the sob that rose in her throat. She didn't feel beautiful. She felt like the trailer trash she'd been called all her life. Lowering her eyes so Nelson wouldn't see what she was feeling, she turned and wrapped her arms around his neck. She kissed him with a desperation that was very real.

"Wynter?" His tone was soft and urgent at the same time. His hands pulled her hips against him, fitting her to him while he once again kissed her. Wynter broke off the kiss and led Nelson down the hall to the elevator and up to the master bedroom.

They made love urgently, passionately. Nelson praised her body, told her how much she excited him, how much he needed her, wanted her, but never that he loved her. She met his urgent thrusts with equal urgency until they both lay gasping in a tangle of sheets. After he fell asleep and his breathing evened out, Wynter rose from the bed and wrapped herself in a long silk robe. She curled up in a chair near the windows overlooking the terrace off the bedroom. The moon was just a sliver in the sky, making the stars stand out even brighter here, away from the lights of the city. As she looked out, silent tears rolled down her cheeks.

She wouldn't leave Nelson. She loved him. No matter how long it took him to bury the ghosts that haunted him, she would stay with him. Wynter swiped the back of her hand across her eyes. There were other things in her life going right. School. Riding. Maybe that would be enough. After all, she admitted, sex with Nelson was incredible. She sighed and stood. Her fingers went to the diamond heart she still wore on the chain around her neck. Love bears all things, believes all things, hopes all things, endures all things. It was something to hold onto. Maybe her love would be enough for both of them.

Wynter walked back to Nelson's side. In sleep he looked so much younger. He'd endured a lot for his thirty-three years. The loss of a wife and child. Injuries that might have killed another man. Yet he ran not only Pheasant Run but a multi-national corporation. Perhaps there were depths to him she hadn't yet explored.

In less than two days, he would undergo yet another surgery, this time to replace the damaged joint in his right hip. She knew he held hope for big changes from this surgery, and she prayed he would get what he wanted from it. Either way, she would be there for him.

Chapter 22

"Merry Christmas."

The words were a whisper in her ear the next morning. Wynter stretched languidly. Although she didn't remember it, she must have fallen back asleep. Nelson's right hand caressed the curve of her hip before reaching around to massage her bottom. She smiled through the tangle of hair wrapped around them, banishing the shadows from the night before. Brushing the hair from her face, she smiled at him and promised herself she would not spoil Christmas.

The shadows disappeared when he looked into her eyes and his fingers slipped across her belly. Wynter sighed and closed her eyes as he touched her softly, teasingly, between her thighs. She lost herself in this man with such ease it was frightening.

He was in no rush this morning. He took time kissing her face and mouth with light, teasing touches while fingers aroused her and made her want even more. She slid her hand over his flat, taut stomach, until she felt the engorged length of his cock. Her hand moved up and down his shaft, drawing a muffled groan from him.

"Stop, Wynter," he urged. "I don't want to rush things."

This time when he kissed her, his mouth parted hers and their tongues tangled in a long, deep kiss that left them both breathless. He rolled onto his back, pulling her on top of him. His slow caresses continued from her hair to her breasts to her hips. His hands parted her thighs so she could straddle him. When she started to guide him inside her, he stopped her again.

"Not yet," he commanded, long elegant fingers once again moving cleverly, caressing her between her thighs until she collapsed forward onto his chest with a moan of pleasure.

"Now," he whispered and lifted her onto his hard shaft. She rotated her hips against him.

"Slowly, Wynter, unless you're ready now."

Her answer was to tighten the muscles of her stomach when she leaned forward, branding his lips with her kiss.

It was late morning before they stirred from the bedroom. Nelson dressed in khakis and a soft cashmere pullover. Her favorite old jeans were mighty tempting, but she fought the urge and instead pulled on a pair of black leggings and a bulky fisherman-knit sweater. While she made sandwiches from the cold cut tray in the refrigerator, she heard Nelson answer the phone in the study, a short conversation then the tap of the cane as he walked down the hallway.

"You might need a few more sandwiches—your mother and Wythe are on their way over." He chuckled. "Do you just want to wait until they get here to open gifts?"

She nodded and gave him a brief smile. She wasn't sure how her gift would go over. She hoped with all her heart it would be okay. It took everything she'd saved up for a computer to get it for him. Oh, she knew he would have given her whatever money she needed, but Wynter liked having her own money. Nelson walked across the kitchen and stopped right behind her. He reached around her and grabbed a couple of olives and popped them in his mouth.

"Ugh!" she said, disgusted. "You eat those things?"

Nelson nodded and grinned. "Have you ever tried one?" At the vehement shake of her head he laughed. "Wynter, you should never knock something before you've tried it." He picked up an olive and moved closer.

"Nelson. No!" she cried and tried to back away, but the counter hemmed her in. His blue eyes danced with devilment. "Don't you dare."

"Just try it," he coaxed. "You like salty foods, you might just like this." He held it against her lips. "Be adventurous, Wynter."

She opened her mouth to protest and his fingers brushed her lips when he popped the olive inside. After her initial shock, she let it sit on her tongue a moment before she chewed. "Mmm. These aren't half bad."

They'd managed to feed each other most of the olives on the cold cut tray before she heard the doorbell. She slipped out from between Nelson and the counter and hurried to the door.

If possible, Mama looked even more radiant. Wythe grinned from ear to ear and looked over Wynter's shoulder to Nelson. He winked at him conspiratorially. "That item we discussed is in the back of the jeep."

"Will it be all right there for now?" Nelson asked. "I thought we'd save that for last."

"Shouldn't be a problem," Wythe supplied as he shut the door with a foot, balancing the gifts he carried in his arms.

While Nelson and Wythe went to the living room with the gifts, Irene and Wynter went to the kitchen to get the food. When the two women paused by the counter, Wynter glanced sideways at her mother. She looked so much younger. It startled her to realize Irene was still a young woman—she'd just never had the chance to show it. Plenty of women her mother's age were just starting to think about marriage, not dealing with a grown-up daughter.

"Merry Christmas, Mama." Wynter gave her a hug. "You look so happy."

She squeezed her back. "I am, Wynter. Unbelievably happy. Now I want my daughter the same way."

She ducked her head. "Does it show?"

"Only to me. I know you too well, honey. Just make sure you're not bringing your unhappiness on yourself."

"What do you mean?"

Her mother stroked a stray strand of hair from her face. "It's easy once you find something wrong to continue until you find everything that's wrong. Stop and think of the positive things. You might find there are more than you think."

Wynter nodded. She didn't want to talk about it, not even to Mama. She felt childish and selfish resenting Nelson. She knew he cared for her at some level. It would be enough. It must be.

When Wynter and her mother reappeared, the two men were seated near the family tree in the living room talking basketball. After everyone had eaten their fill, Nelson looked at Wythe. "Would you mind passing out gifts, Wythe? My leg won't let me get down there, at least not yet."

Wythe sat and handed Irene a gift from Nelson and her. He handed Wynter a large soft package from her mama. Irene exclaimed over the pearl pendant designed to match the one Nelson had already given her. Wynter unwrapped the package from her mother. Inside was a soft green cashmere sweater. Her eyes flew to her mother's hands. She knew how much her mama's fingers sometimes ached, and to have knitted this on such a fine gauge must have been torture.

"Oh, Mama," Wynter choked. "This is beautiful!" She slid off the stool where she was perched and knelt in front of Irene's chair. She lifted her mother's hands and pressed her forehead against them. "You shouldn't have!" she said, massaging them.

"I wanted to, Wynter. It was a labor of love."

"I'm going to put it on right now!" She jumped in surprise when everyone said at once, "No!"

At her startled expression, Nelson said blandly, "You might want to wait until after we've opened the other presents."

Wynter shrugged and retrieved the package she had for Nelson. She could tell from his expression it was heavier than he expected, and his eyes widened. Wynter sat back down on the stool, studying him while he opened the wrapping. She saw his gaze dart her way when he saw the name on the outside of the box. His fingers almost caressed it as he pulled the camera body out to examine.

"Good heavens, Wynter," he said as he stroked the camera. "Where on earth did you find this?"

"Is it okay?" she asked. "I talked to the photography professor in the arts department. He helped me find it."

Nelson attached the lens and looked through the viewfinder. "It's gorgeous." He set the camera aside and pulled Wynter onto his lap. "First the miniature, now a digital camera." He kissed her on the cheek. "You have a unique talent for finding gifts, Wynter. How did you know?"

She stroked the soft sweater still resting on her lap. "Mrs. Caudle told me you used to shoot a lot of pictures. I thought maybe this might get you going again. I love the photos you have hanging on the wall." She smiled at him. "You have a gift for capturing people through the eye of the lens. I charged the batteries and everything, so you can go ahead and use it."

Nelson smiled. "I might just do that."

Wythe handed Wynter a couple more boxes. There was a laptop computer from Nelson along with a cellphone. She half-paid attention when Nelson explained the phone's capabilities. He said something about satellites and being able to locate the phone, but Wynter wasn't listening. She was so relieved and happy he'd liked the camera. Finally, when the boxes were unwrapped, Nelson looked over at Wythe and Mama.

"What do you think? Should we go outside and get the last present?"

Wynter walked next to Nelson as everyone returned to the front hallway. She noticed as they went out the front door he carried the camera with him. She was about to comment on it when she heard a mournful cry from the back of the jeep, followed by a couple of high-pitched yips.

"Someone's not too happy," Wythe said.

"By all means," Nelson said as he stepped back to balance against the car, "let's not wait any longer."

"Wait right there." Wythe pointed to Wynter as he went around to the back of the jeep. She saw him lift the hatch, and when he came back around the side, he set down a wriggling mass of fur and energy.

"Call her," Nelson said a little nervously. "She's yours, Wynter. Merry Christmas. I hope you like her."

She looked at them in wonder then fell to her knees. *A puppy.* Nelson had bought her a puppy!

She called, and the pup spun and raced toward her. She was black and tan with curly hair and a clown of a face. Wynter laughed when the dog jumped on her and lapped her cheek. She wore a red and green bandana around her neck. Wynter jumped up and ran around the front driveway with her, laughing as the puppy stumbled over her big feet.

Wynter stopped fifteen feet from Nelson, winded, and smiled at him. "Oh, Nelson, thank you. I always wanted a dog, but we never had the money. What breed is she?"

Nelson lowered the camera and smiled back at her. He looked happy, hair tousled and cheeks red from the cold.

"An Airedale. She'll get pretty big, so you'll need to spend some time teaching her manners."

"She's beautiful," Wynter said and ran over to Nelson to wrap her arms around his neck and give him a hug before kissing him all over his face. "I love you, Nelson Anderson!" she declared and danced away from him again to the puppy. It was the best Christmas ever.

* * * *

It was evening when Wythe and Mama looked meaningfully at each other and made their excuses. They would see them at the hospital the next day. It was like a splash of cold water, the reminder Nelson would be undergoing major surgery. Wynter nodded and hugged them both when they left, then she and Nelson made the puppy comfortable in a covered kennel in the back of the house by the garage. He said it had been there for several days, but Wynter hadn't noticed it. She was still running in the mornings but along the road instead of in the woods. So she hadn't been back behind the house this last week before Christmas.

Wynter hated leaving the pup out there, but Nelson insisted. The dog would have to stay outside until he recovered from this latest surgery. He'd already told her what would happen during the operation, and she knew his recovery would take some time.

It was still dark outside when Nelson shook her awake. After tossing and turning the night before, she had fallen into a very heavy sleep. She struggled to remain alert, but a bad night's sleep didn't help. On top of that, Nelson was tense and snappy as they negotiated the narrow highway to Durham.

They left his duffel bag in the car for after the surgery when he would be settled in a room. Wynter walked by his side. Tension radiated from him, and his face was pale. The nurse started to suggest she stay in the waiting room, but at Nelson's quiet but insistent "No," she acquiesced.

He was nervous and trying to hide it. A slight tremor in his hands while he donned the hospital gown gave him away. Silently, Wynter folded his clothes before helping him onto the bed. His chiseled profile was harsh in the glare of the fluorescent lights overhead.

The nurse reappeared a short time later and handed him a pill and a glass of water.

"This will help relax you before surgery. Dr. Wallace should be in shortly, followed by the anesthesiologist." Her tone was brisk and matter-of-fact. She glanced at Wynter. "Are you staying with Mr. Anderson until he goes into surgery?"

"Yes," Nelson answered before Wynter even opened her mouth. She smiled at the nurse who surprised her by grinning and winking. Wynter covered her mouth to hide her own grin. After all, Nelson could see her, and right now he was glaring.

The nurse turned back. "That pill will take effect in just a couple of minutes. You might find yourself getting a bit sleepy or a little happy… like being tipsy."

The room was silent a moment after she left, then Wynter crossed over to Nelson's side, taking his lean hand in her own and stroking the back of it.

"Thank you, Wynter," he murmured. "Thanks for coming with me this morning."

She smiled and brushed the dark, gray-streaked hair away from his face. Always so serious. She wondered if he would ever be as lighthearted as Wythe, but she doubted it. Nelson had carried a heavy burden of responsibility for a long time.

"I wouldn't be anywhere else." She kissed him on the lips. Nelson's other hand went to the back of her neck to hold her there. In his grip, she felt the need he couldn't put into words.

"Okay, none of that," a deep voice said behind them.

Wynter jumped back to see Peter Wallace enter the room. He was dressed in scrubs with a loud polka-dotted surgical cap covering his hair. "Nelson, you're supposed to be relaxing."

Nelson grinned. "That was relaxing."

His words were just a bit slurred. Wynter looked at him again, her eyebrows raised, and he chuckled lazily.

"I see the drugs are working," Dr. Wallace said. "Have a seat, Miss O'Reilly. I'll run through what will happen this morning."

Wynter sat in the chair next to Nelson, whose hand stroked her long braid. Dr. Wallace sat on the exam stool and crossed his long legs.

"After I'm done in here, the anesthesiologist will explain that part of the surgery. They'll also insert the IV's, so all we have to do is connect when we get to the OR. I'm estimating the surgery will take four hours, give or take. A normal hip replacement I could accomplish in half that time, but we have a couple of challenges here. First, because of the amount of muscling around Nelson's hip and thigh, I'll make a larger incision and move muscle out of the way instead of cutting and reconnecting after the replacement joint is in. So that will require some more time. Secondly, because of the trauma he's already suffered, we must be very careful. Do either of you have any questions?"

Nelson shook his head, but Wynter asked, "How soon after surgery may I see him?"

"It's up to Nelson," Dr. Wallace said, "but we let family in to be there when a patient wakes up."

Family. She looked at Nelson, wondering just what he'd told Peter Wallace. Nelson was getting sleepy. He smiled at her. "I like having you there when I wake up."

Wynter felt herself blush as both Nelson and Peter Wallace chuckled. Dr. Wallace extended a hand to her and shook it. "I'll come out to the waiting room as soon as we're through and let you know how things went."

She nodded. The surgeon waved when he walked out the door. After the anesthesiologist finished his explanations, the nurses prepared Nelson to leave. He reached for Wynter's hand, blue eyes unfocused.

"You won't leave? You'll stay, won't you Wynter?" His voice was hoarse. "And you'll be there when I wake up?"

"Yes," she reassured him. "I'll stay, Nelson. I'd go in there with you if they'd let me."

He smiled sleepily.

"You can walk along with us until we get to the OR," one of the nurses offered. Wynter smiled at her, keeping hold of Nelson's hand as they went along the hallway.

He stared at her the whole time, his lids drooping over midnight-blue eyes. "Beautiful," he murmured groggily. "So beautiful. Never leave me. My Wynter spring." His voice trailed off, and his eyes drooped even more.

Wynter's throat was tight. "Never, Nelson. I'll never leave you." She released his hand when they wheeled him through the doors of the operating room and then bit her lower lip when the doors swung closed with a vacuum-like whoosh. Wynter hugged Nelson's clothes as she searched for the surgical waiting area. It was almost an hour later when her mama and Wythe came in. The tension was too much. She burst into tears when she saw them. Mama hugged her while Wythe went to get coffee for everyone.

"It's a routine surgery, Wynter," Mama reassured her. "Nelson will be just fine. You'll see."

"I know," Wynter said. "I just hope it does everything he hopes it will."

Just over three hours later, Peter Wallace pushed through the doors to the waiting room. He smiled when he saw Wynter and strode over to where they sat. Wynter introduced him to Irene and Wythe. The surgeon shook hands then turned his attention back to her.

"Nelson's in recovery right now. I'll send a nurse in just a few minutes to take you up there."

"How did the surgery go?" she asked hesitantly.

"Very well," Wallace reassured her. "It would have been easier from a surgical standpoint to have done it when I suggested last February. But the flip side is he has increased his leg strength since then, so I expect a faster recovery."

"How long will he stay in the hospital?"

"About four days. We'll see how he does. Then he has rehab. I keep most patients here for that, but Nelson can go home. A therapist will work with him there daily, and I understand you can also help him, so doing rehab at home is no problem. The pool will provide some excellent exercise."

Peter Wallace glanced at the clock on the wall and stood. "I need to check on him and a couple of other patients. I'll send a nurse to take you to him."

Wynter smiled when she shook his hand. "Thank you, Dr. Wallace."

A few minutes later, she grasped Nelson's bed rails. He looked so young, so defenseless. She brushed the hair back from his forehead then let her hand linger against his cheek. He was turned to take pressure off the incision, and his legs were wedged and propped to keep everything in position for the time being. She sat in the chair near the bed and stroked a long-fingered hand where it lay on top of the covers.

"Wynter?" His voice was hoarse, little more than a whisper.

"I'm here," she murmured. "How are you feeling?"

"Drugged. And my throat hurts."

She held his hand up and pressed her face against it. He smiled at her. "Thank you for being here, sweetheart."

Her smile was shaky. "I told you, Nelson, I'll never leave you."

Chapter 23

Irene was torn in the days that followed Nelson's surgery. She wanted to stay with Wynter, but she didn't want to leave Wythe. He needed to get back to his law practice, but he didn't say a word. Wynter spent most of the days at the hospital with Nelson, so Wythe and Irene looked after her new puppy, which she'd named Bouncer. Wythe took the puppy with him for long runs, teaching her how to run with someone without interfering.

Nelson had explained he'd bought the puppy to be more than just a companion. He'd admitted he hoped the dog would help provide some protection for Wynter. Irene had seen the uneasiness on his face when he'd confessed he'd pulled the bodyguards tailing her because being watched had upset her so much.

"I must face facts," he'd told them. "My position and wealth make me a target, and it makes those I love a target too. A bodyguard used to go everywhere with Lindy and Allison unless I was there. I would have done the same for Wynter, but she's so independent."

"You mean stubborn," Irene had interjected.

"You said it, not me. Airedales have a reputation for being protective of their family without being aggressive in nature, so I hope she'll fill the bill of bodyguard as she gets older, without frightening friends off."

Nelson had smiled, but Irene sensed he was bothered.

Wythe went with Wynter to bring Nelson home from the hospital. They left early, driving the Rolls since it would be easier for Nelson to get in and out. Irene stayed behind and spent the morning in the kitchen with Mrs. Caudle, making soup and sandwiches for later.

Irene liked the housekeeper. It was obvious she cared not only for Nelson, but for Wynter too. And that alone made Irene like her.

Mrs. Caudle was also a rich source of Anderson family history. Irene found out Nelson had taken over the company just after graduating high school, when his parents had been killed in a skiing accident. He'd worked on a business degree at Duke while running Anderson Electronics under the close eye of the vice-presidents—men who'd been with the company since it had started. He'd pushed Anderson Electronics toward specializing in computer components, fighting a board of directors that laughed at the pronouncement that within fifteen years almost every household in America, if not the world, would have at least one computer in the home.

No wonder the man was already gray, Irene thought. He possessed incredible drive and vision to have brought the family company to the forefront of home computer hardware.

Mrs. Caudle also shared a couple of things about Nelson's marriage. Lindy had been the daughter of a neighbor. The two had started very much in love, but the last year of the marriage had been rocky. Nelson had traveled a lot, and Lindy had been lonely. She had wanted to travel with him, but Nelson had felt one of them should be home with Allison. It didn't work quite as he'd hoped. She'd spent a large amount of time with her nanny because the active little girl had overwhelmed Lindy. The Smith Mountain Lake trip had been an attempt to get away from things and work out some of their problems. Lindy had wanted to leave the baby behind, but Nelson had insisted she come because he had seen so little of her.

Irene shook her head. What a terrible load of guilt he must carry. Not only had he been unable to help Allison after the accident, but had he not insisted she come along, she would still be alive. Irene's eyes welled up with empathy.

She looked at her hands with their crooked fingers. Irene knew firsthand just how far a parent would go to protect and nurture her child. She'd never told Wynter how close she'd come to feeling Colin's out of control temper. Irene had hidden how abusive her marriage was. Wythe had known some of it, but just recently she'd shared it with him. She'd seen the anger in him when he'd listened, but Wythe was also a practical man. Nothing could be gained by that anger. As far as she knew, Colin O'Reilly might be dead. He'd never contacted her in the years since he'd left. Instead of storing up anger, Wythe had caressed her and told her he would always protect her.

The sound of the car brought Irene out of her reverie. She smiled at Mrs. Caudle before she hurried to the front door. Irene wasn't sure what she expected, but it was a bit of a shock to see Wythe lift Nelson out of the car and put him in a wheelchair. Some of what Irene felt must have shown in her expression.

Nelson smiled. He looked tired, but his eyes shone with a resolve she hadn't seen before.

"Don't worry, Irene. This is just temporary. I can get around on my own two legs, just not very far yet."

She smiled back in relief. Wynter came around the car and popped the trunk.

"We have all sorts of toys to play with over the next few weeks, and the therapist will be here tomorrow."

She watched Wynter hover around Nelson. Her daughter was reluctant to fuss but seemed overwhelmed with her need to do so. She was right to hold back. Nelson wouldn't like being fussed over. He'd accused Wynter of being independent, but he was just as bad.

The two of them were the most stubborn people Irene had ever met. They still hadn't worked out everything between them. The tension in the air was as obvious as a neon sign flashing over their heads. They would find their own way, just like Wythe and she had.

Once Nelson was settled in the sitting room, Wynter excused herself.

"I'm going to see Bouncer then go for a run since it's warmer today."

"I'll join you," Wythe added and grinned. "And you can bring Bouncer too. I've been working with her so she can run with you."

"Thanks, Wythe," Wynter said with obvious pleasure.

That left Nelson and Irene in the room alone. He was quiet and tired from the activity of returning home and getting settled.

"Can I get you anything?" she asked.

He shook his head. "I'm just glad to be home. I feel drained."

"You should. This has been tough."

Nelson looked at her, his expression serious. "I did it for Wynter."

"Pardon me?" Irene looked at him with eyes wide.

Nelson's mouth twisted. "Peter Wallace wanted me to have this surgery last spring, and I told him no. I didn't care if I spent the rest of my life crippled and in pain. Then your daughter showed up..." He paused, his expression softening. "I had to laugh. It was like spring walked through the door when I saw her, and her name was Wynter.

"She was so vibrant, so driven, so defensive. Before I knew it, I was watching her and wondering about her. I saw her brochures and paperwork for Duke. I made a few phone calls to open some doors for her, but she didn't need my help getting in."

Irene nodded. She knew what Wynter's test scores and grades were like. They'd opened doors by themselves and made people find ways to pay for her education.

"I soon discovered she didn't need much help with anything, nor did she want it." Longing was plain on his face. "But I want to give it. Wynter makes me feel alive again. I didn't realize just how much I'd shut myself off from everything and everyone until she arrived."

Irene studied his profile as he glanced out the window. Over the years, she'd found it was best to be open and honest, and she intended to do that now.

"You say you want Wynter, you need Wynter, but do you love my daughter, Nelson?"

His expression when he turned was an answer in itself, but when he spoke, Irene understood some of the hidden depth to their relationship.

"More than I ever thought possible, Irene. I love her with every breath I take, but she's so much younger than me. I will *not* tie her to a cripple, so until I know for sure this is a success..." He glanced at his hip, fist clenched at his side. "I won't tell her."

As tempting as it would be to tell him just how much Wynter adored him, it was not her place. They would work things out on their own. It was obvious Nelson looked at the surgery as a way to become whole again. Although Irene knew Wynter never looked at him as being anything less, *he* did. She prayed it would do what he'd hoped.

Wythe and Wynter returned an hour later. Both were rosy from the cold and disheveled from their run, but their eyes sparkled. Irene smiled but saw a twinge of jealousy in Nelson's expression.

Wythe shared a special relationship with her daughter, a degree of communication that was unspoken and deeper, as if at some level they were kindred souls. But it had never bothered her. They were like father and daughter, despite the small difference in age. Wythe looked at ease, and for the first time since they'd come to visit, Wynter looked calm.

She protested when Irene told her they must get back the next day. Wythe explained they would be going to his parents' house to break the news of the marriage. She swallowed nervously, but she had met his parents once or twice over the years and knew they were as easygoing as Wythe. Nelson surprised everyone by inviting them back at the end of January for the Carolina-Duke game.

"I hope to be moving pretty well by then," he added.

This night, though, he was tired. When his eyes drooped, Wynter urged him to let her help him upstairs. As they left the sitting room with instructions for Wythe and Irene to enjoy themselves as long as they liked, she turned to Wythe. He nestled her close and picked up her hand.

"Did you and Wynter enjoy your run?" she asked.

Wythe kissed her fingers. "Yes. She's delighted with Bouncer, and the puppy has already identified Wynter as her person."

Irene smiled. "Nelson and I had a very interesting discussion." She told him the details and finished with, "I hope he won't be disappointed with the outcome."

Wythe shook his head. "Peter Wallace thinks Nelson can return to most normal activities. I think the one thing he cautioned him against was jumping competitively again."

Irene shook her head. "They have a lot to settle between them. I wish we could help."

Wythe put her hand on his heart. "You can help me," he purred.

Irene laughed when his head came down and his lips met hers. Wythe was doing his very best to make up for ten years of lost time.

"Shouldn't we go upstairs?"

"I thought you'd never ask."

* * * *

Winter break was over and the new semester had started. Wynter juggled her academic schedule with her riding schedule. The new stallion she worked, Blast Furnace, was giving her a hard time. She wanted to talk to Nelson, but it seemed she seldom saw him.

Between her work schedule and his, plus his rehab, when they did see each other they were too tired to do anything but hold each other and sleep.

"Can't you get rid of Moose?" she asked one night when Nelson groaned with pain.

"Moose?"

"That no-neck therapist."

"Peter recommends him very highly."

"Then Peter should have Moose work him over a time or two," she snapped. "How can this be good for you?"

"Look, I appreciate the concern, but I'm fine, Wynter. Just leave it alone."

"Fine." She shut the bathroom door behind her with a decided click. Bracing her hands on the marble counter edge, she hung her head and stared into the sink. This was not how she wanted things between them. She flipped the water on in the shower and stripped off her dressing gown. She envied the easygoing relationship her mother and Wythe shared, but that was never going to happen. Neither Wynter nor Nelson was laid-back.

Damn, she was tired.

* * * *

Irene tried to be very quiet in the bathroom while she completed the test she'd picked up at the drugstore. Married less than a month and already pregnant? *Maybe* pregnant, she corrected, and they did anticipate things a bit. After following the instructions, she twiddled her fingers while she waited for the results. How could a couple of minutes last forever?

"Irene," Wythe said from outside the door. "Is everything all right? Do you feel okay?"

She checked her watch again, then looked at the test. Everything was more than okay. She threw open the door and looked at Wythe's worried face.

"Everything's wonderful. It's a little late for requests now, but did you want a boy or a girl?"

Wythe was speechless one nanosecond before he swung her up in his arms and twirled her around. When his chest crushed her breasts, she held herself away from him.

"Careful! These things hurt!"

She laughed when he guided her back to bed. He insisted she stay there while he made breakfast—just no coffee, she told him—and brought it in.

Irene munched on toast and tea, laughing at the foolish grin on his face.

"Wynter will be so excited," Irene said. "I'm so glad we found out before we went for the weekend. Should we tell your parents before we leave?"

Wythe grinned and picked up the phone. "They're early risers. Let's tell them now."

Wythe's mother cried and said she was going shopping that very afternoon. As they prepared to leave for Pheasant Run, Wythe started to help Irene out to the car, but she pulled away from him with a laugh. "It's a baby, Wythe, not a fatal disease. You've got eight more months, so settle down, big boy."

They were spending one night with Wynter and Nelson. Wythe turned down Nelson's invitation to make a mini-vacation of it because he was in the middle of some legal work for the Butlers. Wythe didn't say much, but Irene knew their finances were going downhill.

She had also watched him pick up a lot more reading material about Anderson Electronics. Irene hoped it was just out of curiosity, but sometimes she'd caught a strange, thoughtful look when he'd read through the material.

Now that they socialized a bit, she'd heard the rumors that Payton Southard Junior was considering selling the farm that had long-been in his family. Irene felt such a decision meant their finances were on the rocks. She asked Wythe, but he just shrugged it off and didn't want to discuss it. That was also strange. It wasn't like Wythe to be secretive.

He said he wanted to leave early for Pheasant Run. It would give her more time with Wynter, and there was something he wanted to discuss with Nelson. Irene shrugged. Whatever bothered him, she knew he would tell her eventually.

Wynter wasn't back from class yet when they arrived, and Nelson was working in the study. He invited Wythe and Irene to the sitting room, but she figured this was a good opportunity for Wythe to talk in private with Nelson. So she told them she wanted to catch up with Mrs. Caudle instead.

As she started down the hall, she heard Wythe's voice, quiet and serious for him. "Okay, Nelson. What the hell are you doing?"

The urge to stop and listen was almost irresistible, but she wouldn't betray Wythe that way, so she forced herself to go on to the kitchen. He would tell her when he was ready.

Irene was just finishing a cup of tea when Mrs. Caudle said, "I hear Miss Wynter."

Irene met her daughter at the door. Wynter smiled when she saw her mother, but traces of fatigue around her eyes were plain. Irene hoped her news would make her happy.

"Wythe and I are expecting," she whispered in Wynter's ear while she hugged her.

Wynter let out a whoop like Irene hadn't heard in some time and dropped her book bag. "Oh, Mama! I'm sooo happy." She laughed and cried as she hugged her mother, then stepped away and looked at her, holding Irene's hands out from her sides. "You don't look any different yet. When are you due?"

Wythe walked to the hallway to see what was going on, Nelson right behind him. Both men looked a little tense until Wythe saw Wynter and Irene and realized what was going on. His expression lightened. Irene looked back at them, knowing the tension was from their discussion.

Wynter ran across the hall to Wythe and jumped into his arms. "Oh, Wythe! You're gonna be a daddy? I can't wait!"

Nelson smiled at Irene. "Congratulations to both of you. I can't think of two people who will make finer parents than the two of you." He held out a hand to Wythe, who paused for a heartbeat then smiled and shook it.

Irene sighed in relief. Whatever the problem was between the two men, they appeared to have come to a truce, if not a complete meeting of the minds. They ate an early supper so they would get to the game in plenty of time. Nelson's handicapped sticker would put them close enough to Cameron Indoor Stadium to make getting in and out of the arena easy, but they still battled the traffic to and from the stadium.

Wynter tried to convince Nelson to use the wheelchair, but he brushed the suggestion away. Irene shook her head. They were both stubborn, prideful people: Nelson about his physical condition and Wynter about money.

The two men traded trash talk concerning their respective alma maters while Wynter and Irene sat in the backseat of the Rolls Royce.

"When did you find out, Mama?" she asked while Nelson drove toward Durham.

"Just this morning. I used a home test, but I was already pretty positive. I'll call my doctor and make an appointment when we get back."

Wynter giggled. "You know, Wythe will be one of those men who will be with you at every appointment."

Irene smiled at her. "I wouldn't have him any other way. I want him as excited as I am about this baby. As excited as I hope you are?"

Wynter squeezed her hand. "Almost nothing would make me happier right now." Her eyes darted to the back of Nelson's head when she said it, but she shook her head and smiled at her mother.

"Nelson's been trying to get me cranked up over this whole Duke-Carolina rivalry, but you know how I am. If it's not something I'm doing, I hardly know it's there."

She'd made it plain. Her emotions and her relationship were not topics of discussion, so Irene left it alone and did her best to understand the ins and outs of Blue Devil-Tar Heel rivalry. It became more real when they entered the arena and took their seats. Students painted varying shades of blue—all screaming—rocked the rafters of an arena that looked much smaller in person than it did on TV.

* * * *

Nelson and Wythe soaked up the noise, but Wynter seemed terrified by it. Nelson looked at her in surprise when she clutched his hand. He smiled reassuringly, but she paid him little attention. Something had distracted her so much, she kept searching the arena as if looking for someone.

Some of her unease communicated itself, and Nelson surveyed the crowd inside Cameron. Who or what had she seen that upset her? Jesus. Even if she'd seen someone, figuring out *who* among the thousands of people rooting for their favorite teams was almost impossible.

Nelson turned his attention back to the game. He'd bet Wythe five hundred on the Blue Devils. It was a close game, with talented players on both sides. In the end, Carolina came out on top by just one point. Nelson reached inside his pocket and pulled out his money clip before peeling off what he'd lost to Wythe.

"Next time," he commented, knowing how the rivalry swung back and forth like the click of a metronome.

Rather than battle the throng of people flooding out of the arena, they waited. Nelson had no desire to walk through such cramped quarters. Wynter was still on edge, and he found himself searching the crowd again for anyone she might know, but without success. She relaxed when they reached the house, so Nelson dismissed it. Since she wasn't accustomed to big crowds, that might have been the problem.

Chapter 24

Wynter kept so busy, she wondered if she should schedule free time, but the irony was too much to grasp. After two horse shows in Florida last month, it was the end of March and she was in-flight to Atlanta. Nelson's jet had flown her to most of the shows, so she'd missed as few classes as possible.

Every now and then she stopped long enough to think how life had changed in just a year. She was now familiar with negotiating airports and stepping into limos, but she still found it hard to believe, and she worried she'd wake up and find it was a dream—that she was still trailer trash O'Reilly.

Just the thought of the names Pay Southard had called her made a mental image of him pop inside her head. The last time she'd seen him was a lot more recent than anyone knew. Some way, somehow, he had been at that Duke-Carolina basketball game. She had looked back after they'd arrived and had seen him just inside the door. She'd also seen the words he'd mouthed when he'd caught her gaze and held it. *Fuck you, bitch.* When he'd drawn his finger across the base of his throat, she'd shivered and turned away.

Wynter had always known he'd hated her but not the depth or the reason. It had seemed way out of proportion to her having set two dozen foxhounds on his car. It was weird, really, because she had borne the brunt of Pay's teasing for years. If anyone had a reason to be pissed off, it should be her.

She'd never told Nelson, nor had she mentioned the feeling sometimes that someone watched when she and Bouncer ran. It wasn't as if they were invisible. With the colder weather, she ran along the edge of the road because the footing was more consistent. Hell, as paranoid as Nelson was, Wynter was afraid if she said anything he'd have the entire Duke University Police Force trailing her around campus, and she already drew enough attention. For all the size of the campus and the student body, when you lived with someone like Nelson Anderson, word got around.

Right now all Wynter wanted was to get through the weekend. She was showing both Rosie and the Dalton's big stallion, Blast Furnace, and it had not been an easy season so far. Rosie was doing well, gaining experience and a name for herself as a solid, dependable performer. Blast, on the other hand, was as tempestuous as his name.

Their first show in Florida had been a disaster. He'd been distracted and irritable. After being one of many clears in the first round, Blast had dropped rails at the first two fences in the jump-off then crashed through the Liverpool and had almost dumped Wynter in the water. She hoped for better things this weekend in Atlanta.

Once they cleared that out of the way, they had scheduled a break until the mid-May shows in Virginia so she could get through final exams. Nelson flew with her this time. He'd planned several business meetings but said he would be there for her Saturday night rounds.

She glanced at him from under her lashes. He sat across the jet, working at a table. He looked so much better. And he seldom used the cane. There was just a slight hitch in the way he walked that gave away some of the past pain.

As if aware of her regard, he glanced up and caught her looking at him. Wynter felt herself blush, and he laughed. Even his laughter was a lot freer these days. Several times, he'd seemed almost on the point of saying something, but then he'd shake his head and turn away or change the subject.

It made Wynter uneasy. She wondered if he was becoming bored with her. She saw the sophisticated women who hung around on the show circuits. She could never compete with them, and honestly, she didn't want to. They were too brittle, too adrift. Just when her fears would have her biting her lip, Nelson would take her in his arms, take her to bed and banish her worries. Their lovemaking had improved after the surgery, and it was always good. Now it was a lot more frequent. She felt the heat rise in her cheeks again.

Nelson pushed away the table with the laptop fixed to it.

"We've got a few minutes before we start our descent. Come, sit with me before business and horse shows intervene."

This was one aspect of his recovery she enjoyed. She sat on his lap and buried her face against his neck, inhaling the rich, familiar scent of him. He seemed content to hold her, stroking her hair. Beneath her ear she felt the steady beat of his heart. It made her feel lonely and secure at the same time. She knew he would always protect her but felt he held back a part of himself, which he shared with no one. The closest she had come to seeing that side of him was the night he'd dreamed of the accident and had admitted he would do almost anything to see his daughter once more.

Nelson shifted her weight and turned her face up to his. The kiss he pressed against her lips began with such gentleness it took her breath away, but it changed when he teased her mouth open. Molten heat welled inside Wynter, and she moaned against him. His fingers slid beneath the silky skirt she wore and stroked the inside of her thigh. She caught her breath when his fingers touched the thin fabric of her panties.

"Nelson," she gasped. "The pilot..."

"Is busy," he growled. "He won't be back."

His hands worked magic while he fondled and stroked. His hard cock pressed against her buttocks. "Haven't you ever wondered what it would be like to make love in an airplane?" he murmured.

"Right now?" Her breathing was uneven.

"Right now." His voice was thick with need. Setting her on her feet, he slid the silky panties down until they fell to the floor. When she stepped out of them, his fingers went to his belt.

"No. Let me." She bent over him, kissed him deeply, and worked to free him from his clothing. His hands caressed her breasts and thumbs stroked her hardened nipples. Slowly, she slid to her knees between his strong thighs and took him in her mouth. He groaned in pleasure, and his fingers tangled in her hair while she stroked him. With a stifled curse, he pulled her up to straddle him and guided himself inside her. When she sank onto his hard shaft, his hand pushed between them to continue caressing her.

They thrust together, need driving them until Wynter gasped with pleasure, throwing her head back while wave after wave of heat washed over her. Nelson's hands grasped her hips, and he drove himself into her again and again until he tensed in release, gripping her bottom. He gathered her close in the aftermath, stroking the length of her back while he whispered soft nonsense words.

They landed in Atlanta ten minutes later. Nelson's suit and tie looked immaculate when he deplaned. Wynter smiled. He never ceased to amaze her: hot and passionate one moment yet a consummate cool-headed business tycoon the next. In fact, it was one of the things she found so exciting about him.

The Atlanta show was a success. Rosie turned in a stellar, dependable performance that won their division. Wynter was worried about Blast until they took the first fence. Then she smiled at his forward-facing ears and the eager pull on her hands. He took on this course without the usual attitude. It was good enough for a win. Nelson was in the stands to see it, so she was relieved he wouldn't witness another debacle like in Ocala.

The Daltons were excited and insisted Wynter and Nelson attend the exhibitors' party that night. She smiled and nodded, stifling a sigh. Blast had pulled all the way around the course and the jump-off. She felt the ache in her arms and back, but they paid her well to ride him, so she would be there.

Nelson noticed how quiet she was while he drove the Lexus he'd rented back to the hotel.

"If you're too tired, Wynter, call the Daltons and tell them. They'll understand." He touched her arm and she flinched. "Sore?"

"Blast is just so damn strong." She rubbed the back of her neck. "And he pulls like a freight train."

Nelson smiled. "I know just the thing you need."

Fifteen minutes later, Wynter was in the hotel spa. It had already closed for the evening, but that didn't matter to Nelson. Within minutes employees were there, waiting on her with a smile. A massage, facial, manicure and pedicure later, she headed back to the room feeling much happier and far more refreshed. Nelson looked up when she walked through the door to their suite and smiled.

"Ah! That's better." He patted the couch beside him. When she moved past him and sat, his fingers plucked open the belt of the terry cloth robe she wore.

"Nelson!"

"Just one more finishing touch to your session of pampering." Her eyes widened when he pressed her back against the couch and parted the robe.

"Nelson?"

He smiled wickedly. "Just lie back and relax." His hands and lips caressed her from the top of her head to the tips of her toes before he brought his talented fingers and lips back to the very core of her. She gasped, clutching his thick hair in her fingers.

It was late before they arrived at the party at a neighboring hotel. Wynter saw several familiar faces destined to be riding the next day with a hangover, not something she desired. The Dalton kids were already yawning when they arrived. Wynter apologized for being so late but offered them no explanation. Her job was to ride their horse—attending

Laura Browning

the party was good manners. Nelson excused himself after a few minutes and headed for the bar.

She chatted with the Daltons. Behind her, Wynter overheard part of a conversation between two amateur riders from Virginia.

"I heard they're selling the farm because his daddy's lost so much money in the stock market."

"No! I knew he'd left school. I just figured he flunked out. You know how Pay's always been."

"Tory left Salem and transferred to Tech. Seems her family invested in some of the same things."

Wynter turned her head and glanced at the two women. She recalled they had been pretty chummy with both the Southards and the Butlers last fall. She turned back to the Daltons, smiling but distracted while they continued to talk plans for Blast, but she still listened to what was going on behind her.

"Pay's been going wild. His daddy can't control him anymore and doesn't know where he is half the time. Somebody told me he's doing drugs, but I don't know where he's getting the money for it."

While it saddened her that the Southards faced financial ruin, she would not have been human if she didn't feel some small shred of satisfaction. Payton Junior and Payton the Third treated her like nothing better than the dirt under their heels. Now it appeared the roles were reversing. She hoped she never forgot enough of the past to treat anyone like they'd treated her.

* * * *

Saturday turned out as well as Friday evening. The Daltons were pleased. Wynter called Miss Olivia, who had stayed home this time around, and she was ecstatic too. Nelson was moving with ease around the showground, which made Wynter smile. Although he still carried the cane, he seldom leaned on it anymore. When he caught her staring at him, he smiled almost boyishly and snapped the lens of the camera. It was always with him, and she very often found herself the subject in the viewfinder.

They flew home that night, and he showed her some of the pictures he'd downloaded to the laptop. There were pictures of her riding, grooming. There were pictures of her at the party talking with the Daltons, but she gasped when she saw the last picture he'd downloaded. He had taken it just moments after they had made love. Her hair was tangled across the pillow, and she had one bare arm thrown over her head while she focused on something out the window. Her eyes were half-closed in the aftermath of passion, her lips soft and swollen. Wynter stared at the picture a long moment.

"Please don't show that to anyone else, Nelson," she said softly. "It's too…" *Naked? Raw? Soul-baring?* "Personal," she finished.

He stroked a wisp of hair behind her ear. "It's how I see you, how I remember you when we're apart." His voice was quiet. "Soft, feminine. A breath of spring in my life."

* * * *

Nelson left the following morning for New York and then on to Silicon Valley. Wynter returned to her classes, studying, riding and daily runs with Bouncer, who was now a constant companion. She had worn down Nelson to let her bring the dog in the house. It took a couple of weeks, but the puppy was learning manners.

Almost every evening, Nelson called. New York had gone well, but he'd run into problems with a project in California. Since it was something he had developed, he felt obligated to stay and work out the kinks. It was not what Wynter wanted to hear. Finals were approaching, and the week after she was scheduled for a show in Northern Virginia, followed by Devon a week later. And then summer school would start. Nelson was tired and frustrated, and so was she. When Wynter dared to say something about his schedule, he growled he was the CEO of a company with assets in the billions and obligations to fulfill. In turn he'd pointed out she was still scheduling course loads at Duke as though trying to finish her degree in two years, when there was no need. If she would just back off on the course load, she could accompany him on some of these trips.

"And do what?" she snapped, irritated by his tone. "Be the trophy fuck on your arm?"

There was dead silence on the other end of the phone. "Wynter!" His tone was both furious and exasperated.

"Never mind, Nelson!" she spat. "Just do what you must. You always do." She slammed the phone and put her head in her hands.

Chapter 25

Nelson frowned at the hotel phone. He was in the penthouse of a luxurious hotel. No expense had been spared to achieve the understated luxury and open, modern floor plan, but at the moment, he felt any hotel would be the wrong one because he was not in the one place he wanted to be.

"Fuck!" He spun on his heel and stalked out to the rooftop swimming pool designed solely for the penthouse guests. He stripped and dove into the pool, taking out some of his frustration in swimming laps until he paused at one end to catch his breath. He swept the back of a hand across the surface of the water.

It was starting again. Just like it had with Lindy. The business trips, the separation, the simmering resentment. Why couldn't Wynter understand? This was his business. This was something he had given almost half his life to, building it up from just another electronics company and dragging it forward to fulfill his vision. It was a vision many of the executives had doubted, but time had proved him right. He couldn't walk away from it.

And what was this whole thing about being a trophy fuck? Didn't Wynter understand what she meant to him? Was it too much to ask her to back off her studies a bit? Even when he was at home, the demands of her class schedule, studying, riding and showing left them little time together. Nelson often felt they met together in bed for sex. Great sex, but still only sex.

He climbed out of the pool, his wet, naked form gleaming in the moonlight. A trace of a limp remained when he walked to the hot tub a few feet away. After slipping in, he leaned against the rim.

What did Wynter want from him? He remembered the rough-edged, tough-talking teenager who'd showed up on the doorstep a little over a year ago. She had matured and changed. She had become Galatea to his Pygmalion, but had they both lost something along the way?

He sighed. If he could just smooth out some of the contract issues holding up things right now. Maybe putting the heat on would get things wrapped up before the end of the week. He'd take some time off, and they would go somewhere and sort things out. It was time to change some things and figure out where they were headed, or call it quits. Nelson frowned again.

He couldn't envision a life without her. In the past year, she had become essential, a part of everything he did or was. If she wasn't there, life would be empty, as meaningless as when he'd lost Lindy and Allison. He let his head drop back and squeezed his eyes shut. He loved her. God help him.

* * * *

He didn't call her the rest of that week. Finals had started, and Wynter still hadn't heard anything from Nelson. She was distracted and tired by the time she left the library the night before her last exam. She had stayed later than she'd intended, needing to look up some information in the reference library.

She had almost reached her BMW in a far corner of the parking lot when she felt something hard poke her back.

"Don't say a word, bitch, or I swear I'll shoot you now. Just keep walking to that van ten feet in front of you."

Over a year had passed, but Wynter would recognize Pay Southard's voice anywhere. It still held that malicious satisfaction but something more too—a hatred so basic it sent chills down her spine. She remembered seeing him draw his finger across his throat. It was no joke. He would kill her.

She kept her mouth shut while she walked to the van. Pay slid the side door open and shoved her inside. Pain shot through Wynter's wrist when she crashed on top of the hand she'd thrown out to break her fall. Before she could recover, he yanked her arms behind her and wrapped duct tape several times around her wrists. She tried to kick him, but he slammed a fist against the side of her head, dazing her.

"Why?" Wynter gasped.

She had never seen such hatred on anyone's face. He tossed back his overlong blond hair and snarled, "First, because I never liked you, trailer trash. You always thought you were better than the rest of us." He laughed. "There you were in your thrift store clothes, thumbing your nose at everyone because you were so smart. Second, because of that bastard you're fucking. He's ruined my family over a little car accident."

A little car accident? Pay had caused an accident that had killed Nelson's wife and child and almost crippled Nelson for life, and he called it *a little car accident?*

"Well, he's gonna pay now!" Pay slammed the door shut then hopped into the driver's side. When he backed out of the parking spot he looked back at Wynter with contempt. "We'll see just how much he wants you back. Of course I can't guarantee what you'll look like when I'm done with you." He paused. "*If* you're still alive."

She clenched her jaw against the pain in her wrist and head. She would not give in to panic. She must keep a clear head. Payton Caldwell Southard the Third had transformed from a spoiled kid into a dangerous man. Wynter felt the cellphone she kept tucked in the deep, baggy pocket of her pants. She would be patient and wait for her chance to call and pray no one called her. Even though the phone was set on vibrate, he might hear it.

She couldn't tell where they were headed. It seemed as though they'd driven for hours, but because of the constant stopping and starting, she never got the feeling they'd left Durham. She saw almost nothing out of the front and rear windows of the van. When they did stop, Pay threw her over a shoulder and stumbled inside a nearby building. It smelled old and disused, as though it had stood empty a long time. His footsteps echoed when he walked across the hard floor. He paused to open a door and then let her slide onto a thin mattress covering a metal cot set in the corner.

"Welcome to your new home, bitch."

"Pay…" Wynter soothed.

"Shut up!" he snarled. "I don't have to listen to anything you have to say. It's your turn to listen to me, you piece of trash."

He turned on a small light. The windows set close to the ceiling were blacked out, so she doubted the light would even be visible from outside. Pay paced back and forth, the gun dangling from his hand. She watched him nervously. In addition to the desperation and rage she saw on his face, there was something else. He was nervous and agitated. Sweat gleamed on his pasty face. He was, she realized, stoned out of his mind on God knew what.

He paused beside her and yanked her braid, twisting it around a hand to force her face up. "So what's it like?" His tone was chilling. "What's it like fucking a cripple? Can he still get it up, or do you have to work at it before he can put it in you?"

Because of the way he held her hair, she couldn't turn her head away. Instead, she closed her eyes against the look on his face.

"Look at me, bitch!" He snarled the words. Wynter opened her eyes and glared at him in utter contempt.

"I bet you don't even know what your high and mighty Nelson Anderson has been doing while he's been screwing your brains out. Do you?"

She kept her head still and tried her best to hide her feelings as she stared at him.

"Let me tell you." Pay released her hair and continued pacing. "It took me some time to figure it out. Daddy kept getting excited about investment opportunities, sinking more and more money into them. But they would go belly-up after just a couple of months. He kept risking more, trying to recoup the losses, and each time he lost more. I started doing some checking. It wasn't hard to track it down. The investments were legal, and the person who'd set them up lost money. Guess who that person was. Guess."

She didn't need to, and the answer must have shown on her face.

"That's right. The bastard you're fucking. The whole time he's doing you, he's getting revenge for his dead wife. How's that make you feel? In fact, I wouldn't be surprised to find out he was doing you because he somehow found out I've wanted a piece of you for years. I almost got it too. If it weren't for Bradshear, I would have." He paused and looked her up and down. "I wouldn't pay fifty dollars now because I can have it for free."

Wynter struggled then, kicking against the duct tape on her ankles and yanking at her wrists, trying to find some weakness in the bonds he'd tied.

"Think about it," Pay snarled. He turned and rifled through her book bag, coming up with her wallet. She was glad she had carried her phone in her pants, but she still wasn't sure how she would get it. She watched him smile in triumph when he pulled out a wad of cash. He stuffed the money in a pocket and laughed.

"Don't worry, bitch! I'll be back, and we're gonna have some fun, just me and you, and you can tell me how much better I fuck than your crippled sugar daddy."

Wynter struggled while he shoved a dirty rag in her mouth. He slapped her when she continued to fight, and then he left. *Shit!* He was crazy. She wrestled against her constraints several minutes, working to get the rag out of her mouth so she could scream, but it wouldn't budge. When that didn't succeed, she tried twisting her hands far enough around in the hope she could reach the cellphone in her pocket. By the time she gave up, she panted for breath. Nothing was working.

She almost cried with frustration but stilled the moment she heard footsteps echo outside the vacant office area she was in. The door opened. Pay had returned, and her hopes sank. He appeared less agitated, though. He'd probably used her money to get himself a fix. Maybe that would buy her some more time. He tucked the gun in the waistband of his jeans. She could try talking him out of whatever he'd planned. But when he approached, Wynter saw his previous agitation replaced with a cold, calculating look. She could no longer write off his threats to the need for drugs, and it dawned on her just how much danger she was in. She twisted against the tape in earnest. There must be some way out.

Chapter 26

It was late when the phone rang. Irene had been sound asleep but awoke when she heard Wythe's end of the conversation.

"No, we haven't heard from her, Nelson. Not since last weekend." There was a long pause. Wythe turned on the light and sat up, frowning.

"No, you're right. That's not like her."

Irene sat up too, fear gnawing at her.

"Is Mrs. Caudle still at the house?"

Irene was already getting out of bed and throwing on clothes. Something was wrong with Wynter. Irene felt the baby move, and she put a hand to her belly. *Your time will come. Right now your big sister needs me.*

"How soon can you get back?" Wythe drummed his fingers on the night table. "We'll head that way now. Do you want me to call the police?" Another pause. "We'll call you as soon as we assess what's going on. Give me a number where I can reach you in-flight." Wythe jotted it down before hanging up the phone.

"Wythe? Has something happened to Wynter?" Irene was trembling when she neared where he still sat on the bed.

He drew her between his muscular thighs, holding both her hands. "She didn't come home this evening. She called Mrs. Caudle after her last final and said she was going to the library for an hour, and that's the last anyone knows of her whereabouts."

Irene glanced at the clock. It was just past midnight. "Wythe, that's six hours ago. She said her last final ended at five today."

"Calm down, Irene," he said. "We'll head there. It's probably something simple. Her car might have broken down, and her cellphone could be dead. Wynter's very capable of taking care of herself."

Irene looked at Wythe and backed away from him. She had the strangest feeling. "Please, Wythe. Get dressed and let's go. Something's very wrong. I can feel it."

The cellphone rang half-way to Pheasant Run. Since Wythe drove, Irene answered.

"Irene?" It was Nelson. He sounded haggard and strung so tight he might snap. "Campus police just called. Wynter's car is still in the parking lot next to the library." He paused, and even through the bad in-flight connection, she heard his hoarse voice crack with emotion. "Her keys were on the ground beside it."

Irene gasped. "D-did they find anything else?"

"Nothing. Damn it! My pilot's pushing the jet to the limit, but it will be early morning before we arrive."

"We'll do everything we can. You know that. She's my daughter, Nelson. I'd give my life for her."

She heard him take a deep breath. "I know. I've called a detective friend. He'll meet you at the house. Call the police at your discretion, once you get there. If anyone contacts you," he said, his voice thick, "I will do anything, pay anything they ask, if they will just return her."

The connection went dead. Irene stared at the phone in frustration. They were going through a dead zone. She put the phone down and stared out the window.

"We'll get her back, Irene." The icy determination in Wythe's voice made it sound as if each word had been fired from a pistol.

* * * *

"I've left a message for your lover," were the first words out of Pay's mouth. "But it looks like it might take some time before he gets it. So let's have a little fun to take our minds off things."

He grabbed Wynter's braid again and pulled her head back. "Why don't you give me some of what you've shared with Mr. Anderson Electronics?" He ripped open the front of her shirt. "You always did have nice tits." He squeezed one of her breasts until tears filled Wynter's eyes. *God in heaven*, she thought, *he's crazy!* She pulled her knees up and kicked. The blow caught Pay just above the knee, sending him stumbling backward, but before she could roll off the cot, he was back, his face a mask of fury.

"You want to play rough, trailer trash? Is that what your cripple likes? Does it get him hard? Not a problem!" He slapped her hard across the face, dislodging the rag from her mouth. Wynter screamed, and he laughed. "There's no one who'll hear you, whore! Save some of that energy for me."

Pay grabbed her by the arms and yanked her up to a sitting position, fingers biting into the flesh of her arms, making her wrists strain where they were taped behind her back. Then it got worse. He bent his head and kissed her. It was foul. When he pulled his mouth away from hers, pure reaction took over, and she spit in his face. "Go to hell!" she swore at him.

"You. Fucking. Bitch," he snarled, wiping the spit. He drew back a fist, and the last thing she remembered was watching it smash her nose, then everything went black.

* * * *

Nelson stared out the jet's window, lips pressed together and a muscle twitching near his temple. *Where was she?* As angry as Wynter might have been at him, she would never do anything to worry someone else.

Why hadn't he left the guards on her? Bouncer offered some protection at home, but she was vulnerable anywhere else, and Nelson had never explained his fears, the risks that went along with his wealth and position. Risks she'd needed to know.

He'd never talked about anything, he realized, at least not where it concerned their relationship and how he felt.

Nelson flipped his cellphone open again and started to dial her number, but something made him hesitate. What if someone had kidnapped her? Would they know about the phone? He shook off the feeling and punched in the number, but wherever they were right now, no signal got through. Nelson shoved the phone back inside his pocket. He reached into the breast pocket of his suit jacket and pulled out the picture of Wynter he always carried there. It was the snapshot she'd asked him not to show anyone. The one he'd taken in Atlanta right after they'd made love. His hand shook when he looked at it. The photo blurred in front of him, and his throat tightened.

Not again, he thought. *Please don't take away what I love more than life itself. Not again.*

He felt the jet descend, and he pressed the intercom button.

"What's up? Why are we descending?"

"Fuel," the pilot's disembodied voice came back. "We'll get it done as fast as possible, Mr. Anderson, and get right back in the air."

"Thanks."

Nelson drummed his fingers on the arm of the seat and fastened the seatbelt once again. The trip had never seemed so long.

* * * *

Irene couldn't describe the emotions she felt, knowing Wynter was in danger. In danger, and there wasn't a damn thing she could do. Worry, fear, rage—they warred within her. So many thoughts jumbled together. *Who would harm Wynter? Why had Nelson not kept bodyguards on her? Why did she ever fall for someone like Nelson Anderson?*

Irene knew in her gut things were not all right. Wynter was somewhere hurt and hurting. And right now Irene was powerless to do anything. Moreover, she was limited because of the new life she nurtured inside her.

The private detective had already arrived when she and Wythe reached Pheasant Run. When Mrs. Caudle escorted them to Nelson's study, they saw an impressive array of electronics set up. "If someone calls," he explained, "we'll do everything we can, as fast as we can, to trace the call. We're also hoping Wynter might somehow be able to call. We'll use the GPS on her phone to find her."

Irene looked at the equipment, then at Wythe and the detective. "You already think something's happened."

The detective ignored her comment, and that told Irene more than she wanted to know. "Mrs. Bradshear—if you wouldn't mind—please go through Wynter's belongings. See if you can find anything out of place. Anything that might give us a clue what's going on?"

Irene nodded and headed upstairs. Nothing appeared to be missing. Wynter's clothing was there. Irene found nothing in the bathroom medicine cabinet other than a bottle of ibuprofen and her daughter's birth control pills. She couldn't even find comfort in knowing at least Wynter had been taking a few more precautions than Wythe and her. Wynter's calendar lay open on the desk where her finals were noted in red: the one from today and her last exam the following day. None of it gave any indication she might have considered leaving Nelson. Irene walked down the hallway to Nelson's room. Although she felt as if she intruded, she needed to be realistic. Wynter had spent more time here than in her own room.

Framed photos of Wynter hung on one wall near the bed. Smiling, laughing, wistful, studying, playing with Bouncer. Irene sat on the edge of the bed. Nelson had caught her moods brilliantly. She wasn't sure how long she sat, staring at Nelson's photos of her daughter. The sound of the front door slamming startled her. She ran into the hallway, hoping to see Wynter come bounding back in the door, swearing like a sailor over some problem with her car.

Nelson stood in the hallway. Irene looked down from the top of the stairs. She saw the same disappointment in his face she felt. His eyes were red-rimmed from lack of sleep and what might have been tears. His skin was pale and his hair disheveled as if he'd spent hours raking fingers through it.

"Any word?" he rasped.

"None," she said with a choked sob and ran down the stairs.

Nelson met her at the bottom and hugged her. "We'll find her, Irene. I promise."

He greeted the detective and Wythe. He seemed unsurprised by the amount of equipment but disappointed at the lack of contact.

Wythe stared at the computers and asked, "Nelson, have you checked your email at Anderson Electronics?"

Nelson crossed to the PC in the study and logged on. After just a moment, his shoulders slumped and he said, "It's here. It's Payton Southard the Third."

"What does he want?" Wythe asked.

"Ten million dollars by noon, or he'll kill her."

Chapter 27

Some natural light filtered through the windows when Wynter awoke. It took her a few minutes to remember the horror of what had happened… what was still happening. It was hard to open her eyes, but turning her head to see around her was even more painful. She was alone, and that was a momentary relief. She shivered and glanced down, almost retching in disgust. Her clothes were ripped and in disarray. He'd undone her feet, so he could do what he'd promised he would do. She felt the stickiness between her thighs, swallowing hard against the rising wave of nausea she felt again. He'd raped her. He'd knocked her out and raped her. A dry sob escaped. Everything hurt. Her face felt swollen, and she couldn't breathe through her nose. She felt what she guessed was dried blood on her face, but she couldn't be sure. Her hands were still bound behind her back.

Slowly, painfully, Wynter rolled onto her side. He'd dropped her pants in a pile on the floor. She hurt so much it was hard to think, but she knew she must. Pay had gone over the edge. Deep down in her bones she knew he would kill her before this was over. He might have ranted about money, but it was more. It was personal, a vendetta from their last encounter when Wythe had horsewhipped him. Wynter listened but heard nothing from outside. She eased onto the floor. When she did, she saw the bruises on her legs, but since so many other things hurt, those barely registered. Carefully, she scooted around until she put her bound hands on her pants. She worked blindly, feeling with her aching fingers for the telltale lump of her cellphone, sending up fervent prayers he hadn't found it.

Then her searching fingers felt it. *It was still there!* Working with more haste, Wynter pulled it out and flipped it open. She turned again. With a bare toe, she pressed the power button followed by the number one until she heard ringing on the other end. Wynter wept with relief.

"Hello?" It was Nelson. He sounded tired and hoarse. "Hello!"

Wynter fell onto her side and put her mouth near the phone. "It's me," she managed in a whisper through cracked lips. "Please help."

"Whatever you do, don't hang up, sweetheart!" his voice was urgent, frightened. "Where are you?"

"I don't know," she replied, aching and terrified. All she wanted was to feel Nelson's arms around her. She needed him to erase Pay from her mind, from her body.

Another voice was on the phone at the same time, one she didn't recognize. "Tell me what you see around you," the unfamiliar voice ordered.

A harsh sob caught in her throat, but she looked through swollen eyes at her surroundings. "Empty office. High windows. Blacked out. It sounded hollow coming in. Big and empty."

"How did you get there?"

"A van. Pay pushed me in. He's got a gun. We drove a long time, but I think we're still in Durham." Wynter paused to listen again because some sound penetrated her stupor. "I have to go!" she hissed in desperation.

"Don't hang up!" It was Nelson again, frantic. She'd never heard his voice so tight.

"Oh, God." Wynter shuddered. "He's coming back."

Part of her was cold and detached from what was happening, and that part made her swivel around and kick the phone under the narrow bed with her bare foot. Somehow, Wynter got off the floor and back on the cot before the door opened. She scooted as far up against the wall as she could.

"You don't look so uppity now, trailer trash," Pay Southard drawled. His pale eyes slid down her bare thighs. "How's it feel to know you've been with a real man?"

"Stay away, you bastard!" she hissed.

Pay laughed. He shoved a pill in her mouth and forced water on her until she swallowed. "That should relax you some. I'd prefer you awake the next time…just not fighting."

"Nooo!" Wynter wailed. The bastard had drugged her. "Stay away from me!"

She rolled away from him, and he laughed again. He had always been spoiled and malicious—now he was also insane. Wynter kicked out at him, but Pay was ready. He grabbed both her legs and forced them apart then fell on top of her. His breath smelled sour in her face.

"You are such a bitch, trailer trash. Such a hot bitch. Do you make Nelson Anderson moan? Does he give you what I've got?"

Wynter turned her head to the wall. The scream that bubbled up died inside her mind. This couldn't be happening. It wasn't real. Nothing this terrible could ever be real. Could it?

* * * *

The detective reached over and hit the mute button on the phone so Payton would hear no noise from their end, but he didn't hang up. Muffled as it was, they still heard what was going on. At Wynter's loud "No!" both Nelson and Irene jumped up.

"Oh, God!" Irene gasped, looking around at Wythe, the detective, then Nelson. "Do something! He's hurting my little girl."

Wynter's screaming came through the phone, and Nelson stumbled back as if he'd been slapped. Eyes wild and frantic, he turned to the detective. "Have you gotten a lock on the GPS yet?" he growled.

"One more minute."

The sounds coming from the phone made Irene press her face against Wythe's chest. Even his breathing was ragged with tension. Solid, dependable, unflappable Wythe. She felt him shake. She wasn't sure if it was fear or fury.

Nelson prowled the room like a caged animal, blue eyes almost black with rage when he heard Wynter crying. His glance darted to the computer screens.

"Well?"

"Got it."

"Then let's go!"

"You've got to call in the police, man!" the detective snapped. "The guy's armed!"

"Where are they?" Nelson snarled as if he hadn't heard him.

"Inside the old Anderson Electric building."

"Bastard!" Nelson growled, eyes glittering like shards of glass. He swung back on the detective. "Don't call the police yet. He'll kill her!"

"Nelson! Please," Irene pleaded.

Wythe stunned her when he stood and said, "No. He's right. Pay has nothing left to lose. If the police surround that building, he'll kill Wynter and himself." He turned calm brown eyes on Nelson. "Now what do you know about that plant to help us get inside?"

Nelson, it turned out, knew a lot and shared it with the group. In addition to having schematics in the computer, he had crawled, walked and run through it as a child. He knew places in the building he wasn't sure anyone else was even aware of. What he knew best was the hidden staircase in his father's former office. It led to a door obscured by old shrubbery at the rear of the building. He told them he was pretty sure from Wynter's description she was in the clerical office located just outside that room.

"Do you have keys?" the detective asked.

Nelson retrieved them from a small safe behind the desk. Irene listened while the three men went through their plan. Time was short, and they knew it. The detective would distract Pay—lure him out of the office so Nelson and Wythe could get inside.

"What about me?" Irene asked.

They looked at her blankly.

"I am not staying here. This is my daughter."

Wythe looked at the other two men, resigned. "She's right. And Wynter may need her." He turned back to Nelson. "Just one thing."

"What?" Nelson barked.

"When we have Wynter safe, we call the police. You can't keep this under wraps, Nelson."

Nelson's face was pale and his voice cold. "I know. Let's go. We're wasting time."

* * * *

She had no pride left. She was empty. The drug he'd given her had made her lethargic and heavy-limbed. Pay rolled away from her, and Wynter didn't move from where he'd left her. Her mind and heart rejected what he'd done. Her soul felt as if it withered and died inside her. She didn't even care that Wynter O'Reilly might fade away. No one would come. They would never find her in time. He would end up killing her. Did it matter? *I'm fading.* She lost touch with who she was and why anything should matter.

She was thirsty and sick, hungry, yet ready to vomit. And she ached, oh how she ached. Tears no longer rolled down her face. None remained. But she couldn't have shed them anyway because her eyes were swollen almost shut. It was a blessing. It meant she no longer had to look at him, no longer had to see that gleam of hatred mixed with triumph or the sick lust in his face.

See what you created, Payton Junior? With your constant indulgence of your only child. And Nelson, too, with your need for revenge. Somehow, Wynter had become the pawn in their power play. Weakness and cold stole over her. It would be over soon, though. Even if he didn't kill her right away, she would lose herself. She was already retreating into a far corner of her mind, trying to find some small place where it was still safe, where people didn't hurt her body and soul. She moved reflexively, curling into a ball. With her knees close to her chest, she turned her face to the wall.

Pay laughed when she moved, but his laughter stilled a moment later. "Someone's out there, damn it!" And then he swore even more viciously. She felt his breath on her, knew from where he stood there was just one thing that could have him cursing like that. He must have seen the cellphone under the bed.

"What have you done, you cunt?" He kicked her in the back and bent to grab the cellphone. Fingers bit into her shoulder when he rolled her to face him.

"Who did you call?" he punched buttons on the phone to no avail. The battery had long since died. He threw the phone, striking her in the face just above her left eye. Warm wetness trickled across her face. *Blood?* Pay picked up the gun from the one desk still remaining and headed for the door. He glanced back at her. "You're dead, bitch! I'll kill you when I get back. Screw the money!"

The door slammed behind him. Wynter blinked and turned once more to the wall. *Dead.* That would be a relief. There was a momentary pang of regret she would never see Mama's baby. Maybe that new son or daughter would help ease the loss of Wynter. Her grip on reality slipped a bit more. *So cold.* Maybe if she just went to sleep, she could die before he returned.

Wynter heard a faint noise from across the room, a mouse or a rat she supposed. She had seen a couple of them since arriving, but she just couldn't care. She didn't even care when she heard the door open and shut again. Now he would kill her. Now he would end this pain, and it frightened her somewhere deep inside. Not the dying. No, the fear was because of the terrible relief she felt that it would all be over.

Firm hands grasped her shoulder and turned her over.

"Kill me," Wynter croaked. "Just get it over with."

"Wynter?"

Not Pay. She tried to open her eyes and heard a moan of animal-like pain, deep and keening and lonely. She didn't know if it came from her or from the man staring at her. Nelson. She heard a buzzing that grew louder, and her vision faded out like an old TV show going to black at its end.

Chapter 28

Irene called the police from Nelson's cellphone when she saw the detective round the building with Pay Southard in a firm grip. She got out of the car and regarded the boy with pity. It was hard to think of him as anything else because he had never learned to be a man. Even now, he stood there sullen and defiant.

She looked at the detective and said grimly, "I have to go. She's my daughter."

He nodded his understanding. Irene found the door around the side of the building and raced up the steps and into the old musty office that had once belonged to Nelson's father. The door to the next office was half-open. She saw Wythe and Nelson both bent over a cot on the far side of the room. Irene raced in, heart pounding.

Wythe took a step toward her. "Irene," he warned, but she brushed past him.

"Oh Holy Mary," she whispered when she saw her daughter. Irene had brought a blanket with her and covered Wynter with it. "Call an ambulance!"

Wythe held her shoulders. "I already have, love. They should be here any minute."

Nelson sat like a stone on the edge of the cot. When Irene glanced over her shoulder, she saw him cut the tape that still bound Wynter's wrists. He eased her arms from behind her back and tucked the cover around her. He touched her blood-matted hair with a hand that shook. While she watched, he bent his head, his shoulders shaking as he wept.

The paramedics were brisk and efficient. They treated Wynter first for shock then catalogued her injuries. Irene caught snippets of their conversation. Broken. Lacerations. Hematoma. Tearing. Semen. Evidence. Nelson stayed with her, even when they tried to push him aside. His hoarse "No!" echoed around the room.

Irene had never seen a man as haunted as Nelson Anderson. He clutched Wynter's scratched hand, walking beside the stretcher when they took her out to the ambulance. Wynter never moved, never opened her eyes, and Irene wondered if she would lose her daughter. Maybe not to death, but Irene knew only too well how such treatment at the hands of a man changed a woman forever. It left scars that went a whole lot deeper than physical ones. Those faded quickly in comparison.

Wythe came over to her from where he'd been talking to a police officer, and he put his arms around her shoulders. "They'll gather evidence. They don't need us anymore. Let's go to the hospital." His voice was so gentle, so tender. Irene looked up at him. Tears glistened in his eyes and on his cheeks. "Will she ever come back?"

"I don't know," she murmured. "Pray. Just pray."

When they reached the hospital, Nelson was frantic. While they had let him stay with her in the ambulance, the emergency room staff would not allow him back in the examining room reserved for sexual assault patients, and they had already called security to restrain him. Nelson's eyes were wild in his pale face. "They won't let me stay with her. I'm not family." His eyes sought Irene's, and she saw the plea in them.

"I'll see what I can do." She stared at both men. "I know what she's going through." Wythe jerked back. She had told him of some of the abuse Colin had dished out, but not all of it. She returned a few minutes later. "They'll let me back when they've finished treating her, gathering evidence and cleaning her up."

Appearing unaware of the curious stares he received, Nelson sat in a chair in the waiting area and buried his face in his hands. His long fingers curled into fists in his hair. "It's my fault. He came after her because of me. I should have kept the bodyguards on her."

Part of Irene wanted to comfort him because he was in such obvious torment, but the mother in her was furious, so much so it frightened her. Wythe had told her about the careful set of investments Nelson had concocted to ruin the Southard family. And he had gone through with it, knowing Wynter's connection to that family. He'd gambled with her safety. And now, as a result, Irene didn't know if she would ever have her daughter back.

She turned away from Nelson, unable to look at him, and rested her cheek against Wythe's shoulder. It seemed like hours before the nurse came out again. She looked straight at Irene. "You may come in now, Mrs. Bradshear." Nelson and Wythe both stood, but the nurse shook her head.

"Only one person will be admitted because of the extent of Miss O'Reilly's injuries, and just immediate family. You can see her once she's in a room but not until then."

Digging his balled fists into the pockets of his slacks, Nelson spun away.

Irene followed the nurse down the hallway. The ER bustled with activity and noise. Patients were separated in small, private exam rooms. She was grateful. Wynter wouldn't want to feel as if she was on display, but Irene knew that was something her daughter would have to cope with. Because in the eyes of most people, it wasn't Wynter O'Reilly who was raped and beaten. It was Nelson Anderson's girlfriend. Again, Irene felt a stab of anger at Nelson. He'd not only failed to protect her daughter physically, he hadn't even protected her reputation. So in addition to coping with a brutal rape, Wynter would face the publicity too.

Wynter had her head angled away from the door. With the blood washed off her face, it was possible to see what injuries Pay had inflicted. Her eyes appeared to be shut, but when Irene entered the room, Wynter lifted a shaky hand off the cover.

"Mama." It was a whisper so faint Irene strained to hear it.

Her throat tightened when she looked at her daughter. "I'm here, Wynter."

Irene grasped her hand, stroking the scratches that were now clean, and stared at her, swallowing at the sight of Wynter's bruised and swollen face. He'd broken her nose. Both of her eyes were blackened. There was a cut above her left eye that had been stitched. She also saw the bruises on the pale flesh of her upper arms and could imagine where else she was bruised.

Wynter said nothing else, just clasped her mother's hand, refusing to let go. Irene sat beside her a long time. The nurse came back in. "We have a counselor here to talk with you, Miss O'Reilly."

Wynter shook her head then grimaced in pain. She whispered, "No."

The nurse protested, and Wynter's jaw hardened. "No!" She grasped her mother's hand even harder. "Mama."

Irene looked at the nurse. "It's a waste of time right now. She won't talk. Leave her be."

When the nurse left, Wynter squeezed her hand. It was hard to understand her when she spoke again because her words were slurred by her injuries and fatigue.

"I'm losing me, Mama."

With her free hand, Irene brushed tears off Wynter's cheeks and swallowed again. "Hold on to me then, Wynter. Hold onto my hand. I won't let you get lost, baby girl."

Time passed. Irene felt Wynter's hand relax at last and realized she had fallen asleep. Still, Irene held her daughter's hand. The orderlies came in to move her to a room, transferring her to a gurney as they moved the IV tubes she was hooked to as well.

The older man looked at her. "You her mother?"

Irene nodded.

He smiled, "Good. Come with us. We're taking her up to a private room."

Wynter didn't awaken the whole way. They bumped into the elevator and then down the hall to an airy room that didn't resemble a typical hospital room, and she still slept. They moved her onto the bed, their hands careful to avoid touching the bruises on her body. Irene moved back to her side and took her hand once again. Wynter stirred and whimpered in her sleep, and Irene heard her mutter, "Nelson."

The two men arrived a few minutes later. Nelson had regained control once more. Although his face was pale and his eyes still haunted, his jaw was stiff as he surveyed her. He sat on the opposite side of the bed from Irene and held Wynter's other hand while he stroked her hair.

"Wynter." He whispered, so Irene wasn't sure she had even heard it. But Wynter did. Her eyes flickered. Slowly, deliberately, she pulled her hand out of his and turned her face away from him. Nelson's hand on her hair stilled, and he swallowed, pain twisting his features into a pale, remote mask. Irene turned away. Part of her was glad to see him suffer even a fraction of what Wynter was going through.

It was just after lunch when a tall, distinguished-looking doctor came in. Nelson greeted him by his first name.

"John! Thanks for coming. I know Wynter will want you to be the one to treat her." Nelson introduced John Holt to both Wythe and Irene. Holt's face was grim as he looked at Wynter. She still slept.

He picked up the chart at the end of her bed and flipped through it. Looking at them he asked, "Has anyone gone over the extent of her injuries with you?" When they shook their heads, he continued. "There are the obvious things you can see. Broken nose, split lip, the laceration above the eye and a couple of cracked ribs in back where he appears to have kicked her. There's a mild sprain with some swelling to one wrist, but that's minor." Holt paused. "There was also some vaginal tearing."

He turned to Nelson. "I had put her on birth control pills. Was she using them?"

Nelson nodded. If possible, his face went even whiter.

"They've put her on a course of antibiotics and also tested for any STDs. Everything came up negative."

He watched them. "Those are the physical injuries. Those I can treat. But there will be psychological injuries too. I understand she refused counseling?"

Irene nodded. Holt looked back at Wynter again. "I know she's a very strong, young woman, but I doubt she can cope without some help. Just be alert as the physical injuries fade." He looked at Wythe and Irene. "It was nice to meet both of you, I just wish the circumstances were different." To Nelson he said, "I'd like to speak with you outside."

After they left, Wythe sat beside Irene and she leaned against him. The baby moved and kicked, and Irene placed Wythe's hand over her rounded belly. He smiled when he too felt the rolling movement. He looked back at Wynter.

"She'll be all right, Irene. She has you for a mother."

* * * *

Nelson thought the pain and anger could get no worse. But when he stood in the hallway outside Wynter's room, he discovered he was wrong. As John described in more detail what their examination of Wynter had revealed, Nelson put a hand on the wall to brace himself against the powerful wave of fury washing through him. It took his breath away and weakened his knees so much he thought he might fall. What Payton Southard did was beyond anything. *The kid was insane!*

"She will need time and care to recover, Nelson," Holt explained. "You should be prepared that she might experience difficulty having any males near her." He paused and pursed his lips. "And the idea of any sort of physical relationship may well be traumatizing."

Nelson's temper flared. "Are you suggesting I would even consider that right now?"

Holt put up a hand to stay his outburst. "I'm just relaying facts and being realistic. And the fact she's refused any counseling might make it even more difficult."

Nelson relaxed. "I'm sorry. I'm a little on edge."

Holt studied Nelson. "You'll work it out. I know you." The doctor patted him on the shoulder before heading down the hall, the tails of his white coat flapping behind him.

Nelson walked in the other direction to the empty waiting room at the end of the hall. He needed some time to assimilate everything he'd heard and seen. Nagging at the back of his mind was the feeling it was his fault. His hand shook, and he raked it through his thick hair. His breathing was ragged. He leaned against the wall in the empty room, head tipped back toward the ceiling and eyes closed. He didn't even brush it away when a lone tear escaped the corner of his eye and traced an uneven path down an unshaven cheek.

All he'd wanted to do was love her. His Wynter. She'd brought the warmth and rebirth of spring back to his life, and he had unleashed a hurricane in hers. Could he even begin to repair that damage? From the beginning, he'd set out with the intention of making her a pawn in his revenge against the Southards, and though he'd told himself he wasn't using her, she still had ended up being a pawn. Payton Southard the third had known exactly how to get back at him.

Nelson clenched his teeth. He'd craved satisfaction, a way to get even for what a drunk teenager had cost him, but he now realized nothing would ever bring Lindy or Allison back. He must move forward before his desire for revenge cost him Wynter too. The problem was chances were good he had already lost her.

Chapter 29

Pain. She felt pain. It was something, Wynter thought. At least she felt something. She remembered little of what had happened since…since that second time. She didn't remember Wythe and Nelson coming in, though Mama had told her. She didn't remember the hospital. At least not the details. Snippets came back to her: Mama holding her hand. Nelson stroking her hair. They had kept her overnight then sent her home. Her body would recover.

Nelson wanted to talk to her, but Wynter couldn't. Not yet. She hung on to Mama. Maybe that wasn't fair, but there was something between them. Something Irene knew Wynter needed to know, and she couldn't let her go until she found out what it was. Wythe returned home, but her mama stayed. Wynter didn't protest. Irene kept Nelson away since she couldn't face him, didn't want to see the pain in his eyes. She had her own pain to deal with…physical and emotional.

Bouncer refused to leave her side. She stayed with Wynter wherever she went, and Wynter was glad. In just the week since she'd come home, she'd seen Bouncer turning from a puppy into a dog. She would look at Wynter with her funny clown-face and cock her head as if trying to figure out what was different. The dog seemed to see deeper than the bruises on Wynter's face. At some level, that was more comforting than anything. She hated having everyone hovering around her. After two more days in the house, she pushed up off the couch in the sitting room.

"I'm going to change clothes. I'm going to the barn."

Mama opened her mouth to protest and then stopped. Nelson didn't exercise that same control.

"Don't you think you're rushing things?"

She spun around on Nelson. "No, I don't. I'm not planning on riding, Nelson!" She closed her eyes briefly to keep from ranting at him that no, she wasn't planning on riding anything at the moment. After all, that bastard had torn her. Wynter shuddered when thinking of what had happened or of being with anyone in that way again. She wanted to get away from her thoughts, away from the memories. She opened her eyes. "I just have to get out. I can't stand being confined like this!"

When Wynter hurried past him, Nelson reached out. She flinched away from him as he moved. She couldn't help it, nor could she stand to see the reaction.

"Let her go, Nelson." Irene's voice came from behind Wynter.

The barn brought some relief. Bouncer followed her in and sat in front of Rosie's stall, almost as if she stood guard. Rosie blew against Wynter's cheek, and she stroked the mare's big head.

"I'm sorry we had to withdraw from last weekend," Wynter whispered, glad to put her mind on something else for a change. She ran her fingers along the horse's smooth neck. "You just don't know how much I want to get on you and ride away, but I hurt too much to ride right now. Maybe Devon. Maybe we can make Devon."

Wynter ran her hands down Rosie's back and along the length of her clean, strong hind legs. "If I can just stay busy. I won't think about it. Devon. Yes, that's what I need."

* * * *

Wynter called Dr. Holt the next afternoon. She needed to ride again. He didn't say no but said to use discretion. Her body would tell her when she was ready. After Wynter hung up, she knew it wasn't her body—it was her soul. And her soul told her she must ride. It was how she'd found herself as a girl. Now as a woman, she needed to find that balance again. She must take back Wynter. She might be forever changed, but she must rediscover that central core before she faded away.

She distanced herself from everything and everyone around her except Bouncer and Rosie. Her mother gave her space. Nelson just looked frustrated and angry. The following week, Wynter called the University. She talked to the professor whose final she'd missed, and he waived the exam. He had read the papers. Hadn't everyone? Nelson Anderson's girlfriend didn't get the same kind of privacy other rape victims did. At least, thank God, the reports didn't cover all of the details. John Holt, the nurses and physicians in the emergency room knew.

The next afternoon Wynter put on riding jeans and paddock boots, which elicited some reaction. Mama protested. Nelson raged. Wynter ignored them. Nelson put a hand on her arm to stop her from going, and she jerked it away.

"Don't touch me!" She couldn't help herself when she shrank away from his touch. He dropped his hand as if he'd been burned, his expression tense and closed when he turned away from her.

An hour later, she was in the saddle. Thomas just shook his head and walked back to the barn telling her to "Be careful with that mare." Wynter smiled slightly. It was the closest to normal she'd felt in days. Thomas was more worried about the horse than her. That was something sane, something normal that had not changed. Maybe she could still find herself.

Bouncer lay next to the ring, her fluffy head resting on her paws while she watched. Wynter circled the mare at a walk. The rhythmic thud of her feet on the arena and the gentle swaying motion of her gait helped soothe Wynter. When she felt nothing more than a little stiffness, she eased Rosie into a trot, asking for exercises to make the mare round and come down onto the bit as a matter of habit. As Wynter concentrated, Rosie became suppler, and Wynter did too. Tension flowed from her like water down a drain. They cantered. The movement of her body made Wynter tense for an instant. It reminded her of … *No! Never of that.* That was violent and frightening. She concentrated on the rhythm, the power she felt in Rosie as they settled into a collected canter and turned toward the first jump. It might be too soon, but Wynter realized she must do it. She had to take her mind off what had happened. She needed the physical and mental challenge of it. She craved it.

When Rosie gathered and pushed off, Wynter knew she had been right. She might be sore tomorrow, but this was what she needed now. They sailed around the arena, negotiating a tight triple and a huge oxer before Wynter slowed the mare down again. It was enough. She didn't dare push her still-aching body any further. Wynter let Rosie walk on a loose rein and wiped the tears of release from her eyes, covering her face with her shirttail. She found what she'd sought. She was still Wynter. Pay hadn't killed her. She had asked him to kill her, but he hadn't—not her body and not her soul either.

She let the shirttail drop and looked up. It was then she saw Nelson standing beside Bouncer. His white knuckled hands clutched the top rail of the ring in a death grip. When he saw her expression, though, he wiped a shaking hand across his eyes. For a brief second he leaned forward and rested his forehead against his hands. Then he climbed over the rail and strode toward her. When he was just a few feet away, Wynter vaulted to the ground. Nelson hesitated.

"Wynter?" There was so much in that one word. Pain, regret, fear, longing and hope. His face was pale, and his Adam's apple bobbed as he swallowed. He looked young and vulnerable when he spread his arms. "Wynter?" It was soft, almost a plea for forgiveness.

She let go of the mare's reins, let her helmet fall, and sucked in a shaky breath. She walked into his arms. They hardly noticed when Thomas walked across the ring to take the mare. It was just Nelson and Wynter. It was a moment in time that would shape where they would go from there, whether it would be together or apart. They didn't need the words. They said it in their hearts.

She curled her fists against his broad chest and cried—wrenching sobs that came from the very depths of her. She poured out the rage, anger and fear. She let it flow from her, held in Nelson's arms. She'd almost let Pay Southard win. She'd almost let him take her away from the man for whose very soul she yearned. There would be time later to talk. Now she just needed to feel Nelson close to her. If she could have melted into him, she would have. She was vaguely aware of his shaky breathing as he whispered in her ear. She understood the words at last. They weren't nonsense. They were so soft, so urgent, so aching with need.

"Never leave. My love. My Wynter. My spring."

"I will never leave you," she answered him. Her hands cupped his face, and she searched the depths of those beautiful eyes.

"I thought I'd lost you." His voice broke. "I was so stupid and it almost cost me the one thing in life I need. I was so blinded by my desire for revenge, I didn't see what happened. I didn't see how vulnerable I left you."

Wynter shuddered when memory grasped at the edge of her mind. "Not now. I can't talk about it. Not yet."

* * * *

Irene was alone when Wynter and Nelson returned. Wythe would be coming back this evening. He had promised to be there for Pay Southard's bond hearing the next day. The magistrate denied bail at first, but Pay's attorney had appealed.

Irene saw something different as soon as they entered the room. Wynter still looked haunted, but Nelson was more relaxed than Irene had ever seen him. Nelson bent to slip off Wynter's paddock boots. She allowed him to touch her. That was some progress.

"How was your ride, Wynter?" Irene asked.

She turned. The swelling was gone, but her bruises were just starting to fade. "Wonderful, Mama. It was what I needed." She smiled at Nelson when he stroked her hair. "I feel much better."

Irene smiled too and then jumped as the baby kicked her under her ribs.

"Is something wrong?" Nelson asked in sudden concern.

"Just the baby letting me know her big sister isn't the only one jumping around." She laughed. "This is a very active baby."

Wynter glanced at her mother's stomach with a wistful expression on her face.

"Would you like to feel?" Irene asked softly.

Wynter's eyes lit with a pleasure that had been missing, and she scrambled to her knees in front of her mother. Irene placed her hand on the right side where the baby kicked the hardest. It took a moment or two before a very distinct thump beat beneath her hand.

Wynter's eyes widened with awe. "Oh! Mama," she murmured. "That's so incredible!"

Irene glanced over her daughter's head at Nelson and was surprised to see the most wistful, tender expression on his lean face. "Nelson?" Irene pointed to her stomach.

He averted his eyes and cleared his throat. "No. Thanks, Irene." His voice cracked. "I just can't." He grimaced before adding, "I have some work to finish. Excuse me."

Wynter laid her head on her mother's lap, and Irene stroked her silky hair. *Things are better,* Irene thought, *but they still have a long way to go.*

"Your bruises are fading, but how do you feel inside?"

Her daughter stiffened. "Fine," she said tensely.

Maybe it was time to tell her. She continued to stroke her daughter's thick, dark-red hair. It was so like her father's and such a painful reminder sometimes.

"You don't remember much about Colin O'Reilly, do you?" Irene murmured.

Wynter shook her head.

"That's a good thing," her mother continued. "But I do think you should know about him...and me."

Wynter looked up at Irene, her green eyes still shadowed.

"You look like him, you know," her mother whispered. "Colin was a very handsome man." Her hand stilled on Wynter's hair. "But inside where it counts, you are nothing like him, thank God. When you were just under a year old, we lived in an apartment near Martinsville in a pretty bad part of town. Colin wouldn't let me work, but he also wasn't reliable in providing for us either.

"You were fussy and colicky one evening. Colin had been drinking. The night wore on, and his rage built. I couldn't get you to settle down, and the more nervous I became, the more upset you became. Finally, he jumped up, knocked the chair over and started toward your room. It wasn't much more than a closet. I saw his out of control anger. I knew he would hurt you, and I couldn't let that happen. I jumped up and blocked his path. He tried to shove me out of the way, but I wouldn't budge. He was a tall man, but I was a mother desperate to protect her child."

Irene stared out the windows while she continued stroking Wynter's hair. Neither woman moved—only the sound of their breathing disrupted the quiet room.

"He yelled at me, 'Get the fuck out of my way, you worthless bitch! You aren't worth a shit for anything. You can't even keep your damn kid quiet! But I can. I'll teach her to whine and cry like that.'

"He shoved me again, and my head slammed against the doorjamb. 'Don't touch her, Colin!' I screamed at him. 'Or I swear I'll kill you!'

"He laughed at that," Irene continued, studying her daughter's head while she relived the events from so long ago. "But it diverted the anger from you to me. He slapped me around the room. When I tried to defend myself, he punched me in the nose. The pain was incredible, and he just continued hitting me. In his drunken rage, he couldn't stop.

"He shoved me down on the floor and dropped to his knees beside me." Irene swallowed, and Wynter looked up at her with tear-filled green eyes, somehow knowing what was coming. "He raped me. He took me with such brutality I wondered for a long time if I would ever heal— inside or out. Then as I lay there, bleeding on the worn-out carpet, he stood up and stomped a heel on both of my hands. 'Just so you don't go calling the police anytime soon,' he said before he walked out the door."

Irene looked at Wynter and smiled at her. Tears rolled down their cheeks.

"I haven't seen or heard from Colin since. I never want to see him again, but I couldn't let him destroy me, Wynter. He'd beaten me. He'd raped me, but I couldn't let him destroy *me*. I couldn't let him win. I had you to take care of. And you brought such love into my life. Recovery took a long time because I didn't have people around me who loved me like you do—people I could talk to. But I did have you, and I did recover because I didn't lock myself away from your love.

"Don't shut yourself off, Wynter," Irene pleaded. "Don't shut out love. If you do, you let the Colin O'Reillys and the Pay Southards of this world win."

Wynter nodded and touched her mother's face. The healing had started. Oh, the hurt was still there, but that inner strength which had sometimes made Wynter such a stubborn child was returning. Feeling they were no longer alone, Irene looked up and saw Wythe standing in the doorway. His haunted eyes showed he'd heard most of her story. Nelson stood right behind him. Both men looked shell-shocked, staring at the hands with which Irene still stroked Wynter's long hair. She leaned her cheek against her daughter's hair. Now Wythe knew it all, knew just how vicious Colin's abuse had turned.

* * * *

Wynter had almost sought out Nelson that night. But something still held her back. He came to her room before he went to bed and kissed her goodnight, but when the kiss heated up, Wynter pushed him away. Panic, unwanted and unexpected, flooded through her.

"I'm sorry!" she gasped. She felt as if she was on the verge of hyperventilating as her fists clenched the comforter on her bed. "I'm sorry."

Nelson backed up a step. His lean face was white and pinched with tension. "No. It's my fault. I didn't mean to frighten you."

Wynter looked back at him, still fighting the panic that now held a newer edge—the niggling fear she might not be able to let him touch her. "Please, Nelson. Give me a little time. I just need time. I'll be okay. I'm sure."

He stroked her hair. "It's okay, sweetheart. Goodnight." He left without another word, and even Bouncer, curled next to her feet, couldn't dispel the loneliness left behind. As much as she felt alone and wanted him near her, she just couldn't bear being touched. The thought of it made her nauseous, almost as nauseous as the idea of going to court the next day.

* * * *

"Wynter! Come on!" Wythe yelled from the bottom of the stairs while she forced herself to leave her room the following morning. "We'll be late!"

She trudged down to where Mama, Nelson and Wythe waited. "I don't think I can do this," she said in a voice tight with strain. "Please don't make me."

Wythe tilted her chin up. "Honey, the prosecutor wants the judge to see you when he makes the decision. After what Pay did, do you really want him to make bail?"

"Wythe! That's enough," Nelson cautioned. He stood behind Wynter, his hands resting on her shoulders.

Wythe turned suddenly-hard brown eyes on both of them. This was Wythe Bradshear the attorney. "Both of you need to understand this is a war. You must make your points in each and every skirmish." He softened when he looked at Wynter again. "He'll be in manacles, Wynter. There's no way he can hurt you or anyone else."

She nodded. The logical part of her brain recognized the truth in what he said, but the emotional part...

"Okay," she mumbled. "I'm ready."

By the time they walked into the beautiful glass and concrete building, Wynter's teeth chattered. She trembled like someone standing in freezing cold weather. Nelson was right by her side, and she clutched his hand in a death grip. It must have hurt, but he neither said a word nor tried to get away. Instead, he and Wythe were both busy shielding her from the media gathered outside the courthouse. Wynter slipped on sunglasses to hide the bruising on her face. She tried to keep them on in the courtroom once she saw a camera in there too, but the prosecutor turned in the seat and whispered to Wythe.

"You've got to take them off, Wynter," Wythe urged.

It was almost like being violated again, knowing everyone wanted to see what had happened to Nelson Anderson's live-in lover. She slipped the glasses from her nose just when the deputies escorted Pay Southard in through a side door. His wrists and ankles were bound to a chain around his waist, so he shuffled rather than walked.

Even that brought horrific memories back of having her arms and legs duct-taped. Wynter's stomach lurched, and she swallowed down the bile. Nelson laid his hands over hers as they trembled in her lap. She knew the Southards were in the courtroom too, but Wynter refused to look at them.

Everyone rose when the judge entered the room, and Nelson's hand was under her elbow for support. Her nerves screamed at fever pitch. Panic choked her. Pay Southard might be manacled, but he had lost none of his arrogance.

The prosecutor and defense attorneys both made their cases. Wynter saw the judge look her over, and she forced herself to keep her head up. There were still visible bruises on her face, arms and wrists. The judge went over the list of charges. First degree sexual assault, aggravated assault, assault with a deadly weapon and crimes against nature. He looked Payton dead in the eye.

"These are serious charges, young man. I also see here you have a previous conviction in the Commonwealth of Virginia." The judge paused and looked up at Nelson. "All things considered, I believe you to be a flight risk. Bond is denied." The gavel smacked with finality. "Trial date is set for August eighth."

The Southards gasped. Wynter sagged with relief, but her relief turned to horror an instant later. When the deputies led Pay past, he looked Wynter up and down. "Fucking your crippled sugar daddy again?" he jeered.

Irene gasped, and Nelson leaped up and was already halfway over the partition between the spectators' area and the attorneys' tables. "Why you son-of-a…" he snarled.

Wythe grabbed Nelson by the shoulders and pulled him back. The deputies stopped, hands on their guns, and the judge paused on the way out the door, staring back with a hard frown on his face.

"Nelson!" Wythe snapped. "Let it go! He's not getting a slap on the wrist this time. We'll make sure of it!"

Nelson shook him off, straightened his coat and tie, and ran shaking fingers through his thick hair. Wynter sat, staring straight ahead now, her face felt frozen. This was going to be much harder than she'd envisioned. She would see Pay every day during the trial. Nelson stretched a hand down, and she grasped it like a lifeline.

"Please get me out of here," she whispered faintly. "I can't take any more of this."

Nelson set the dark glasses back on her nose. As they left the courtroom and the building, she noticed he had donned sunglasses too. The media was even more insistent.

"What did he do to you, Miss O'Reilly?"

"What's the 'crimes against nature' charge?"

"Mr. Anderson, is it true this is the same kid responsible for the accident that killed your wife and child?"

"What's your relationship with Nelson Anderson? Is that why Southard targeted you?"

Each question was like a white-hot brand searing Wynter's brain. By the time they reached the Rolls, she felt shell-shocked. If she'd ever wondered how "high-profile" Nelson Anderson was, she now had no doubts. It was like being in the middle of one of those paparazzi frenzies that plagued athletes and movie stars.

"Get in the back!" Wythe ordered Nelson and Wynter, keeping one arm around Irene's shoulders. "I'll drive." The two men bundled Wynter into the backseat. While Nelson hurried around to the other side, Wythe put Irene in the front then sprinted to the driver's door. Photographers pushed up to the car windows, but the tint prevented them from seeing inside. When Wythe put the car in gear and pulled away from the curb, Wynter turned her face into Nelson's shoulder.

His arms held her tightly. "It's okay, baby," he whispered over and over. He slid her sunglasses off. With a hand on either side of her face, he commanded, "Look at me, Wynter. It's okay, love. You're okay."

She had seen such stark pain in his eyes just one other time. "Don't leave me, Nelson," Wynter begged in a whisper. "I need you. I can't do this without you. I can't."

He gazed into her eyes, searching for something. "I will never leave you, Wynter. I love you. I will always love you."

He had said the words. It took him a year, but he had said the words. He stroked a wisp of hair away from her face, his hands shaking. She held onto his gaze afraid to look away. Every other noise faded until there was nothing but the reassuring, deep-blue steadiness of his gaze. Slowly, Wynter calmed. An immense fatigue overwhelmed her. She had slept very little since Pay had abducted her. Feeling Nelson's heart beating beneath her fingers, the gentle hands stroking her hair and her back, Wynter's eyelids drooped. She relaxed against him at last, feeling comforted by the hard feel of his chest against her cheek.

"I'll make it right," he whispered against her ear. "I'll make it right."

She awoke when Nelson lifted her out of the car. "What are you do... you'll get hurt!" Wynter protested, starting to panic. He held her in his arms with what looked like every intention of carrying her into the house.

"Shhh," he soothed her, the sweetest expression darkening his eyes. "I can do this. I want to do this. It's my turn to carry you like you've carried me the past year."

She looked at him in confusion, but he just smiled. When they reached the front hall, he continued to hold her as he faced Wythe and Irene. "Make yourselves at home, and please stay the night. Wynter and I have some talking to do, but after that I want to talk with you too."

Wynter protested again when he carried her up the stairs, but he just laughed and ignored her. He didn't even pause when he turned toward the master suite, nudging the door shut with his foot. He set her on the edge of the bed and knelt between her legs. When her eyes widened, he took her hands.

"This is me—Nelson," he reassured her, "and I love you more than I can tell you. I can feel my very soul reaching out for you like it's never done for any other woman, even Lindy. Tell me what you want me to do, Wynter. If you never want me near you again, I'll do that. I will do anything to make you happy again. You are my spring, Wynter. You renew me. Tell me what you want."

She said the words so Nelson had to lean closer to hear her repeat them. "Make me forget, Nelson. Make me forget any touch but yours."

Chapter 30

He bent and removed the black leather flats she wore. His gaze held hers as he eased his hands up each leg to slide her stockings down. When she tensed in fear she couldn't control, Wynter clutched his shoulders, never letting her gaze wander.

"It's okay," he soothed and reassured her. He tugged her to her feet and turned her back to him. He slid down the zipper on her dress to where it ended at her hips then slipped it from her shoulders and down her arms, keeping his mouth to her ear and reassuring her over and over. "I love you, Wynter. No one but you. I will never hurt you, never leave you."

He turned her as her dress pooled at their feet. He kissed away the tears on her face and laid her on the bed. Wynter saw the control he exercised over himself.

"Do you want me to undress?"

When she nodded, he stripped off the coat, tie and shirt. As his hands reached for the belt, he paused when he saw her tense. "Wynter," he commanded softly, "look at me!"

In his blue eyes she saw nothing but a deep, burning love. "I don't think I'm ready for that yet," she said shakily. "Can you just hold me?" He smiled and knelt beside the bed. "I will go as fast or slow as you want. You tell me."

He stroked her face with long, lean fingers and pressed gentle kisses against her cheeks, nose and lips. Wynter was still tense, but now there were other feelings, welcome ones.

"My sweet Nelson," she whispered against his lips. "Kiss me."

He moved slowly, deepening the contact when he felt her willing response. After she opened her mouth, he opened his. When her tongue brushed his lips, he answered. Their breathing grew ragged. Nelson pulled back slightly. His hand rested just below her breast. "Wynter?" he asked.

She nodded, not letting her gaze leave his for even a second. His fingers were like the brush of a butterfly. He hesitated as they slipped under the straps of her lacy bra and his look sought permission. Wynter nodded, still not taking hers away from him. This was Nelson, no one else. He would not hurt her. Still, she tensed when he touched her breast.

"Okay, sweetheart?" His voice sounded worried.

"It's all right." She breathed shakily.

He eased his lips down the curve of her neck over the soft swell of her breasts. Their fingers entwined.

"I love you, Wynter. Remember I love you."

His lips traveled lower to the soft skin of her flat, taut belly. His hands released hers and eased over the waistband of her panties. She answered the unspoken question with a tense nod, but she shivered, a reaction beyond her control.

"I can stop, love. We don't have to continue." Nelson looked stricken, his worry evident.

She lifted her hips, so he could slide off the silky panties. "Don't stop, Nelson. I have to do this. I need you to make me forget. Everywhere he touched me, make me forget." The last came out on a sob.

He lay beside her, cradling her. "We have plenty of time. We don't need to do this right now."

"Please!" She sobbed against him. "I need this. I need you."

His hands moved once more, sliding her underwear down until he pulled it free and tossed it on the floor beside the bed. His gaze held hers while his mouth traveled down to the bruises on her thighs. Lowering his thick lashes, he pressed his lips to each mark.

"Let me take away the pain," he murmured. "Relax."

Wynter's body shook while she tried to banish the memories and replace them with new ones. Memories of Nelson, her love, her soul. *Ah!* At last, the first stirrings of desire deep inside. "Nelson," Wynter whispered his name like a prayer.

He raised his gaze. When he saw the look on her face, he slid back up alongside her and once again pressed his lips to hers. "Do you want me to stop?"

"No," she whispered.

Nelson skimmed his hands along her body, elegant fingers brushing her nipples before tangling in the soft curls between her thighs. "Do you want to take the lead here?" he murmured. "You can go at your own pace, as fast or as slow as you want."

Wynter nodded, and he lay back against the pillows, watching her through half-closed lids. "Then love me, Wynter. However you want. I'm yours."

Tears rolled down her face while her shaking hands fumbled at his belt. He covered her hands, and she looked at him. At the unspoken question Wynter said fiercely, "I can do this. I have to."

His hands traced the outline of her face. Fingers pulled the pins from her hair, letting it fall around them, curtaining them and cocooning them together. His touch calmed her, so she undid his belt and slid her fingers inside his pants. She removed the slacks, but her hands shook when she stared at the front of his shorts. Her teeth chattered and she looked at Nelson beseechingly. "I..."

"I'll do it," Nelson murmured before stripping off his shorts. Wynter shook, her eyes closed and her teeth chattering. He stroked her hair again.

"You don't have to do this, Wynter," he repeated, this time more firmly. He gathered her to him and she stretched out along the length of him. "Easy, sweetheart," Nelson whispered over and over. "No one will hurt you. Not ever again. I promise." He raised her chin and kissed her. This time desire stirred deep in her belly.

She shifted against him now, his erection no longer striking fear. This time it was different. "I want. I want..."

"You do it, Wynter. Take what you want, as much as you need."

She straddled his hips, her shaking fingers circled him. Stroked him, and guided him. She sobbed when she sank onto the hard length of him. *Oh God! Oh God! Oh God!* She started to shake again.

"Wynter!" Nelson's voice was soft but firm. "Open your eyes and look at me, baby. It's me, Nelson."

She clung to his steady, loving gaze as if it was a lifeline keeping her afloat in waters so stormy she feared she might drown. The shaking slowed then stopped. Nelson held her hips and eased in and out. She kept her eyes on his, their gazes locked. The love she saw there erased fear, replacing it with a slow, burning desire. When she moved her fingers across his chest, tangling them in the thick mat of hair, his fingers slipped between their bodies and massaged the small nub he sought. She kept her gaze on his until slow waves of pleasure rolled over her. With a long sigh that was both sexual release and a cathartic letting go, she collapsed onto Nelson's chest.

"Wynter?" he asked, concern roughening his voice.

"I'm all right," she murmured against him. Lean hands held her hips while he drove in and out of her until he climaxed. He shifted her onto her side. He faced her, twining her hair over and around them, binding them together.

With one finger, he turned her chin up. "I promise you, Wynter, I will erase everything he did. I will love every inch of you, but not right now. I just want to hold you."

"It's okay, Nelson."

He laid a finger over her lips.

She must have fallen asleep. When she awoke some time later, he still held her cradled against him. The afternoon sun slanted through the windows. In the palm of his hand rested a small velvet box.

"Open it," he mumbled against her hair. Her fingers shook as she did what he'd asked. A ray of sunlight caught the square cut emerald inside, setting it alight with a brilliant green fire.

"Marry me, Wynter," Nelson whispered into the quiet solitude of the master suite. No other sounds disrupted their island of peace and healing. "Make us both whole. Come be my spring, my life, my laughter. Teach me to love again. Let me love you and show you we can find happiness together."

She stared at the emerald in awe. This man who could have anyone he wanted, wanted her. After everything that had happened, he still wanted her. It cleansed her soul as much as their lovemaking had purified her body.

Nelson must have misunderstood her silence because his voice tightened. "Please say yes. I almost went mad when I found out you were missing." He laid the box in the palm of her hand, stood and walked naked to the window.

"It's my fault, you know." He turned, his expression filled with a pain almost unbearable to witness. "I set out to ruin the Southards. Pay figured it out and decided to come after me. But he was smart enough to realize you were my weak spot. So he went after you." Nelson ran a shaky hand through his hair and stared at her with haunted eyes. "But that was my first mistake. I let my need to make the Southards pay for the past blind me. I let my need to make you happy blind me too. I took the bodyguards off you because they had upset you."

He crossed the room and knelt at her side. "I'm lost without you. It's not the past that matters. It's the future with you that does. Please say you'll marry me."

She touched his face tenderly. "Nelson, you have already given me so much. I love you, and I will be anything in your life you want, but I bring nothing to you. I'm a nobody."

Nelson laughed. "You brought everything to me. You walked into my life last year and brought spring back when I thought it would be winter forever. At perhaps the lowest point in my life, you gave me a reason to care, to live. From the moment I saw you, you fascinated me with your beauty, your tough, independent spirit, and a laser-like intelligence that saw to the heart of everything. Marry me," he pleaded again.

Her heart hammered in her chest, almost choking her, but she squeaked out the words, "Yes, I'll marry you."

* * * *

"Calm down, Wynter," Irene soothed. She sat in the chair in front of her mother while Irene brushed her hair and twisted it in a long French braid. Her teeth chattered as they always did when she was nervous.

"Oh why did I let him talk me into a big wedding? We should have just done it like you and Wythe, in the hallway at the house."

Irene smiled. "Wynter! Wythe and I have never 'done it' in the hallway at your house."

There was a brief pause. Then Wynter laughed. "Mama! That is not what I meant, and you know it. Shame on you." She glanced at Irene over her shoulder, and they smiled at each other. At least Wynter's teeth had stopped chattering. At that moment, the baby kicked and Wynter's eyes grew even larger. "I saw it, Mama. I saw her kick."

Irene put a band on the end of the braid just as Wynter turned and laid her cheek against her mother's stomach. The baby kicked again, making Wynter giggle. It was such a good sound to hear. Irene had her daughter back. Over the past two months, Nelson had drawn her back out and banished the shadows in her lovely green eyes. Irene knew the reason why he'd convinced her to plan a more elaborate wedding was to help take her mind off the upcoming trial. Between a couple of horse shows, summer school and wedding plans, Wynter didn't even have time to sneeze. What time she did have, Nelson was there to distract her. And distract her he must have, because she looked radiant. Her nose had healed with just a slight bump at the bridge, only noticeable if she ran her fingers along it. The scar near her left eye from the stitches would soon disappear, and it was nothing a little makeup couldn't cover.

Wynter looked up at her mother, her green eyes sparkling. *My two daughters.* She touched Wynter's face and rested her other hand on her rounded stomach. A knock at the door preceded Wythe's head peeking around the edge. Brown eyes softened when he saw them together... Wynter with her head on Irene's stomach and her arms draped around her while Irene's hand rested on Wynter's head.

"I hate to break things up here," he said with a grin, "but the groom's expecting you in fifteen minutes. And just so you know, Wynter, he's nervous too. But never fear, as his new attorney, not to mention the best man, I've calmed him down with the promise I would check on you."

Irene waved at Wythe. "Out, out! We'll be there."

The door shut behind Wythe, and Wynter stood. "I guess we should get my dress on before we finish my hair."

It was a beautiful dress, ideal for the evening wedding they had planned. Made from a heavy oyster-colored satin, the strapless gown molded her breasts in front and plunged midway down her back. The detachable train hooked at the bottom of the deep V and swirled around her. Instead of a traditional veil, Wynter opted for a wide hat with a veil that came just below her chin.

When everything was in place, Irene looked her over from head to toe. It was easy to see why a man like Nelson Anderson had fallen in love with her daughter. He had seen what lay beneath the rough, angry exterior of the teenager who had showed up on his doorstep. Wynter had blossomed into a stunning woman. She smiled.

Wynter looked confident and sounded it when she said, "I'm ready, Mama."

Thomas waited for them outside. He'd agreed to give Wynter away since Wythe was acting as best man, and Irene served as matron of honor. At the sight of Wynter, Thomas's blue eyes lit up. "Are you ready, lass?"

Wynter nodded.

"Now how many people did you say Nelson invited?" Irene inquired.

Wynter laughed. "A thousand, I think. I believe he wants no doubts he is marrying me."

Irene almost faltered when she stepped through the doorway of Duke Chapel. Guests crowded both sides of the long nave. Nelson and Wythe seemed a long, long distance away. When she reached the end, Irene smiled at the two men. Wythe smiled back, but Nelson's gaze was already riveted on his bride. Dressed in formal evening attire, he looked even more handsome than usual. His gray-streaked hair was combed back from his face. He looked every inch the powerful businessman he was, except for that curious brightness in his eyes, she thought.

When Thomas placed Wynter's hand in his, it was obvious the bride and groom both trembled slightly. The service began. As huge as the chapel was, and as many guests as there were in attendance, it was intimate in the area surrounding the altar. Nelson and Wynter's vows were exchanged with obvious commitment, their gazes never leaving one another. It appeared they had banished the ghosts of the past. Now there was just one more hurdle to go: Pay Southard's trial, which had been shoved back to the end of October.

Irene realized the minister was doing the benediction.

"Ladies and gentleman, let me present Nelson and Wynter Anderson." Lowering his voice, he added, "You may kiss the bride."

Nelson smiled and stepped close to Wynter. Lean fingers brushed back the veil from her face before he tilted his head and lowered his mouth to hers. Her arms twined around his neck, and it looked for a moment as if both of them had forgotten where they were. The minister coughed and the two parted, both looking dazed. There was a moment of silence before the entire congregation applauded.

Wythe and Irene followed them down the long aisle and outside. Like Nelson had warned them, a swarm of media awaited. Evening shadows dimmed the sunlight of the long summer's day as Nelson stopped and kissed Wynter once more on the steps of Duke Chapel.

Cameras flashed. One of the reporters shouted, "Is there some reason you've rushed this wedding?"

Nelson looked at Wynter and smiled. "I hope so," he answered. "But we haven't 'rushed' this. I've waited my entire life to find this woman."

Before they could ask any more questions, Nelson helped Wynter into the limousine. Wythe handed Irene in before bending his long frame to join them. Wynter leaned back, a tired smile on her face.

"Do we have a sit-down dinner we have to attend now?" she asked wearily.

"Our *guests* have a sit-down dinner to attend. And for the amount of money I've spent on it, I hope they have a wonderful time." Nelson grinned. "We're going back to the house to sit around the pool and have drinks and a cookout."

Wynter pulled off her hat and threw her arms around Nelson. "Ooh! I love you!"

* * * *

It was late. Wythe and Mama had already excused themselves to drive over to the cabin. They were staying there until they could find a place closer in North Carolina. Wythe had accepted Nelson's offer to head Anderson's legal department and wrapped up his practice in Virginia. Thomas and Miss Olivia had left much earlier too. They were the only other guests in Nelson's private reception.

That left Nelson and Wynter alone next to the pool. In the distance she heard the calls of tree frogs in the woods. Nelson touched her hand, and a shiver of awareness sparkled between them. Wynter felt that familiar tug in the pit of her stomach and continued to marvel at how he aroused her with such ease.

"Now that we're alone," he purred, "I'd like a private swim with my bride—sans suits." His sensual blue gaze traveled over the curves of her body. Again she felt that instant leap of desire. The fear was gone.

Wynter smiled and stood. Nelson rose and with just a flick of his fingers untied the knot that held her bikini bottom on. She unsnapped the front clasp on the top and both pieces fell to the ground between the lounge chairs. Wynter stepped closer to Nelson, hands sliding his trunks off. Her lips kissed the scars on his right hip and thigh. Nelson sucked in a breath on a soft chuckle.

"We'll never get to the pool if you keep that up, Mrs. Anderson."

She grinned at him but stood back up. "Oh, I intend to keep it up, Mr. Anderson—all night long."

Taking her hand, he led her down the steps to the warm water and into his arms. Soft jazz music played through the speakers on the pool deck, and Nelson moved them to the music. Wynter smiled and leaned her head against him, her hand skating across her stomach before she slid it upward and twined both arms around his neck. This would make a wonderful story to tell their children. A wedding dance waist-deep in the backyard pool. As Wynter felt Nelson's erection press against her, she thought that maybe their children shouldn't hear the *whole* story.

They made love on the steps with the water lapping around them and then once again in the lounge chairs next to the pool. An evening shower sent them running indoors, still naked, up the stairs to the bedroom where they made love once more, languidly touching and exploring every inch of each other. When they had finished, she curled along Nelson's side and whispered, "There will never be anyone but you."

She brought his hand across her hip, resting it against her warm, flat belly.

"There is something else I need to tell you," Wynter confided. "It is a good thing we 'rushed' this marriage like that reporter so tactlessly put it."

Nelson went still behind her.

"Why's that?" he asked.

"Because I'm pregnant."

His hand trembled when he caressed her belly. "Are you sure?"

When she nodded, he turned her and hugged her. "When? How long?" he murmured against her lips.

"Dr. Holt confirmed it yesterday. And Nelson, there's something else you should know."

"What's that?"

"He went ahead and did an ultrasound—something about the Anderson family history," she finished.

"Twins," he choked. "We're having twins?"

She felt him shake. *Oh no, maybe he hadn't meant it when he said he wanted a family!* She had stopped taking her birth control pills after he'd whispered the idea of starting a family on the day he'd proposed. She rolled over, saying, "I thought you'd be happy!"

He tilted her head back, so she saw his face in the dark. It was then she realized he was laughing. "I'm not upset, Wynter. I'm ecstatic!"

"Then why are you laughing?" She huffed in a rush of irritation.

Nelson kissed her hard on the lips. "You just never do anything halfway, do you, sweetheart? Tell me this. Will you have gotten your degree before they're born?"

She shook her head ruefully. "No, but if everything goes according to plan, I should graduate just a few months later. I might have to work something out with regard to my midterms, though."

Nelson laughed even harder.

"Nelson!" Wynter scolded. "I fail to see what's so funny!"

"For all of your impulsiveness, you are driven by a master plan more precise than most corporate tycoons." He sobered and looked at her. "Including me. I've resigned as CEO of Anderson Electronics."

"What?"

He traced his fingers over her face. "The announcement will be in the papers Friday. I'll still retain my position as chairman, but Wynter, I don't want to make the same mistake this time that I made with Lindy. Our marriage was pretty much on the rocks when she died. I was seldom home, and when I was, I was still working. I won't do that again."

"Nelson. I won't take you away from something you love!" She pushed his tousled hair back from his face. "I'm not Lindy."

Nelson smiled. "Trust me, you are not like Lindy. You are my other half. And I want to spend time with you. Anderson Electronics has consumed my life since I was nineteen. I want to step back for a period and enjoy my wife...and family." He hugged her tight against him. "God that feels so good to say."

She snuggled against him. "I will have more free time too. I'm afraid Thomas is going to have to find another rider. Dr. Holt wants me to stop riding. He says for a single pregnancy, he'd be less adamant, but with it being twins he doesn't want to take any chances."

"I suspect Thomas will be able to find someone...although not as talented as you," Nelson said casually.

They decided to forego a honeymoon until Christmas time since Wynter already carried a heavy load of summer classes and had scheduled a heavy fall semester. She had even added a few more to keep to the schedule Nelson had found so amusing. So while he had a lot more free time, Wynter found herself spending more time on campus. Nelson's resignation had sent a ripple through corporate America. There was plenty of speculation about his health, which made both of them chuckle.

Toward the end of the month, Nelson surprised her by saying they were headed to the mountains. Thomas had added in a show for Rosie and Blast to give the new rider a warm-up before the Lexington National in August. Wynter was curious. She had yet to see who'd replaced her. Whenever she had asked Thomas, he would say only that he'd found someone with experience who rode during the day while she was at class.

Wynter missed Rosie, but she did not miss Blast Furnace. They had never quite clicked, so he had dragged her around courses until she felt her arms would snap off. He lived up to his name in every respect.

Olivia Rutledge waved to them when they arrived. She gave Wynter a quick hug and looked her up and down. "I understand from Thomas that congratulations are in order. You're looking well, Wyn. Have you been sick?"

Wynter grimaced. "Not much. I'm a bit put off by a couple of foods, but that's it."

"Excellent. Why don't you come over to the ring with me? The Daltons are ready to ride. I know they would be so disappointed if you missed them."

She gazed toward the barns. Nelson squeezed her shoulder. "We'll check on everything for you, okay? Then I'll find you later."

Wynter smiled. That would have to do for now.

The show was crowded. In addition to the regular crowd, summer tourists milled about too. Both of the Dalton kids rode splendidly. Their daughter came in second, while their son stayed just in the ribbons with one rail down.

"I think I'll go find Nelson," Wynter said, starting to get up from the stands. The glare from the sun made it hard to see the barns or the warm-up area.

"Oh, don't go yet, dear." Miss Olivia tugged her back down. "They're starting the open jumper division, and this will be a small class."

Wynter sat back down, looking over her shoulder to see if Nelson was around. The first horse and rider on course turned into a demolition derby. The rider had enough sense at last to retire before she and her mount toppled any more jumps. The jump crew ran in to reset the course, measuring distances on spreads to make sure everything was set exactly as intended. When the crew finished and ran out of the ring, the announcer intoned, "Next on course, Blast Furnace—owned and ridden by Nelson Anderson."

Wynter's head jerked around, and she saw Nelson halt Blast before he dropped his hand and saluted. He wore a scarlet coat and a neat, white stock tie, white breeches and custom-made boots that fit his calves like a glove. Involuntarily, she started to her feet in fright. What on earth was he doing? Visions of the broken man she'd first met leaped into her imagination. She had opened her mouth to cry out for him to stop when Olivia Rutledge pulled her back down without ceremony.

"Don't disrupt his concentration!"

"Olivia! What the hell is he doing? Damn him! He'll get hurt!"

"Nonsense! He's ridden that stallion since it was just a colt."

Even with her heart in her throat, Wynter paused a moment to study the pair of them. It was the same horse in the picture of Nelson, which Wynter loved so much. They sailed over the stone wall and headed toward a triple oxer, and she relaxed. Blast was jumping keenly, ears pricked forward. They were a team, just like Rosie and Wynter had become, just like Nelson and her.

Wynter watched their round in awe. Nelson was not just competent—he was brilliant. When they sailed over the last jump on the course, Wynter saw him laugh, eyes alight with pleasure, face carefree. She inhaled sharply, letting her breath out on a laughing little sob. He surprised her at every turn. Less than a year ago, she could no more have imagined this than she could have imagined flying to the moon. Gone was the man whose face was etched in lines of pain and grief. In his place was a man so vibrant and intense it was like standing with her hand over a flame to be near him.

"Excuse me," Wynter mumbled to Olivia, hurrying out of the stands to find him. He was standing near Chris Stevenson, Blast's reins hanging in his hands.

When he turned and saw her face, he handed the reins to Chris with a mumbled, "Do you mind? I won't be long."

Wynter rushed toward him and into his open arms. He lifted her off her feet, twirling them in a circle.

"I'm sorry if I frightened you, Wynter. I wanted it to be a surprise."

"It was! Oh, you were brilliant." She buried her head in his neck and shivered. "But you frightened me to death. I am so annoyed!" He set her back down when she leaned away from him and frowned before she pushed him with her hand.

"How could you do that? I guess everyone knew what was going on but me? And what's this about Blast being your horse?"

Nelson's blue eyes sparkled. "I sold him to the Daltons after the accident, but I bought him back the moment I saw you ride." He laughed. "For a very hefty sum, I might add. The therapeutic riding school was a big help when I decided to rehab. Then Thomas and I worked things out while you were at class every day."

"I thought Peter Wallace told you no competing?" She frowned at him.

Nelson just laughed. "Peter knew that was why I had changed my mind about the hip replacement." He lowered his voice for her ears alone. "Among other things."

Wynter blushed, and Nelson smiled. He bent his head to kiss her fast and hard on the lips. The announcer started calling everyone for the jump-off.

"Gotta go," he whispered.

"Good luck!"

Chris beat him by a tenth of a second. The two men shook hands and grinned at one another after they finished their victory lap.

"I'll get you in Lexington!" Nelson promised as they rode up to Wynter.

Chris Stevenson glanced at Wynter and said with a grin, "As someone once told me—eat my dust, rich boy!" Then he laughed and rode off.

Nelson slid out of the saddle, careful to land with more weight on the left leg. He might be riding again, she thought, but he was still being careful. She was glad. She would never ask him to quit something that gave him so much pleasure. He gave Blast a pat before he stripped off the helmet and came back to her.

Wynter leaned against him and hugged him tight. "Have I told you, Nelson Anderson, how very much I love you?"

He tilted her face up. "I will never tire of hearing it."

Chapter 31

The weeks flew by. Midterms were fast approaching, but that wasn't the only thing looming. So was Pay Southard's trial. Wythe took Wynter to meet with the prosecutor. He made Nelson stay behind. When Nelson had protested, Wythe said, "You can't hold her hand while she testifies. She needs to know what's coming and be prepared to deal with it."

After a grueling meeting with the prosecutor, Wynter didn't think there was anything that could prepare her for what would happen in court. The staff in the prosecutor's office laid it on the line. Pay's attorney would be doing her best to discredit Wynter, to make it look as if she was somehow to blame for him beating and raping her. When Nelson asked how it had gone, Wynter shrugged and said very little. She didn't want to think about it, at least not until it was unavoidable. She much preferred to concentrate on the two babies she carried. They were very active, making it difficult for her to rest. When one was awake, the other was asleep, leaving her almost no time without being prodded or kicked.

The night before jury selection, Nelson held her close, stroking her stomach with gentle hands. He turned Wynter on her side and massaged her shoulders and back, working his way down her hips and legs until he sat on the bed at her feet. Thumbs rubbed along the length of her narrow feet, easing the tension and lulling her to sleep.

It had taken two days to select jurors because of the publicity the case had drawn. Once the jury was seated, by the end of the second day, the judge recessed until the following morning to begin opening arguments. Wynter had no appetite. Nelson coaxed her to eat some soup before he carried her upstairs to bed. His fingers were gentle as he unbraided her hair and brushed it out. When he had finished, he held her.

"I love you, Wynter."

"I'm frightened, Nelson," she admitted. "I don't want to relive what happened. I just want it to go away." She buried her face against his naked chest. "It was so awful. I don't want to tell people what happened. I don't want them to know." Wynter shook, her teeth chattering, reminding them both of what she had been like in the first few weeks after Pay's attack.

"Shhh." Nelson worked to soothe her with hands and lips. "I'll be there. Just hang on to me. I won't desert you. I won't stop loving you, no matter what you have to say, no matter what you think I don't know. Nothing will change how I feel—ever."

Hands cupped her face, and he kissed her deeply. Wynter's mouth opened to him, and she groaned. She couldn't seem to get enough of him. Her hands flattened against his chest and slid down over his tight stomach to his lean, hard hips. His erection was hot and hard against her belly. One of the babies kicked and Nelson chuckled.

"Would you like me to rock them to sleep?" he growled.

When she nodded, he rolled her onto her back and spread her legs. Kneeling between her thighs, he kissed her rounded stomach, his lips and tongue traveling lower to taste her.

"I will never get enough of you, Wynter," he murmured. "Not in a million years."

He guided himself inside her hot, wet passage and rocked his hips against her. The babies moved once or twice, then seemed to settle down, even as Nelson's rhythm picked up pace. He kept himself under exquisite control, teasing her with his fingers as his hard shaft stroked back and forth, and Wynter gasped his name in a soft cry of pleasure. Through half-closed eyes, she saw him stiffen and throw his head back when he found his own release.

Amazingly, she slept well that night for the first time since the kidnapping. Nelson kept her cradled against him protectively.

* * * *

They had to leave early the following morning. Nelson looked confident and in charge in a dark business suit with a conservatively-patterned red tie. Wynter wore a navy maternity suit with flats, and clasped the pearl pendant Nelson had given her around her neck. Wythe and Irene waited for them outside the courthouse. Once again, the media gathered. Although Wynter was accustomed to seeing them, she did not want to talk. All she wanted was to get the trial over with. She knew the prosecutor would call her to the stand as the first witness following opening statements.

Nelson kept a tight hold of Wynter's hand on one side, while Wythe and her mother flanked her on the other. When they entered the courtroom, she saw Pay's parents. They turned at their entrance, Payton Southard's eyes widening when he saw Wynter's obvious pregnancy. She returned his gaze as she absorbed his appearance. He looked like a beaten man. The arrogance that had characterized him was gone. His hair had receded since Wynter had last faced him in his study. It seemed so long ago. He looked old, and Mrs. Southard wasn't in much better shape. Wynter noticed the expensive jewelry she'd always loved to drape herself in was missing.

The door at the side of the courtroom opened, and the deputies brought in Pay. Wynter stiffened. She hadn't seen him since the bond hearing. Several months in jail had changed him too. His hair was trimmed and he wore a suit, but his hands and feet were still manacled. He looked thinner and more mature. The spoiled expression of someone who thought the world had owed him was gone, replaced with what Wynter could only describe as a look of sobriety. Pay Southard looked as if he might be stone cold sober for the first time since she had first seen him in school.

Wynter looked away in distaste. Nelson tucked her closer. She drew comfort from his nearness at the same time she offered comfort to him. The jury was seated, and a few minutes later the bailiff announced the judge.

Wynter tried to concentrate on the opening statements, but the nervous thumping of her heart drowned them out. Every sound in the courtroom was accentuated—the shuffle of someone's feet, a discreet cough, the sound of the ventilation system. When the prosecutor called her name, her heart leaped to her throat. She stared at Nelson, trying to control the fear that clutched her. He reassured her with a smile and pressed a clean, white handkerchief in her hand before helping her up.

"I'm here Wynter," he whispered. "I love you."

It seemed as if every gaze in that courtroom was on her when she approached the witness stand. Pay Southard's widened when he took in her pregnancy. After giving her oath, she eased into the chair. The prosecutor began by asking her to tell him what had happened after her final exam the day she had been abducted.

She told the story, and he prompted her when she hesitated. Periodically, he would supplement what she said with evidence to be introduced in the case.

"What happened after you were able to make a phone call out on your cellphone?"

She knew the question would come. He had told her he would ask it. Wynter twisted the handkerchief in her hands, and the familiar scent of Nelson wafted to her nostrils. She searched for her husband, and when she caught his eyes, he nodded his encouragement.

"I heard him coming back, so I pushed the phone under the cot and managed to get back up on the mattress before he came in."

"Then what happened, Mrs. Anderson?"

"He forced me to swallow some sort of pill." Wynter paused, the nightmare closing in on reality. "He said he wanted me relaxed but awake this time. I tried to fight him, but I couldn't." She paused. "He pushed my legs apart, and he raped me."

"Did his assault end with the rape?"

Wynter twisted the handkerchief and looked for Nelson again. His deep blue eyes still met hers with the same steady, loving expression. "No."

"What else did he do, Mrs. Anderson?"

The pain and fear came back. She bit her lip but couldn't quite stifle the sob that escaped. "He turned me over," her eyes found Nelson's in a silent plea, "and he forced himself on me again from behind."

"Do you mean he sodomized you?" the prosecutor asked.

"Yes." Wynter's eyes never left Nelson's, and his gaze never wavered. She wiped her cheeks with the handkerchief, his scent calming her. She looked at her hands as the ripple of shock went through the courtroom.

"Was that the end of what happened?" the prosecutor prompted.

"No. A while later, I don't know how long, he heard a noise outside and spotted the cellphone under the bed. The battery was dead, but he realized I had made a call."

"What happened then?"

"He threw the phone at my face and hit me here." Wynter touched the scar by her left eye. "He left, and the next thing I knew, Nelson Anderson and Wythe Bradshear somehow reached me."

The prosecutor looked at the judge. "I have no more questions for Mrs. Anderson at this time."

The judge looked at Pay's defense attorney who was in conference with her client. She rose and said in an irritated tone, "I have no questions, your honor."

The prosecutor helped Wynter down from the stand and across the courtroom. When she moved between the lawyers' tables, Pay Southard raised a hand to brush a piece of hair from his face. She jerked away—she couldn't help it as she covered her belly instinctively. Wythe and Nelson were there in an instant to help her back to her seat.

The judge called a ten minute recess. Wynter leaned against Nelson, shaking from head to toe. He held her against him, cradling her head against his shoulder while he whispered in her ear, "I love you, Wynter. Remember that."

When the judge returned, the prosecutor called Nelson to the stand. He described the call he'd received from Mrs. Caudle letting him know Wynter had failed to come home after her exams.

"Was this something out of the ordinary?"

"Yes. Wynter is very organized, particularly when it comes to her education." He smiled at his wife, and it warmed her. "She has a plan from which she does not deviate—even for a honeymoon or the demands of carrying twins. So deciding to 'go out' when she had a final exam the following day would not have happened."

"What did you do after you received the call?"

"I contacted her mother and stepfather, along with a detective who I knew would be discreet but capable of employing the latest technology to help us find her."

"You didn't think this was an overreaction?"

"No," Nelson responded. "Like I said, Wynter is very focused on her education. Doing anything that might jeopardize that would have been out of character." He paused and looked at Wynter again. "I was also concerned because my wealth and position made her a possible target for kidnappers."

"That being the case, Mr. Anderson, wouldn't it have been wise to have a bodyguard for her?"

Nelson stared at Wynter with such regret on his face it pained her. "I hired two men, but she objected to being followed, so I took them off to make her happy. I never thought someone would take her from such a public place."

Nelson described the phone calls that followed, and how they had used Wynter's phone to locate her.

"Did you have any knowledge, at this point, of who might be responsible for her disappearance?" the prosecutor asked.

"Yes. After logging into my company email account, I discovered a message demanding ransom. The message was from Payton Southard."

The attorney glanced at the stenographer and the judge. "Let the record show both printed and electronic versions of that email have been submitted into evidence." Turning back to Nelson. "Explain what you did after pinpointing her location."

When Nelson described breaking into the plant's office and seeing her, his voice broke. "She was curled tight like a ball. Her face was covered in blood and her nose and eyes were swollen. I—I wasn't sure for a moment if she was even alive." Nelson paused and swallowed. "Her clothes were torn, there were bruises everywhere and more blood between her—thighs. She opened her eyes when we got to her."

"Did she know who you were?"

"No. She begged us to kill her, to 'just get it over with.'"

"What did you do then, Mr. Anderson?"

Nelson clenched his jaw. "I cut the tape from her wrists, and we covered her. Her mother had already called the police when she saw the detective with Pay, and Wythe called an ambulance."

Once again, Wynter saw Pay Southard lean over to tell his attorney something before she told the court she had no questions.

Next on the stand was the paramedic. Wynter didn't remember him. He was a tall man with dark hair and a kind face. After describing the scene when they'd arrived, the prosecutor asked him to go through the initial assessment of Wynter's injuries.

"She appeared to have a broken nose, severe bruising around the eyes. There was additional swelling along the left side of her head, under the hairline, and a wound along the left brow, which we closed with a butterfly bandage until it could be sutured. We found bruising to the back of the rib area with a suspected fracture. In addition, there was bruising on the arms and legs and the inner thighs that indicated the victim had been raped."

"Objection!" Pay's attorney said. "The witness is not a physician and cannot draw medical conclusions."

"Sustained."

The prosecutor looked at his notes and changed his tack. "In your job as a paramedic, how many rape victims have you transported?"

"Numerous. At least two a month, and I've been doing this for ten years."

"Based on other rape and sex abuse victims you have transported in the past, would you say her bruising was consistent with a rape victim?"

"Yes. The injuries I observed were consistent with those sustained by other rape victims, so we treated the scene with that in mind. Per our instructions in such situations, we left the potential evidence intact and prepared her for transport."

"Did you notice any additional injuries?"

"She sustained some vaginal trauma."

"Tearing?" the prosecutor asked.

"Yes." The paramedic glanced at Wynter.

She dropped her gaze to her hands, which still twisted in her lap, but she looked up toward Pay Southard when she heard his attorney again announce there would be no cross examination. The judge looked hard at the lawyer before announcing a lunch recess. Pay Southard turned when he stood, his glance taking in both Nelson and Wynter. There was something different about him, she thought. But she was so terrified just being near him she averted her eyes and stepped closer to Nelson, who wrapped an arm around her shoulders in a protective gesture.

Wythe took them to a small restaurant nearby, but none of them were very hungry. After nibbling at a sandwich, Irene pulled out her cellphone to check on their baby daughter, born just a few weeks earlier. Wythe had been afraid the trial might be too much stress so soon after the infant's birth, but Irene had insisted. Wynter was glad.

She picked at the salad she'd ordered, forcing some food down for the sake of the babies. They were rolling around, kicking. Nelson smiled and rested a hand on her stomach just as a strong kick landed, making his hand jump.

"I think these babies are going to be as obstinate as their mother." His smile turned to a grin. Irene smiled and Wythe chuckled then reached for his pager when it chirped. He checked the message.

"Pay's attorney and the prosecutor are meeting with the judge in chambers. They want everyone back in court as soon as possible."

"Is that good news or bad?" Irene asked.

Wythe shrugged. "It might be procedural issues, but my gut feeling from what I saw in court this morning is that Pay will change his plea."

"They're not going to plea bargain the charges are they?" Nelson's voice turned cold.

"I doubt it. Neither the prosecutor nor the judge seemed too willing to deal on this one." Wythe rose. "We'd better get back to see what's going on."

The two men flanked Wynter and her mother while they made their way back to court. The reporters weren't asking questions now. Wynter guessed they had heard all they needed in court that morning. They sat back down. Once again the Southards were already seated, and if possible, looking grimmer than before. Pay returned, but this time he kept his eyes down and didn't look at anyone.

The judge settled on his seat, getting down to business. "Mr. Southard, please rise. It's my understanding from your attorney you wish to change your plea. Is that so?"

"Yes, sir." Pay's voice was quiet but firm.

"How do you plead?"

"I wish to plead guilty to all charges." A gasp went through the courtroom. Wynter clutched Nelson's hand, almost sagging with relief this might be over at last.

The judge studied Pay. "These are serious charges, son. Are you sure this is what you wish to do?"

"Yes, sir." Pay looked at the judge. "May I say something, your honor?" The judge nodded.

Wynter cringed when Pay looked at Nelson and her. "I wish to tell you how very sorry I am." He looked at them steadily, even though his voice shook. "I don't expect your forgiveness. In your shoes," he paused, "I don't think I could ever forgive what I've done. I can never repay you. I can never bring back what I've taken from you. Just please know, I'm trying to change, and I am so very sorry." He turned back to the judge. "Thank you, your honor."

The judge nodded, thanked the jury for their service and dismissed them. After the jurors left the courtroom, the judge looked back at Payton. "Payton Caldwell Southard the Third, please rise."

Pay stood and squared his shoulders when the judge sentenced him. Wynter heard the words "life in prison" before a sudden roaring filled her head. Nelson pushed her head forward between her knees. She fought to sit back up. Her eyes went to Pay Southard. She heard his parents crying, but Pay stood dry-eyed. He looked at Wynter one last time before he left. She saw the sincerity in his gaze when he said, "I'm sorry."

Wynter looked from Pay to his parents. The older Payton looked right through her, and his wife looked away, wiping her eyes with a crumpled handkerchief. Wynter looked back to Pay and nodded her head in acceptance. That was all she could give him. Forgiveness might come but not yet. It was just too soon.

Epilogue

"You did it!" Irene gave Wynter a quick squeeze, balancing her daughter on her hip. "I am so proud of you, Wynter. You are the first person to graduate from college in my family."

Nelson and Wythe stood nearby, each of them cradling a baby boy in the crook of their arms. Wynter smiled at them and unpinned the mortarboard from her hair. When the sleeves fell back from her bare arms, she glanced up to see Nelson's smoldering blue gaze travel the length of her arms to where her fingers had removed the pins from her hair. Heat rose in her cheeks. This man possessed the power to arouse her with just a look. But there was so much more than just the sex. Wynter knew she could trust him to the ends of the earth. He would never leave her, never stop loving her, no matter what. They had already been to hell and back together.

Nelson handed the baby he held to Wythe. The twins were now three and a half months old. Wynter had made it thirty-four weeks before Matthew and Marcus had insisted on being born. As Wythe balanced the two gurgling boys, Nelson turned and pulled Wynter into his arms. He bent his head and inhaled just as Wynter did. She could never get enough of the warm scent of horses, leather and spice.

"Congratulations, sweetheart." He held her away and smiled at her. "I suppose grad school starts next week, and you plan on being finished in a year?"

"No," she said slowly, "I've decided to change my plans." A sudden silence followed her words, and even the babies were quiet.

Nelson recovered first. "You...you're changing your plans?" He staggered backward in mock horror.

"Stop it!" Wynter laughed. "I just decided I'd like to spend some time with the boys—and you," she added for his ears alone. "Maybe I'll take a year off and just relax."

"It'll never happen," Wythe said.

"I have to agree with that," Nelson added.

"Never in a million years," Irene finished.

"Yes it will!" Wynter protested. "I have it all planned."

Meet the Author

From the moment Rhett walked out on Scarlett, Laura's been hooked on romance. Deciding truth really is stranger than fiction, though, she chose a career path in journalism. Laura now teaches English and has returned to her first love—writing fiction.

She lives with her husband and son in central North Carolina, along with a menagerie of animals that includes two rowdy Jack Russells and a gentle white mare named Tweed. When she's not reading or writing, Laura enjoys riding, photography and baking the best darned carrot cake you've ever tasted.

Laura's Website:
http://www.laurabrowningbooks.com
Reader eMail:
Laurabrowning613@yahoo.com

Turn the page for a special excerpt of Laura Browning's

Bittersweet

Can love survive a night he can't remember but one she'll never forget?

Anna Barlow is giving herself a fresh start, leaving everything about her old life behind. With a new name, a new career and a new look, everything about her has changed since the night her daughter Becca was conceived. Anna finds out just how different she looks when an emergency farm call brings her face to face with her baby's father...and he has no idea who she is.

Chris Stevenson is on hiatus from the world of competitive show-jumping. He's returned to the family farm to get his life back in order. Nothing's been right for the past year... not since the night that has remained a blank in his memory. When he meets the area's newest veterinarian, Chris feels two things—instant lust and that he's met her somewhere before.

As they struggle to reconcile the night he can't remember, both Chris and Anna must learn to trust each other and the idea of what family really means.

On sale now!

Chapter 1

The cellphone on Anna's hip buzzed. She had turned off the ring in the hope that Becca, nestled in her carseat in the backseat of the pickup, would stay asleep at least for a short while. Days and nights of colic had drained them both. The programmable swing at home wasn't a luxury but a necessity. Miles of uninterrupted driving making farm calls also seemed to soothe her daughter. Saturday night dinnertime had already come and gone, both hers and Becca's, and Anna felt the pressure to nurse. She had been about to pull over to feed her when the phone had vibrated against her hip. Not now. Just this once.

"Dr. Barlow," she murmured into the phone as she slowed the truck and pulled to one side of the secondary road. The clinic answering service secretary was on the line with an emergency farm call. Anna jotted the address and the directions the operator gave her. Still somewhat new to the area, she was learning her way around, so directions were a must. Getting lost on her way to an emergency was not an option. And at this hour on a Saturday evening, no one called a veterinarian for anything routine, but the nature of the emergency wasn't what made this call different. The owner's name made her stomach jump with nerves.

"Please let Mr. Stevenson know I'll be there in five minutes." Anna hung up, checked there was no traffic and pulled onto the road. She found the first available driveway to turn around and head back the way she had come. She glanced at the address again. Main barn, Fincastle Farm. Of course she had heard of it. Who hadn't? The farm had been the signature of the Stevenson family for several generations.

She had held hope that Fincastle would never appear on her client list. Naive of her to think she wouldn't see him. Some sort of veterinary call had been bound to happen sooner or later. Later would have been much better. Never even more so. Maybe she'd luck out and the Mr. Stevenson in this instance would be father rather than son.

Anna swallowed as she turned down the long driveway bordered on each side by tall, white-paneled fences. In the paddocks left and right, high-dollar horses grazed in the glow of the spring moon. Ahead lay a long, pristine white barn. A darker color trimmed the doors and windows. It would be green, she recalled. Forest green, like the curtains around the Fincastle tack stalls at shows. Light blazed from one barn, which must be her destination. Most barns would already be settled for the night.

Okay. She was headed into the lion's den. Chris Stevenson, the man she so did not want to meet. Anna hoped he wouldn't be there. Sure, she'd known the possibility of meeting existed when she took the job in Redfield. Let him not be there. Not tonight, when she was tired and needed to nurse Becca to the point that her breasts ached. The show season had started, after all, so he should already be on the road at some of the smaller warm-up shows.

She took a deep breath and let it out. It didn't matter. She could do this.

After she parked in front of the barn, Anna shoved two more nursing pads inside her bra and muttered a quick prayer she and Becca could wait a while longer. One glance over her shoulder showed her infant daughter still slumbered in the carseat. She rolled down the windows before she got out and checked on the baby one more time. A gentle tug brought Becca's blanket back to where it belonged. After releasing a soft sigh, Anna straightened away from the truck. She pulled the zipper higher on her cotton coveralls and threw her stethoscope around her neck.

"Dr. Barlow?" someone inquired in a deep, masculine voice.

For an instant, she swayed. That voice. So much for being on the show circuit. Anna stepped around the back of the pickup into the view of the man who had emerged from the lighted doorway of the barn. Even as one part of her brain told her it was him, she shook her head in denial. Not with his reputation, and not on a Saturday night. There must be some horse show groupie somewhere who was willing to jump his bones, and that would take precedence over actual work.

"You're not Dr. Barlow? Where is he?" the silhouetted figure asked. Anna could not see his face, or much else, since the light behind him cast his front in shadow. As much as she might have tried, she would never forget his voice. She didn't need to see his face to know the speaker was Chris Stevenson.

Now, though, irritation kicked in. Where was he? She sighed. In this day and age, women veterinarians were more the norm than the exception. Of course, her height, or lack thereof, also played a role. She had encountered similar questions before, so she shouldn't have been surprised when it came from a man like Stevenson.

"Sorry, my mind was on something else. I am Dr. Barlow. I understand you have a horse in need of stitches." Anna's jaw hardened as she sensed his reluctance as well as his outright hostility. "If it will make you feel better, I would be happy to show you my credentials, Mr...." That was a nice touch. She'd make him think she had no idea who he was.

"Stevenson. Chris Stevenson."

"The man himself." As soon as Anna voiced it, she wanted to kick herself. She hadn't meant to say that aloud. He had half-turned, and in the glow from the barn, she saw his frown at her tone, but she was not going to back down now. Stevenson was nothing to her. Not anymore. Not ever. Once he'd been her hero, the object of teenage fantasies. But that was in the past. There was an injured animal to treat, she had a hungry daughter to feed and a painful need to feed her that only increased as time passed. She'd do her job, get the hell out of there and be done with it.

"May I take a look at the injury, or would you like me to call the answering service to see if someone else is available to take the call?" At the moment, she couldn't care less that Fincastle was one of the clinic's biggest clients. She was tired and wanted to go home, so if he wanted a different vet, that was fine with her.

She braced herself as they walked into the light of the barn. As the fluorescent lights illuminated his lean features and fair hair, she realized he looked different. He was harder, but also healthier. The dissoluteness that had begun to leave its mark last summer was gone.

"You'll do," he grunted in response. "Follow me."

Anna cocked one eyebrow at Stevenson's retreating back. At least he was polite enough not to sigh as he said it. Still, what an arrogant jerk! Thank God she need have nothing to do with him outside of professional calls, and thank God he appeared to draw a total blank when he looked at her.

She supposed she should be used to people questioning her abilities because of her petite size. She had received odd looks through veterinary school, and even had to answer some pretty pointed questions when she talked to people about joining their large animal practices. Just over five feet tall, she was slender to boot, and at the time, she had been very pregnant. At least the vets at Redfield were able to overlook her appearance in favor of the credentials she'd set in front of them.

Her biggest relief was Chris seemed not to recognize her. She shouldn't be surprised. She knew she looked a lot different than when he'd seen her, but part of her hardened with hurt and anger. What was she hoping, that he would remember the night they met? He would fall at her feet like the prince with Cinderella? There was no reason for it to stand out in his memory, not like it forever would in hers. He spent plenty of nights bedding besotted bimbos. She'd been another in a long line.

Stevenson stopped so abruptly in front of the stall midway down the aisle that Anna almost walked into his backside. Quivering at the rear of the stall was one of the biggest Thoroughbreds she had ever seen. The horse snorted and rolled his eyes. On his right hip, she saw a jagged tear about eight inches long, a messy wound that would require careful stitching.

Stevenson turned to look at her, his eyes challenging. "Still ready to take this on?" he asked with a sardonic twist to his lips.

Anna gazed at him without batting an eyelash. "I'll get my supplies. Would you prefer to bring him in the aisle or would you like me to do that when I return, since he seems a bit rattled?" Her tone dripped ice.

Stevenson looked her up and down. "I'll bring him. He's a stud, and I give you fair warning, he's always had more than his share of attitude."

Anna bit back the retort on the tip of her tongue about him having something in common with the horse besides their hind ends and nodded before spinning on her heel. She had dealt with bigger horses' asses than this one, and she wasn't referring to the horse.

She sighed with relief when she reached her truck and saw Becca still slept. "Bless you, sweetheart," Anna whispered to the baby.

She checked to make sure her daughter was still dry and stroked a finger over her soft cheek. With one last sigh, Anna opened the tailgate. She always kept a plastic caddy ready to grab, which she stocked with the supplies most often needed. After picking it up, along with a few other items she'd need, she hurried along the aisle. Chris was snapping crossties on the stallion as she approached. The big horse stomped his front foot before kicking out with his right rear leg as if trying to dislodge whatever it was causing him pain. Anna set her supplies several feet away and slipped the syringe of sedative inside the front pocket of her coveralls.

As she approached the horse, she murmured to him, watching his ears flick backward and forward as she continued talking.

"You can release him, Mr. Stevenson," Anna directed in the same even tone she used with the horse. Once he turned the halter loose, the horse quit stomping and stretched his nose toward her.

Anna stopped in front of him. Her face was scarcely higher than the horse's flared nostrils. He puffed at her and she blew back. The horse's head relaxed and both ears came forward.

"That's it, big man. Why be scared of something as tiny as me?"

Anna touched him on the cheek before stepping to his side and stroking his neck. Before either the horse or the man was aware of it, she slipped the hypodermic with the sedative into the horse's vein and delivered the drug. She continued to talk to the stallion as the horse's eyes drooped.

Anna bent to look at Chris from under the tall Thoroughbred's neck. "Do you have a step stool close by, Mr. Stevenson? If not, I can get the one I carry in the truck."

Stevenson's pale gray eyes had lost their sardonic expression, but not the hostility.

"Sure," he responded in a clipped voice. He stepped away, returning in a couple of minutes with a lightweight mounting block. "Will this work?"

Anna smiled. "Perfect. Thank you."

She sensed Chris's critical gaze on her but dismissed it. He'd have to deal with his own hang-ups without her help. Right now she had a job to do. Anna worked with careful efficiency, first cleaning the wound before checking for any underlying tissue damage. She was relieved to see it was only a tear to the hide and did not involve any muscle.

"How did he do this?" She lifted a brow in inquiry. Even standing on the second step of the mounting block, she stood barely above eye level.

"A fool of a groom who was careless with the gate when he tried to bring him in tonight. Bart caught himself on the latch coming in."

"That explains the tearing more than cutting," Anna mused as she returned to her work. She used small, neat stitches, tying off the sutures as she finished each one. As she was knotting the last one, she heard Becca wail. Oh no! Just what she needed. She hoped she might be able to get away from the farm without Stevenson realizing there was a baby in the truck. A baby she preferred he didn't see.

His head jerked toward the barn doorway. "What the hell?"

Anna felt the tingling in her breasts that signaled her milk letting down and knew she was leaking. Becca's cry was like an instant trigger to nurse, and she was already long overdue. She hunched her shoulders and jumped off the mounting block. There was no way around it. At least he hadn't recognized her, and at the moment, that was a plus she would accept with gratitude.

"My daughter. Your stallion should start to wake in the next fifteen minutes," she explained even as she packed. "He should be fine to go in his stall. I'll check on him in the morning."

Anna shoved everything into the caddy and the buckets she had brought with her and turned to escape. The leaks from her breasts grew heavier as her daughter continued to cry. Her entire focus was on getting away and finding a place to nurse. She was not sure how long the nursing pads would hold.

"Whoa!" Stevenson commanded. Anna stopped, her mouth tightening. "I want you here until this horse recovers from the sedative."

Anna frowned then looked along the aisle to the truck parked on the edge of the light spilling from the end of the barn, and the increasing volume of the hungry wails emanating from it.

Stevenson ran a hand through his sandy hair in obvious frustration. "This is my best stud. I want you here in case there's a problem. Can't you call your husband or boyfriend or someone to take her?"

Anna's eyes narrowed. "No, I can't. She's not a puppy, Mr. Stevenson and she's hungry now." No way was she going to let him know there was no husband, not even a boyfriend.

He expelled his breath. "Go get her and bring her in."

Nowhere had she heard a please, but what had she expected? Anna shifted. Now was not the time to worry about manners. "Fine," she mumbled.

As distasteful as she found him and as tempting as it might be, Anna knew she couldn't afford to anger one of her clinic's biggest clients. The job was too new, she needed it too much, and if she alienated someone like Stevenson, it would leave the vets who owned the clinic little choice but to get rid of her. She might be excused for taking a tone with him after he questioned her identity and credentials, but ignoring his wishes about this was different.

She hurried from the barn. As soon as she picked up her daughter, the baby reached for her, making smacking noises with her lips. Anna laughed and felt everything inside her melt. As she cradled the baby in one arm, she used her other hand to unzip the coverall. She bared her swollen breast and leaned against the pickup with a sigh of relief as Becca latched on and suckled. Her tiny fingers pushed against Anna's breast.

"Is everything okay?"

She almost jumped out of her skin as she heard Chris's impatient voice. She threw the blanket dangling from her hand over her half-bared front.

"She was hungry," she replied in a somewhat shaky voice as she angled herself away from the man coming around the side of the truck.

"You can give her a bottle inside where it's light," Stevenson added as if he were granting her a huge favor.

"I'm nursing her, Mr. Stevenson. She won't take a bottle."

"Oh."

Anna almost laughed as she saw him halt. He was tall enough his face was in the light showing from the barn over the top of the pickup. For the first time since she arrived at Fincastle, Chris appeared at a loss for words, and she felt a small spurt of cynical amusement. Of course he would be unprepared to deal with the normal result of the sex act. The only thing he was interested in was the performance, not any repercussions.

He cleared his throat and coughed, his gaze skittering away from her. He shifted his weight from one booted foot to the other, and if the light were better, Anna would have sworn a blush stained his tan cheeks.

"You may still come inside if you'd prefer. Sit in my office, and I'll keep an eye on Bart."

Anna darted another quick look at the man. Perhaps he was human. As soon as the thought popped into her head, she shook herself. No, not bloody likely. "Thank you."

Stevenson looked anywhere but at her as he led the way to his office. It was spacious and furnished for comfort rather than style, with a large antique desk and a couple easy chairs in addition to the leather chair behind the desk.

"Make yourself comfortable," he murmured with an automatic kind of politeness she was sure had been drummed into him, but the words cut off on a choked cough as Anna sat. The receiving blanket slipped, giving him a clear view of the baby nursing at her breast. She pulled the blanket back in place. Anna had long ago lost any embarrassment about feeding her child, and though she didn't push her breast-feeding on people, she wasn't going to apologize for it.

The door shut with a hasty click. Anna leaned back in the chair and sighed with relief. The pressure eased, at least on one side. Now Stevenson had disappeared, she removed the blanket, burped the baby and switched her to the other breast to get some relief there too. If there was one thing she had learned, her daughter had no problems nursing. The baby was strong and efficient. She had finished burping her again and put her own clothing to rights when he knocked on the door.

"Are you... Is the baby through...uh, nursing? Bart's waking, and none too happy."

The impatience was back in his voice, and it hit her the wrong way. Anna stood. The weariness of the long day was catching up with her, and she lost patience as well. As much as she wished to keep him at a distance, sometimes options ran out. "I can't juggle him and my daughter. If you'll hold Becca for a minute, I'll get him settled and in his stall."

Chris looked almost as if she had instructed--"here, take this large, poisonous snake and give it mouth to mouth." To give him credit, he recovered in an instant and held out his arms, uncertainty plain on his face. Anna hesitated a moment before she put the baby on his shoulder, her gut clenching as she gazed at his sun-bronzed forearms and work-toughened hands that rose to cradle the infant. He hadn't recognized her, so it should be safe to let him hold the baby this once. Beyond that, though, she didn't want him near her daughter. She settled Becca's bottom on his muscular forearm and placed his other hand at the back of the baby's head.

"There you go." She left him standing in the middle of the office, a nervous, almost frightened look on his face. Serves you right, Anna thought with a small spark of vindictive satisfaction as she walked away. The only thing that would make it better would be for Becca to either spit up or poop, both things she excelled at doing. Imagining such a scenario made Anna smile.

The horse's ears swiveled forward when he saw her. He quit stomping once again and this time blew at her enough to make a small nicker. Anna's smile widened. She loved horses—always had, and somehow they knew it. Without hesitation, she walked to the muscular animal, stroked his head before clipping on a lead shank, and unhooked the cross ties. To make sure he was steady on his feet and the stitches weren't pulling, she walked him the length of the aisle a couple times before leading him to his own stall. The horse followed her and munched the hay in the feeder as soon as she escorted him inside the stall. After unclipping the lead and looping it in her hand, she shut the door and watched him for a couple more minutes. Finally glancing at her wristwatch, she hurried up the aisle to the office.

Chris stood rooted where she'd left him, as if he were afraid any movement might startle the tiny person in his arms. Curiosity had replaced his earlier frightened expression. Becca had her face turned toward him and watched him from her big, blue-gray eyes. Anna swallowed. The baby had a reputation for not liking strangers, so her daughter's quiet observation of the man made Anna uneasy in a way she did not want to examine. Part of her had hoped Becca would scream bloody murder the moment he touched her, and at least her daughter could have covered him in spit up. Traitor.

"Thank you," she said, reaching for her. "I can take her now."

"I've never held a baby before." Stevenson's deep voice was rough, and he sounded a little embarrassed. He handed her the infant.

His awe made Anna drop her hostility. For just a moment, she felt like she glimpsed the man behind the public persona--and he appealed to her. When she smiled, she saw Stevenson's eyes widen, then narrow with speculation. Her smile turned to a chuckle. "I know."

His gaze swiveled from her to the baby and back. "That obvious?"

Anna pursed her lips. "Yes, but at least you were brave enough to take her." She laughed again before quieting at the curious look he gave her.

Time to go. Right now. Curiosity was not good. The last thing she wanted to do was make Chris curious about her in any way. They had nothing in common, nor should they. She would not take such a risk.

She kept her tone cool. "I'll stop by in the morning to check on your stallion. Good night, Mr. Stevenson."

"Good night, Dr. Barlow."

He turned back to the barn, and she gathered Becca and the rest of her things and headed toward the truck. That was it. He hadn't recognized her. She was relieved. Of course she was relieved. It was the best thing. Her lip trembled and she clamped on it with her teeth until it hurt. He was a despicable human being, which she knew better than most people ever would. The farther she and Becca stayed away from him the better.

www.ingramcontent.com/pod-product-compliance
Lightning Source LLC
Chambersburg PA
CBHW020749250626
47155CB00003B/989